Love, DECEIT, and War!

Book 1: Emergence

By Tommi Swartzando

Book 1

Authors Notes:

Hello Everyone,

I want to explain how my book works really quick before you dive into it, I wrote this book with Greek Tragedies and TV Episodic like so each chapter would count as or close to a full episodes worth of information (I realize there are some shorter chapter but for the most part they all will follow that mindset). Second The space between paragraphs is to denote the passage of time or scene transition. I do attempt to emphasize when a transition is happening but if it is not clear please take note of this message. Third, this is a story and is completely fictional. Fourth and most importantly, please enjoy my book and the story I am attempting to tell.

About the Author:

Tommi is autistic Author and Creator from Nebraska. His struggles with mental health issues and acceptance of his disability lead to the creation of many universes including the 'If Left to our own Devices' Series, 'The Eternal Cycle' Universe, and The Giant Cosmic Owl Known as 'TheGM' found on YouTube. He spends most of his time trying to come up with new universes idea's or filling orders for Misfits Inc, A Legal think tank, Mr. Swartzando helps run. He is very reclusive and prefers his privacy but is very open to conversation. He expects to finish the rest of the series in the next couple of years.

Prologue
A Word from the Future's Future

"Plato once said. Only the dead have seen the end of the war. I think those who remain are just surviving till they end the war themselves." - Lylah Soffrireterna, May 30, 4999.

My mother once warned me. How can you save the universe if you can't save yourself? I never understood she was preparing me to answer the questions I didn't know I had. Like what would I do when she's gone.
I am a soldier like my mother before me, but I can't help but wonder what she went through in her war. How she dealt with killing, how she dealt...with loss. — Lisa Soffrireterna's personal diary, May 30, 5050.

Preface: Part 1

Regret only Leads to Heartbreak

1 week before the Great War Started
Magness Prime
Horatius School of War Arts

Luke Akya
9:00 A.M.
March 12th, 4999 A.D.

"Welcome back I hope you aren't too eager to go on your break that you have forgotten we must get back to the matter at hand. There is a question as old as war itself," The room was tense, the Commander wanted to get the lesson today. Commander Montgomery stood before thirty-nine cadets. Her one good eye examining each and every one of them as she looked around the room. The holo projection of a fight during the Founding War illuminated most of the room. The Scenario was of a Single Pike Class Destroyer vs Thirteen Battleships. Luke had seen this scenario before it happened to be one of his favorites. "The Commander of this Pike," The commander shifted letting her words fill the room with tension, "William Archer, had out maneuvered the battleships and canned himself seven kills in this fight. 8 hours and Archer had lost a third of his crew," She let the words sink in further, " They were down to eight rounds in the man cannons, their drone defense was shot, kinetic barriers didn't exist."

She paused again before drilling her point home, "but back in those days he was an insurrectionist. Not a Founding Member of the Federation." Luke shifted in his seat as he watched the Commander in front of them as she went about today's lesson, Commander Montgomery, a slender woman, her back tense, who had a single scar that ran from her right temple across her eye blinding it and finished down by her right cheek, making a small crescent moon on her hardened pale skin. Her years of experience and hardship showed in her tight jawline as she looked around the room, her years of teaching and war allowing her to have the entire class's attention. She walked around the classroom, her eye continuing to move from cadet to cadet. Her steel blue jumpsuit zipped up to the bottom of her breast line. A black tank top shown through the opening and old fashioned dog tags dangling around her neck as she moved. Letting the cadets feel the tension. She stopped and rolled up both sleeves before continuing her walk around the room letting the question sink in, "Cadet Akya. Why is Commander Archer's fight today's lesson?"

"Sir, This fight is one of the best in terms of tactical maneuvering and using brains over brawn. The Assembly was way too over confident and Archer used the overconfidence of your opponent against them, completely decimating two battleships before two hours had passed." The young cadet yelled, his voice booming across the classroom. The Cadet stood, he was in true peak fitness and stood a better foot taller than the other cadets. He had moss green eyes that gave him a calm feeling despite his massive frame of muscle. His jet black hair was slicked back today giving him an old 1950s greaser feel. He wore a green jumpsuit, the patch of cadet first class shown clearly even in the low light.

"Good Cadet now let me ask you something?" Before he could breath she was there staring him in the eyes, " If you had the same choice," She threw her head towards the holo, "I wonder how you would handle the oldest question in war? Do you know what that question is?"

"No, Commander Montgomery, I do, not" he said as his eyes flicked around the classroom for aid, trying his hardest to not show his insecurity at not knowing an answer, his jawline clenching at the insecurity.

"Then let me enlighten you, you may sit," She nodded slowly, an almost softness crept into her voice as she continued to make rounds looking every cadet in the eye as she spoke, "In this fight," She waved her hand and the Simulation played out as she spoke, "Archer had only two options. Fight and maybe save yourself and your crew and give them false hope of victory. Even if you aren't even sure it is possible to live but probably become a Martyr," The first ship explodes quickly followed by the second as the destroyer took off dodging shots around the room, Using holo asteroids, hollowed out planetoids and debris fields as waves of shots and missiles followed in a wave of devastation, "or die a coward, disgraced, scared and pathetic trying to run."

Her eye connected with Luke's before continuing, "Archer was faced with the oldest question in war. If someone is trying to kill you, is it not thrust upon you to kill them first, to take his life to save yours and maybe hundreds more, to ignore politics and try to survive, the consequences didn't matter as long as you lived?'Archer would take a single Destroyer and not only cap two ships," the simulation flashed with the third and fourth ships as they were being taken by boarders as the simulation followed her words, "for the non existent Federation and still managed to slag five more in the process," The other five vessels exploded as the three ships set upon them, "Are you ready to take after Archer's example? Are you ready to kill and die for the Federation?!" The Simulation slowed down to a holo projection of the Commander on his ship. His arm was up in triumph, his men cheering the start of the 'Foundation to the Federation'. Luke always admired how normal Archer looked for a man of his Legend; his soft features and dull brown hair and eyes made him look like he belonged on a farm or in some fancy suit, not on the bow of the most famous Destroyer in history.

"Sir, yes, SIR." The Cadets responded with pure conviction that had been drilled into them all since the day they had arrived at the training facility.

"Sir, what happened to Archer's Destroyer? 'The Eclipse of Saturn'?" Someone asked their feminine voices dancing around the room as Montgomery eyed them.

"The Eclipse of Saturn was lost to time after the ship was abandoned somewhere over Pentawar as Archer and the Federation worked to conquer the Celta Quadrant. No one has seen or heard from the ship and it is presumed lost to time." The Commander paused her eyes flashing around the classroom before she continued,

"You all still have a lot to learn. When the time comes I hope you all remember my lessons." Commander Montgomery commented looking at Cadet Akya as she spoke with no nonsense expression. Even in the darkness of the room he could see the warning in her eye, "You all will know what I mean when the time comes," the bell's harsh grace filled the room as if planned perfectly to save them all from her gaze. "Class dismissed," she said, Then stopped her back relaxing, "Class do not forget about the weekly drill this afternoon. You are all expected to show even those going off planet." Her eyes connected with Cadet Akya's one last time as he made his way out of the classroom.

A loving hand is gently placed on his shoulder as he stares off into the distance trying to comprehend today's lesson. It had been haunting him for the last hour. He barely had even noticed that time had passed. Luke looked around the cafeteria; its blue marble glistened gently in the sunlight. The room was almost the size of the training deck which could fit the crew of a full cruiser of almost nine-hundred people. The air was still with little to no movement or action happening in the off hour before the long break. Most Cadets would be in the squad pods or walking the courtyard on a day like this to waste time. The rains had stopped bathing the courtyard and the surrounding area in a purple iridescent glow.

"Huh...sorry I was just thinking about what Commander Montgomery said," He said, looking at his closest friend, his moss green eyes searching her pale face for answers. She stared back with her calm gray eyes almost complementing his. She weighed in at a little over fifty-five kilos. Her trained frame was stiff from her physical training she just endured right before meeting Kyle. The most identifiable part of her was her hip length raven laced hair; her navy blue highlights that were entwined intricately made her hair look almost a midnight blue.

"It was just Commander Montgomery speaking in riddles again. You know how she is," Lylah signed, trying to comfort her friend, "I wouldn't think too hard about it, although all that eye contact made it really creepy." She continued trying to lighten the mood. Rolling her eyes and flashing a soft smile trying not to show her worry.

They half laughed but Luke couldn't forget Montgomery's face; it was beyond serious and the eye contact was menacing in a soul warning way. He looked at his second grade friend and wondered if she knew more than she was letting on. He stared at Lylah's baby smooth face, She looked up and met his eyes with her gentle gray ones. He had loved her for so long. How could she not see it? He smiled uncontrollably at her, starting to fade into a memory.

"Op!" Lylah cried trying desperately to form the words she knew she couldn't make. Lylah wiggled back and forth trying to sign but failing because she was also having to defend her sides from Luke attacking her ticklish ribs.

"Saying stop will not save you now," Luke grumped at her and continued tickling her. They were only eight and just got out of school. Lylah's Dad had picked them up, as they waited for Luke's dad to get off work, Luke continued to attack her ticklish ribs in the living room. The room was almost as big as Luke's Room, his dad's master bedroom, and the living room combined. His dad was a wealthy trader throughout all sectors so it's not like they were poor but this living room alone was massive. Pictures of all three of them and some of just Lylah and Luke lined the ever expanding walls. The champagne white walls were lit with rays of the sun making the room look even bigger. He smiled and raised his hand as Mr. Soffrireterna walked by with a huge grin on his face.

"Tag Mr. S." Luke cried and smacked Mr. S's hand.

"Now you're in trouble," Her dad chuckles and dives over the couch tackling them both as they all fall to the floor. Mr. S was a well built man but by no means husky. His mid shoulder length hair hung gently around the crick of his neck as they laughed all just enjoying the beauty of the day and each other's company.

Lylah smacked Luke on the shoulder and signed, "Luke! You're doing that thing where you stare at me awkwardly."

"Huh," Seeming to finally get his attention as he was pulled out of the memory.

"I'm sure it was nothing Luke, I really think it was." She once again signed, patting her friend on the back as they silently looked around the now empty room.

Luke smiled trying to move the subject and responded, "You should turn on your mental recognizer."

"Ugh you're gonna make us late with all your damn day dreaming." She sighed loudly as she saw the time tapping the red crystal in her neck as she stood in a rush.

Luke shook his head empathetically. "You started it." He mumbled slowly standing beside her.

"Oh fuck you," she laughed her voice echoing her minds projection of what she thinks she sounds like. Lylah shoved Luke towards the hallways as Luke marveled at her, "Come on don't make me regret getting you special seats, front row." Luke looked at her with sudden disbelief.

The Academy had managed to get a set of their favorite bands to do a concert to start their spring break. The line up was Sexiest Ba Booms, Poets in Falling Space, Lin Parker, and City of Owls. Lylah was a huge Sexiest Ba Booms, and City of Owls fan and Luke loved Poets in Falling Space and Sexiest Ba Booms as well but did enjoy Lin. The Front row was supposed to be reserved for only finalists in the Best Commander tournament but everyone knew that they had more seats than competitors. Even though they were not allowed to complete.

"You need to be stopped." Luke chuckled as he allowed the five foot one shorty to "push" him, "If your dad..."

"My dad is the one who ordered them to give me the seats." Lylah said curtly as she stopped trying to move him and kicked at his shin. Luke looked at her with disbelief hopping in an over dramatic fashion, "You're awful."

"And you love me for it." She smiled coyly and swung around in a huff.

Luke was very aware that her dad, the Commander and Chief of the Entire Armada had not ordered anyone to do anything. Most likely she had hacked the system and used Luke's illegal body double program to make herself look like her father and had a false ping to earth that would appear at least to no one looking too terribly hard that the orders were from earth. He looked at her knowing only she could get away with such an insane plan.

"What did you even say?" Luke mocked trying to imagine that amount of sass the Commander and Chief would have if Lylah was the speaker. The thought brought a slight boyish smile to Lukes lips.

"Now assuming I had managed to hack your pad, use a highly illegal program also created and hidden by you, to score you and I sweet ass front row seats that so happens to have both of our favorite bands which somehow happens to be at the very school we attend. All of which is highly suspect and your question is 'What did you say?' Do you think I planned a speech or something?"

"Why do I allow you to get away with this shit?" Luke sighed as they rounded the corner of the squad pods.

The corridor wasn't anything different from the rest of the academy; the granite walls had sixteen doors etched into their long stretches. The doors were made of glass and slid on their own having privacy settings and lockdown procedures available. Compared to the rest of the high tech School the Squad pods were remarkably plain and out of date. Most had a basic holo computer and a bunk that held two wall dressers underneath the mattress all of which was etched into the walls . The pods themselves were isolated units that were completely self-sustaining. On one side was the entrance, the other was a commons with a full armament in case of an assault on the academy. They had enough space for a fireplace, a decent side kitchen and full pantry, and a bit of furniture that was circled in the middle of the room. The bathrooms and showers on either side of the room rounded it off.

"Cause you benefit too." Lylah said curtly as she walked passed Lukes's Pod, which was the third pod on the right from the entrance.

"I wonder sometimes who gets chewed out worse, me or you." Luke mumbled to himself as he stopped in front of his pod.

"Two minutes." Lylah smirked as she walked away.

Luke watched after her. His heart skipped several beats as he slowly awaited for the right time. *Tonight is the night.* He decided as she disappeared into her pod the last pod on the left and went to change into civilian clothes himself.

The concert, as to be expected, was beyond amazing; after the concert they had backstage passes and met some of their icons Lin even gave Lylah her number so they could stay in touch. The whole thing cheered everyone up, even the almost always stoic Commander Montgomery. As the masses moved out of the great hall and went their separate ways. Commander Montgomery ,who was still in uniform, waved as they approached the train platform.

Luke and Lylah nodded as they moved to put distance between her and them.

"Cadets if I might have a word?" She motioned for them to approach and stand with her.

"Ma'am," They droned back knowing what was next.

"How did you enjoy the concert?" She said, staring forward as the cadets tried acting like civilians, failing to not stick out as none civilians.

"Luke and I had favorite bands in the mix for this year ma'am." Lylah said taking in the surroundings and noticed a group of undesirables eyeing them. She used low hand signals to inform the other two. Three men with hidden weapons and what looked like a bounty I.D. pad. The Pack held it up at Luke, Lylah and the Commander. The men were probably looking for a rape hit. The head mob bosses of Magness Prime used sexual assaults and torture to get what they wanted and most importantly they hated female officers in the military. Magness Prime was one of the Best Military schools in the Galaxy hidden deep within the Delta Quadrant which was rank with Corruption. Unfortunately for the men that had the I.D. Pad, they happened to size up the best Squad at the Academy and worse they probably didn't even know Luke, Lylah, and the Commander were Spec Ops.

"Yeah that's the damndest thing isn't it?" Command Montgomery mocked, ignoring the men and turning to look full at Lylah.

"Ma'am," Lylah sighed and tensed up as four more joined the pack of three. Lylah relayed the info and Luke walked up behind dropping the act and putting himself between Lylah and the Gang forming but beside the Commander. His arms crossed staring a hole in the group, a few laughed in response.

"I will reprimand you back at the school." Command Montgomery said as she nodded to Luke and turned to light a Cigarette. Lylah stood rigid wincing when she heard bones crack or break: she kept her back turned to the chaos of the fight.

Luke surged forward with the nod his first hit, a clean knock out on the nearest thug moving at blinding speeds. Turning Luke snatched an arm out of the air. Immediately twisting to tense it before using his palm to snap the elbow joint inverted. Blood splattered over Luke as he caught a hard right to his jawline. He twisted with the momentum gaining a quick recovery and dived for a double leg take down. Luke was far better then the now group of seven as Luke used his size to quickly mount and pummel the man with two decisive haymakers cracking the man's skull under the pressure and showering his arms in blood. A leg lands solidly on the side of Luke's head exploding his ear and jaw with pain. Sharp ringing plagued Luke as he rolled to avoid further damage giving him a fraction to recover and face the remaining four, arms up ready. Luke relaxed as blood slowly trickled down his eyes as he stared at the men with a hunger lusting in his eyes. Two gulped nervously as they stared at each other for a second debating if continuing this was worth it.

"That's enough Cadet." Commander Montgomery barked, thick smoke exploding from her lips as she spoke.

"Fuck their Spec Ops." One of the Thugs said as he double checked the hit and shook his head in fear.

"Fuck the pay out." Another Responded and they ran off leaving the other three to whatever fate was in store for them.

"You can turn around Cadet," Montgomery said, patting Lylah on the shoulder as she walked passed.

"Let me see." The Commander said, walking to stand beside Luke. The size comparison is like a Gorilla to any normal woman. Lylah turned slowly and saw the fallout. One man was cradling his blood soaked arm that hung limply in the wrong direction. Two of the men were on the ground, one an indention in his skull , his nose cavity was caved in and it looked like he wasn't breathing. The other was face down a few feet from her twitching as if his neck had been broken. Lylah's stomach turned and she threw up, turning her head.

"Still can't handle blood?" Luke said patting her softly on the back for a big guy he could move fast and helping her move her hair.

"Fuck you," She said through gritted teeth. She knew he wasn't trying to be mean but it bugged her that she couldn't stand the sight of blood. She shivered at his touch but his hand was oddly soothing on her back. She suddenly didn't want him to stop touching her.

"Come on," He said, helping her stand without messing her hair up. Lylah looked over Luke, his City of Owls shirt was dirty and spotted with his own blood, his cargo slacks were covered in dirt and blood and he had a blood smudges on the left side of his face but his arms, from the elbow to his fingertips was dripping, some globs even starting to crust over in the heat of the day.

Luke looked her over. Her punk mini skirt and fishnet stockings were perfect as usual, balanced out by her short sleeve Sexiest Ba Booms belly shirt covered with a net brassier . Her hair, its beautiful raven mane hung loosely around her shoulders, a perfect mix of mess and style. He let a soft smile form. She looked at him and slapped him in the chest reminding him of the fight he just endured for her.

"Did you kill him?" She pointed to the man with his face pushed in, "If you got me fucken paperwork on vaction I will literally..."

Montgomery walks over, raises her wrist map and opens a bio reader, "Nope he's alive." Purposefully interrupting Lylah in the process.

"A thanks would be nice." Luke said, rubbing his chest gently as he looked from woman to woman.

"Baby," Lylah sassed, trying not to laugh as she glared at him.

"That really hurt. Like more than getting kicked in the head hurt." He said as he continued to rub his massive chest sprouting a puppy dog face.

"Fuck off." Lylah choked a laugh back trying to look away to allow a smile to form, blush gently teasing her cheeks.

"You two in my office first thing Monday till then have a good spring break." The Commander said, reminding them both she was still there, "And whatever this is," She raised her finger in their direction with an uncharacteristic sly smile teasing her left cheek, " Hold onto it."

"Ma'am!" Lylah blushed hard turning a burning cole red looking away quickly and taking a massive step away from Luke in embarrassment.

"Mo..am. We aren't...we can't...us...can't..."Luke Stammered quickly raising his arm to the back of his neck trying to find the words before trying to dismiss the notion all together. Lylah smacks his arm and pulls him into the tram as it arrives, her face crinkled in rage and fury.

"The fuck was that?" She hissed her emotions overwhelming the mental recognizer as it struggled to convey her overwhelmed emotions. They sat down and the tram left the station with a jolt. Lylah's face is a mixed bag of worry, rage, and embarrassment as she wrestles with her own inner monologue.

"I...what are you mad at?" Luke said with a hushed voice back, quickly retreating to make sure they were on the same page as he attempted to get closer so only the two of them could communicate. Lylah shuts down and starts speaking in sign language as she turns off the Mental Recognizer. "We can't?" She raged, her facial expression rapidly changing as she tried to convey in emotion and signs what her words were completely incapable of saying. She rapidly changed her starting before taking a deep breath. Signing. "What if I wanted an us?" She finished her venomous fingers pointing from him to back at her. Luke's heart skipped several beats, she beat him to it.

"Do I want...an us? Is that." Luke signed back slowly allowing Lylah a moment to register his question.

Lylah rolled her eyes and shook her head, "Do you...want an us?"She quickly responded, her arms racing with insecurity as she signed back. The world raced back and forth because the tram was traveling at just shy of moch 2 from town to town. Magness Prime hazed over with the deep purple rains of this planet's winter season, giving an unnatural beauty to Lylah's deep raven blue hair. Luke lost how long he stared at her.

"Yes," He signed slowly. Finale. A soft smile chiseled on his face. The people came and went but neither noticed or cared; they both sat staring at their hands trying to deal with their own mixed feelings. They had said it. The world slowly started to return to normal as Lylah tapped Luke on the shoulder and signed "Luke," She hesitated before finally controlling her emotions to speak with her words, "you aren't just trying to get down my pants?"

"You would have run me off long ago. I think you know the answer to your own question. I," Luke said softly and with unnatural insecurity in his voice, "I have wanted you for as long as I can remember." Luke's heart bound as he waited for her response. Lylah girlishly lowered her hand onto Luke's hand and laid her head on his chest waiting for their stop. They didn't need to speak or sign in that moment words couldn't explain the sheer emotions they both held towards the other. The trip from that point on to the party wasn't as eventful. They walked into the party, Lylah being escorted by Luke, everyone of their squad noticed them interlocked and took a moment to register the news before exploding in excitement and cheering.

"Luke! Luke!" The guys crowed and cheered viering him away from Lylah. She smiled and shook her shoulders as the woman dragged her in the opposite direction. Gawking at him as she rolled her eyes, getting lost in the sea of people in the bar. Luke took a moment to take in the bar as his fellow brothers guided him to the actual bar and some stools. The dark seductive red tapestries and outlining teased the black ambience of the room. Their air of vampiric goth and alcohol bombard Luke's senses as candles seem to whisper sweet nothings to him. Luke froze realizing someone had just laced him with something. His eyes floated back to Lylah as she saw him staring at her and winked as if to confirm his suspicion. He allowed a smile to form knowing Lylah realized he wouldn't have been able to relax without dosing him.

"Shot's for the Luckiest man in the entire galaxy." Dakota said, slapping the bar and bringing Luke back to the here and now. Dakota was plump for a spacecoresman. His sandy blonde hair and unregulated beard made him appear more homeless than a soldier, beside him was Aaron, a flaming flamboyant pottymouth with hella good sniping skills. His unregulated ponytail was allowed due to religious reasons and Mark, who was the squad's douchebag, was bald with a scrunched face and little mass, maybe a buck fifty in weight. None of the boys had much bulk on them and looked more like officers than actual engineers who were expected to move giant pieces of ship siding, pipes, you name it to all over the starship if needed. However despite this, all three were on the Apache squad, the best squad in the entire academy and already slated to replace everyone of the command officers on the F.S.F.V. Ellen a brand new Medical Carrier class-dreadnought. A ship capable of slagging forty carriers without having to reload or deploy fighters. Its overwhelming firepower was nothing to its state of the art medical facilities complete with auto-repair beds, Macrobot regeneration pods and helmed by Doctor Mal the direct descendant of the man behind the cure for autism in the early 25th. Now Genetic augmentation on Molecular changes ensured everything from sex, to hair color. When the child is finally born and grows to the age of maturity, in this case sixteen, the child gets a free genetic modification to change anything about themselves. Luke shook his head trying not to get lost in the fact that everything they take for granted on that ship will be repaired and fixed by these three idiots. Luke marveled at his friends and smiled realizing how amazing his life truly was.

"So what's it like being second in command, chief tactial officer, AND," The booze stank so heavily on Dakota's breath when he elongated the and Luke almost lost his patience, "Are gonna be fucking the captain?" Luke took his shot and downed it in one quick guple before smashing it into Dakota's head knocking him out on the spot. The other burst out laughing knowing the absolute right Luke had in retaliating to a comment like that.
"He's your chief, I wouldn't be laughing'." Luke signed so they both knew it was an order, "You're in charge of him." The other two quickly stopped what they were doing, their training kicking in and pulled Dakota away.
"So?" A bratty voice purred at him, "You and the Captain huh?" Luke's tolerance for distractions was starting to weigh extremely thin at this point as he simply wanted to be alone with his thoughts and a smooth drink.
"What is it with people and running words tonight?" Luke said into his drink, raising his hand and tapping the table three times for a triple shot, the bartender walked over waiting for a type. Luke mouthed Whiskey.
"What?"The voice asked. The bartender compiled before finally Luke turned on the stool to look at the voice. The voice belonged to Beth Sorginfierer. A skinny, low self esteem, entitled Delta Quadrant model. Her asian descendance is more visible than ever with her skimpy kamoto and hair style. Luke despised her for disrespecting her own history. Luke quickly downs the drink taping for another.

"When you're done with the captain can I have a turn?" She cooed, moving provocatively towards him, the booze doing her no favors as she tried to grab his crotch. Luke quickly used his shoulder to roll her off him and onto the bar top before Beth sat up and smiled awkwardly at him. Luke shook his head, a splitting headache forming; the drink arrived with perfect timing and he slammed it down, ignoring his own gag reflex and asking for another before catching the bartender and changing the number to three.

"Oh my, it seems you were naughty tonight." Beth said, looking him over and seeming to get sexually aroused by the bruises and blood that he had forgotten to wipe off before entering the bar.

"I would have let you been raped." Luke said into another triple downing the drink in disgust and shook his head from the strength of the cheap liquor that burnt like ash down the back of his throat.

"Now now, don't threaten me with a good time." She cooed back, dropping towards his crotch before Luke shot up.

"You're done, Bartender, this is a military personnel please call the MP's and have her escorted home. She was attempting to violate me." Luke said, revealing his ID to the bartender without taking his eyes off Beth while he spoke. Letting the bartender know why what he was saying was a big deal.

"Right away." The Bartender hurried away. Luke looked back at Beth and nodded as her mouth was anchored to the floor and slammed the rest of his drink. Leaning closer to her so only she could hear him, Luke whispers, " I'm only taking away your vacation. Next time I will leave you in the brig for two months alone. And when I finally let you out you'll be cleaning the toilets for work with your tongue. Don't ever make an advance on me. If I hear about you advancing on someone else without their consent, I will personally feed you to Lylah's dogs. Am I understood?" Luke hissed, grabbing her by the throat and pulling her closer to him as he spoke. Luke had no intention of following through on any of this but the best thing he could do was scare her straight.

"Ye...yes, sir." Beth almost turned into a ghost in his hands as Luke roughed her up. Luke released her and made sure she was stable as the MPs arrived.

"Now be a good soldier and go wait for graduation." He ordered dismissing her and the MPs with a nod.

Luke took another shot from the bar and turned in his chair and went back to admiring the bar. Extravagant old gothic church stone and cloth decorated the pack party. The pillars and columns were perfectly aligned but not so perfect you could tell someone actually made the stone and that this was not just some giant holoroom. Lylah had probably paid out the ass for contractors to only get frustrated and just designed the entire thing herself. The Girls had Lylah around one of the many black booths on the other side of the bar. The low light helped slightly with the blood red lines that laced the walls in places and outlined most of the furniture. The Candle lite tables flickered softly casting sensual shadows dancing over Lylah's soft face as her eyes flashed his way and she smiled gently before he turned his back to think.

"Treat her well or I will kill you myself." Luke stiffened like a board because he knew that voice by heart. The world grew fuzzy and almost tunneled as the booze slammed hard into Luke. Of course this weasel would show up now when Luke was already drunk.

"I will," He said, still frozen, watching with longing eyes at Lylah, "I thought you had business in the Alpha Quadrant?"

"I know when my daughter acts up." Luke turned to face The Commander and Chief of the Armada. Mr. S. had his long mud brown hair in a tight low ponytail. His native skin seemed more alive in the dark of the bar. His piercing steel ice eyes tearing pieces out of Luke every second. He was covered in a long coat and deep hat to avoid being spotted. Luke looked at the man in complete disgust.

"How?" Luke raised an eyebrow fully aware the Commander couldn't beat him any longer. The man raised his wrist pad and swiped his hand and the picture on the screen was of them entering the bar with the headline, 'NEW POWER COUPLE TAKING OVER THE GALAXY'. Luke nodded in acknowledgement. And downed another drink.

"You're a good man son, but they will never find your body if you hurt her." The Commander spat as he stood and patted him on the shoulder. Trying his hardest to control the situation.

"You don't get the right." Luke rolled Mr. S's hand off his shoulder and quickly pulled the completely smaller man closer to him. Mr. S struggles, unable to move the mountain of man. Panic and fear quickly plaster themselves as Mr. S desperately tries to free himself, making a slight commotion as he flails about.

"I made myself clear five years ago. When we left." Luke whispers sinisterly, refusing to concede, flexing slightly which starts to apply a blood choke on Mr. S. Luke waits for panic to set in before stopping the flex and finishing. "Leave her alone and never come back." Luke snarls finally as Mr. S turns bright red and Luke tosses the vial man on the floor, for him to scamper away. Luke looked at the bartender who's eyebrow was raised.
"Last time I swear sir, my apologies." Luke quickly recovered and made a generous tip to the man's tip jar. The Bartendered eyed him suspiciously but nodded allowing Luke to continue drinking in peace.

Lylah watched as Luke never stopped being the good soldier even when she saw Beth approach. The other girls in their squad had talked major shit on Beth of course but only because Lylah was a bigger hit right now. Her and Luke finally become an item.

"This one is so my favorite," Michelle cackled reading the headlines, "Gray hair beauty has joined the?" She paused and looked at Lylah before raising her fingers and put quotations up as she spoke, " 'mile high' club as she tackles the mountain on her path to the top." Lylah playfully shouldered her friend who rolled her eyes realizing finally after they had pumped her full of margaritas and had their fun they needed to ask.
"So like how is it you never saw the signs?" Michelle stated and the other girls nodded getting close as it was finally time for answers.
Lylah snapped back to the table and ordered another Margarita as the waiter passed by trying her best to ignore the question before turning to the others and signing,"There weren't any."

Michelle was on Lylah's left, a skilled close combat expert soon to be the Chief Security officer and Advanced Boarding Leader. Her coal hair was slightly brighter than Lylah's. Her soft features and ebony skin didn't match the bark she possessed. To Lylah's right were the twins Alice and Selaris, gingers through and through topped with green eyes and freckles. Smart and Sciency like Lylah liked it. They were shorter than Michelle but taller than Lylah. And on the left edge was Maddie, the local hardass. She stood a massive six foot two and weighed in at around two-twenty. Her pale white skin almost glowed in the low light matched only by her bright blonde hair. She has height, weight, and beauty that made up for the lack of brains. She was the only one in the squad who wasn't an officer.

"The fuck there wasn't, bitch I looked at Alice and Maddie yesterday and was all watch those two gonna make babies." Michelle rambled drunkenly as she struggled to compose her thoughts as the two mentioned nodded.
"Alright," Lylah signed as her ninth drink came and she took a sip before continuing, "Tell me. What signs of this 'not coming outta nowhere' can you find." Lylah rolled her eyes in irritation as the others gave her an incredulous look.

Michelle laughed obnoxiously before being taken back, "Ok bitch first off, You wouldn't have tailor designed this entire thing so he could get in your pants." Michelle was interrupted as Lylah exploded with signs, "Fucken first off," Lylah raged, "I had nothing to do with any of this," She waved her hands around at the bar. Michelle raised an eyebrow but waited for her to continue, "so fuck your first point."

"Fine second off," Michelle stared at Lylah with a booze induced frenzy desperate to win.

"Even I knew," Maddie said with a grin as the others giggled with delight at the bomb. Maddie was not known for her ability to lie. She was the respectful silent type. Lylah quickly started to reconsider her stance.

"Whatever," Lylah dismissed before turning on her voice, "Y'all the worst." She took another drink mocking Michelle's accent.

"And you love us for it." Selaris inserted, sending the girls into a fit again.

Lylah laughed and took a moment to glance at Luke. He hung gloomily at the bar downing shots. His shoulders low and his head lower. He was losing himself to his brain again. Lylah also couldn't help but notice the bartender's nervous looks towards Luke.

"So when will you be sharing bunks?" Michelle proded, "I bet you he has a."

"Wow! Now that kinda talk needs more tequila for answers." Lylah said, shoving her hand in Michelles mouth and waved down a waiter with the other, ordering shots as Michelle drunkenly failed to get Lylah off her mouth.

"We know you set this up, Captain. Your money trail is almost more secure now." Selaris leaned in winking.

"SHOTS." Lylah said with relief as the waiter came back; the girls seperated the booze and prepared for the shot tradition. Lylah had started it the first year. Whenever someone has good news or gets in a relationship they shot. Everyone at the table had to have at least one thing. This was their fifth year of the tradition.

"Lylah you first." Alice said, nodding.

"I got the captain's chair!" They shotted. Michelle was next. "I beat Luke this morning in hand to hand!" They shotted. Lylah raised her hand and gagged slightly.

"He let you win."

Michelle punched her shoulder, "No way he even said I won fair and square."

"Unless you can take seven guys and beat three, he let you win." The giggles stopped as the girls noticed the odd specifics of what Lylah was saying.

"What?" Alice said her face was horror stricken, her drunkenness leaving for the moment.

Lylah smiled, "At the tram station a gang of guys tried to rape collect and Luke took them all by himself." Lylah said, realizing what she had just said. The booze makes things painfully clear and the world slows to a screeching halt. Her emotions overloaded the Recognizer and signed the rest, "Command Montgomery...was with us Luke was just following orders." Lylah signed frantically.

"Luke..saved you?" Selaris signed back.

The floor disappeared as she sank out of her own ignorance. Lylah turned to Luke.He was still taking shots and the bar area was almost empty now. The dance floor was roaring in front of the stained glass of some saint as mostly everyone had their drinks or dates. Luke was notorious for being a loner...except when it came to Lylah. Lylah's head swirled in a fantasy.

"What are you guys gonna do next year? Stay enlisted and be officers or take that shiny piece of bullshit and run?" Alice said as she slurred her words, the booze hitting her harder than normal as Selaris shook her head.

"I'm gonna take the captain's chair of the Next generation. I don't have credits to pass. So I will be the rookie's Captain like ours." Maddie said her thick slavic accent blaring through, patting Lylah on the shoulder, "You gonna take the Commander's position Cap'n?"

"I'm..." Lylah said, losing track of herself to a daydream, "gonna marry him." She saw their wedding, and I do's. Their children, a girl with beautiful raven hair and her eyes a beautiful moss green to match her daddy's. They would watch her go to the very school they were at now. Lylah smiled to herself seeing herself in old age . Luke a few feet away gray and wrinkled with time napping before the grandkids arrived. The thought was comforting.

"I wanna do one for someone." Maddie said and brought her back out of the daydream. Everyone came to and prepared to take another shot.

"To Lylah for finding her partner for life." Maddie raised her glass and everyone else did as well. Lylah smiled and held back tears of joy. They had four more rounds of the thankful shots and the girls allowed Lylah to return to Luke who sat across from them. Lylah walked her way to Luke and rubbed his back gently. He looked and smiled, his eyes pained with the torture of his own thoughts. Lylah offered her hand and a soft smile accompanied with it. They retired back to the hotel next door together.

Preface: Part 2

Do all Miracles come with conditions?

1 week before the Great War Started
Magness Prime
Horatius School of War Arts

Luke Akya
9:00 A.M.
March 12th, 4999 A.D.

Luke lay still listening to the soft breaths that came from Lylah and looked up at the ceiling. The air was still and the moon shone brightly through the windows. The traffic cast moving shadows as they passed. He smiled and closed his eyes. Her soft breaths provide a rhythm for him to relax as a hover car goes by teasing the walls with light. Lylah saw his eyes blink.
"This is real right?" Lylah spoke softly, her head still tucked into his massive shoulders she wanted to use her words for once.
"Yeah." He whispered back and moved slightly to pull her that much closer.
    The air was still again before she struggled to speak."You wanted this right? Us? Me and you?" She asked, trying to settle her own self confidence issues. Another car goes by making a light shadow that danced up her exposed soft back. Luke smiled at the ballet of light and shadows on her back as the drunk crowd went home.
    He kissed her forehead gently then spoke, "You are the only one I have wanted. You're my first and last. My future, my past and present. My Universe." Lylah coughs a laugh trying to hide tears struggling to fight to make sure her words are spoken correctly."Using My favorite quote against me huh? Totally something you would do." Lylah said, raising herself to look at him. The Ballet dances around Lylah's breasts, collar bone, and as she lay atop Luke. Luke being drawn in as the rains once again picked up showering the light with iridescent pulsating R.B.G. that now seductively danced on her upper body.
"I learned from the best teacher...Are you sure this is what you want?" Luke smiled as he signed, trying not to stress Lylah out and choosing to sign.
    "For the first time in my life I have never been so confident in my choice as I am choosing you." Lylah spoke, staring at his eyes in the low iridescent dance which allowed them to almost glow as cars would pass by. The air seemed to tease the senses. They kissed again, getting lost to the emotions of the night.

The phone rang, bringing the couple out of their blissful dreams. Luke reached over, blinded by the light in the room trying to not wake Lylah more. He hit the holocom sensor and answered.

"Yello?" Luke grumbled, slumping his head back on the pillow.

"Ah, Good Morning sir, would you care for some breakfast?" Lylah lay still not wanting Luke to know she was listening.

"Yea let's do, Pandercakes vanilla, with Peanut butter drizzle and syrup," Luke rubbed an eye and continued an inside smile formed as he spoke, "and I want the biggest breakfast meal you have." Pandercakes were giant four inch pancakes filled with chocolate or whatever delectable treat the orderer would like.

"Alrighty sir you said the Pander or Pan Cakes." Lylah smiled uncontrollably because Pandercakes were an Alpha quadrant speciality dish, one she particularly liked and one she made sure her hotel had.

"Pander please, and my account." Luke opened his wrist map and hit the holo screen till he got to his cards and flicked the card forward to initiate the transfer of information. "All of it."

"As you wish sir. Will you need anything else?" The assistant asked with a hint of misunderstanding in his voice.

"I don't think so, I have everything I need right here." Luke smiled curtly.

"Good day, sir." and the com went dead.

"You suck at stealth by the way. You caught your breath when I said pandercakes." He said moving his arm out from under her and standing up to stretch.

"You don't have to be so cute when ordering food." She signed, smacking his ass to get his attention before Lylah ran by and giggling heading to the bathroom.

"Don't make me come in there." He said as the shower turned on.

"Don't threaten me with a good time." She giggled her words playful as she peeked around the corner, still nude.

"I told you that in confidence! That's it, Munity" Luke falsely claimed running in after her laughing. Lylah's joyous giggles and excitement echoed around the room as they "showered".

The food came some time after their shower. Luke got his first good look at the room in the light of day. Lylah had gotten last night. The Suite was gigantic, probably one of the penthouses. The bed sat on the far side nestled between two large windows. Luke strolled over to one taking in the Dark Gothic themed decorium. It seemed to match the same as last night's bar. Luke looked at the bottom right hand of the furthest wall. He smiled seeing a giant dark oak dresser in his way. Luke smiled and easily moved the ton dresser out of the way and saw what he was looking for. In the Corner was Lylah's S over L signature. Luke quickly put the dress back and figured out Lylah's secret. She had built the bar and Hotel which were now making her money, which meant she paid for literally everything and there would be a huge money trail leading back to Lylah. He looked around the dark oak walls and varying blood red lines that ran down the walls. Luke heard Lylah leaning against the bathroom walls. Finally Luke turned to Lylah, "You bought a Hotel and Bar?' Luke asked.

"I have a deep trust fund." She dismissed and headed to the bed looking for something in one of the bed draws.

"Jesus." Luke said looking at Lylah before signing, " We are," He stumbled before changing his signs. "Us. there is a real us."

"Last I checked." She said her body relaxed, pulling out a bong raising an eyebrow. She slowly starts to load the bowl, seeing Luke's worried face, Lylah stops before Luke asks. "It's not that Delta shit again is it? Cause that shit was a bad two days." Luke said, shivering, looking at the green being packed into the double vortex bong.

"Alpha Centi Six." She said, "Last night was my first time..." Her recognizer became quickly overwhelmed leaving the last part of whatever she said an unknown mess.

"Mine too." Luke signed awkwardly, moving to sit beside her and taking his side of the bong wishing to end the conversation.

"Luke..." Luke wasn't hearing it and light, pulling hard on the bong which forced Lylah to cover and breath in the drugs. The world started to mix and match, spinning wildly. Luke felt himself leave his body and return to it a few times before he adapted. He felt the relaxation and ease flood over his body as Luke lay, extending his massive body over the bed. Thankfully Lylah had thought ahead, making sure the bed could fit with an extra large bed, the was big enough that even he looked slightly small in size which was not an easy feat.

"Holy shit." He coughed a thick fog coming from his mouth as he finally spoke allowing the smoke to slowly seep from his lips spouting like a geyser of smoke that slowly hung in the air.

"Good stuff." She nodded and agreed, smiling as she stared at him. Lylah laid her head on his chest and extended her body across the bed. They talked about everything and anything they had ever wanted to and wandered off getting lost in each other and the days to come. In their heightened state the six remaining days flew by and they were back to business in the academy preparing for graduation.

Luke Akya
Less than a Day before Graduation

"Cadets come in." Commander Montgomery stated; the door slid open as Lylah and Luke walked in. Her room was unlike anyone else's. Instead of marble, her office was made of wood, a nice deep mahogany. Shelves lined the walls like an old archaic library. Luke and Lylah sat in the wooden chairs that complimented the Desk and the walls. The air of strict discipline hanging like damp dew, complimented by soft sandalwood that teased at the edges of the Cadet's noses. "They lived." The Commander jumped right in staring at the holoscreen in front of her refusing to acknowledge the two as she read, "They received medical attention and were sent on their way with an offer to exchange for information on someone higher up or forced conscription. They chose to be conscribed and will learn their lessons."

"Ma'am." Luke said knowing fully well most conscribed men took beatings and depending on their squad gang rapes of their own to show them humility and expose them to the exact thing they were trying to do to the military.

"That isn't my issue." Commander Montgomery scolded, and swiped the holoscreen aside and stared at Lylah, " I have told you many times if you dont pulse the sensor ping it wouldn't be authentic." Lylah's face exploded in shock, "If I hadn't found it before anyone else you would be flagged and canned, do you understand me? They would have taken your damn ship away." She twisted, jumping down Lylah's throat with her words, "And you, boy, if you don't make the passwords more original I'll lock you out of your own bunk until you come up with something stronger than a three hexagonal bypass password." The two cadets stayed stoic as they waited for the rant to end.

"For fuck sake!?" She explain in desperation, "How the fuck am I supposed to approach the brass with you two?" Changing her tone to a complete belittling, she continued, "Oh here is the best crew we have the brass wants for the MOST ," She started to scream, her face turning red in rage, "Advanced ship in the fucken ENTIRE Armada. But fuck niether of them know how to or just simply won't follow basic rules," Slammed her fist into the table before pointing at Lylah, almost climbing over the desk in rage as she spoke, "You can't stand blood, simply refuse to follow the change of command and," She breathed, "I am convinced ENJOY giving me heart attacks with your sheer gall. And," She wields herself upon Luke,"and YOU. ARE. so stupidly loyal and naive I CAN'T fathom even how you got in Apache squad let alone understand how you are it's XO. How in the fuck are you gonna run The Ellen if you two can't control your own crew? You gave your own chief engineer a concussion, locked up another for charges of unwanted advances. But when it came time to press charges,"

"And I Quote," as she reads the report she brought it up, "release the fish." She throws out her arms in rage and genuine disgust at what she was reading like a rambling parent, "And back to you," Quickly turning on Lylah who had been suppressing a laugh, " Have, and this is by far the strangest one, have literally." Montgomery continued to rage as it turned to sheer astonishment as she looked over Lylah's files, "and I mean literally have broken every fucken rule we have." Montgomery started to sass some of the rules, "Assaulted several M.P.S, Possible sedition against a fellow cadet or squad," Montgomery's eyes almost glossed over as she continued to read, " forty-seven reports filed. Misallocation of Military property. Twenty-four times. Assaulted fellow cadets and/or," Montgomery raised an eyebrow.

"Teachers. Eighty-six reports." Mongtomery lowered her head in defeat as she returned to looking at the Cadets, "How can I expect your men to follow god damn rules when their captain and XO are literally BREAKING all of them multiple times." Montgomery composed herself further wrapping up. "But you're so popular on media and propaganda sites I can't fucken fire you or the Armada comes into question. Even with both of your wrap sheets." She continued to eye them before her rage returned, " You two are a fucken terrifing NIGHTMARE and are menaces to my goddamn health. And do I even need to take a hair follicle?" She stood up and walked around the desk getting closer to the couple. "But here the fuck you are following fucken orders like good soldiers," The commander nodded sarcasticly, "If I catch you fucking it up before graduation. I'll cut your dick and your titts off and proceed to throw them into the nearest Solar storm to see what would happen. Am I fucken understood." Standing at attention. The two stood and saluted in sync, "Sir, understood, Sir." "To class with the both of you." She waved dismissively. The two bolted and the rest of the day went without incident.

The final warning bell rang and everyone left the commons to head back to their pods. The Apache Cadets were giddy and smiling, all dressed for bed. Lylah hung off of Luke most of the time and they cuddled on the couch the rest as they waited slowly for the hours till graduation ticked by. Finally the bell rang and they made their way to the pods. Luke stopped in front of Lylah's pod and kissed her gently. The two lovers stared into each other's eyes almost lost in a shared fantasy.
"Jesus. What PDA." Beth shook her head in disapproval.

"Oh and you think we don't know Dakota sneaks into your room every other night?" Lylah signed as Maddie headed to her room catching Lylah's signs and Maddie slid into her own room so Beth wouldn't see Maddie holding back laughter. Beth scoffed and entered her pod before the glass closed and the privacy setting activated.
Michelle took stray shots with her fingers at Lylah's ticklish ribs and smiled before disappearing into her pod leaving only Luke and Lylah alone in the hallway.
"Tomorrow, I will be with you forever." Luke whispered to Lylah causing her heart to stop, her head hanging in his dinner plate sized hands.

"I love you." She whispered back and Luke kissed Lylah gently once more before they parted and Luke went back to his pod. He sat on his bunk looking at the wall before deciding to lay down, his mind completely restless as he traded staring at the wall for staring at the ceiling. Luke breathed deeply unaware of how much time had truly passed as the night lay still. The soft pssff alerted Luke to the fact he wasn't alone as the door slid open. The whisper of movement told him that this wasn't a drill. He rolled as the weapon came crashing down where he had been a second ago sending sparks as metal cut metal. Before Luke launched himself blindly at the door and connected with something solid, grabbing it with every ounce of strength he could. Luke roared, lifting the assailant with all his might slamming them straight down from Luke's massive seven foot six height. The force was estimated to be able to explode all the internal organs of anyone not wearing armor and make power armor completely useless.

The Dark almost black made it impossible to ID the attacker or the weapon that was now somewhere on the floor. The Black shape grabbed Luke's leg, seeming to recover unflappably fast. The man jerked the leg out from underneath Luke causing Luke to flip backwards landing hard on his back Luke attempted to recover before finding himself sliding across the floor. The man must have power armor on to throw Luke, who happens to weigh three hundred and eighty-eight pounds, like a child would throw a doll. Luke cracked against the wall leaving a small indention in the marble whereLuke collided with the wall. The Glass door slid open as Beth saw the shape. Beth didn't even hesitate, her training taking over as she jumped on its back clawing at its face successfully digging her nails into its eyes and showering Luke in a dark green chunky magnetic like liquid. Luke rolled forward taking the opportunity to slide under Beth's legs as Beth rolled backwards off his shoulders. Luke with a great gutturalw coming from deep and using all his strength once more, lifting the man again and suplexing him against the wall trying to break the thing man's neck or at least the armor system. Beth had managed to find the weapon in the darkness as they heard debris slowly bouncing off the thing giving a fair warning it wasn't full dead.

"Luke!" She screamed and slid the blade using her foot. Luke used the echoes in the room to catch the weapon and immediately turned it on the man. The man snapped up in the next instance quickly grabbing Luke's arm as if it could see in the dark. Twisting inwards and over Lukes shoulder the man caught Luke in a shoulder bar. The man quickly reclaimed the weapon from Luke, lobbing it into Beth's head as she surged forward and tried to free Luke. The man seemed to relish the fight and let Luke up. He moved his hand over the light sensor. As the light flicked on. Luke stared at what he thought was a man as it started to decloak. A scar tissue covered face emerged, a humanoid face, but this was not human. Its unnatural paleness wasn't white but like a very bad bleached skin color.

Black voids filled the holes that would normally be eyes and stared at Luke. Luke knew Beth had damaged those eyes but couldn't help but feel she hadn't done any damage. There was no mouth, just scar tissue layers. Its neck and body quickly followed revealing massive skin tight plate armor covering various parts of the body being infused to the scar tissue as opposed to over with some sort of suit. A greenish coal colored liquid travels through tubes that snake along the thing's legs, body, and arms. Luke saw three summer sausage size fingers and toes with a mandible fourth finger on the inside. The thing was just slightly bigger than Luke. The creature walked over and grabbed the blade out of Beth's head causing the head to bobbly lifelessly. Even though Luke knew Beth had damaged it, the only indication was the deep tear lines colored that sickly greenish black, making the creature look like it was a weeping willow of myth. Luke finally got a good look at the weapon. A long blade that had been serrated down both sides of the main blade leading to a clean looking delta quadrant inspired handle. It passed the sword back and forth before shifting forward. The blade hung in the air as the creature snached the handle with its feet just to show its versatility or an intimidation technique Luke cared not for the real answer.

"Come on," Luke roared as the creature swung at him, slashing wildly to the left before transitioning the blade to its lower leg as it missed changing its tactics, stabbing at Luke instead. Luke slid effortlessly along the safe flat of the blade closing the distance and quickly grabbing the creature's wrist before it could react. Luke snarled to the creature, "Wrong fucken room." Luke slams his head into the nose area of the thing and quickly takes advantage attempting to snap the creature's elbow, burrowing his forearm deep into the creature's elbow joint. Luke misjudged the creature's strength minorly as the creature managed to pull its arm back, slashing at Luke's hip. Flesh tore and ripped along the attack as the serrated edges gleefully did it job. Luke hollowed in pain before ignoring all his own rules calling on his ancestry. The creature tilted it's head as if it knew what he was doing as Luke launched emerald green lighting into the creature. It screeched and dropped the weapon as it spasmed, wrathing as burns started forming on its arms and legs, the lighting growing brighter almost to a neon color as Luke screamed continuing to fry his enemy. Luke roared letting go of the lighting and skidded forward grabbing the blade and spinning abruptly decapitating the thing with ease before throwing the body in a glass door shattering it on impact as some of the others, Lylah, Alice, Selaris and Michelle peeked around the frame to get a good look at the inside. The body smashed through the door as Luke dropped.
"Fuck." Luke cries as the adrenaline wears off, dropping the blade quickly clutching his side in pain as the cost of his actions appear, soaking his side in blood and torn flesh.

"Holy shit! Medic, Luke and Beth are hurt, Medic." Michelle hollered her training kicking. She moved towards Luke who nodded, raising his hand towards Beth as the air started to dry. Michelle walked over, checking her holopad and shook her head back.
"Fucken christ move." Chelsea rushed in, having to shove Selaris and Lylah out of the way. Chelsea the Squad Medical officer had some of the steadiest hands in the whole quadrant. She had an hourglass figure and dark pink hair make her semi seasoned face. Her wise old mother's gaze was earned. Chelsea was the oldest of them and regarded as the squad's mind and heart. Chelsea rarely left the squad pods, being a motherly recluse and officially was only there to keep them alive through training before the next elite squad rolled in.

"Get the medic kit from the commons," Chelsea barked, moving Luke's hand to get a good look at the oozing torn flesh. "Don't go alone." Chelsea added as Alice turned to run after Michelle.
"Fuck Luke." Lylah said, moving past everyone and almost throwing up immediately.
"Beth...jesus what the fuck happened." Lylah said her recognizer barely conveyed her feelings as she looked around the room.
"What is this?" Selaris said entering the room and examining the thing. Alice came to a skidding stop and handed Chelsea what she asked for before turning to help her sister dissect the creature. Maddie and Michelle had their backs turned watching out for more of these things.
"Did we lose anyone?" Lylah barked at Maddie and Michelle who quickly left to check on everyone else.
"Fuck!" Lylah signed

"We gotta move him." Chelsea nodding to Lylah as they slowly lift Luke. Luke winced but did not fuss.The lights lighting the hall flickered as she spoke. Lylah and Chelsea slowly moved Luke down to the commons. An explosion and fire fight broke out somewhere down the hall echoing crisply against the marble reminding everyone of what little time they

had. Maddie and Michelle armored up. Grabbing a S.T.A.R. (Standard tactical assault rifle) and grenades. Chelsea quickly applied some Skin Flesh allowing Luke to have restricted movement without tearing the damage area open again.
"Who'd we lose?"

"Dakota, Beth, Aaron, and Mark. All K.I.A." Michelle relayed as two soldiers charged down the hall. Michelle put a quick one in the first and Maddie took the second. The Cadets were armored up with Standard Alterran Gravity Suits that allowed for zero-G engagements, with the highest defensive rating possible without sacrificing maneuverability. The only major drawback was the suit only covers up to the neck which needs a helmet piece to be attached. Most technicians could get soldiers in armor in five minutes with the aid of machines. Apache could do it in one minute without machines. S.T.A.Rs, a full complement of breaching and lethal options, side arms with thirteen mags per person all the while setting up a machine gun nest amongst the ruined commons in a matter of five minutes. The cadets knew their training well, refusing to give and inch or submit as the hours slowly started to tick by. Two hours pass as they take turns manning the gun and refilling. Bullets, spent phase casings, bodies, and pools of blood littered the now swiss cheese hallway. Trenches up to the waistline of the dead bodies lead into the commons as tracers and flares fly to and fro.

Snaps and explosive gun fire echo at an eerie regulator as more men attempt and fail to siege the killzone hallway. The Apache refused to be merciful, forcing the reinforcements to push through the mounds of bodies that littered that end of the hallway making the "Trenches". The mound both protected and funneled the enemies creating a linchpin trap. The enemy couldn't clear the bodies but they couldn't advance without sacrificing way more men then any commander could be proud of. Luke eyed the enemy as they entered their fourth hour, coughing softly to himself as he watched from the machine gunners nest. Everyone was spread out making sure every angle was covered and ammo was distributed. Those who need a rest could without fear of dying at least right now.

"Let me see." Chelsea whispers and motions for Luke to give her access to work. Luke rolled his eyes and motioned Alice to take the gun rolling on his back against the inside of the couch, hich had been flipped to provide a headboard for the gun. Fortunately there were enough dead bodies to reinforce the surrounding area creating a mound of literal death. Luke was struggling to breath with his helmet on as she once again examined his wound and shook her head.

"I'm gonna have to reapply the liquid skin, take it easy, we are running low. On slightly better news, I gotta stitch up the tares first; like we need nano paste to fix this without surgery." Luke shook his head in disbelief at his luck and nodded, turning to watch the hallway as Chelsea worked. He cringed every once and a while as Chelsea set the thread. "Alright, ready." He nodded. Chelsea smiled and quickly asked, "Is Lylah pregnant." Lukes face stared mortified as she lit the stitch to cauterize all of the tears. Luke shook his head as his suit covered the injury in a phase shield.

Alice's head snapped back before they heard the shot go off. Luke saw Alice's face, a mix of shock and horror as Luke finally noticed the burning hole that now made its home in her head. Alice fell for a long time before she ragdolled in air, landing on Selaris as Alice's body made contact with the base floor. Luke quickly rolled back onto the gun killing fourteen men in a hellfire of gunfire as another firefight began to break out. Selaris wailed in horror as she realized she was covered in her own sister's brains.

"Banger!" Chelsea calls as she ducks in the "Mound". Lylah and Maddie scramble to elude the banger. The seizure-like effects rack both of their bodies; unfortunately, they drop in that exact moment seven additional men attempt to storm from a hidden location coming out of Luke's pod in force. Luke realized they were cutting through the walls as he fired at one of the men who was getting too close. Luke tried to quickly adjust as one of the soldiers threw themselves at Luke. The soldier's desperate lunge was met by Luke who simply lit the target up in a hail of bullets however the man's angle was good, only taking a few shots before colliding with Luke launching Luke and the Soldier tumbling backwards as they wrestled for dominance. After a few seconds Luke found his advantage quickly pulling his blade and plunging the narrow tip deep into the soldier's neck before quickly retracting the needle-like blade, cleaning the blood off in one swift movement. Quickly Luke reascended the Mound to get back on the gun. As Luke started manning his position as more soldiers began besieging the "Trenches".

The other six quickly opened fire suppressing Luke and Chelsea who was still in the Mound calling targets and taking pot shots. Lylah tossed Maddie a S.T.A.R. as they come to from the stroke-like effects of the banger and they each kill two soldiers immediately. Lylah spins behind the kitchen island and quickly pops up from cover killing another in the process as they manage to bypass Luke. Maddie tries to grab Selaris out of the way. Maddie is dragged backwards from the close ranged shotgun blast Selaris takes, sending Maddie sliding across the marble floor from the moment of the blast. Maddie quickly regained control, turning quickly as she slid sparks angrily erupted from metal on metal contact.

Maddie took the prone position never losing momentum however as she placed two clean kill shots through the man's head catching her balance as her feet found the wall. Maddie quickly righted herself seconds later. Luke grabbed his own banger and lobbed it quickly, popping back on the gun while laying down suppressive fire once more. Lylah watches as Maddie is tackled. Lylah quickly turns in a fraction of two seconds to catch her own charging assailant with two bullets to the chest rolling around the man trying to get a shot at the man on Maddie. Maddie rolls around struggling for control as Lylah spins again grabbing at her side arm to kill another. Lylah aims the weapon at Maddie's attacker as Maddie screeches in pain, the world starts going in slow motion, spinning the man off her as Maddie reveals the man's knife in her ribs, rage and horror filling Maddie's face as she attempts to cope with her pain. Lylah raised her gun only to be tackled by a hidden eighth man. Luke's gun fire and Chelsea calling targets told Lylah where their eyes were.

Lylah was barely able to hold the man up before grabbing at his side arm making the man think she wasn't in control. The man fell for it as Lylah kicked the soldier in the chest creating some distance and launching the man to his feet as he stumbled backwards. Lylah did not hesitate to blast the man with her side arm. The explosive force of the side arm's discharge flung the man away from Lylah and launched pieces of his stomach flying everywhere. Lylah took a deep breath in, struggling to control her own breathing, trying to keep her nerve as she tried to take in the scene once more from her hunched over position, sweat poured down her face as she tried to recover.

"Bitch." The final man screamed, swinging a foot at Lylah. Lylah quickly raised her arms as she battered the man's shins with her forearms. The counter allowed Lylah to swing her body weight inwards bringing the man down by grabbing between his crotch and ripping the thigh out of the socket. Lylah was not as strong as the others and the man's armor allowed him to fight off her attempts as they both desperately struggled to get Lylah's knife. The man kept trying to get out of her hold as Lylah and the man struggled for almost a minute before the unthinkable happened. The man got Lylah's blade into his hands and Lylah quickly rolled away to gain distance. The man smiled as he realized he had gained the upper hand. His smile was quickly replaced with shock as he fell forward, his own knife plunged into the back of his head. Maddie smiled for a quick second before falling backwards, blood staining various locations of her armor as she slowly started to close her eyes.

"Medic!" Lylah cried as Michelle came up from to her nap at the cry. Michelle quickly scrambled out of the pantry and took overwatch for Chelsea. Chelsea looked at Maddie not even needing to check the data before shaking her head toward Lylah.

"We need a way out." Michelle cried over the coms as a bullet caught her armor launching her back into the two of them at the bottom of the mound.

"Take the Air duct." Luke ordered quickly shoving Michelle back off the tower as an explosive shell barely missed her head as she tried to reascend. Debris fell harshly around all them for a second before Luke returned to the gun.

"You can't fit in the Duct with armor and you'll die without it." Chelsea said, realizing his plan.

"No fucken way." Michelle added.

"Then I'll hold here and you get help. Clear the other end out and come save me." Luke yelled as he unloaded again.

"I'm staying then." Chelsea said turning to the girls as they looked at each other and she signed, "I'll keep him alive."

Lylah nodded as Michille pulled herself into the air duct. Lylah signed, "we are coming back." and got in the vent.

Luke turned to Chelsea and set to work, for the next hour they held the line.

"Go after them." Luke coughed finally overcame his exhaustion evident.

"With respect but fuck you number one, if I am to die I will choose where the fuck I die. If I have to die trying to save the people I have grown to love as my own children then I will die there and do it with a fucken smile. Now stop trying to be a hero and let us save you." Chelsea scolded, killing two men as they tried to crawl over one of the trenches.

"Why did you choose our squad X.O.?" Luke finally asked, making sure the bodies wouldn't get back up.

"You really are a good hacker aren't you? Only place that I'm listed as a X.O. is sealed." Chelsea said coming over and giving him ammo as she checked his wounds.

"Doesn't answer the question." He said positioning himself so he could watch the door continuing to cover his position.

"I couldn't command troops. It takes a special someone to motivate troops to want to die for them. I had that but not the stomach." She said solemnly. "So I choose to follow. Why did a Fairsist follow the Chief's daughter all the way from earth to a war school?" She responded after admiring her work.

"They all died almost a thousand years ago. Even if I was one, I would be doing a lot better than I am," Luke said shifting uncomfortably. "I came here because I love her."

"You're good but I'm a better kid. That creature had targeted lighting so unless you have a weapon I don't know about." She tilted her head seeing his nervousness, " I won't tell anyone," She shifts to move back down the mound,"but now you know why I stayed."

"Luke...we made it. Target mixed thirteen, E.T.A. If the Sexiest Ba Boom is here we will return to the City of Owls with the Poet in the falling space." Lylah's voice echoed over the coms and they both smiled; they might just make it.

"Chelsea...You good?" Luke said from across the room. The bodies had made a small wall staining everything in the area around the entrance. It had been almost an hour since they had heard from Lylah. The sweat from his fever makes it hard to aim as she patrolled. Luke eyed Chelsea as she slowly patrolled the trench.

"Yeah..You ok?" Chelsea responded.

Luke looked at the puddle he sat in, "Yeah...I'll make it." Turns out that shooting and sweat also could disrupt the flesh skin, which had fallen off almost ten minutes ago, reopening the wound with a slight trickle.

"You take a shot?" Luke said, struggling to reload.

"Yeah graze on my hip and shoulder." She said over the coms as she slowly walked to the line rolling her shoulder. Luke understood they were gonna die. Why hide it?

"The skin fell off..." Luke said. Coughing up a little blood.

"You got a fever yet?" Chelsea asked before popping a round through someone trying to enter.

"...I love...Lo...l.lyl..." He said through heavy breaths, trying to keep his eyes open, feeling death's final embrace approaching.

"Luke!?" Chelsea screamed from somewhere as her mic cracked and distorted. He heard Chelsea running, gun rounds going off. Then something slammed into Luke stirring and shaking the giant man as the next couple of minutes didn't seem real. Lylah and Commander Montgomery seemed to just appear as silhouettes of motion securing the mound around him before he finally allowed himself to fall unconscious.

"We got a route if we can open this corridor here. The problem is we have to use depth charges and damage it enough. that will cause a lot more problems then we already have. There are a lot of them if this room has anything to say." Someone was saying in the darkness of Luke's mind.

"How long till the fleet arrives?" Montgomery responded.

"7 hours probably less depending on which fleet they send and its ready status." The man said back.

Luke opened his eyes realizing he still lived. Taking in the scene, Luke saw thirteen regulars, a doctor, and Commander Montgomery standing around a holo table discussing plans. Luke shook his head but his eyes locked on the pantry and the now partially covered dead body of Chelsea who seemed to have died on a makeshift operating table. Closing his eyes Luke allows himself to shed a single tear for his fallen squadmates before standing catching a now unconscious Lylah before carefully righting her and moving towards the others..

"At this rate we can last but they won't," The Commander nodded in the direction of the cadets as Luke slowly limped over. Somewhere along the line a blood vessel had popped in his left eye and he was covered in sweat and blood. Bruises, cuts, a swollen left eye and his damaged armor made Luke the most battle scarred person there other than Lylah.

"Ma'am, who are they?" The Soldier asked, nodding towards Luke and Lylah.

"You don't know where you are, do you?" Montgomery said to the others as well, "Look around at the markings or there in the lack of. The old tech doors? The Bodies. You're in Apache Squads home. Their home they are dying defending." Montgomery pointed at the dead bodies of Luke's friends all now covered in memorial flags, "So if your next words were why are they so important, save it because I think I just made myself painfully clear. They are the actual future of the Federation and there are two left. The only Squad who survived by itself without aid. Now more than ever we need to keep them alive." The commander said moving into the middle of the room."The future of the Federation is in our hands gentleman, let's make sure we get one." She said looking at everyone in the room.

"What's the plan?" Luke came over and looked at the holo taking in the information.

"Using these trenches to create a crisscrossing x attack pattern. We can navigate semi safely through the trenches. The only problem is once we pass them there has been no word from anyone, anywhere passed the mess hall. So it's gonna be a fight no matter what." Commander Montgomery informed Luke of the plan. Luke shook his head in disagreement.

"With respect to you, Commander but," Luke waved his hand updating the holo with his observed information, "It's exactly what they want you to do. We need to use their own holes against them. Funnel the fighting into the tight controlled rooms where skill has the advantage." Luke said recalculating the holo for his own purpose. "This is how we escape using their own cheat sheet against them. To them, that's a safe zone. The trenches aren't."

Lylah seemed to appear out of nowhere, " They are also really good at setting traps. They can't fight us one on one; they need multiple men and a lot of luck to take even one of us. As long as we work as a team we won't die." Lylah backed up; her realizer not once cracking or distorting her emotions or feelings.

"You heard them, let's move." Montgomery barked, nodding at them with a sense of pride as she relinquished command to the two Cadets. The moment of hope was silenced with a snap as the two guards at the hallway entrance dropped. Montgomery rolled and rifled her weapon, firing a burst down the hallway. No tracers were returned as they prepared for exfil. "Peace, if I may come down the hall without being shot, maybe I could reach an agreement where no one else dies." echoed down the hallway and a white flag could be seen from the now over eight foot high trenches.

Preface: Part 3

6 hours in Hell

"Peace, if I may come down the hall without being shot, maybe I could reach an agreement where no one else dies." The voice echoed again as Luke looked at Montgomery who shook her head listening. Time slowly trickled by seconds seemed to be going on for an eternity as Luke stared at Montgomery, he felt something off then eyes saw the unusual strain on her face and a single drop of sweat started to roll down her face, in the wake of the droplet pools of lighting danced in the trail. Luke scowled as time started to slow as he realized he shouldn't have ever been able to see her sweat lighting again. Not on Magness Prime. Not on this day an age as Luke realized where his mom had gone. Luke slowly blinked his eyes as if time was slowing down. A sigh of defeat escapes Luke's lips as he realizes this is what he had been dreading this day for over five years. The location of which no one was allowed unless you were born with it. A place of wonderfully destructive power. A place few dared to ever see and even fewer are chosen to call it home. The River of Freenoena. Luke gritted his teeth before closing his eyes. Feeling the power of The River explode around him blacking the room in near perfect darkness. Luke was only illuminated by a faded soft gray outline that barely had any weight or color.

He calls, *Mom?* Luke's voice echoed around the black room. Luke's eyes snapped to the outline of Commander Mongomery. She snapped her head in his direction seeing Luke's spectral form which was even more different from how Luke saw himself. Instead of the massive mountain of muscle he looked like he was twelve. Luke blinked rapidly and spectral blue light started to outline him with how Commander Montgomery was seeing.

Luke had gone through an old school punk emo phase, complete with emo blue hair cut and skinny jeans. Which now was outlined filling out his definition. Commander Mongtomery appeared in the darkness in her fairsist form: that of a Greek Goddess Athena complete with the owl on her shoulder. Montgomery turned to look at Luke slowly taking him in before smiling uncontrollably, remembering when he was that age. The cheek under her left eye twitched slightly as she rolled her eyes at him. Montgomery was never short of amazement even in a completely unpracticed state. Luke still felt her enter The River. The Commander stares for a brief second with pride before speaking. *When have you ever been that small?* The Commander's thin smile widened as she spoke, her mouth not moving but her mind conveying her meaning. The Commander's jaw never moved as she took a small moment with Luke.

I was Twelve. About to follow Lylah here. I think you remember that conversation clearly. He said looking back at her acting awkward, Luke's overbearing confidence was replaced with a sudden unnerving tickle as he realized he couldn't see The River. The River wasn't allowing itself to be seen. Luke's spin curled as he realized The River and his ancestors were mad at him for using their gifts without seeing them first. Luke almost got lost to the over thinking before he noticed Commander Montgomery seeming to be lost in memory.

Five years ago, Jesus, where did the time go? Montgomery said, trying to remove a tear that didn't fall as she failed to notice The River's response to Luke. She tried to steel herself as she turned and beaconed Luke over to her. The river would tell her later why they were only in a black void instead of the beautiful blue beach. Time truly had passed since the last time Luke had been here then he was a boy but now, upon his return, Luke was a full grown man. Montgomery took a moment to marvel as Luke walked closer, his hands in his pockets, his steps more of a shuffle. *Plus I haven't been to the River in a long time. I don't think it recognizes me yet.* A smile formed on his face without his mouth moving. He was trying to make her smile and hide his own thoughts.

Your Ancestors are in the stream. You should say hi. She nodded as a small stream of gray light slowly materialized behind Commander Montgomery as blue misty ribbons of energy slowly fill the black box with a deep waving ambient blue light.

The ground below Luke formed a slight indentation changing to the texture of sand but staying that soft blue outline. The River was done hiding from Luke as he finally closed the distance down the now forming beach. Trees grew from the ground growing their entire existence in moments enclosing either side of Luke and Montgomery as a clearing forms around them before a thick canape forms the edges of the clearing. The river grew soft grass around the edges of the peaceful sand leading to the menacing jungle. The water itself, a spectral blue, starts flowing almost like thick fog from right to left gently covering the far side of the bank in dense jungle like vegetation and a soft dew blue under light. Dark Teal colored firefly like creatures softly expand beetle like wings and take off from the banks forming swarms of soft teal trails like bird formations soaring around the river. A baby blue sun rises somewhere in the distance casting deep soft baby blue dew lines through the trees.

I am only here to make sure you don't die, Me and the Ancestors, Luke threw his head in the direction of the river quickly changing his tactic, *We don't have the time for such a.* Luke paused as the River tried to compel him to tell the truth. Montgomery knew quite well how much power and force the river could wield when it wanted something; however it never astonished her how powerful Luke had become without her or the Ancestors' guidance. They were trying to compel him to finish his words however something unexpected happened.

Shall we. He held out his arm and pointed to the door that had materialized behind Montgomery. Montgomery grew colder as they entered the door leading to the mind of whoever was on the other side of the trenches with that flag. Luke blinked, instantly the scenery had changed, landing in what looked to be a dinner party maybe late 15th century made by Hollywood standards. The lavish drapes and marble white matched perfectly, no dirt or grime, or the slightest indication of realism meaning they were in someone's dream not the person's actual mind. They shouldn't see an active scene furthering Luke's suspicion someone knew they were coming.

Columns stretched out on either side of the massive hall. They landed in front of a magnificently crafted table. The wood had a story etched along the table's surface of some war between what looked like humans and fire which was pouring down from the skies. There was a man at one side of the dinner table waiting for them. The man looked more like a spoiled king of old than a soldier in the 50th Century, his brown cowlicked head and terrible mustache almost froze when he truly finally got to see them. The King's deep blue eyes danced in recognition. His sharp muscles and angular face did not match the poor hairstyle choices. The King's stache seemed to twitch in disbelief before the child king spoke, seeming to choose his words way more carefully as if playing a part.

"Ah I wondered when you'd make it here. If you'd make it here, And yes I can see you," The child-king seemed to get slightly giddy before continuing with a smirk, ",both of you. I had my servants make some prime rib. I don't wanna assume but you look like you'd enjoy a big juicy," The King seemed to be able to make them out better before he raised a knife at Luke, "Wait," The King menaced, waving the elegant steak knife at Luke. The King threw something in his mouth chewing on it, something as his eyes locked on Luke who seemed completely unimpressed, "are you my quarry? I mean, you...anyway..well...you are at least one of them. I was led to believe Lylah was the other Fair..." Freezing mid sentence, The Child-King turned to Montgomery, "But if you're not the soul. That would make you?" He paused, almost smiling with unfiltered joy.

"That makes you." The King seemed to recognize her more in depth now as Luke and Montgomery walked up either side of the massive table. "Momma bear." He almost whispered, seeming to be taking a different tact then before slighting the point of the knife at Montgomery as he tried to put things together. "Interesting for sure." The King pauses for a second to consider some unseen options,"Sit, sit, sit." He said, motioning them forward as if not liking his option but willing to play this out.

"Who are you...and how did you know we would invade your mind?" Montgomery said cautiously as they approached, her eyes evaluating all threats and dangers. Choosing her tactic very carefully in the unknown mind. Montgomery had invaded many minds, many far stronger than this "King". But it nevertheless made her very weary of everything from the servants, to the drapes, to the dark corners, to especially the food.

"Ah well, lucid dreaming is something I am really good at to say the least." The Child-like King sassed back trying to feel like he was in control by slouching as he shoved more food in his mouth however The King's intention made him come off as bratty rather than in control.

"You're not the man in front of us, you're asleep elsewhere. Controlling him from in here...that take's lot more power then I pegged you for having." Montgomery said as they were getting closer now being able to completely see this "King".His Clowlick extended into a full mullet with almost incompressible beautiful jewels lining the man's ears, neck, nose, and eyebrows. A sorta Hillbilly Xerxes. Long twelfth-century King's robes hung loosely around his body.

Luke and Montgomery sat on either side of the table. "Luke, right." He said changing the subject as servants came and gave them all dinner. They knew it wasn't real but didn't make it any less tempting. Montgomery slowly shook her head indicating to the food with her eyes.

"Yeah and you are?" Luke's voice echoed stronger than the form the King was seeing, taking the King's attention away from Montgomery as she took her moment to breach the King's mind. Luke rolled his eyes as he saw the sweat drop trailed by a dance party of electricity and knew they won but for the first time in a long time was happy she had let him come along.

"Bailey-five." Montgomery said mindlessly back as her eyes suddenly disappeared falling from the top of her eyes as she locked them on the King: her face so stoic it almost made Montgomery feel menacing herself. She had taken mental copies of all of King's memories and could now use them against him. Smirk firmly planted on her face Montgomery released her shoulders, leaning to the left and placing her elbow down she rested her head on her palm two fingers rising her up, the others around her chin. Montgomery's face was no longer menacing but way too over confident and completely in control of what happened next as she simply waited no longer on a heightened alert.

"Yes. Well now that no one can die while we talk, what do I have to do to not put you in any more danger." He said looking at Luke then Montgomery as he spoke, starting to dig into his food. Luke sat back looking at him with malcontent and a slight hint of disbelief as Luke strokes his chin.

"Leave." Luke said finally after allowing several tense seconds to pass, falling into the Child-king's game.

"I'm sorry Luke, but I'm afraid I can't do that." The Child-like king said, a smirk twisting itself into his cheeks.

"What's the Problem?" Luke irritatingly asked back, leaning forward and moving his feet close to the king, locking his arms in a prayer-like clasp.

"Oh I think you know why, I can't. This mission is too important to let you or anyone else jeopardize it." The Child-like King mocked, cutting more into the Steak and then stabbing the meat, bringing it leisurely to his mouth before speaking. "However Ms. Soffrireterna, she's," Seeming to become aroused at the thought of Luke's girlfriend, the Child-like King continued with a heavy sigh on the must, "A must for our plan. So either you come down the hall or we will siege this hallway endlessly and eventually she will be ours, You are just an added bonus chip we could use." The words cut into Luke with devastating efficiency. His twelve year old appearance shedding off of him as the mountain of a man returned. The King quickly shot back in his chair which nearly tilted over; fear and horror at the sudden giant caused the man to shake uncontrollably. The Child-like King's eye darted around the room looking for safety from Luke.

"You're lying through your teeth." Montgomery interrupted, stopping Luke from completely neural overloading them with the added bonus of not allowing Child-like to continue either. Montgomery moved her hand up and down towards Luke before relaying her intentions in sign. She then turned to the "King" and motions him to sit up before returning to her relaxed state once again somehow reasserting her control over the situation before continuing. "You're running outta time till our fleet arrives. We don't have seven hours, we have maybe less than four. We have a lot of soldiers down here with us. All of who are willing to put up with your shit for that long, maybe less. You'll be overwhelmed and killed, failing your objective all together." Montgomery mocked back leaning forward making the "King" tense up, "You're so close, just on the other end of those trenches made by cadets. What happens when the Viridian Guard shows up with The Ellen? Or worse T.O. may already know about your attack and have this all planned out." Montgomery motioned around her, "this is your last hope of walking out of this alive. You need them alive or your sorry ass isn't walking off this planet and when I say them." She leaned closer, a sick smile on her own face. " I mean both of the Cadets."

His face cringed with irritation, "Damn woman you are good." He said, seeming to get excited at her interruption, putting his silverware down and grabbing a drink trying to remove stuck food with his tongue.

"You can't win this fight but you can surrender and meet with diplomats at..." Montgomery said stoically, staring through his bullshit without breaking a sweat or trying.

"So we agree that we are done here? I can't have them without you trying to kill us. And they won't come willingly. We will do as the ancients did and kill each other for valueless pride." He said and smiled before pinching himself causing them to be jetted back out into The River. Montgomery turned moving towards her body wanting to wake up.

She can't know. Montgomery stopped dead in her tracks slowly turning as Luke looked at Lylah feeling the baby forming inside her as he used the Rivers powers to see her in the real world frozen in time and highlighted by peaceful blue outlines. A soft dark Emerald glow coming from her pelvic area. His face torn with sorrow. *I can't leave her with the pain of this if we...* Luke almost breaks as he softly touches Lylahs tummy. His fears of failing and losing them both were breaking him into pieces. His spectral form started to splinter, sending chunks of outline spewing away from Luke as if in space before becoming ambient beauty.

If you mess with her head and that truly is the next generation's mother and she finds out. You risk losing them both forever. Montgomery said with a worry, her fear echoing The Rivers turbulent waves as heavy deep gray waves started building against the shores casting haunting shadows to reflect the dark decision being discussed.

She can't know that she bore the next generation of Fairsist. A true Second Mother. Luke said, shifting on his feet planting them, *Lylah would not allow for that to happen , You know how they see us. We need to move her away from doing anything that could stop the next generation from being born. Maybe then you and the Ancients will relax about this Next Generation shit.*

Together then? Montgomery said, holding out her hand, a soft teal blue smoke ribbon danced around her hand and fingers before wrapping one around her wrist and reaching with her towards Luke. The River was even willing to help. *I will help by leaving a shadow of you just in case...you and I...she will remember. Someone will be there for her leading her down a path that is best for everyone.*

Luke reached out his hand before stopping and jerking back momentarily. The ribbon, almost coiling back in shock as it went back to dancing around Commander Montgomery's fingers and hand, waiting for words to be spoken. Luke stared hard and long at Montgomery's hand.

Luke returned the next second later, a single droplet of sweat dripping downing his own head, green lighting trailing in the tail. Montgomery smirked as Luke stared at her looking at each other in a brief moment of self reflection lost in each other's minds as well as their own. Lylah shifted under his weight trying to look at him causing Luke to wipe his head hiding the sweat trail making it clear that him returning to the river was a one time thing. Montgomery nodded and turned to everyone else hiding her own sweat only those two truly knew what was next.

"We are gonna surge through the Trenches." She spoked.
"What?" The Medic said with fear.
"Attack." Luke coughed, "Charge the trenches and we will live."
"Isn't that sucide? I thought we just discussed this?" A Soldier spoke up fear teasing the edge of his tone.

"They don't have enough time to risk damaging why they are here. If we surge they won't risk the crossfire hitting their targets. We have the advantage they need to make accurate shots while we use us as protection." Luke said, nodding to Commander Montgomery who nodded as if coming to the same conclusion.

"I'm asking you to trust me one last time. I have trained most of you. I wouldn't do anything I didn't know was best for everyone." Montgomery followed up as the soldiers slowly nodded. The others looked at each as if they too felt like they were missing something that had happened in the previous few seconds before nodding in agreement.

Luke pulled Lylah aside and signed, "Where's Michelle?" Lylah quickly responded, " Me and her got separated in the ducks. One of those things attacked me, ripping us right out of the fucken vents." Lylah hesitated trying to gather her thoughts, "She shoved me out of the room after a quick scuffle. Michelle had kept using me as a shield which I freaking hated until now. She saw It wasn't trying to kill me, it was trying to hurt me. But. I was thrown from the room and Michelle locked the room with command codes behind her. I heard screaming and ran to get help but there was a lot of blood in the room when we finally got the door open. We think, it escaped how we got in."

Another tear fell this time uncontrolled from Luke's eyes, the two of them were truly all that was left. Luke looked around realizing he had led everyone to a slaughter. A moment of horror as he contemplated Chelsea's words about leading soldiers. Luke scowled, No one else he cared about would die this day. Luke looked at Lylah, his eyes softening for a fraction of a second as he knew how far he would go to save her and their little one to come.
They stacked with the others who had the clearest visual side of the trenches one by one they all went prone, almost drowning in blood and unidentifiable substances. Inch by inch they slowly crawled only using the edges of the trenches stopping at the slightest hint of movement. The slog forward only lasted about two minutes. The air quieted and Montgomery slowly rose up the wall leading into the safe zones, a fellow soldier climbing the other side of the wall as they slowly nodded. Montgomery pulled a banger lobbing it in the pod, a quick flash as they all surged forward. Four soldiers writhed on the ground as their meal contributing to the shadows that now haunted the warzone. As they all quickly surged the room four friendly soldiers quickly cuffed and gagged the now spasming enemy soldiers. Luke looked at what used to be his home.

The normal beautiful white marble was chard or bloodstained with nothing in between. A soldier-sized hole is drilled through the north wall leading to a junction for every other trench and safezone. A trench jets from the next room in a diagonal fashion leading to the other side of the trenches and Lylah's side of the pods. Luke scanned the quiet trenches realizing just how much the child-like king was willing to sacrifice. There must have been thousands if not double digits of thousands; moaning, dead, dying, or torn to shreds. The child-like king did not care if you were dead or alive building the now eight foot tall body walls of both the living and dead. Luke hadn't realized the Apache's ferocity till just now, just trying to survive. A shot whizzed past Luke as he quickly snapped back, spinning quickly; he realized he had full movement without pain and returning to instinct he easily killed the shooter with a single bullet. Lylah stacked up relaying Montgomery's orders with signs.

Luke nodded slowly backing him and Lylah up as she held onto his belt to make sure he stopped when needed as another soldier took Luke's current position. Montgomery stacked up with the rest on the other side and nodded at the soldier guarding them. Luke handed him a banger while Lylah pulled her own. Luke nodded his head so they could keep beat and then mouthed one, two; the three soldiers in almost perfect sync popped out of their position lobbing bangers at various points of the trenches. The soldier that had popped out with them was quickly blown off course as a shotgun blasted him backwards plasma scorching the front of his body. Luke caught the assailant who had posted themselves on the other side of the wall. Grabbing the barrel with his right hand while he shifted to the left, getting the barrel away from his direction. Quickly Luke overwhelmed the human, snapping the gun back into the man's face before turning away the shotgun in Luke's hand and putting a shot in the killer's chest blasting him against the wall. Luke lobs the gun over to the dead body, quickly grabbing his S.T.A.R. from his back and taking the lead so his armor's partial shield could take some more of the damage. In that quick instant a rave of gun fire and bullets racked the wall where Luke had been literally a second before. Luke saw the flashes using his armor to reach speeds of a hundred miles an hour as he dashed across the trenches, almost mistifying a soldier who had attempted to catch Luke mid dash.

Luke quickly stopped himself turning as the other soldiers seemed to be frozen as they stared at him. Luke smiled quickly, moving with unnatural speed as he ducked, the furthest soldier shooting at him. Luke launched himself towards the closest soldier using the weight of the armor and his own massive frame to snap the armor rig that connected the armor to the spine in half causing the man to convulse as his mind began erasing itself from the neural overload of the armor.

Luke quickly rolled forward as the other soldier panicked, barely able to track Luke as he almost danced around the shots. While he danced he slipped his blade out of its home, quickly ending the man's life as Luke stabbed the blade through the juggler. Luke ignored the shock and fear from the man's face as he realized the man was going to die. Luke covered the man's mouth but a muffle was heard before the man stopped struggling and went limp. Luke shifted placing his back to the hole that led to what used to be Aaron's room. His knife still in hand stepping three steps back and crouching.

"Intrud..." A soldier was attempting to say as his head exploded sending brain matter through the door. Luke clung to the wall as he heard another soldier move before another hiss. The distance impact of human flesh bits and the phased sniper round Lylah had fired from across the tench had not been friends as Luke looked at the corpse in the next room before moving into Dakota's old room. Dakota was still in his room, a death cover had been placed on him with the correct flag which slightly irritated Luke for unknown reasons.
The butt of a gun slams into Luke's bicep as another soldier attempts to subdue the giant. Luke slowly turned his head, staring at the man in his deep blue eyes and cracked the man with his elbow as the soldier's nose spewed blood. The blow's power also caused the man to be thrown off his feet.

"Left Clear." Lylah reported over the coms as Luke pulled his pistol on four men surging from the last room, what used to be Chelsea's old room. Luke caught the barrel of the first gun to come through the hole spinning across the threshold putting two rounds in the man. Luke wrapped his arm around the body of the gun as he did so. The other soldiers attempted to raise their rifles as Luke used the now dead body of the man as a shield and threw it at the other three. As Luke threw the body he surged forward. The men unfortunately had been in a diamond formation allowing Luke to use them as body shields against everyone else and control the tight pocket created by the hole. Luke's home was in the pocket as the man to his right attempted to pull his gun. Luke quickly took his wrist, side stepping as the man pulled the trigger in panic. Luke had control as he reversed their direction, swinging the first man into the other two as Luke put bullets in their heads as they attempted to rise. Luke cleared the room only stopping to linger on a picture of all the apache squad in bathing suits at a local lake. Chelsea had placed the holo recording on her small desk. Luke felt the sudden weight of sadness as he realized they could never have those times again with any of them. They encountered no one as they slowly made their way into the main hall, which was littered with silence and creepy tones that were accompanied by bodies and blood trails of victims scattered among the low-lit halls.

More than once people cried out for mercy or in pain. The cries were minutes apart but each cry made everyone hesitate and pause as they waited. More than once the lights flicked and an explosion would echo through the halls. Then more cries of pain and horror before the return to deafening silence. With each cry or shot that echos Luke gritted his teeth, hating his enemies that much more. They halted as a firefight broke out in front of them only a few hallways down. The cries of civilians echoed as they begged for mercy. Soldiers screaming for the fallen brothers before a snap and they joined them in the beyond. Lylah cried to herself, keeping her head down so no one would see.
"We have to help." Luke hissed as they waited for the screams to die.

"You're too important to die. I think they just want everyone dead. We can't let this go unpunished. But you wanna go charging into that faceless battle. Sure why not. I don't think they're gonna show you mercy anymore." Montgomery scolded.

Lylah shifted in place at the harshness of the words but kept her mouth shut. The silence once again engulfed them and Montgomery nodded before they continued the trek to the shuttle bay. The time seemed to never pass as they encountered no one else. As they approached, Montgomery raised a fist. They stopped and moved against the walls. Luke shouldered his S.T.A.R. falling into Formation with Lylah and the others. He felt a pull before finding himself in the Spectral River again.

You look more like you. Montgomery mused at him. Luke blinked, seeing himself as he is now not as the River remembers him.

It's a trap. She said getting back to it before raising her hand.

I know...what if we head to the tram station? He said back.

No...we'd never make it because we'd have to double back almost thirty clicks. She shook her head. *We have thirty minutes what if we just secured the bay and used the shuttles as close ranged air.*

Wait, there's only one fighter docked because the others...were in orbit: on top of that the only one's here qualified are me and...Lylah...You don't think we will survive do you. He said horror stricken.

You two can use the shuttle to stay in atmo; their ships in orbit can't follow you into the lower atmo without you guys catching them and damaging their ships beyond repair. Me and the others will hold as long as we can. She explained.

You're coming with us. I can't do this without you. He cried.

Don't make me make you. She said with sorrow in her face. *I'm gonna kill everyone in the room before we return.*

Luke watched as she splintered every door with her mind slowly raising her hand to the middle of the doors before quickly making a fist. The doors compressed on themselves and shattered into a million pieces before also turning into beautiful blue ambience. Luke's mind flashed back to his fight with the creature.

It's time. She said walking back and he came to.

Preface Epilogue:
The Worst Truths are Goodbyes

Lylah Soffrireterna
2:00 A.M.
March 12.1 , 4999 A.D.

"Wake up," A female voice called to Lylah through the endless void of darkness.

"Wha...What happened?" Lylah questioned groggily, trying to adjust to the blinding white light that now flooded her eyes. This wasn't; Lylah quickly closed her eyes as the light blinded her so bad it almost made her eyes tear up watering but failing to start a flow. "How do you feel?" A Gentle voice followed somewhere in the blackness, it was a man's voice; she blinked trying to force her eyes to focus but this effort only brought tears to them.

"I feel like shit." She spoke, stopping and reaching for her neck, her recognizer crystal was missing, Lylah once again tried to open her eyes only to bring a fresh wave of tears but this time not from the light."It doesn't matter." She stuttered unsure how to phrase her words. Her mind flashes to them for a brief second bringing a new wave of pain, fighting tears and closing her eyes remembering the day's events. Flashes started to form before Lylah shook them away unwilling to face them.

"What are you thinking about?" The voices prodded together. Lylah stayed on her back blinking rapidly, fighting tears and starting to make out shapes, as things started to focus. She found herself in a pure white room, she was laying on some kind of bed and those voices were so familiar. The room wasn't very large in size, maybe fifteen square feet. The room had an ancient 1970's feel. There was an old school black and white box TV placed on the opposite side of the room. A love seat was placed directly in front of the TV with a lazy boy off to the left. A table set for four was placed along one side; matching chairs of marble placed neatly and squarely at the table itself. A vase of white roses placed lovingly as a centerpiece. A shag rug was in front of the TV, and fake wood vinyl on the surrounding walls.

"What?" She said rudely. Lylah felt the world freeze over and the dots started to connect, her eyes widened and her mouth tried to anchor itself on the ground. She slowly looked to Lukes left and nearly lost it as she came face to face with Commander Montgomery. Lylah shook her head fighting what she was seeing.

"Luke? But...but..." She started but a finger raised to her lips tears forcing their way out of her eyes.

"But...what? Last thing I remember you had told me you loved me and kissed me." He said looking around. He was clad in a traditional chinese monk outfit made of black and gray, the only color in the room but it made him appear to be the focus of the room. Commander Montgomery was dressed as the Greek Goddess Athena.

"Luke you're...I saw you...Neither of you can be here...because..."She tried to explain, the words fumbling over themselves as her disbelief swelled.

Luke gently raised her chin so that he could look her in the eyes, she tried to blink back tears but they trickled down her face. He wiped away a tear and grabbed her hands with his sausage fingers. She saw a twinkle in his eyes, something she hadn't seen before. He pulled her up so she was standing less than five inches from him and lent his head down, she closed her eyes waiting for the thing she had longed for since the start of the attack. The thing she had dreamed every night, his lips hit their mark; she felt a familiar hunger for him. Lylah's heart started to surge through her body, he was real. She suddenly longed for more, her body demanding more than a kiss and she fought it with all the strength she had but the urge overcame her defenses. She grabbed the back of his head and pulled him to her. She ran her hands up and down his back, through his hair, and she started to lift up his shirt but the lip lock was broken and she opened her eyes only to see him looking to the right as if trying to decide to proceed or not to, his face was filled with humility.

"What's wrong?" The world fizzled as if it was missing something. Luke turned away from her and walked toward the door not uttering a word, "Luke, hunny what's a matter?" He turned his head toward her but didn't look at her, keeping his eyes on the floor. Luke's shoulders lowered in complete defeat before whispering. "I can't. Not like this. I won't do it this way my love. It's not goodbye." He turned the knob and opened the door, a surge of blinding white light, engulfed him and the entire room.

Lylah shot up gasping for air screaming, her bed drenched in sweat as she came back to the real world. She scowled as she turned over in her bed, a familiar dingle rang on her holopad.

"Would you like another sleeping aid," The voice echoed from behind Lylah as she stared at Ellen's metal work.

"Yeah, better make it stronger this time please." Lylah said not wanting to leave her fetal position.

"Yes ma'am." The voice echoed back and she felt the air slightly pick up as the sleeping aid was pumped into her room. Lylah felt its power but couldn't stop the tears from falling as she lulled herself to sleep trying to not think about the academy.

"Wakie wakie," A playful voice called to her through the endless void of darkness that reflected a time already passed.

"Wha...What happened?" Lylah questioned groggily, trying to adjust to the blinding white light that now flooded her eyes. This wasn't, Lylah quickly closed her eyes as the light blinded her so bad it almost made her eyes tear up watering but not failing.

"How do you feel?" A Gentle voice asked somewhere in the blackness once more it was a man's voice; she blinked trying to force her eyes to focus but this effort only rewarded her with tears.

"I feel like shit." She spoke, reaching to tap her recognizer crystal only to find it was missing. Lylah once again tried to open her eyes only to bring a fresh wave of tears but this time not from the light's pain but from the pain within her." How would," She stuttered her eyes fluttering back and forth in the blinding light unsure how to phrase her words choosing to play along with this idiotic dream. "How um, would you feel if someone you had only really recently gotten to know. For the person," Her mind flashes to them for a brief second bringing a new wave of pain, "They are," She croaked, tears running deep lines as she closed her eyes remembering the day's events. Flashes started to form before she shook them away. She couldn't face them, not here, not now.

"Who is that, if I am ask?" The voice prodded. Lylah stayed on her back blinking rapidly, fighting tears and the painful light as she started to make out shapes; things started to focus at a blinding speed as Lylah's brain struggled to keep up with the detail she was absorbing. She found herself in a pure white room, she was laying on some kind of bed and that voice, it was so familiar. The room wasn't that large, maybe thirty square feet. The room had an ancient 1970's feel. There was an old school black and white box TV placed on the east side of the room. A lipstick kiss red love seat placed directly in front of the TV with a musty brown lazy boy off to the left. A table set for three was placed along the side of the room but along the fair north side of the room across from the kitchen; matching chairs of wood placed neatly at the table and the bar extension for the kitchen. A vase of white roses placed lovingly as a centerpiece on the privacy window for the cook. A shag rug was in front of the TV, and fake wood vinyl on the surrounding walls.

Lylah flipped her head in the opposite direction completely missing the figure as she took in the other side of the house. A window was placed in front of a fake vinyl staircase leading to an unknown upstairs like some 1970's sitcom. A door with elegant lines that made beautiful fire outlines as if the door had flames rising up from the bottom; slight gray barely visible outlined the edges and only if one was looking, which Lylah was, could they see it was some sort of war. Humans vs Fire as it spews down from above.

"Their name was," her voice wavered in pain as she blinked back the tears, " name was.". Lylah's head turned as she finally noticed the black shape in the only dark corner of the room, in front of a south side fireplace next to the door and the TV. A shape stood almost a black stain on this beautiful home. The world froze as Lylah recognized that stain and the dots started to connect, her eyes widened and her mouth tried to anchor itself on the ground. Luke stood before her clad in a traditional chinese monk outfit made of black and gray, the only off color scheme in the room but it made him appear to be the focus of the room even in his corner. His eyes glowed such a bright emerald green Lylah wasn't sure if he was real as she almost stepped back from the brightness.

"Luke? But...but..." She started but a finger raised to her lips, tears forcing their way out of her eyes as she stared at him the light outside suddenly dimmed as every Light in the house flashed on in sudden display of beauty. The firepit light casting an uncomfortable calm over the two of them as they stared at each other. The flames being the only illumination after all the lights finally dimed to the blackness of space. A sudden burst of lighting cracked their background as Luke's eyes still a piercing Emerald finale jeweled over as Luke blinked once more removing the overwhelming brightness but leaving the intense color.

"You're a Fairsist." Lylah looked at him as she finally put the piece together slowly standing to her feet. The table she was on dematerializing into blue ribbons quickly which faded out of existence. Luke nodded slowly as he waited for her to continue staring at her. His face solem as if he couldn't decide if what was happening was good or not.

"Luke...I." Lylah said before Luke once again put a finger over her mouth shaking his head finally coming to a choice. He slowly signed for her to just watch and listen, but Luke refused to open his mouth or even utter a word. Lylah nodded slowly and Luke lowered his hand slowly grabbing hers, pulling her gently towards the love seat.

"Luke, we don't have time for this." Lylah tried to say before Luke once again put a finger over her mouth. Resigning for her to just listen and watch as Lylah rolled her eyes just allowing him to lead, for once. He sat them down and grabbed the remote, turning to the T.V. and pressing power.

The screen flickered and static shot from the box as a surprisingly detailed show started.

"And now we return to our normally scheduled show." A terrible 1970's parody news anchor was saying. The screen flashes with a color test screen before a casting roll starts. The main title plows above a gorgeous Magnus Prime sunset. As the starring credits start and characters are introduced, Lylah's heart almost overloads itself. She watched as the old 80's family introductions start as the First Character turns. First under the Starting of the actor and stars list was Lylah herself. Followed by Luke, Michelle, Chelsea, Selaris, Dakota, Aaron, Alice, Maddie, Beth, Mark, with special Guest stars Commander Montgomery and The Child-Like King played by Bailey-Five. Lylah turned to Luke who nodded towards the T.V.. Lylah sighed, turning almost freezing on the spot as she watched the events of the Acadmey play out. Lylah's eye's widen as she watches Luke enter The River. Lylah quickly covers her eyes as she watches Luke's fate play out once more, tears falling down her face as stares mortified at the TV unable to turn away in pain.

"Why would you show this to me?" Lylah whispers as her voice cracks under the pressure of this dream.

"I have tried to help you understand why I did what I did. Some of that was influenced by other forces at times, yes." He nodded and blinked, regaining his thoughts, "I have tried other ways to show you something you need to know but...your mind has rejected all of them so I took the most direct one I wanted to do from the start." Luke continued. "I know something that I left out of the movie, our movie, that you need to see. But I want you to understand I need you to understand me before I showed you this."

"Who was your parent?" Lylah growled as she struggled to control her emotions, this dream was starting to get a little too personal.

"You mean the Fairsist Parent? My mother." Lylah stared blankly at the TV as that made way too much sense.

"This...this is." Lylah said, shaking as she turned to look at Luke tears once again falling down her face.

Luke shook his head as Lylah burst out and threw herself onto him just to feel his warmth once more. Luke allowed Lylah to have her moment taking his time after an untold amount of minutes and a lot of crying later. Lylah was finally calm. She turned to the TV and the scene started. The scene of Luke and Montgomery discovering Lylah was pregnant, the words were not the same and did not matter for Lylah wasn't listening. Her eyes were locked on the Emerald light coming from her pelvic region. Her head snapped back to Luke, tears falling like waterfalls as she nodded not even being told what to do. There was no need.

Chapter 1:
Remembrance and Reverence

3 Wormhole months After the Attack on
Magness Prime
The Ellen

Lylah Soffrireterna
5:59 A.M.
March 12.3 , 4999 A.D.

Lylah walked on to the Bridge of The Ellen as the crew snapped to attention. Lylah waved her hand for them to continue what they were doing as Lylah took in her bridge. The bridge was state of the art; her father truly had not wasted a single detail, back-up stations and Personal Emergency pods that would snap around the officers so they could remotely control the ship if the shields died. The pods would eject downwards as the ship would turn on its belly as crew and personnel escaped. Low holo lights filled the voidlessness of wormhole space. Wormhole space was humans long old question of faster than light travel, well Lylah sassed to herself at least the Light Drive was.

The wormhole space was linked to the same location in time and space just without mass, a type darkspace. Lylah walked around the bridge and gave herself the lesson, reminding her that all her training wasn't going to waste. The tunnel was linked and held open by sub-light to faster-than-light lightning-like strands that opened the hole long enough for a ship to enter. Once the hole closed you were in the void and needed computers to plot and help you escape back into real space.

Lylah shook her head as she sassed herself. Lylah rolled her eyes, almost hearing Luke's voice arguing. *Lylah you know for a fact if it weren't for the 1 to 1000 A.U. (Astronomical Unit) time differential range. They couldn't go across the galaxy in a matter of seconds. But there is a major drawback to wormholes. They may be traveling extremely fast, but even this trip took ten months to complete inside the wormhole space.* Lylah nearly jumped out of her skin as she turned and saw Luke in full spec ops gear propped up against a wall watching her. His arms folded as his back leaned against the wall as he stared at her, contempt in his eyes as he shook his head. Lylah blinked at the exact moment an officer blocked her view of Luke with a question.

After two seconds Lylah looked back and felt her spin freeze. Luke was gone. Lylah told the CO to watch the con as she chased after Luke, her mind slipping back into the events she was so desperately running from afraid she may have missed something.

Luke turned to Lylah as they approached the door and signed, "Me and you in the fighter. She will order us to leave but." Lylah put her hands over his to stop him nodding as she understood. The two were the last two to stack up as the Commander held up three fingers for a countdown. One finger went down as Lylah shouldered her rifle. Lylah could feel her left thigh tensing and untensing as another finger went down. Lylah found herself flying away from the wall as the explosive sent her skidding over the marble. Lylah shifted catching someone's leg as she skidded sparks and metal screeched behind her before Lylah smashed her foot down holding onto the person's ankle. Shots rang out and words were shouted but Lylah barely noticed; she had found her flow state. A shot rocked Lylah's right shoulder launching her forward as she lost control smashing into the wall as something leaped at her; Cratering Lylah into the wall as the two elite units brawled. Lylah quickly punched the thing as it raised its arms crashing down on Lylah trying to crush her power supply. Lylah screeched quickly stabbing that brute like creature repeatedly in the ribs before spinning the creature into the hole.

Lylah slams her head into the creature ignoring the coms, sweat starting to pour down Lylah's face. Lylah's eyes snapped to her head's up display as her motion track sent a warning, something she had been pretty much ignoring, began to scream as a rocket came inches from hitting Lylah. She turned nailing the creature onto the wall as Luke spun infront of her and cradling her as they were blown into the creature. If it had any hope of surviving that was now gone. Luke had a pained cough as he held the rubble off her. Despite her head snapping and cracking the marble Lylah used what little power her suit held to eject it from between Luke's legs.

"I hate it when you do that." Luke twirls Lylah in his arms as he blocks shots as the door is finally forced open.

"I know you'll always be there to save me."

Lylah skids to a stop. Spinning wildly in the cross section almost getting herself lost as she searches for Luke.

Why do you run towards me and away from the truth? Luke's voice echoed all around her. Lylah spotted his smirking face heading towards the hangers almost two miles from where they originally started. Lylah with tears falling down her face took after him snapping around the corner before seeing him running away from her at top speed down a walkway over the hangers. Lylah lowers her head and ignores her breaths as she takes off after him once again slipping into a memory.

"Shift thirty by nineteen, raise eight and use turret four and six at ninety port side." Luke hollered as the vessel responded to Lylahs commands and turned the guns of her favorite hovercraft on the men trying to jump onto their craft, ripping them to pieces as she tapped her pad. Lylah's head snapped around the cockpit as she read the sensors and made adjustments.

"Just like training." Luke hollered as they continued to support the marines. Lylah breathed in as a tracer round zings off of the cockpit. Lylah stays stable holding the controls with confidence. The Pl-89 interplanetary hovercraft was the best non-jump non-capital ship someone could get their hands on. A fighter designed for fighting bigger ships with hidden crew, playloads, and stupidly powerful plating: the vessel was the embodiment of built for everything but the biggest problems.

"Lylah!" Luke cried pulling Lylah outer her daze as the g-forces flung her back against the seat as the fighter struggled to maintain hooverability.

"Pad's one, three, and four are." Lylah couldn't make out over the rest as she lost control as two missiles capsized the fighter from below flipping and completely downing the vessel in a heap of metal, smoke, and fire.

"Luke." Lylah blinked again, losing herself to corridors before seeing him walk down a hallway to her left as she continued after him.Though thoroughly lost she wondered why he was playing games with her. She rounded a corner before stopping as she froze staring at herself and the events of the hanger playing before her, tears slowly started to fall as she watched.

"Luke," She blinked, smoke billowing from all around her as she dropped, having to remove debris from where Luke should have been in the copilot's seat. Only dust greeted her and struggled to get out of Lylah's way as she darted from the back of the craft fearing the worst. Lylah froze for a second staring at the weapons rack and the now missing weapons. Lylah knew Luke was using.

A snap and scream of terror caught her attention, completely ignoring every danger as she darted towards the screams unholstering her pistol and lowering to look under the smoke. She started to crawl, finding it easier to see. Another scream pierced the night as Lylah caught her breath seeing two pairs of feet walk in front of her not three feet away from Lylah, she quickly rolled to the left. The pairs of shoes are not Federation regulation. Lylah knew without her armor she needed to try to stay out of combat and being closer to the ground made it easier to see through the ash that stung at her throat and eyes. The soldier stops as he stares at the ground. She stared at the blood streak and caught her breath. She had just been on that.

The soldiers were looking for him too. The soldier lowered his head trying to get a better look as Lylah coiled like a snake and blasted the two men with quick shots to the chest that sent them hurtling, pieces and all, into the smoke. Lylah slowly breathed out as she rolled back out of cover and started to follow the smears, "Luke." She said with a whisper. Turning her head towards the sound that brought her crawl to an end as the noise echoed in her ears.

"Fuck you!" Luke's bellowing voice echoed as she desperately jumped to her feet and tore into the smoke with a panicked fear. The sounds of fighting grew louder as she saw the fight through flashes that cast shadows showing the battle that Lylah was just too far away to be in. Lylah sprinted as hard as she could as she stared at the battle

Luke and what looked like Commander Montgomery were defending themselves from a constant wave of enemies. Back to back flashes of what looked like lines of green lightning flashed like strobes around them. Luke turned to catch a man before throwing the man with unnatural strength, grabbing his pistol in the shadows as the quick blast of a shot sent the man flying as Luke continued to use the weapon until it was empty, mowing his way through at least twelve men before using the empty weapon as a club. Lylah side-stepped a man who came crashing down where she had been a second earlier trying desperately to help as the battle started to back up onto one of the docked destroyers. Lylah stopped staring at the flashs trying to gauge where the Commander and Luke were heading before the battle was lost to the bowels of the destroyer.

"NO," Lylah roared as she turned around away from the memories forcing herself back to the here and now, coming face to face with Luke as he looked at her with pained eyes. She shook her head as she stared at the portal to the memory. Tears now heavily fell down her face as

she turned to Luke. Her eyes pleading with his, begging for this to end. To not watch his fate once again.
Luke placed his hand on her chest and with a quick shove pushed her into the memory. Lylah's eyes wide with shock as she was sucked into the memory so she couldn't escape it, was forced to confront the truth.

"Luke." She coughed louder and heard the scuffling of someone struggling before the snap of a pistol. She jumped at the snap and rushed towards the violence, shaking uncontrollably. Lylah had lost track of them when they entered the ship and slowly she stepped through the now body ridden hallways, Lylah couldn't imagine the casualty count because this simply wasn't worth it. Nothing was worth this much death. Heading towards the best choke points of this Mardine-Class Destroyer before stopping mid strid staring at several non-human bodies one in particular had Lylah's knife forced through its skull a bit of crimson painted its chest, someone else's knuckles prints painted various points of other creatures as well. Lylah noticed what looked to be some kind of intense burns scorchings target locations much like that other body had. She caught her breath as she saw the doorway and the apache wall of bodies that had been built. Damage extended outwards like lines of death. Lylah gulped before checking how many shots she had left, 2, stacking up at the only entrance point.

Taking one final breath she hardened herself before storming the room only to collapse in the doorway at the sight of Luke slumped up against a chair with thirty or so odd men around him. Most of the bodies were beaten to death but just as many had huge lighting burns going through their chest. Tears fell steadily as her mind recreated the fight. She watched as Luke had been forced into a chair taken by more than a few men as Luke killed them. They had tried to restrain him as Lylah's face had deep waterfalls of tears falling from her eyes as she continued taking in information, her eyes locking onto restraints that littered the floor. Burns and scorch marks extended from Lukes body damaging walls as if some giant discharge of electro-plasmic energy tore through everyone. Luke's head was back, his arms hung loosely off the back of the chair unbound. His face was almost unrecognizable from all the broken bones and damage he had taken. They had taken their time once he was restrained and tried to force him to speak but. Lylah starts to sob as she continues to read the room building the finale, he couldn't handle it.

Somehow Luke had forced that discharge to end it all. Lylah broke emotionally running over to Luke in pain, throwing herself on him as she wept, his body lifeless reacting to her pain. All her friends, her mothers, and now her lover were gone. Lylah wailed, her cries echoing like a banshee for an unknown time. The air had dried to an unparalleled degree when she finally stopped cradling his body. Lylah painfully opened her swollen eyes trying to see the silvery object in his left hand, the glint being the first thing that had caught her eye. Lylah leaned forward, disbelief and horror continuing as she reached for the glint.

"Identify yourself. You will only get one warning." A booming voice called from the entrance. Lylah could hear whispering as lights flooded the room illuminating all the horror for those to who had just arrived to behold. She knew what they saw. Bodies torn to pieces, two soldiers, one in a chair dead, a grieving friend who was covered head to toe and stained with blood. They needed to know if she was a danger but Lylah cared not. She couldn't stop living how Luke had killed all of the men, either with his fist, their own weapons; it didn't matter he had forced them to kill him and all because these idiots couldn't respond fast enough. Lylah cried harder as small wails started to escape her lips, panic filled her body as her recognizer struggled to read her mind as she crumbled into the fetal position broken by pain.

"You're too LATE." She wailed finally the only thing the device was able to muster in the four hours it took to remove her from that room being forced to take Luke's body at risk of life and limb.

Lylah snapped back and looked down at her left hand feeling something metallic in it. Lylah noticed the portal and Luke disappear into blue ribbon like specs but the thing in her hand took all her attention as more pain and tears extended over her face as she stared hard and long at the blood stained dogtags of Commander Montgomery. Lylah stared at the Commander's information none of which she ever knew.

```
Commander Annábella Jane Montgomery.
Service date admission: Nov. 10, 4950
Date of Birth: Nov. 10 3960
Killed in Action: March 12th, 4999
Home Planet: Anastasia's Tears
Ranks held: Commander-First Class of Special Operations Forces. First Mother's
Imperial Protection Detail. Planetary Defector.
Clearance Rank: Tier Two (Federation), First Mother's personal archives
access.
Children: 2, All living
Spouse: 1, All living
Parents: 1 Living, 1 Deceased
```

The tags slowly changed in front of Lylah's eyes. Lylah blinked rapidly trying to absorb the information as it quickly updated making Lylah question what she saw originally. Lylah noticed one thing had actually changed, the children and how many were alive.

```
Commander Lisa Jane Montgomery.
Service date admission: Nov. 10, 4950
Date of Birth: Unknown
Killed in Action: March 12th, 4999
Home Planet: Unknown
Rank held before death: Commander-First Class of Special Operations Training.
Clearance Rank before death: Tier Two.
Children: 2, 1 living
Spouse: 1, All living
Parents: Unknown
```

Lylah's heart broke knowing they never found the Commander's body. The Commander had shared a special connection to Lylah, like a mother Second only to Chelsea. The Commander had always watched Lylah's back, she slightly jumped as someone spoke from behind her as she crunched in reaction, restricting herself. Lylah forced herself not to swing in response.

"Ah Captain Soffrireterna, just the person I was looking for. I know since you have been brought on board there has been no time for a medical examination but I am pulling the procedure book on you and must insist you come with me before I am forced to take your wings away." A males voice scolded her from behind. Lylah spun around sliding the dog tags into her back pocket palming away from the Doctor as she faced the head medical examiner. Doctor Malarious "Mal" Jabezes. His soft cow brown eyes and slight salt and pepper beard complimented his wise old doctor look. Slight wrinkles teased his aging face. The Doctors had crowsfeet that lightly caressed the edges of his eyes only complimented a white with red outlined jumpsuit identifying him as medical. The red outline designated him as Lead medical officer on board. While everyone else wore white with blue. Mal actually hated being on the bridge so he usually used one of his many assistants to maintain the bridge for him while he worked.

The man himself is said to be quite a pleasant person to be around though Lylah had only read his file before coming on board and over the last month in the wormhole had avoided him like the plague making sure they were scheduled on either side of the massive vessel and using her advanced knowledge of the ships inner works to keep track of all medical staff so she couldn't be ambushed, yet somehow here she was. Lylah mused how they had even tried catching her while she slept until she rewrote the ship's A.I. 's protocols to only send outgoing holos. To say that him finally catching her is a big deal.

I haven't earned that title yet, Lylah sassed to herself, "Of course Doctor. I do apologize but I have had a lot to deal with." Lylah said curtly and waved her hand only stealing a glance to see if Luke was watching but saw no one. She turned her head and conversed with the doctor dodging most of his major questions before getting blood drawn as he quizzed her about the events to make sure she wasn't suffering from brain damage.

"All done. Look, it only took fifteen minutes, ten of which was getting here." Doctor Mal said smiling trying to reassure Lylah as she nodded and a light smile formed. Lylah tried soothing herself by reciting information in her head. She looked around the infirmary for more in depth detail knowing the facts of the ship but wanting first hand knowledge. The beds were self diagnosing and self treatment to save staff for major things, if she had been paying attention she could have just used one of them and been able to tamper with the results. The nurses all looked professional and she could tell that a lot of the gear and tools laid out were for extreme measures once they got back into the fray. Once they landed at Earth and rearmed, debriefed, Captain Lylah would be leading The Ellen and forty other ships to take Magness Prime. Lylah leaned back on the medical bed as the scans continued deep in thought before being interrupted.

"Well congratulations are in order." Mal said, continuing to read the information, keeping his back to her. Lylah stopped breathing for a second as Mal continued, "Do you wanna know the sex? Looks barely over a week along." He paused, taking in the information in front of him, "I assume this is your first?" Doctor Mal said, finally turning back to her after reading the information.

"Um..."She coughed, her body stiff-as-a-board as for a fraction of a second she didn't believe him. A tear slowly fell understanding the message Luke was trying to send."Yeah. The father died in the attack." Her eyes wandered away from the conversation trying to keep her composure as another tear fell. The irony of the situation not being lost on her as some divine comedy.

"So, The true question is, are you gonna keep the child?" Mal responded carefully, noticing her pain and trying to invoke emotion.

"What kind of question is that?" She flipped on him, locking him up in her sights. Standing and pushing Doctor Mal against the wall fist raised, Mal showed no fear in the sudden movement and shook his head at the nurses who turned to get involved and patiently waited for her to finish."Of course I am gonna keep our..." She stopped realizing what she was about to say.

"Our? As in the young man that took hours and forty of my friends lives to peel you away from and who is now sitting in cryo?" He said with tactful eyes. The Doctor had used his words wisely to draw her into revealing the truth without her realizing it.

"Yes." She said sitting down again. Emotions overloading her face as tears begin to flow down her face.The area started to spin and she drifted back into those final moments with him. She saw his body and what they had done to him, trying to get him to crack, to give them their prize, her.

"Loss is hard, I understand." The Doctor's face softened, "what it's like to lose the love of your life." Mal finished almost not even talking to her but taking a seat beside Lylah before removing his glasses and tapping his cowlicked hair with a towel under the extreme pressures of the situation."You need to grieve. Ma'am. you have done nothing but plan and form strategies and make sure everyone is ok since you came aboard. You haven't stopped analyzing those implant downloads looking for weakness. No one blames you for the law of survival or pain. But you have done everything," He said, closing his distance with her to lift her eyes so she could tell how much the doctor actually cared, " but you need to grieve," He started adjusting his glasses back into place as he talked and crossed his arms relaxing before once more speaking, changing his tone, "Now tell me something weird about yourself."

"The file is right there," Lylah signed reflexively before pointing at the screen, and saying "All you need on me is right there."

The Doc smiled softly actually knowing what she said, "Not your medical file. The file doesn't make you, you. I want to know something about you, like what is your favorite romance novel, "He signed quickly back sarcasm being laid on thick in his movements and face. "Or if you're not ready for romance, how about your favorite type of taco?"

Lylah burst out laughing, "My favorite type of taco? What the hell is wrong with you?" She signed back.

"He's a damn doctor. So everything." A roaring voice came from behind Lylah startling her a little. She turned to look at the Colonel looming over her. His massive frame cast her in almost a complete shadow. Reminiscent of their first meeting.

"Says the giant." Mal retorted with a smile as they all burst out laughing. The Doc and the Colonel were obviously good friends which made Lylah smile, knowing her staff liked each other. Lylah shook her head as images of Michelle, Alice, Selaris, Chelsea, Maddie, Dakota, Aaron, Mark, and Luke danced in her head sitting around one of the tables at the academy enjoying the meal before afternoon classes.

"I was going to go for breakfast if you two would like to join." Spage said. Lylah snapped to the here and now taking in her savior once more. Colonel Murtus Spage was very much the same size as Luke if not just a slight bit taller. The Colonel however was not as stacked with muscle, defined yes, muscles on muscles, no. The colonel had a full head of mud brown hair reaching towards his shoulders, a very tidy chinstrap goatee covered his face. His uniform is almost completely wrinkleless as any Spacecore's uniform should look, tight and clean. After a small walk through the main hallway which was much bigger than the crew halls all three arrived at their destination. The mess, a six story mall like atrium which was packed with crewmen getting on and off shift. The hustle and bustle could leave one in a daze if they got lost in it. The crew allowed the Spage, Lylah and Mal to move ahead as Lylah stared at the seemingly endless choice of food. Lylah's eye landed on a pandercake line and she moved over waiting for her turn.

"What are my options," Lylah said greedily not realizing how hungry she was as her turn in line arrived.
"Anything you choose, Captain." The chef avoided his eyes as he spoke. Lylah noticed the man's reaction and shifted on her feet.
"What's your name crewman?" Lylah asked, trying her hardest to stay composed.
"Crewman Micheal," Lylah got a good look at the man and almost broke down as he moved out of the shadows of the Kitchen.
"Oh my God. Micheal." Lylah sighed as Michelle's little brother came into view. He was only fourteen, two years younger than his sister and Lylah.
"Ma'am. Would. Is." Micheal stammered as he tried to ask the questions as they both teared up trying not to break.
"We couldn't find the body." Lylah said a tear falling down her cheek once more as she raised her eyes, took a look at Micheal tears pouring down the poor kid's face, "I won't let her death go unpunished. Michelle was..." Micheal shook his head up and down as Lylah's crystal failed to finish the sentence.
"I'll uh take vanilla please." Lylah quickly snapped back into her act and continued through the lines before meeting back up with Mal and Spage, her hunger vanishing as quickly as it came.

Spage nodded towards a table next to a window and settled into it. Lylah did her best to hide in the shadow of the Colonel trying to avoid the rest of the crew member's gazes. YouThe tension in the air was unmistakable as she passed, table after table, men could be heard whispering. She strategically placed herself with her back to the rest of the mess hall to help her avoid eye contact but she felt the gazes. After a few awkward moments of silence the Doctor spoke.
"Would you tell me about Luke if you're ok with that."He said, choosing his words very carefully.
"He...he was a brave man. When the shooting started he didn't hesitate to jump right in." She said, staring at her food aimlessly, losing her appetite once more. "But that's not what made him...him. He had this way of just making everything ok, you know. It was always like him to save me. No matter where or when. I would go play hero or badass and he was always there to save me, being a bigger hero," She smiled a soft smile, a tear slowly falling down her face. "I remember this one time when we were kids and it started to become increasingly harder to hide the fact of who my dad was, this bully decided he was gonna pick a fight with me. I'm the Chief's daughter so I must be a socialite right?" Doctor Mal and the Colonel smiled at each other as Lylah shifted in her seat. Lylah left her desire to be a socialite out of the story. "So he pestered me relentlessly for days, right? I finally snapped and went to crack him hard. In the split second it took for me to launch my attack, Luke had caught my fist and I mean in mid air," She showed the motion, "mind you, this is in his emo days so no hulk of muscle. I mean as if he could see what I was gonna do from a mile away. Well naturally I stared him down and yelled, 'The fuck Luke?' The bully tried to take advantage right." The other two started to chuckle and she tilted her head, "and without missing a beat he pivoted and knocked that smug prick out." She slammed the table as the other two burst

out laughing, "I was so mad at him. Motherfucker stole my kill." Lylah found herself struggling not to giggle. "And I mean it was a two hit combo, Luke hit him and that bastard hit the floor." She stared at her drink before finishing." Suffered a broken nose and major concussion from one hit. And I mean Luke weighed maybe a buck fifty. He.."The others nod acknowledging the hit laughing.

"Well of course I wanted the glory right, so I got up in Luke's now smug face," She tried to imitate getting some chuckles, "and I proceeded to scream at him for the next fifteen minutes as we waited for campus security to show up. He just sat there tapping his toe. Unbenounced to me this was his whole damn plan." The Doctor and Colonel got closer enthralled by the story being told; wide grins spreading on their cheeks holding back laughs. "I continued to scream, I was so furious with him that I hadn't been aware of the security members sitting there for the past 5 minutes waiting for my crazy ass to calm down." The men started to lose it, " Luke just nodded after a while and I turned hoping for more enemies. Nope, what was there instead you ask? An officer who came over and I fucken I quote, 'Sir you two are free to go, I have no desire to explain why I had to taz the Commander and Chiefs Daughter to be very honest I am way too lazy to even attempt to fill out that kinda paperwork. So you two have a great rest of your day ok'. We walked away scot free because he knew I would go fucken psyco on him and he could weather it." The combo of Mal and Spage both spat out the drink and filled the now almost empty mess with laughter as they tried to control themselves.

"No way an officer would do that. No way." Mal laughed.

"Fuck yes he would. Man was a genius. Just let the Commander and Chief's daughter go psyco for a bit and it will freak them out." Spage chuckled. "I probably would have said and done the exact thing. Fuck that shit show." Sending them all into another burst of laughter.

"Worst part is that it is completely true," Lylah said through laughter, "I got grounded for a solid month." She rolled her eyes heavily, "After my father found out six months later. Not for starting a fight but for making the officers wait fifteen minutes to approach me," The men lost it, "Luke walked me home every night to make sure I followed my dad's instructions,"The men slowed and tilted their heads, "so I wasn't lonely. I think my dad knew how Luke felt. Luke just was...a whole different kinda human. A kind we shouldn't have lost." Lylah said, stuffing food into her mouth with a sudden renewed hunger, "Jesus christ what is this liquid stims?"

"He sounds like a good man." Spage said a slight smile teasing his lips at the sudden outburst before taking a sip of his coffee and finishing his steak and eggs.
"The best." She said as she stared at the passing void missing him more than ever as she stared, a quick decision was made as she contemplated everything.

Chapter 2:

Only the Darkest of Secrets Allowed

Only twenty-two hours since the Attack Magness Prime
Earth Orbital Space dock: Executive Docking Bay 34
Catwalks and Loading ramps Leading to The Ellen
Lylah Soffrireterna
8:21 A.M.
March 13th, 4999 A.D.

    Colonel Spage, Doctor Mal, and Lylah walked down the open hangar ramp of the F.S.F.V. Ellen to a standing ovation from the crew and most of the Space Station staff who had been waiting for the three of them to exit. The Air stunk of shame and dark deals as they saluted and continued down the ramp. The Space dock had ships, varying in size from frigates, to full dreadnoughts that dotted the ports around the Ellen. Those who weren't at the ceremony were doing their jobs taking quick glances to try and see the excitement. Lylah looked warily at Dr. Mal who just nodded. As the crowd split in half, a man stood at the back of the pack barely visible along the nearly nine miles of ship, Lylah now looked down. She didn't have to guess or even see who the highly decorated man was. Lylah's eyes started to tear up. The three of them took almost twenty minutes to get down the ship. Lylah and Spage stopped and saluted in sync, the Chief saluted back and opened the door of the armored limo for them. The Chiefs face was cold and calculated Lylah could already tell this would not be a pleasant ride. They all got in and waited for what was to come. The tension had all the time to build as the limo barely started before the Chief Spoke.
    "Colonel Spage, report, if you please." The Chief ordered, his temper was short as the morning had been filled with bad news after bad news. Lylah observed his left leg having trouble staying still, her eyes wandered up her father's uniform of black and gray. Tassels, awards, medals, and the most exquisite looking gold trim completed her father. A sudden sour taste filled Lylah's mouth as she despised who wore the most important uniform in the Galaxy.
    "Camera analysis from the academy combined with the videos from high orbit and the hangar, plus," Spage paused to take a quick glance at Lylah, "implant recordings that

could be recovered, we have determined that they employed precision strikes and full stealth tech. Their fighting patterns are similar to Alec Nartine from the 31st century including his knack for brutality." Spage reported his voice dropping with boredom as he continued. Lylah watched the debriefing play out but did her best to ignore everything staring at the floor and listening to the conversation, her mind elsewhere. "The creatures we have dubbed 'Brutes' are very resilient and don't seem to have an overheating threshold for their personal cloaks which makes it extremely hard to pinpoint. They wrecked four squads. The One encountered by the squads had very few weaknesses other than overconfidence. Their ships' cloaking works in a similar way but we can see them in visible space, which will be how we wanna use combat targeting till we can find a way to identify their signatures. Plus their ships are simply too fast for tracking computers to compute, unfortunately boardsiding was the only way to hit them or us. We lost most of our sensors and coms but no damage was reported and shields held at 70% even under the stress of the Electro-Plasmatic based rounds. EP rounds for short. Our EMS (Electromagnetic scaling) shielding stopped all E-warfare attacks, and we were able to deploy drones. We maintained an 89% accuracy rating for all drones, fighters, bombers, and remaining, Frigates and Cruisers. The rest of the squad sent was not so prepared, Electro-plasma ripped straight through shields and melted hulls. We registered massive EM damages to weapon system complements and shields. We think the Electro damage being done is by nano tech design, maybe acid infused. We will need to do more investigation for more information."

    Spage took a breath in. "I lost all six escort destroyers. They were torn to shreds before anything could be deployed. Known casualties are the F.S.F.V. Saratoga. Full crew complement of one thousand six hundred and eighty-eight including ground forces. F.S.F.V. Kirk. Full crew complement of one thousand seven hundred and one including ground forces. F.S.F.V. Kobayashi. Full crew complement of two thousand one hundred and fifty-five. F.S.F.V. Beta. Full crew complement of one thousand two hundred and thirty-one. F.S.F.V. Likened Home. Full crew complement of two thousand eight hundred and ninety-eight. Including ground forces." Lylah's head lifted, listening to all eighty nine ships he listed before discovering how devastating the battle actually had been. Lylah had been so focused on what she endured she forgot there were more aspects to the battle like the space battle now being reported. "All causality reports from both atmo and ground combined are four hundred-ninty eight thousand two hundred and three dead excluding enemy casualties. Once the Ellen tanked through their main attack line we launched all eight cruisers and fifteen frigates with fighter escorts, bombers and drones. The two back up troop transports launched with me on board to collect survivors." Lylah listened intently, not having briefed on the battle in orbit or even thinking about it till just now.

    "Our response quickly routed all eighteen cruisers, four Battleships, and what we assumed was a dreadnought or carrier." Spage shook his head as he continued, "Their attack on Magness Prime was effective on a global scale. The orbital station hadn't had a chance before it was destroyed in the first twenty minutes. The enemy used targeted debris strikes from pieces of the orbital station to rain down with pinpoint precision and destroyed most of the city or academy defenses looking like a meteor shower. After they had broken atmo their main landing force besieged both the city and the academy claiming it in the name of The Freedom Initiative. No previous record of an Association exists on record. We were forced to retreat and draw all ships back into the Ellen. A response fleet of nine hundred ships returned maybe forty minutes later. I wasn't going to risk any more ships or lives."

    "Who filed the report?" The chief's demeanor slowly worsened as he took in the complete information being presented.

"Due to her over-exposure on the ground, figuring at least ten hours of close quarters combat, combine with her being the only known survivor of the attack on the Academy, your daughter did sir. I filed the Space and afterbattle reports as I could fill in the blanks she wouldn't have been aware of sir." Colonel Spage started trying to defuse the situation.

" Let me refresh that," The Chief venomously spat, "Why did I not know she was alive? How the fuck did such a attack happen? More importantly ,why did I walk into work this morning only to find out one of the most secure facilities in the FEDERATION had been taken in the name of others? Who even the fuck are these guys? Those are the questions I wanted to fucken answered. Instead." The Chief spat, throwing all the blame at Spage.

"Fuck you." Lylah hissed at her dad, purposefully interrupting him, being completely done with his bullshit. The room froze before exploding in a flurry of tension. Shock plastered its way onto the Colonel's and her father's face. The doctor turned trying not to laugh, trying to shield his smirk with his forearm as he coughed towards the window.

"Excuse you." The Chief retorted, recovering his composure trying to take control back attempting to get in Lylah's face as she forced him back with her forearm, simply and easily overwhelming the Chief who stared horrified at his daughter. A moment only Lylah caught. Her simple strength forced the chief back as he grabbed at his chest as he coughed.

"Your excused Chief," Lylah's crystal flared as she spoke her emotions forcing her to change her words and tone. "If I was anyone of your other soldiers you would have already ripped me for the patches in the report. You would make me take Noxsite so it would make me spill my fucken guts before finally hooking me and my damn implants up to HoloReality and making me live the attack over again and again just to make sure that I'm telling the truth but instead you're chewing Spage out for doing his fucken job. Stop acting like..."

"Shut your mouth. You are my daughter. I could never..."The chief interrupted as a loud crack interrupted him once more as Lylah's hand found its target. The silence that followed had the Colonel and Mal look at each other in disbelief as Lylah tore pieces out of her father with her hatred, her eyes filled with so much fire the pair thought her father might internally combust from the heat. Her point had been made. Blood slowly trickled from the force of the slap as a red marker tattooed itself on the Chief's face as he stared.

"No. You. Shut the fuck up S*ir*," Lylah sassed before becoming the soldier she was supposed to be. "I am just another soldier. Don't start acting like you gave me much of a choice. Now live with that fucken choice." Lylah's words tore through the Chief as he stared frozen at the sudden outburst, "Now fucken act like it." Lylah took a deep breath in calming herself, " Please continue Colonel." She said turning to the now shocked soldier and nodding before looking out the window to zone out.

Lylah looked out of the window choosing from now on to ignore whatever happened next as the city zoomed past. Earth hadn't changed much since she left. Giant cityscapes ran for almost two hundred miles in every direction. One could easily lose themselves in the almost thousands of stories they now hovered over. Earth was still the overcrowded dying world she remembered. Lylah noticed a holocron newsreel showing shattered hulls of ships and the battle that had taken place while they were in wormhole space and docking. The scrolling message below, *The Federation wins but at what cost? How many died in the attack and where was The Ellen? Was the Attack a response to upcoming elections?* She almost scowled at the blatten slandering of those soldiers. No one was prepared for this war let alone her father. Lylah's eyes darted to his direction as a scowl formed. Lylah once again took in the vast cityscapes, following the holoways (Vast freeways of holocars flying through various levels of the deepened city), and holosigns could keep her busy till they hooked her up to VR for implant recreation. Lylah blinked, feeling something she had never felt before the feeling of a slight tug on her subconscious so she grabbed it with her mind.

"How did you do that?" Luke said slowly as if Lylah wasn't supposed to be there as he emerged through the smoke from behind Lylah in the hanger of his death. She turned and saw his emo phase and couldn't help but smile.

"Where? Why am I here?" She said looking around and realizing nothing was actually moving but them two. The scene was exactly as it was the first time she lived this nightmare. Lylah felt a sudden surge of accomplishment for no apparent reason as she took in everything once more waiting for Luke to respond.

He shrugged finally, his hands in his pockets, he moved them out till the hoodie wouldn't let him and she smiled deeper. She uncontrollably moved her long hair behind her ear and looked at him longingly.

"Why here?" She said looking around and she turned her head down looking at the two of them as he had died. The feeling of every little nerve ending standing at complete attention as the scene remained frozen; Lylah wailing in pain as Luke hung limply on her body. Her head extended toward heaven in defiance. Hints of pleading teased her cheeks begging for an unforgiving God to bring him back.

The scene started to reverse startling Lylah as Luke's left eye crinkled as he stuck out his left hand slowly rolling his wrist to the right. The scene sped up slowly replaying the events in reverse. They watched as Luke sprang from his chair, his face slowly fixing itself as the damage was reversed until they were on the side of the destroyer. Luke looked at Lylah with a solemn sorrow in his eyes as he put his hand back in his pocket. The scene snapped to play as Lylah watched the struggle up the side of the destroyer. Luke moved like a mad man as the commander and him retreated up the walkway. Four men attacked Luke with batons in their hands as Luke easily overwhelmed all four with his superior skills and size, slaughtering them in quick succession. His moves are cold and calculating as he ends them; the battle continues into the ship slowly as the numbers game starts to take its toll on Luke, his breaths are deep and purposeful. Luke clenches up catching another man's leg before snapping downwards with his forearm shattering the man's thigh bone causing it to explode out the other side. The scene slowly froze as Luke looked to Lylah once again, seeming to debate something before quickly changing the scene to the moment's before Lylah found Luke.

The Commander and Luke had been the only two to make it this far. Commander Montgomery was looking at Luke, her face torn in pain as if she knew her only options and it was time to say goodbye, Luke's face was damaged but not gone yet as he stared blood and sweat mixing down his face as his eyes past her at the now surging horde. The Commander's eyes and face almost pleading with an unknown force. Time quickly returned to normal speed as the Commander turned away from Luke as she screamed towards an unforgiving God. Acceptance and pain on her face as a single tear slowly makes its way down the Commander's hardened face, the only thing visible under the mud, dust, blood and sweat seeming to clear a line that exposed clear skin, Lylah's eyes widened. Luke's left hand flew from his hoodie as he quickly slowed down the scene so Lylah could take in all the details. Lylah watched her eyes widening as she stared at what came next. The tear started to gain static electric build up before emerald green lighting started to flash all around the Commander and in the tear trail. The Commander's eyes exploded in Emerald green rays as she nodded to Luke shoving him back into the chair, where Luke was found after the flash by a full squad. Another horde entered the room, Luke launched his left out of the hoodie and slowly returned to the flash so Lylah could see what happened.

In the moment the Commander had turned, raised her arms and launched all her pain in the form of something Lylah only read the Fairsist could do for myths and legends. A cacophony of emerald green lighting started to surge through the air. Licking and twisting its way as its ever growing lighting arced through the men as the Commander slowly started to dematerialize screaming in pain and joy before eventually completely dematerializing into green ribbons as she screamed. Electrifying everything in front of her as she finally smiled, her body returning for a second. Tears ran down her face as the Commander seemed to stare at Lylah for a quick second then staring fully at Luke eventually fading into blue ribbons before completely disappearing. Luke stared at the now scorched ground that used to be the Commander as he rose, catching a soldier as more surged in almost an endless tide of soldiers until Luke could no longer take any more and the horde managed to get him in the chair. The scene slows to a stop as Luke turns to leave, seeming to have seen enough.

"What happened next?" Lylah said rivers are now flowing down her face, her eyes swollen and red.
"You know what happened next." Luke whispered in her ear as she turned to look at him. Somehow he got behind her. Lylah almost shied away but steeling herself as stared ahead.
"Who was Commander Montgomery to you?" Lylah asked before turning to stare into his deep emerald eyes. Shaking as her mind flashes to all the theories and ideas she had dancing around.
"You know the answer to that question already." Luke raised an eyebrow, "You just don't wanna hear yourself say it." Lylah's eyes poured tears as she looked once more into his eyes and he nodded, "Say it."
"She was your mother." Lylah whispered in response, her heart shattering into a million pieces as she stared at the ash pile, a fresh wave of tears falling down her face.

"Can I tell Mr. Akya that Luke has fallen," She said, snapping back to the present completely changing the subject at hand, "I know him the best," she said, working her magic on her father. " Dad, I mean sir. I think I should be the one to tell him. It would do Luke honor and we would have returned today to show off our diplomas sir, I don't know if you were aware of how close to graduation we were; he should know from me not some face in the Federation Space Force that Luke died saving me. I...I need to tell him. You can't send a nobody not for Luke. Please." She choked out realizing the depth and pain of what she was asking for.

The Chief thought for a moment, and nodded, getting ready to leave the vehicle, "Cadet," making himself clear, "you do realize that he will take it hard knowing that his only son is dead. Despite your history with him, he may be angry at your survival. Are you ready for that kind of spit?"
She nodded, holding back tears.
"Granted. But when you get back I expect your full cooperation." He said, staring at Lylah with one foot out and one foot in.
"She will have it but once she is done with you, sir. I will need her as she Volunteered for Project: Gods." The Chief's face froze as he stared at them before slamming the door leaving the other three to stare at each other awkwardly until till their respective stops.

West Lafayette, Indiana
10 hours Later

"Cadet, are you ready?" The words echoed around Lylah's ears. She stared emptylessly at the back of the limo. Her face stoned over as the limo stopped. The fine black leather seats with golden embroidered outline with soft pulsating blue back lights could calm anyone but Lylah down. The echoes of those she killed still ringing in her ears after holoreality. Eight times they ran her through the nightmare. One for each dead squad mate. Her father's direct orders, revenge for him realizing he could no longer over power her with strength.

"Yes, Private Sotof." Lylah droned back as she closed her eyes trying to relax her nerves as they arrived. The three armed escorts, Private Sotof and Cadet Lylah, got out of the limo in front of The Akya estate. She walked up the sidewalk. Instinct almost took over and it took all she had to not walk in the front door. She pressed the doorbell and only knew one thing, this would be the last time she walked into her home. She heard Mr. Akya come down the stairs in a hurry, excitedly. Lylah's heart teetering on the edge. Mr. Akya threw open the door trying to surprise what he thought were the kids. The plump two-hundred and eighty-nine pound man stopped mid-skip as the twinkle quickly faded from his eyes. Mr. Akya had his jet black hair slicked back and Luke's lime green eyes stared at her; his face rapidly changing emotions as his eyes darted towards the limos and the lack of Luke. Mr. Akya's eyes finally locked on the folded flag Lylah now held in her arms. His breath caught and his eyes watered as Lylah bit back tears of her own. The weight of what was expected started a small stream of tears to fall from Lylah's eyes. Her breath caught at the sudden realization he hadn't seen the news this morning dawned on her. He started shaking his head in pain, his eyes pleading for her not to start. Tears already swelling his normally happy-go-lucky face as he struggled to control himself. Lylah saw the party decoration and almost lost her nerve then and there as she wrestled with the gravity of what she truly asked.

"Mr. Akya," Lylah managed to squeak out as Mr. Akya started to shake his head, hard tears threatening his chubby cheeks. She took a deep breath trying to control her emotions and continued, "I regret to inform you that Luke Wade Akya has been killed in action on...," She choked. His eyes started to let tears out as he held back wails of pain, " He died serving," She knew this wasn't how it was supposed to happen through her own pain she went off script, handing the flag to Sotof and cradled her second father, "He wouldn't let me died, he died saving...me, I...let you and him down by not being able to save him, he died in my arms...he was.." She broke down and cradled Mr. Akya as he wailed and cried holding her back trying to resist her sympathy before embracing her back after a quick minute they separated as they both tried to control their emotions.

"Special, he was special, I know. I read...in the announc..."He continued struggling through tears "I wanted to surprise." He choked on his words as he stared at her, crossing his top lip over his bottom before continuing, "God he loved you." The pain truly sank in as the man collapsed in grief screaming to an unforgiving God." My boy." He wailed not noticing Sotof grabbing the second flag and the uniform outfit. Mr. Akya's eyes widened and more and more as tears fell shaking his head as he stared at the second flag, unable to handle his own grief. "No, no no." He shook his head, tears once again flooding his face as Sotof failed to read the room correctly.

Sotof started, "Mr. Akya, I regret to inform you of your wife." The wail that followed stopped time as Mr. Akya screamed again, silencing the soldier and making the man step back Mr. Akya launched himself at the Private. Lylah quickly grabbed Mr. Akya and cradled the grieving man as Mr. Akya panicked in her arms, grief-stricken screams in agony. "You all need to leave me." He screamed at the Private, his voice breaking in pain, Lylah once again pulling into him to make sure he couldn't hurt the privates as Mr. Akya screamed, attacking towards the private. "You all need to fucken leave. Go the fuck away." Tears and spit flew as Mr. Akya almost tried to throw himself for a final time at Sotof but Lylah kept him firmly in his spot, easily redirecting the grieving man inside as he wailed helplessly in her arms despite the size differences.

"Come on." Lylah waved the others away as she moved the man in the house easily. He screamed again, staining her uniform with his tears, snot, and saliva. She moved him with ease as an adult moving a baby and sat him on the sofa in the living room. She seemed to stand and move almost too fast to Mr. Akya as she moved to the door pushing Sotof out of the house while slamming the door in his face. She navigated one of her childhood houses with ease, got kleenexes and poured both of them some whiskey, a drink Lylah particularly didn't care for but Luke loved. The man continued to cry as she sat down offering him the drink. He took a sip and tried to control himself as he tried to come to terms with his grief, the light in his eyes completely gone as he stared empty at the floor.

"I'm sorry." He said choosing to speak first, rubbing long tears off his face and blowing his nose.

She let a slight smile tease her face before signing, "I requested this."

"I know baby girl, I know." He signed back, looking out the window before taking another sip, his hands shaking in shock. They sat a long time in silence. They sipped their drinks looking out the window and getting refills. Lylah more than once took in her surroundings. They sat in front of a fireplace. A beautiful genuine Egyptian green rug in front of them. The holo tv stand was on top of the fireplace lip. They sat on beautifully soft deep emerald couches. There was a good eight feet for the screen to spread in each way. Behind them was the doorway that led to the front door and a staircase. Pictures of her and Luke hung along the walls going up the stairway. She couldn't believe they were only sixteen as she looked at their pictures. Toothy smiles and cheesy poses in pictures at pumpkin patches; real pumpkin patches not those holo patches. The first dance they had gone to was with a chaperone. Luke scowled in every picture as both an emo punk and military soldier at her dates and it made Lylah smile uncontrollably. The green walls and white trim had just proved how goofy they had been. None of the rooms in the house had the same colors Mr. Akya had wanted to repaint the house, insisting Lylah and Luke be his official "color pickers". If she walked up the stairs there was a tight cluster of rooms on her immediate right, the rooms belonging to Luke and Mr. Akya. To the left were the holoroom and bathroom. Mr. Akya could afford to have a personal holoroom and the bathroom was filled with real stained marble. The hot tub sized bathtub had jets and showers to make sure no matter the angle, you were getting wet.

The marble sink and toilet were remarkably planned and almost complimented the tub. If you went into Luke's room you'd see an old school electrical computer set with a 21st century HD screen. Luke could hack into the holonet easily from there and never be traced. Holonet doesn't use I.P.s, they are all connected to your DNA. His paper posters of a game called Halo. Lylah mused because she did like the absurd idea of sentient life outside. *God if they had only known how empty and truly alone the galaxy truly is.* Lylah quibed to herself. Directly next to that poster was a poster she had always wanted to know about, A giant badger holding the capital letter H. Underneath was the words Hufflepuff. Lylah never had asked what the hell a Hufflepuff is and why a Badger cared about the H. The thought of never knowing brought a tear to her eyes onces more as she continued her tour. Luke had various things from the early 20th century all the way up to the 39th century hung around his room on shelves, real wood shelves not holo-shelves. She never knew how he got his hands on the Fairsist Dagger seeing as all legends have them as peace loving species but when Mr. Akya had it tested, came back positive and got a special visit from the T.O. or The Others. Her father's personal kill squad, slash a hush squad, slash Bully Squad, slash what her father needed them to be. She knew it was being run by a man Lylah had heard her father only refer to once as the Peacekeeper. She suddenly pulled herself out of her mind and realized in all her years here she had never seen Mr. Akya's room. "I'm sorry." He finally said, snapping her out of her tour.

"I'm more sorry," She signed back looking at him. His head was still down and he eyed his drink.

"He was such a good boy." The man cried to himself taking a light sip trying not to burst into tears again.

"She was the mom I never knew." Lylah signed as she once again began tearing up trying to control herself.

"You knew?" He said, looking at her helplessly.

"I figured it out." She leaned forward as she gave him the dogtags and he started to cry again.

"Thank you." He whispered back, "She finally found what she was looking for."
Lylah watched as the happiest tear of grief seemed to slowly crawl down the man's left cheek as he stared at the tags.

"If you need," she started before he raised his hand.

"Just leave." She nodded and stood to leave as she walked by, he caught her dangling hand.

"He loved you," Mr. Akya said, pain once more flooding his face with grief.

"I loved him. I wanted him to live because the world needs him more than it needs someone like me...He..." She said before being interrupted by Mr. Akya.

"If you are here and he isn't, that's because he knew better." Mr. Akya's sudden outburst made Lylah wonder if he knew more than he was letting on which left a slight chill that teased her back. She walked out of the house and looked back at Mr. Akya through the window. His face blank as he stared at the wall. He blinked slowly and turned towards her, staring at her before nodding his head and getting another drink.

Lylah walked down the path to the limos, remembering that stare but never turning back, refusing to look back. G.O.D.S. would start soon and she wouldn't allow herself to lose this shot at revenge on her father.

Project Name: G.O.D.S.
Original File date: 12-██-495█
Redacted Date: 12-14-49█
Subject: ██████████████████ and possible ███████ of the ████████
Reporter: Doctor Malarious Jabezes
Redacted Reporter: Doctor Malarious Jabezes

In my initial report I stated it was not possible to make what I call genetically superior soldiers let alone bring back the ███████ through such a process. Using the previous ██████ and a ██████████ we could perfect the ██████████ Upon review I have deemed the ███████ not only would work but could lead to the re-emergence of the long ████████████

During deep space exploration of ██████████████████████████ in the █████ ████████ I have found the long fabled and almost mythic ████████████. In my research and through lots of failed experimentation, we have discovered the needed ███████ is not the only needed item. We need a ████████████ but one who has ███ all but ██ thing. A █████ They must have watched their ██████████ be ██████████ and ████. A █████ can be ██████████ but to create a ██████████████ I would advise ██████████ for a ██████ break out. If the ██████████ is truly what's needed to ██████ the ██████████████ then there are alot of drawbacks that need to be ██████████████. Below are all the ████████████ from ancient ██████████ on ████████████████████ are located in █████ ██████████████

The first ████████ of a ██████████ must be a ██████
███ must have watched her ██████████ go up in ██████
███ must be with ██████ when ██████ comes ████████████████
███ must be willing to accept something called ████████
███ must be willing to accept being ██████████
███ must be willing to survive ████████

Major Drawbacks.

First drawback comes from the ██████████████ itself. Due to its high ████████████ rate to ██████ no amount of training will prepare for the effects. On a full ██████████████ will result in ████████████████ The mind of ████████████ coupled with the ██████████████████████ of the ████████████ will overwhelm anyone over the age of ██████████████

Second drawback comes from finding a██████████████ to ████████████ such things let alone trying to ██████████████ such a horrid thing.

These are just a few of the problems let alone funding. However as requested by the current Chief I have included a full ██Page summary.

Chapter 3:

The Devil's Bargain

Deep in the Tributary

"This is serious," Luke was saying, sitting in front of a fire. He wore a fishing jacket, his black hair hung across his eyes with one eye still visible as he stared at Lylah as he poked at the fire. She looked around, soaking in the memory. They were on the top of a mountain on Magness Prime a few days after arriving on the planet. The forest cleared in this one spot and you could see the valley for miles and miles. The city was almost forty miles in the opposite direction. Magness Prime itself was nearly the size of Jupiter. The forest was made up of a weird pine, ironwood mix like mix. Its deep natural lakes are flooded year in and year out. Long months of continuous rain filled the deep valleys creating deep caverns that ran through the entire planet. The leaves were all shades of purple and pink to indicate the Autumn season. Lylah closed her eyes as the sun was starting to sink behind the north mountain range filling the sky with shades of bright green and yellow. Water glistened a crystal like color adding to the beauty of the mountain range as it danced in the light. She smiled and felt a soft breeze blow past her. The local Marceetes, a mix of minx-like reptiles danced in the underbrush as their nose twitched sensing their environment for potential friends or predators. They had six legs and fur-like scales; they could harden their fur to protect themselves. Lylah had watched scientists try to figure out how these things had natural hardening abilities to use as prototype shield tech and the results were promising as the "fur" was able to shrug off three shots from Ll-98 Officer's hand Cannon (Lylah's pistol) until exposed to extreme heat where the fur simply could not harden under the heat. The soft sounds of nature dancing through the mountains as Lylah continues to take in the memory, closing her eyes again and enjoying.

    A soft smile teases Lylah's lips as another gust teases her hair but she knew this gust, she felt its presence before or should she say whose presence. Lylah's eyes open to stare at the incorporeal form of Commander Montgomery as she slowly materializes as green ribbons of energy that explode out of nowhere, spinning Commander Montgomery as the energy seemed to build her causing Luke to jump away from the fire in shock, almost falling over as his mother formed. Lylah almost laughed as Luke stared blankly at his mother.

    "How did you do that..." Luke whispered to himself as he stared at the now solid form of his mother tears teasing the edges of his face.

Lylah was ripped away from the dream as an explosion rocked the Earth Orbital Space Station, snapping Lylah awake by the anti gravity blanket activating. Lylah shook her head as she looked around feeling like she hadn't really left her dreams yet but ignoring the feeling listening for the emergency responses and orders.

    "General Alert. Boarding Parties on levels sixty-eight though one hundred and sixty-eight. All civilians evacuate. Evacuate. All Response squads report In." Lylah's training took over as she removed the nano blanket and felt true weightlessness take over. Lylah let out a slight smile from remembering how Luke had lost control on their first day of Zero-G training and crashed into her causing them both to take major injuries and concussions sidelining them for a couple of days. A flash of green energy exploded outside her door as Lylah kicked off the wall spinning to her back as she collided with the wall across from her. Grabbing the Zero-G bars she waits trying to flatten herself so she could use the ceiling to gain momentum. Another muffled flash as arcs of Green Lightning kiss the outside of her door. Lylah gulps as she watches the reflection in the window, no sound echoing around her, only silence as she watches. A robed figure hovers past the door stopping in a millisecond as it turns. Staring at the door to Lylah's room seeming to know something was off. Though no eyes could be seen, it sniffs the air as an explosion flares in the window from somewhere else in the station blocking all reflections of Lylah. The creature slowly hoovers forward into the doorway as Lylah gulps, sweat starting to run down her brow as its hand raises slightly. No skin was visible as green lightning ricocheted off the window pinning Lylah against the corner of the room writhing in agony. The creature, seeming to know he caught someone, launches a continuous stream of lightning into Lylah, burns start to form on Lylah's arms as every nerve screams out to be released from her body at once. The explosion of sheer pain almost deafens Lylah as the creature rounds the corner. Letting its lightning go as it caught Lylah's smoldering body.

"Do you want this power?" The creature coughed when Lylah recovered her skin had long trails of white steam spewing off of her as she stared at it. It let her go waiting for her to rise, floating just a few feet from her.

"What will it cost me? A wiseman once said, 'Nothing is ever free if someone says it is. They are either a liar or trying to sell you something'." Lylah signed to the creature while staring at it. The creature gave off nothing but emptiness, long robes just floating for no reason. Lylah knew one thing however, the pain she felt was real. If this wasn't a dream and it could give her an advantage she was willing to listen. After a few moments she followed with. "SO, which is it? Are you a liar or are you selling me something?"

The creature almost seems to relish in her words, "It will cost you, everything, including your soul." It hisses back.

"Then I'm getting the better bargain." Lylah signed back.

The creature almost seems to laugh with glee playing Lylah's little game. "Why?" It hissed mockingly, raising its hand already knowing the answer.

Lylah smiled, "I don't have anything left to give, including a soul." She said as she shook hands with the creature.

The creature laughs maniacally as it comes alive in sudden animated displays. A tornado of black energy exploded from the bottom of the creature as the winds ripped off its hood revealing Commander Montgomery. Lylah's eyes widen as the Commander roars, the tornado of energy latches light tendrils to Lylah's face. The commander's face slowly starts to deteriorate. More tendrils explode towards Lylah grabbing her wrists and ankles, Lylah fights back struggling against every angle as she is caught. Lylah's eyes widen with fear as she is stretched outwards by the black energy tendrils. Trying to plead with the Commander who pulled her closer, almost no skin was left on the Commander's face as a piece of skull started to shine as more pieces flew off her face peeling like wet paint. The Commander's eyes rolled backwards and her mouth unhinged like a snake. Lylah's eyes locked onto the back of her throat where a poisonous bioyu sat, a festering pool of black ichor that started to bubble and boil building energy. Lylah's screams can not be heard in the void of space as tendrils latch on the back of Lylah's head as she struggles, unable to move as the ichor erupts, completely covering Lylah's face as she is down in the stuff. Lylah drops crumbling as stains of black energy surges below Lylah's skin, almost being drank in by her mouth, nose, eyes, and ears, making dark pulsing lines extend from Lylah's eyes, mouth and ears. Lylah shakes as the pulses start increasing giving off a purplish hue below her skin. The creature slowly deanimates cracking slowly back into its hooded state, watching as the pain of its gifts take hold. Completely a skeleton now, the Commander was no more a creature to Lylah after that display.

   Lylah felt the poison she needed to overcome but her body tensed and sent waves of exploding pain throughout her like every nerve ending just pinched at the same time. Her neck strains as Lylah's jawline begins to lock, muscles spasming. Cracking can be heard breaking inside Lylah's body. *What is this?* Her own mind screamed in horror as Lylah struggled to survive. Somehow this pain managed to be more intense, never pulsating and ever constant. She felt her mind seem to split open from the inside out. She couldn't breath as she writhed, twitching her eyes widened as she stared at her death. Lylah's body starts to slowly stop shaking before becoming completely still. The Creature turns as Lylah's eyes lose all life. Her face was in utter shock. The Creature almost seems to smile as if waiting for the best part as it slowly hovers away.

Lylah's eyes explode open with dark emerald green rays of power. Lylah slowly hovers upright uncontrollably, clasping her hands together, causing the creature to slowly turn. A rose twisted its way into existence from blue, green, and pink energy ribbons as Lylah slowly pulled her hands apart curling her fingers as the rose continued to twist. The rose spun faster and faster, the ribbons spinning the colors of green, blue, and pink making a blurred line of hues as Lylah's facial expressions changed in a moment of clarity as her eyes wave back and forth as if understanding or even making the rose exist herself. The energy waves slowly pulsed adding saturation and cooling the rose. The streams of power slowed before completely disappearing as deep white outlines teased the edges of every pedal giving the rose a soft white outline that made the other colors glow. The steam cracked like glass as black and gray ash marble teased its surface. The void exploded into a sea of soft shifting ribbons that pulsed with colors casting deep ever expanding lines covering every color in the rainbow. A pure smile slowly crosses Lylah's lips, a tear slowly falling down her right eye as she mouths the word, home.

The creature seems to relish as it watches, not wanting to miss The Emergence.

Chapter 4:

The Devil's Due

Earth Orbital Space Station
Lylah Soffrireterna
8:14 AM
The Ellen
March 31st, 4999

Lylah screams as the anti-gravity blanket shatters, sending Lylah crashing into the ceiling of the Earth orbital space station as the massive station gets rocked by an explosion, The power fully re-cycles flickering the lights and igniting the emergency power. Lylah shook her head as the automated gravity kicked in, dropping her almost eight feet into the bed as she bounced crashing to the floor with a thud.

"What was that all about?" She said, rubbing her head as she looked at herself in the mirror. Her face seemed to glow softly in the shadow casting low-light. Lylah immediately felt nauseous as her brain almost took off absorbing beyond enough information to make Lylah hurl. After a few painful minutes, the doorbell rang as Lylah looked from her porcelain altar, standing and wiping her mouth. She looked at the button for a moment before pressing it as Doctor Mal greeted her at the door.

"Are you ok? Your vitals went all over the place. We can't," Lylah raised her hand interrupting the Doctor as he spoke.

"Gravity-blanket malfunction and I smacked my head seeing things that weren't there" Lylah dismissed with a wave, "Can we start early. Record what's necessary for the financials and I'll cover the rest myself." Lylah pauses focusing her thoughts. "My father will at some point try to stop this, we need to be done before he gets the chance." Lylah said with unusual conviction not once stuttering or having to change her wording.

"Of course. This way then." Lylah nodded, fully zipping up her jumpsuit.

"So I assume you read all the files?" Mal said as they navigated through The Ellen towards the medical wing.

"All that wasn't redacted." Lylah mumbled back as Mal stopped sharply staring at her.

"We don't know what this will do to you. The last people to use this method." Mal hissed beneath his breath at Lylah.

"That's why it has to be me. Now." Lylah hissed back as a group of soldiers saluted and walked past. Mal took her in, his eyes flashing around her body to get a full read. He stared for a quick second before nodding as they took off again. They arrived almost four hours before the operation was supposed to start, which would be preceded by a two hour briefing before they could even start with safety measures. Lylah looked at herself in the mirror. If all goes right she will be in recovery by then. Lylah stared at herself knowing full well when she laid back Lylah Sofferentera would no longer be alive. Someone or something else would take her place, making her strong enough to save her baby from having to grow up only knowing war. Lylah stared into her own eyes at a mirror that was to her left, reminding herself of her own conviction as she lay on her back a white gown was placed over top of her naked body before a blanket to keep her warm. Lylah took a breath as she stretched out her arms feeling the needles entering her skin. The room had light on almost every angle, almost giving off a blinding white light. Her eyes closed, Lylah waited patiently for a pat that finally came and she opened her eyes, almost crying from the blinding white light as she shook her head. Mal pushed her gently back down before whispering in her ear.

"Look, I can't prepare you for what happens next. It's on you now. Just know. I'm rooting for you kid." Lylah smiled softly as Mal pulled a file off a nearby table sliding it into his hand as he turned to address the camera.

"Lylah, we will be activating a neural dampener as well as giving you a high amount of tetraphilois a complete neural paralyzer. Meaning you will not be able to move or feel a thing till the procedure is over. When you wake up we will have put formulas 'Chromosome 25 and 26' balanced by genetic manipulation and heavy forms of augmentation in your physical body. We also will add heavy forms of physical augmentation that will be directly injected through the needles that are now in your skin allowing you to adapt to your body and new genetic makeup. Do you understand what we will be doing to you? You will not be gaining any chromic upgrades and we will not be replacing any part of the body with non living tissue. Do you understand the procedure?" Mal asked aloud, putting on an act for the camera as he turned the table, moving up as he did so. The camera adjusted so it was looking at Lylah.

"I do Doctor, you may proceed." Lylah said, closing her eyes onces more as Mal's fingers tapped her elbow to pop the vein for the Chromozone injection. Lylah ignored Mal's commentary, an explanation that meant very little to her. Her mind wandered away from Mal explaining all of this to Council. A soft breath, a sharp poke, and Lylah knew no more.

Mal watched as Lylah almost immediately fainted when the injection was pushed into her body. His eyes intently fixed on Lylah's vitals as they began to spike followed by what looked like strokes. Lylah's eyes almost erupted into the back of her head. Alarms and warnings started to blare to the point Mal turned to the assistants shaking his head. Lylah began convolusing on the table, her neck strained and her back arched as if in extreme pain. Her eyes flew open and emerald green light engulfed the room. Mal watched in horror as Lylah's eyes fluttered close. Her body was not physically different until Mal noticed the snow white hair that had now replaced Lylah's deep midnight blue. He stared in shock, afraid he may have succeeded in becoming Frankienstein. His eyes locked onto his white haired monster a tear slowly ran down his face as he weighed what he may have just sacrificed.

Lylah's eyes flew open as she stared around the now abandoned academy. The walls, halls, and atmosphere was the exact same, bringing a soft smile to Lylah's face. The air was quiet before she became keenly aware of someone else behind her. She turned around as she was unable to see her attacker as it attacked at her face with furious bites and slashes pulling flesh off while tearing chunks off her shoulder. Lylah fell backwards, her training and her own will to survive allowed her to pull the creature with her rolling with the weight to gain leverage as she launched it forward into one of the columns. Her face bleeding profusely as she finally stares at her attacker. A six hundred pound extinct Bengal tiger stared at her, eyes locked on hers, it growls slowly trying to be menacing but not yet threatening or intimidating.

Lylah looked at the majestic creature with pure contempt, she spits blood at the tiger in defiance. "Come on!" She roars as the tiger springs at her, Lylah however is ready spinning with pinpoint accuracy she slides under the swiping arms smashing her elbow down on its ribs knocking the tiger of course. Lylah tries to mount the tiger to take the advantage. The tiger, seeing Lylah's mistake, rakes its left paw down on Lylah tearing chunks out of her left breast as she rolls off the giant cat, never taking her eyes off it as the wounded combatants circle each other. The Tiger gingerly side steps as its ribs started swelling from the counter force Lylah had applied as it coughed, seeming to struggle for air. Lylah covered in blood watches as the Tiger's breaths get heavier and heavier, either it wasn't aware of its lungs filling with blood or more then likely it didn't care. Lylah knew its last attack would either kill her or it. They once again started to circle each other. The Tiger's eye becoming blood filled as it seemed to taste its revenge, long shoe strings start to form at either sides of the fangs before it licks its lips. Never breaking eye contact, slowly keeping Lylah's pace as both predators circled each other. A single sweat droplet falls down Lylah's face as she faints forward drawing backwards. The Tiger either in its tiredness or weakness launches once more at Lylah trying to pounce on her. Lylah smiled once more sliding under the animal's arms and punched directly into its chest tearing through the skin, bone, and organs. Completely killing the tiger by disemboweling it with her arm. Lylah shook as the tiger crumbled somewhere behind her. She stood shaking and turned. The tiger was gone. No blood splatter, no evidence of a body or fight. A tear fell from Lylah's eyes as she turned to stare at the nightmare shade she made the deal with.

"I've come to collect those souls!" The creature laughed at her. The walls of the academy shaking and breaking around Lylah like glass as she dropped from its gasp falling into the blackness once more.

Lylah roared awake in Ellen, her eyes glowing as she stood. Blood poured down her face as if she was being attacked. Mal watched almost being blown off his feet by the forces being thrown around in the room. Tables shook as he stared at Lylah before her skin cracked and caked itself in blood as if she was enduring some unknown assault. Her skin exploded and chunks were torn off her body. Mal's eyes snapped to Lylah's voice crystal that lay inches from him; he hadn't even noticed it till just now. As he watched the crystal almost magnetically flung back at Lylah snapping back into her. Her head snapped back, opening her mouth as more energy exploded from her as her skin quickly healed itself.

"Lylah!" Mal screamed into the endless typhoon of energy around him.

of various colors licked the air around him, winds and heat exploded off of Lylah in extreme waves as Mal motions for his assistants to leave for their own safety while he watches. The damage fills in with green rivers of energy before exploding as Lylah crumbles to the ground shaking and smoldering. Mal stared, his bottom lip trembling before uttering the words as he struggled to keep her alive, "I'm sorry, I'm so so sorry."

Chapter 5:

Only G.O.D.S allowed

Kyle Akya
May 3rd, 4999
Time: Unknown

Kyle looked around the atrium. Along with the twenty-three other cadets they were joined by what looked like black-ops soldiers standing firmly in position as the cadets talked back and forth on bleachers waiting for the presentation to begin. Kyle looked up trying to see the top of this building but only blackness greeted him as he tried to figure out how he made it to this black ops site. The room had no propaganda posters, learning posters, and even the color of the white walls seemed to suck the energy from all of them. A door exploded open in noise as someone began speaking over the speakers."Welcome to all of you my name is Dr. Mal, I would like to be the first to explain this opportunity that has been given to each of you." The chatter quickly quieted as the cadets sat down or turned around focusing on the doctor that now walked towards the middle of the classroom sized room. "In this room are twenty-three possible candidates for the project code named G.O.D.S. or GODS. You have all been brought here because you showed willingness to fight and if need be die for the Federation. Training has set you on a course but this project..." The Doctor stops staring at the cadets seeing he had their full attention. The Doctor's eyes seemed to examine them all until he reached Kyle which seemed to almost harden for the doctor before he finally continued speaking. "This project will turn the war in the Federation's favor simply put. You will become stronger than you ever thought possible."

    Kyle noticed a moment of fear from the doctor. "Now I would like you all to meet the one who will train you, should you choose to take on this challenge." Doc Mal said excitedly, disguising his discomfort well. A woman walked in about five foot three inches. She walked with a purpose moving faster then Kyle thought even possible; his eyes struggled to keep up with her. She was well built, long snow white hair almost flowed behind her as moved, she didn't look much older than him but her stance told him all he needed to know. Military born based on her posture, a lot of recent trauma based on her movements. Kyle looked over her body as he attempted to continue to read the woman. The moment she turned he couldn't stop himself from being paralyzed by her eyes. They stuck out more than the woman's hair, deep almost glowing navy blue irises danced around her eye lids as she took them all in. Those eyes landed on him staring for longer than on anyone else as she seemed to assess him just as much as he was assessing her. The woman wore a black jumpsuit with a white tank top meaning she was a commander of some kind. But Kyle wasn't aware of any back jumpsuits that were in defense force regulation.

"Welcome to all of you, My name is Commander Odyne." Her voice pierced the murmurs. "Let me make this perfectly clear from the start.. I am your commanding officer and you will treat me as such." The air was sucked into space as this Odyne made herself perfectly clear. " If you choose to accept this project then like Dr. Mal said you will be put through the ride of your life. I am what you will become in retrospect. I am as of right now the fastest, smartest, strongest, and deadliest thing in the galaxy including blackholes and spaghettification." The teens chuckled at the statement, "Let me prove my point. I would like four people who think they are competent." She said without missing a beat, staying perfectly in check.

"Aye." Kyle said standing up without missing a beat either. Kyle wasn't all that big, maybe six foot even but he could lift which led to Kyle dancing with heavy weapons and heavy mechs before getting the offer for GODS. His dark brown hair and eyes passed him off as some casual frat boy instead of the nerd he actually was preferring to spend his time in deep debate about some fictional world while working on his mechs.

"Anyone else?" She said, raising her eyebrow looking him over once more before looking away dismissively.

"I volunteer too." A girl two rows down said. She had bright strawberry orange hair. She looked like a delta quadrant in appearance as she launched herself down the stairs.

"Me too." Another girl said, rising from her seat. This one was massive, maybe as tall as Kyle. Beta Quadrant for sure Kyle mused as she had to part the cadets to move her way to the steps.

"I will fill the last slot." A boy said; he looked like a giant without the muscle. His ebony skin and tall lengthy body was that of an old earth sportsman, a basketball player Kyle mused as he took his allies.

"Dr. Mal will you get the terracoil? As you all know terrarium is the strongest metal known to the galaxy. I want you guys to bend the coil in half." She said looking at them with her voice steady.

"That's impossible." Kyle blurted almost seeming to activate her trap.

"Is it?" She said, raising her eyebrow. He suddenly felt like a child who had done something wrong. She took the coil from Dr. Mal and bent it in half in front of everyone without breaking a sweat. The crowd was visibly shaken at the abrupt movement as the metal groaned at the unnatural bend. The shock that followed was that of pure silence in disbelief. The tensile strength need to bend a terra coil was beyond nine million p.p.s.cm.

"Bend it back." She ordered handing the coil back to the cadets.

The four of them split up two on each side and started to try to bend it back after about five minutes she ordered them to stop no longer needing her point to be made. Kyle was soaked in sweat like everyone else. He hadn't believed it till they hadn't moved it, no amount of struggling, trying to use the stage as leverage, nothing they did unbent that coil.

"You may return to your seats," Commander Odyne said, "That is just the beginning of what I can do and I assure you all that I have many tricks up my sleeve. If you think you are up to the challenge, rise now." She stated, as if all of them came to the same conclusion at the same time they all stood up.

"You are now Apache. You will choose a new name, this name will identify you as an Apache so make sure you are willing to live with it for the rest of your Military Career. This name must be of an Ancient Greek God." She warned. Kyle raised his hand.

"Yes cadet?" She said, turning those haunting eyes on him.

"Will you be choosing a new name as well?"

"I already have. Now if you all would step forward and read the agreement and sign the contract we will begin."

"Begin with what?" Someone said behind him as the cadets moved into a clump to start getting the paperwork.

"Your new life." Odyne said as she moved out of the room to prepare for them.

Olympus Training Ground
Day 0

Lylah Soffrireterna
May 4th, 4999
Time: Unknown

"How are they doing Doc?" Lylah's back turned as she stared over the bodies of the Cadets.

"Well only eleven have survived. Barely, none of them experienced near the level of damage you did but it seems even with your help some just couldn't handle it. " He said, turning to her disappointment as she stared blankly down at the bodies.

"Eleven? I thought I had saved at least eighteen." She said walking over and looking at the control room panel. The room was a giant observation holo-room. The technicians that ran back and forth kept the vitals of everyone. The bodies were on holo projections and sat around the room as Lylah walked over to the dead bodies staring at them for a quick second feeling the weight of her failures deepening.

"Either their bodies would not accept the twenty-fifth and sixth chromosome or they couldn't accept the river. I mean, you." he said, nodding to a holoscreen to her left as the dead passed across. Lylah seemed to glare at the screen as she read the information, her minding teasing her with her friends around the screen staring back at her smiles and joyous glees being shot her way.

"Who survived?" She said, turning to him and hiding the tear that slid down her face from him.

"Eliza "'Apollo' Suecourt, Shyanne 'Aphradite' Resdicor, Chantae 'Artemis' Le'Nor, Ketsy 'Athena' Nileson, Devin 'Themis' Lacy, Josh 'Phobos' Reed, Dakota 'Nyx' Liop, Chelsea 'Dionysus' Marnic, Laurel 'Demeter' Wheeler, N'vid 'Adonis' Flaecatcher, and Kyle 'Ares' Akya." Doctor Mal said.

"Wait, that last name you said Akya...that's not possible." She said stiffly and walked over to the young man's vitals clicking and tapping making the screen move and reading the information as she quickly read it.

"Well according to this he did," Dr. Mal said, reading from the screen. She sat down and stared at the screen in silence lost in deep thought. Her mind flashing to the dogtags.

"He checks out." Mal said, trying to scan her emotionless expression.

"No it doesn't." She stood her irritation hidden well as she turned to leave. She needed to think and punch things in simulation.

"I also meant to ask you why don't we augment their bodies." He said changing the subject trying to keep her in the room.

"Easy answer is that if they learn to be one tenth or even one twentieth, of my speed before they get the augmentation their minds will crave it and the desire to keep up with me throughout training will make them want it more. Basic raise to the challenge psychology," She stated, "I want them completely ready to go in five hours."

"It took you twelve to get over what we did to you though." He said, turning to look at her as she moved towards the exit. Remembering the slash marks appearing all over her body as she was in recovery. Her muscles would tear themselves open before quickly sealing, gushing a new wave of blood every time. Mal had read about her experience inside the academy and even collaborated to the council on the consistencies of the injuries he documented through the ordeal. What her body went through, A Sibirian tiger was mauling her in her mind and her skin reacted as if the extinct cat's claws were truly real. Eleven maulings she endured Mal thought staring at her.

"Yes but you also augmented my body which took even more time for my body to accept." She said not wavering and turned to fully leave her mind made up.
"They will be exhausted, they will more than likely pass out from strain." He warned.

Lylah just snorted, turning once more to belittle Mal. "You still see the body as such a limited thing. You see what it can and can't do but the truth is it is what the mind can do, the body is irrelevant. If the mind thinks something is real the body will follow that train of thought till the end of time. Five hours to get them ready." She said, turning around on her heels and walking out onto the railing overlooking the now sleeping children and looked down before attempting to walk towards the rooms. Mal trailing behind her as he struggled to keep up not wanting to let her go.
"I'm sorry." He panicked.

She stopped. Her back tense before sighing and in the moment he could blink she was less than a foot in front of him. Her gaze added to the intensity of the color of her eyes."Doctor, you can't just apologize this away. I am stuck like this for a long long." Emotion flickered across her face as Lylah adjusted, changing her tone, "I will be this way for more than a thousand years." She hissed at Mal being very honest out of respect for him. "So I will outlive you, your kids, their kids by the time your grandkids have kids I will only look a little over twenty. I will still be combat ready into my eight hundreds and probably will never lose any physical prowess as long as I am breathing." She shifted on her feet as she looked around the room in deep sorrow trying to cover her face as she desperately tried to explain herself. "I can hear all the heart beats in this entire facility, all thirteen thousand of you. I can tell you every single way I could kill you in front of everyone to the point I would be hailed as a hero or to make them so afraid of me they would never betray me no matter what I chose to do." The fear in his eyes shone like the sun at her sinister implications. "I wouldn't but it doesn't mean I couldn't. If you knew now what you knew then would you do it all over again? Would you make the same call to get this advantage?"
"Of course not." Mal said through chattering teeth finding his backbone as he stared at her.

"That's the difference, Doc. I knew the risk when I signed the paper. I didn't know what would happen when I accepted the River Wrath's power." Lylah softened up and walked back to the railing and looked at her new soldiers. "We will outlive our kids." She stared at them aimlessly before speaking lost deep in her own thoughts. "Parents are supposed to be buried by their kids, it's against nature to go the other way around." Doctor Mal looked at her then to the cadets trying to piece together her thought process before she spoke again. "Doc, I forgave you before I woke up, The moment you blackmailed me I was pissed but I see it was honestly worth it but." He sighed a breath out but she continued, "but do I hate what I have become?" There was a long moment as Lylah considered her words very carefully. "More than anything in the galaxy because I will live to see what will happen next. I will live to see the next war and the war after that and the war after that. You on the other hand will get old and die after the age of sixty-five," She heard his heart skip a beat. The muscles were strained and she estimated that's when the muscle would tear full causing the heart attack. "You will never know the horrors that come after. I have to live with the horrors of the past, present and I get to know the horrors of the future. A fate far worse than living." She said, nailing him to the wall with her venomous words and turned to leave again. "We will always be called upon to make new horrors for wars whose leaders' grandparent's grandparents haven't even been born yet."

"You'll live to see over a thousand?" Mal said, staring blankly at her bold prediction.

"Yes, if I am left to my own devices. I can reach well beyond a thousand but at least you can die, natural or not, no human can kill us. You'd need a fucken nuke and even then we might be able to outrun the blast. If you think that's not hell I don't know what is." She paused. "I will help you win this war but once that's done all of this will end. There will be no more of us made. Ever. The River will not allow anymore to be made if you push it. It will cut us all off. File that in your report." She finished with a whisper next to him. Mal looked at her before a quick blink as she was gone. Mal's face in shock turned and stared at the Cadets as untold thoughts danced around his head. He tried to come to terms with being Victor Frankinstien of his own horror reality. Forced to watch his monster do her thing.

Olympus Training Ground
5 hours Later

Lylah Soffrireterna
May 4th, 4999
Time: Unknown

"Alright listen up, you will be training every minute of every day till December 31st, then you will be put into commission. I know you are all feeling a little strange but we can't wait for you to feel comfortable in your new mind. Any Questions?" Lylah barked at the entrance of the underground academy. The deep walls echoed her words around the Cadets; a door entrance was carved into the wall behind them leading into the base. Three long pathways lead from right to left and lead to the door in the wall. All pathways lead to endless blackness with very little light except for the light revealing the door. The Cadets had been horrified to know that so many of the others had died adding a new level of levity to their struggle.

"Ma'am how will we train in our sleep?" One of the boys said, stepping forward. He is barely smaller than the rest, not well built, Lylah almost was sure that due to his deep almost pulsing golden hair and his now glowing magenta eyes this was Luke's little brother Kyle. For some reason Lylah felt a sudden malice towards the unblooded.

"Virtual simulations will broadcast in your heads through the implants allowing you to sleep but will still be training you on a semi-conscious level." Odyne responded, staring at him.

"If we fail a simulation?" Kyle asked.

Odyne allowed her mind to smile, " I would suggest you don't, now we are going for a run, grab your pack and keep up."

Lylah bent down and picked up her backpack with ease while everyone struggled. She listened intently as they complained and helped one another. Lylah felt a slow gentle smile form wondering if this is how Commander Montgomery felt when she was doing this kinda training. It was gone just as quickly as it appeared as she turned to look at the Cadets.

"Alright now everyone will get into two lines. On this run, if you require aid or help I want you to know no one will help you. If someone helps someone who is struggling you will suffer twelve hour handstands. If someone is struggling you will give them words of encouragement but you will not help them in any way, shape or form. Am I understood Cadets?"

"Sir yes, sir." The Cadets barked and Lylah almost cried remembering the Original Apache members, seeing a few of them as she looked over these Cadets.

"Move out." She said, taking the first step. She knew she had to keep it fair for the first run but after that things are going to get rough. They needed to keep their mind active and running or they risked over thinking everything and ruining their one shot at freedom.

"Ma'am?" One of the Cadets said. She flipped around to see the name. It was the one who asked the question earlier. Lylah almost rolled her eyes in irritation at the fact Kyle reminded her of Luke.

"Yes Ares?" She responded by keeping pace next to him still going backwards.

"What was your name?" He responded almost taking offense to how easily she was keeping with them.

"Odyne." She said turning back around keeping pace with him, Normally her face still stoic and hard, locked forward as they jogged. Not once turning an eye to catch a glimpse.

"Isn't that your name now, I mean what's your real name like the name you gave up to be Odyne?" He inquired rolling his eyes at the sharpness of the response.

"Wanna know what the best part about being in command is, cadet?" Lylah deflected quickly.

"What's that sir," Kyle said knowing a scathing comment was in bound.

"You may ask all the questions you want Cadet, But I can tell you to shut the hell up and if you don't I get to hurt you." She answered, her face still stoic even in the dark shoulder lamp filled caverns, "Am I understood Cadet?"

"Yes ma'am." He lowered his head in defeat.

"Now if there are no more questions to be asked I'm about to increase the speed so keep up."

Chapter 6:

Conning the Devil

Lylah Soffrireterna
May 5th, 4999
Time: 3:12 A.M.

"You know I never thought you could be so cold but damn this takes it to a whole new level." Luke's words teased her mind as Lylah felt her face smile. She could feel the excitement at seeing him explode from her and for this brief moment she allowed herself to be Lylah.

"Why are you here? I need sleep." Lylah said, opening her eyes. They were on Magness Prime again, the same clearing as before but the leaves were a dark blue and purple for the winter season. There was no crystal clear shine, only darkened and angry looking clouds threatening them with a swift drowning. The air was quiet and almost hostile as Lylah waited for her response.

"You are asleep, anyway I wanted to continue our conversation." Luke said, lighting the fire after seeing Lylah slightly shiver. She glared at him and moved to take a seat only admitting to herself the heat felt nice. "How'd you do that thing with my mom, oh and you made more?" Luke taunted trying to lighten the mood for Lylah knowing full well she couldn't answer those.

"Shut up." She hissed not getting the sarcasm as she stared at the flames, the ones they lost to surgery heavy on her mind.

"The Ancientors are pissed as fuck." He said looking at her, A sudden rage flares from Lylah as she screamed to the skies."Oh who fucken cares you murdering fucks." Looking around the now 21st century style campsite after flipping off the skies with the best bird sign she knew trying to find the drinks.

"And what will you do when you lose one?" Commander Lisa Montgomery said, walking up from behind her, a ghost in the storm. Lylah spun allowing a slight smile as she stared at the Commander. She looked normal in short shorts and hiking boots with a shirt and vest on, her hair neatly tucked under a cap. Luke arose to get food and found some meat rolls and patties. Laying them on a metal grate they all ponder the question as it hangs in the air. A few minutes passed as the smell of burning ironwood and meat teased their senses. Grease cracked loudly as Lylah finally found an answer, an answer that she wasn't exactly proud of. "I won't. Not if I can help it." Lylah said, looking at the food cooking on the fire before attempting to steal some. Luke stabs at her with his sausage fork trying to swat her away. "Not yet. Meats not done." He said and added some wood to the fire eyeing her suspiciously. "What happens when they find the stream?" Lisa said sitting down, "And find out your true intention?"

"It won't matter." Lylah said and snatched a roll fumbling with it due to the heat as the Commander rolled her eyes trying not to smile all the while covering her mouth.
"How can you be so sure?" Luke said smiling.
"You're all bits of my mind you should already know." Lylah said, blowing on the roll before scarfing it down.
"Fucken weirdo." Luke laughed and offered her a plate.
"You intended to tell them right off the bat and explain everything in the training tonight." The Commander said, looking around with disgust.

"Go back and finish your game but when you're done wasting lives maybe we will have something to talk about." Montgomery said, raising her hand as Lylah was knocked away. Awakening as the Cadets attempted to knock on her door, she was there before they could knock,"So?" She said, raising an eyebrow scanning over them all. The Eleven survivors looked nervously at each other before Ares was shoved to the front. "We're in."

Olympus Training Ground
Day 3
Lylah Soffrireterna
May 8th, 4999
Time: 10:01 P.M.

She watched him as he struggled to get his bearings. Lylah was never more than ten meters away hiding in the ignorance of her prey. She had felt inspired and wore Amazonian Jaguar leather. This would-be Apache; he thought the mission starts only when they arrive, a slight smile spreads across her face as she planned to take her time. She could feel the others making his mistake. Luke would be disgusted how little his baby brother had learned at his training academy, Lylah thought with such disappointment.

Enough. A voice echoed from the trees but Lylah ignored it and moved in front of her target making sure to trigger his motion tracker and waited for him to discover her. Lylah locked her eyes to watching the skies. Virtual was nice and all but Lylah always preferred the real thing. She heard the grass become disturbed as her prey walked into its trap. Ares never stood a chance.

"So..." A voice echoed slowly over the open field. Lylah could feel her disappointment building as he seemed confused behind that helmet of his. Lylah smiled knowing full well Kyle was making basic mistakes trying to figure out why she would draw him into the opening with no weapon in sight or scanning range. Lylah was well aware he couldn't touch her. She listened to his muscles as they screamed inside his body telling Lylah his every move ahead of time long before their actions were taken. Kyle would be learning how much he really doesn't know about war in a few short minutes, Lylah mused to herself ignoring the aura of rage surrounding them.

"Are you waiting for an invitation?" Lylah sassed standing slowly allowing Kyle to face her fully.
"By order of the..." He started to speak and Lylah almost lost her nerve raising a hand to interrupt him.

"Save the drama for someone you can actually convince to surrender." She ordered, "You know your goal."

Kyle's armor had yet to be modified in Virtual which for some reason made Lylah curious, taking a mental note for later. Lylah almost smiled as she heard the tips of his fingers running along the tops of his darts. Lylah almost smiled, sidestepping the three needles barely moving in the seconds that followed. Lylah had to give Kyle originality. He liked unusual weapons and had a knack for making them work when they shouldn't.

"You flinched." She nodded at him fully knowing it was the fact she could hear both his muscles tightening and his insistent rubbing on the needles as a pacifying action.
"And?" He replied confused.
"It gave you away." Lylah felt the shock from Kyle as he threw seven in less than three milliseconds and she dodged all of them with one fluid movement, sliding effortlessly between the cluster of darts.
"Stop flinching." She droned at him enjoying her power over him, "You have the entire human race of combat training in your head...use it."

Kyle launched a wall's worth of darts in one minute trying to get close as he surged forward shadowing the wall as cover. Lylah surged forward dancing around the few darts that blocked her path as she danced off her back foot, spinning inwards as she wrapped her knee around his thigh and yanking the ankle rolling the opposite direction and dragging Kyle with her. Lylah let the lock go quickly to mount Kyle before the boy could even react, punching her fist through his throat and rolling backwards. Kyle's body disappeared as another reappeared in the millisecond after.
"One to Zero." She stated and let him rise before throwing up her arms waiting for him to attack.
"Score limit?" Kyle said, rolling his neck slowly circling her trying to shake off the death.
"Ten wins." She said, clenching her fists softly as a pacifying behavior.

He shifted on his feet as he launched himself forward, grabbing three darts in his left hand and slashing across her chest before following through with the momentum and launching from a counter clock form. The first punch landed on his upper chest with such speed he genuinely couldn't keep up as she spun around him catching him from behind. Milliseconds passed as she paralyzes him with her forearm to his lower back only to follow that up with snapping Kyle's neck. Lylah walked away in disgust as Kyle respawned. She could see his muscles clenching as he tried to figure her out.

"Two to Zero," She said, waiting as he stood back up. Kyle knew she was good and was supposed to be better than the others but he couldn't help feeling like there would never be enough training for them to be equals. Kyle had heard of Black Ops and how unfathomably trained they were but what she was doing put those myths to utter shame. She looked to her left and raised her hand. A sword flew to her as her other hand threw a banger.
"Defend yourself." She barked as the banger made contact with Kyle, flinching in the moment, unable to tell the danger from friendly.
"Now that's cool." He said out loud before she cut off his head in one fluid movement.

Kyle Akya
May 9th, 4999
Time: 8:01 A.M.

The punishment was everything she promised as Kyle's body almost stroked out from the surge of pain that rocketed up his spine as he thrashed trying to cope with every nerve rebooting. In the next moment Kyle shot up and touched himself all over, panicking as he tried to make sure he was alive. His body trying to cope with dying and the shock of what he assumed was them stopping his heart. Ten deaths. Ten.

"You too?" A girl said next to him. Kyle rolled to his left and could see the bucket of vile sitting beside her and the long eyes of someone's first death experience in VR. Long trails of sweat and deep bags told him all he needed to know. It was her very first time dying in VR ever.

"Yeah, it is." He said, rubbing the back of his neck trying to avoid her fate before a heat surged throughout his body and his mind slipped out from underneath Kyle as he grabbed his own bucket launching the contents of his stomach forcefully forward.

"Laurel..uh Demeter. Mine too." She said lowering her head as another wave hit them both before holding out her hand. She was five foot five, maybe a buck ten. Her bobbed green hair and yellow eyes almost didn't match her rounded face. Deep ebony skin made her yellow eyes seem a golden honey colore almost completing her look.

"Kyle, Ares." He said and looked around as others seemed to be failing but none seemed to be first timers like Kyle and Laurel.

"She get you too?" Another woman walked over.

"Aphrodite, right? Yeah." Laurel said and moved so the only normal-ish looking one of them could sit on the edge of her bed. Aphrodite was taller than everyone but Chantae or Artemis. Aphrodite had native skin that was coated in sweat, her orange cat eyes and long eggplum hair hung loosely around her skin. Her wider frame made her more curvy than any of the other girls. Kyle took in the room they sat in which was referred to as the transfer room. Where the doctors made their bodies fall asleep and took their minds and displaced them in VR. Nurses ran to and fro as the Apache waved the technician away in disgust trying to live through dying in peace. The Eleven beds with neural uplink collars laid at the top of the bed. Each bed was designed for one person meaning only their neural waves could even activate the beds. However the beds were completely self-sustaining. In case of an emergence they would encase each Apache and put them into deep status as the A.I. scrubbed records and would eject them into space if things went to complete shit. When in space the pods would drift together and wait for pick up. In case they were too near to a planet the beds were completely amto rated so even if the planet caught them they had a 70% chance of living through the descent. Kyle didn't know the name of the ship they were on but he found it funny that each person's new name was above each bed in a granit like plaque. A small night table and locker stood to each bed's left for personal effects which usually consisted of back up clothes rather than actual personal effects. Kyle shook his head snapping back to the conversation

"Damn, I only had my head snapped twice," Aphrodite nodded.

"Wait, did we all..."Another screamed and came too, Kyle recognized Devin or Themis. His orange long mullet and white eyes which were unmistakable as he launched up grabbing the bucket to hurl. Kyle was happy to see he survived as he happened to be his bunkmate during surgery. Devin was not what Kyle had expected when they first met, being well versed in many forms of art and promised to show Kyle his works after training. His bleached skin glistened with sweat as he tried to calm his nerves breathing heavily.

"You too." Kyle nodded at him after he recovered from the shock.

"Damn Ares you got big. What the hell did you eat?" He said after recovering, standing and bouncing on his toes, shaking his arms looking over at Kyle. This is the first time they had seen each other since that first run. After the run they were separated and kept in isolation for two days to make sure everyone was ok. They must have moved their bodies into this new area when they were in VR which is why this area was such a shock when he had come to. Kyle and Devin used to stand about the same height, now Kyle hulked over him by a good foot and somehow packed on an additional forty pounds of muscle making him look more like a tank then a soldier.

"It just honestly won't stop," Kyle started trying to continue the conversation, "Did she..."All four of them stopped as a sudden outbreak of loses almost avalanched down as everyone else seemed to launch up throwing up vigorously as more technicians poured in in a panicked rush of movement. The four looked at each other as Commander Odyne just appeared at the stairs, her face stoic as always staring at them. A shadow that was even visible in all this commotion.

"Officer on the Deck," Aphrodite tried to start as the four of them attempted to stand at attention. Others also attempted but failed, returning the buckets of shame and standing once they could after shooing the aids away.

"Unfucken believable." Odyne strode through the lines with purpose, walking around looking at the wary cadets, her eyes poised with pain and fury.

"Not one point." She walked back and forth in the aisle of cadets, her words drawing long lines of spit as she screamed at them, "Not a FUCKEN point." She raged around getting in everyone's face. "Burpees," She pointed at the ground as the cadets immediately obeyed. A few technicians step forward but never got a chance to voice an opinion as one look from the Commander put them in their place. "One, Two." She barked and the cadets dropped and began continuing to count for her. She waited for the first person to throw up. Patiently not a hit of anger or rage for almost two hours till she got it. Technicians who couldn't watch were excused before Laurel shot chunks next to Kyle causing Devin to blow as well and a few others following quickly. Vile splashed and splattered as somehow her rage was back in full swing as she came around with all barrels firing.

"How is it that not one of you managed to hit me?" She asked with complete contempt. The cadets kept their eyes glued on the floor regardless of what was there. It was better than looking at Odyne when she was in a rage.

"How is it that every single one of you has the entire history of war and not one of you used your fucken ablilties. Faster." Odyne continued to rage at the cadets, her words cutting through them worse than any weapon. They sped up throwing up and continuing to blast aids with glares when medical staff and others tried to aid them. Most of the medical staff were watching monitors, unable to sit in the room.

"None of you will ever see augmentation day at this rate." She hissed, "Faster." The Cadets tried to compile as others started to throw chunks, their muscles simply unable to allow them to move. After every single Apache blew chunks, a full four hours after they had woken up she finally gave the order.

"Stand face." She said from her step slowly rising as the cadets stood at attention, defeat and determination plastered on everyone's face.

"You think this is cool." She said raising her hand and the same sword she had cut his head off flew into her hands. She jerked forward grabbing his collar holding the sword to his neck. Her face stoic before relaxing.

"Defend yourself." She then handed the hilt to Kyle. Kyle looked at the sword a moment and waited for everyone to move. He flinched to snap the sword up. Kyle didn't even see her move but he felt the cool steel placed under his neck lifting his head upwards. He froze eyes wide as Kyle's eyes flashed around him looking at his team members.

"Let's see if any one of you learned a thing." Lylah said, grabbing a banger from out of nowhere and flinging it at everyone. Kyle jumped in it trying to mitigate the effects with his body. Devin moved slightly forward before finding the tip of the blade pressing up against his Adam's apple.

"Why didn't you all move?" Odyne said, turning in the circle to look at the others. "You are a fucken team and only two of you defended yourselves. Or tried." She jerked her foot and stopped it a few centimeters from Kyle's face. No one moved to stop her. His face closed as he awaited the kick that never came.

"Exactly why I punished you all this morning. If you think you're invincible as a piece, imagine how powerful you will be when you are whole." She said, looking around, staring at each one of them in turn.

"Start fucken acting like you wanna be here. Start acting like this is the real world because I think you all know what we are now." Lylah continued and lowered her foot offering her hand to Kyle. Lylah turned and looked at the faces of everyone in the room and saw the old apache members. Lylah could hear their cries in a quick flash as she silenced her pain. A tear teasing her eyes as she stared at everyone.

"Do you even understand what you're meant to be doing here?" She looked at them once more leaving the words in the air as she disappeared.

Luke slammed his fist into the side of the bed. The crack that resulted felt both painful and relaxing. Causing a Medical staff to rush and push Kyle onto the bed to fix the damage, ignoring the protests of Kyle.

"How did she pull that banger out of nowhere?" Devin said, looking after her. After Kyle's hand was wrapped.

he raised his injured hand and willed the sword over. The sword flew over with ease and he caught it by the hilt. "We can all do it." He said, shoving the sword onto Devin's chest before heading to the shower. His mind raced over the day's lessons.

Chapter 7:

Do you ever wonder if the Devil is just defending herself?

Olympus Training Month 1

Aphrodite
June 9th, 4999
Time: 11:43 A.M.

"Ares two hundred meter ping." Aphrodite said over the com as she watched her mind trying to find their prey. "Red squad acquired." Not their target but a good decoy. Now where was she? "Fifteen meter trigger on mark. Mark." She rolled her finger backward as her disruptor carbin launched a white almost invisible line out from her gun. The gunner slumped and she saw her team surrounding the objective. Devin, Laurel, N'vid, and Kyle. She was lucky she had four team members this round. The Red Squad of the rest of the apache had their hands held high. Previous matches had seen her vastly outnumbered but for this match there was a balance. Something felt off to both sides as they weren't against each other in this match but a mysterious third enemy. It was a triple threat match where the red and blue squads could work together to defeat a common enemy but they must achieve their objective to not be punished.

"On the ground, on the ground now." She heard her blues hollering over the mic and allowed herself to smile relaxing as she heard the words. "Targets pacified. No sign of the main objective."

Ares looked at Aphrodite from the distance of 600 meters and waved before watching her helmet plate implode as it shattered from a large caliber shot connecting. Kyle blinked trying to comprehend why someone would use such an outdated sniper-rifle. The chances of hitting that shot. Kyle turned finally hearing shots crack echo aimlessly around him as the others dropped, their rifles shouldered. Kyle lowered his head and looked at them with sorrow in his eyes as the ground beneath them exploded. Kyle shook his head and soaked in his failure before jolting up. Vomit flying from his mouth and covering his chest as he awoke from VR. "Fuck." He said in shock, shaking his hands before running them through his hair. He turned as the others recovered.

"Wasn't even your fault." Aphrodite said, raising her hand, stopping Kyle from speaking and storming towards the commander. Odyne sat up and dodged as Aphrodite threw a punch. Odyne reacted slamming each fist into the left side of her ribs making sure to hit the liver. Aphrodite dropped and coughed some blood cradling her stomach as she rolled in pain, her face in shock as she stared at Odyne trying to calm her screaming body.

"Next time you take a nap." Odyne spat over her defeated victim kneeling down so they could stare at each on the same level. Hate and rage spewed from Aphrodite as she glared into Odyne's cold, calm, and unyielding eyes. Mistrust and misunderstandings stained the air as Odyne stood looking around.

"What are you even teaching us?" Ares spat before walking over and picking Aphrodite up, stabilizing her under his arm. Technicians running over.

"They weren't moving, a heavily armed convoy like that would never stop moving. You know that. So it was a matter of time for you all to fall into my trap. You should have left the secondary targets alone. They already knew the plate was there but before they could tell you I took out your sniper." She got in Aphrodites' face, "You should have heard and saw the shot from the six miles back where I had you sighted the whole time. I watched you lay down and take aim. You didn't secure your sectors or attack zones. I even allowed glint to hint at my sights yet you were too concentrated on winning to see my mistake did you." She hissed. Aphrodite looked up at her through hurried breaths as she spoke. "Once she was gone it wasn't hard to trigger the trap and kill the rest of you. My tactic, a reverse trap is day one stuff. Use your enemies' conflicting goals against them. And all of you should have heard my shot and scattered before the explosion. You're fast enough too, running shy of six miles in three and a half seconds is nothing to sneeze at. Stop acting like the idiots who started the war. Humans need fight or flight. We do not. Assess and act, you have the time and you sure have the power. FUCKEN USE IT. That 's it." Odyne continued looking around the room before finishing with. "Kill me before I kill you, that's war. Your mind will allow you to do things you never even thought possible. You had three full seconds to respond to the explosive. Instead we are here and if that had been real. Everyone here would have died. Period. They win. Now what?" Lylah ranted, staring at their squad. "Three seconds." Odyne finished nodding her head in disgust. Her words hung for a long time. Everyone stared at Odyne as she sat on her table. Silence followed as they all contemplated her words.

"What are we?" Aphrodite coughed, breaking the silence.

"Get dressed and showered. Once everyone is assembled we will go for a hike and I'll show you." Odyne said standing and looking at the technicians as they nodded and left. Odyne walked towards the door before stopping refusing to look at them, she turned her head staring at the wall but speaking to the apache. "Humans only get seconds to live, a fleeting blip in galactic history. We will live to see what happens to the blip when all is said and done when that galactic history becomes galactic myth."

About thirty minutes later, deep within the River.

"They aren't allowed. Not us."

"They are us."

"Yes, They can join us."

"Who are they?"The stream argued with itself, many of its voices arguing back and forth as the Cadets looked around in wide-eyed wonderment.

They remind me of you. The Goddess Lisa Montgomery whispered to Lylah as she floated hovering inches off the ground beside Lylah.

"Welcome to the stream." Lisa said with arms wide open, soft blue specs danced off her before turning into butterflies and then ribbons following her as she drifted around the cadets. In her Greek Goddess form Lisa stood a massive eight and a half feet tall. Flowing blue cloth draped around her as she moved. Their air of majesty about her. Something Lylah's wasn't used to Lisa being.

"Why are you modeled after Athena?" Aphrodite said not missing a beat after the wonder wore off.

"The stream chose it for me." Lisa said with a smile. The stream continued to flow silently though Lylah could hear it's arguments; it was hiding the many voices it held from the Cadets ears.

"Why didn't your mouth move?" Ares followed as he looked around startled.

"In the stream your mind is all you need to communicate." Lisa stated.

"So, you can answer our questions?" Devin asked, looking at Lisa.

"They can, yes." Lisa said, turning to the stream.

"A stream can't spea..." Laurel started before becoming completely silent.

"We can speak for ourselves." The stream interrupted as some of the cadets backed up, their tones calm despite the racing thoughts.

"Now you all want answers, time to ask them." Lylah said to them and stepped aside.

"This place is really pretty, what is it called?" Laurel said looking around very much like Lylah had.

"We call it the Stream of Ancestors." Lisa began, "The stream was born when the Fairsist were born."

"Hold on, sorry. Fairsist. Like the fucken boogie-people? The ones who can control people's minds and use...." He froze his mind running through over fourteen million possible endings until he came to the only answer, "holy fuck." Kyle stated before turning to look at Devin and Laurel. The cadets looked at each other as they all tried to handle the truth of what was happening.

"Language." Lisa hissed. "Yes, them. The Fairsist used to be a collective of people with extreme mental and telekinetic abilities. When the Federation was being founded they refused to engage in the conflict and in the crossfire their home planet was destroyed and burned by a tremor missile." The cadets shifted at the news. Tremor missiles were illegal and had been discontinued centuries ago. A single missile was capable of lighting an atmosphere on fire burning everyone and everything in minutes. Tremor missiles however were not fast in the reaction stage. The missile required biological material to mix with which when done lights anything or anyone with the same biosignature or biosignatures aflame. If you launched one at a planet everything on that planet will become ash and molten rock, in a matter of minutes. The Tremor missile was all but useless in space however due to its need for biological material. Lisa gave them a second to recover before continuing. "Fortunately once a Fairsist, always a Fairsist." Lisa paused if remembering another time, "We were able to repopulate for a while before being hunted down by the very federation you now serve. It's not clear which side started it but, as we were already weakened from the loss of our home world, we," Lisa paused as if refusing to allow herself to say something, "we went into hiding. Disappearing from the galaxy and vanishing in the myth, legends, and eventually we became the boogie-people." Lisa paused, seeming to remember a thousand years worth of life before continuing. "Everything that was us...our culture, our very identity, gone." For the first time in Lylah's life she watched Commander Montgomery change tact. "Eventually and unfortunately through repopulating with non Fairsist we diluted our blood. Those who were not purebloods could no longer have children after maybe three generations completely cut off from the river," Lisa paused emotions flooding her face as she tried to find her words, "and..."

"And you started dying off as the Federation hunted you." Aphrodite finished as she stared off trying not to allow emotion to overwhelm her.

"Somehow we have managed to make you twelve, The next Generation of Fairsist to continue our line and more importantly." Lisa started as the stream hissed."Oh hush. You have a sane First Mother. Who can and will help you through everything." The Cadets, unable to control their thoughts, laughed before expressing their fear.

"She's a maniac." Laurel protested.

"You can't expect us to follow the unknown." Aphrodite followed.

Others threw questions before Lisa raised her hand and spoke, "Is she really any of those?" She looked around as the cadets backpedaled. "Do any of you know your Commander's real name?" Lisa looked around at the Cadets as they fell silent. "Do you even know why she is the first? What it even means to be the first of a Generation of Fairsist?" Lisa stepped forward in rage as the cadets fell back further completely misunderstanding Lisa's point as she tried to explain further. "How much pain is involved with watching her planet burn, Her lover..." Lisa started before disappearing into the stream as neon pink, blue, and green ribbons uncoiled snapping around all of her limbs. As Lisa was dragged under her mouth was quickly covered and she frantically moved around shocked and fearful, trying to figure out what was happening before her eyes locked and glared furiously at Lylah as she was submerged below the waves, fury and contempt filled her face as she submitted.

"Now you know, Anymore questions." Lylah said staring holes in everyone as she looked around finishing her stare at the peaceful river as it flowed quietly in front of her.

"You were on Magness...weren't you?" Kyle asked, trying to piece together what little he could for the little he had to work with.

"My answer still stands, cadet. Now let's get back to work." Lylah said and walked away from the stream as the others did the same.

Olympus Month 2

Kyle Akya
July 12th, 4999
Time: 1:26 A.M.

"Give me a firing solution on my mark. Move kinetic barriers and magnetized armoring from aft to bow of the ship and keep on this heading." Kyle ordered as he stared out the bridge of his cruiser through the polarized view screen enjoying the view of space for a brief second. His eyes then immediately scanned the other ship waiting for their move. His ship had been orbiting a gas giant when they were attacked by an unknown battleship. Through the course of two hours and almost having to broadside to do any real damage they had come down to this. The battleship was either gonna charge trying to rack the much weaker ship with it's station blasters or it was not gonna risk the charge and shell them from a distance giving the smaller ship a chance to escape. Eighteen twelve hundred pound mass-throws started to turn as the vessel prepared to come about on them, stationing the massive guns towards them to lay down fire. Thirty missile pods launched missiles that screeched through the black at them. Alarms blared as everyone was quiet waiting for orders.

"Point defense to maximum, Jacks, not'a one gets through. Spin us clockwise against the spin of those missiles." Kyle orders as the missiles launch at them in a circular formation, making a spiraled line of death. The ship lurched and the guns started running; echoes of the guns bounced throughout the ship as all the red bleeps disappeared. Kyle closed his eyes and nodded.
"Sir, it seems four missiles have misfired, all other shots cleared with no debris damage." Jacks reported a moment later.
"Sir?" An officer turned to Kyle fear in his eyes as the three mile long ship turned drifting on a forty-five degree angle under them.
"Do it lieutenant." Kyle ordered, calm plastered on his face.
"Roger Sir."
"Strap yourselves in and prepare for zero-g combat." Kyle said tapping the intercom. "In twenty seconds rotate us ninety degrees portside on a y-x axis and prepare for full volley." Kyle roared as a volley from the blasters shattered the station-sized asteroid behind them as the drift passed. Kyle strapped himself in and tapped his controls taking in every scan as he waited for his opponent to charge them staring at the various view screens filled with information. Kyle could feel her staring back at him from her bridge as an unsettling quiet started. Kyle could feel her debate. *Did she dare risk his escape?* They both knew what happened if she failed to capture or kill him.
Kyle had revolved in the face of Space combat as it is the only place anyone could win against Odyne. Aphrodite, who they finally found out was called Shyanne, had been really close to beating her; he intended to take Aphrodite down a notch. Her guns, though extremely powerful and could easily one shot his ship, would not be able to track them at full orbital thrusters which gave his plan credence. Another round of shots blazed past causing another asteroid avalanche behind them cloaking them in debris as they continued to drift softly.

"Increase Orbital Thrusters to full and prepare to use landing thrusters on the starboard side and take us over her. Have all missile pods and gun batteries fire on a one-ten degree towards the bow for the first volley after the volley has connected free fire. Let Amto guns know they get to play too. E.V. suits and packed ammo. No regs will leave this ship. I need defensive stations around all weapons and engineering. Jacks you have the point defense just in case she tries to turn and unleash another missile storm." Kyle ordered as he read his hud again.

"Sir, yes, sir." His crew yelled.

The ship lurched from the sudden increased speed. "Disable gravity." The air lifted into weightlessness. They all watched as Shyanne's ship came about to charge, forced into only one move. Stop Kyle's ship from escaping. His finger twitched with anticipation. He knew his win was assured now. An explosion shook the ship, jolting him into looking at his monitors.

"Report?" Kyle shouted over the alarms bringing up the alerts.

"Explosion off port silo 1 through 3 and maneuvering thrusts thirty-six through forty-one. They are reporting a boarding party attempting to disable another silo on the outside of the ship. Missile and gunpods 1 through 3 on portside. Offline. Leaking atmo. Reports of missing decks coming in. Atmo guns on decks eight and twelve offline. We have confirmed reports of casualties on all previous decks and a few accidental injuries from maneuvers sir. Gravity zones have been established for the injured." The Lieutenant said as he pressed his heads-up display. Kyle pressed his command console and put in the maneuver for the A.I. to handle.

"Jacks execute maneuver Zeta as soon as their ship moves within range. Officers. Let Jacks fly, focus on medical coordination and gun coordination. Jacks continue as planned." Kyle said, unbuckling himself and pushing off of his seat letting weightlessness take over before activating his mag boots and his feet are sucked to the ground.

"Alert Regs, we have borders. Have my team assemble at airlock twelve for counter hull-combat."

"Aye, sir." The smooth photonic voice of Jacks echoed throughout the bridge.

Kyle moved with all his might as he became shadow, moving so fast that everyone almost seemed to stop. A perk of the augmentation they would soon be receiving was a form of super speed. He didn't feel any thrust or pull as the ship moved because his hyper awareness already knew it was coming. Kyle couldn't feel the gravimetric forces thanks to the wonderful gel layer in the armor he now wore. As he ran another explosion shook the halls but that didn't in any way deter Kyle. Placing a foot on the wall as the ship started to invert itself and darting on to the ceiling as Kyle continued barking out orders."Alpha team prepare for outer-hull high speed counter contact."

"Roger that, team lead. Alpha ready for launch." Laurel said over the com.

He rounded the corner and nodded as Laurel slammed her fist into the release. As she did so he released his mag boots and felt the decompression launch him forward at extremely high speeds. He watched his hud eyes solely focused on his motion tracker. A ping hit and he locked his mag boots back into place, sliding a couple of meters before taking off towards the ping ignoring inertia as his crew closed into formation behind him and a single green blip on his motion tracker moved towards the first two red blips.

"Beta Team, secure the bridge." He commanded over his mic.

"Roger that." Another Apache said over his headset his real name was N'vid, his code name being Adonis. N'vid's changes were on a really high level, having creamsoda eyes and neon white colored hair that did not mix with his rounded face. N'vid had been the other boy who tried to help Kyle on their first day quickly becoming friends with Devin as they had claimed Kyle, becoming self proclaimed Pack brothers. A ping spiked and he saw the disturbance, unlocking his mag boots slamming his foot as hard as he could to get extra momentum using the ship's own speed to propel them faster. The ping's source was the enemy team lead, Shyanne. He gritted his teeth because he really liked Shyanne and would have rather her been on his side. It took less than a minute to collide with her. Catching her completely by surprise, Kyle pulled his pistol flipping in circles as their suits magnetically kept them attached to the ship. He struggled to restrain her.

They rolled along the hull bouncing off the ship as Shyanne pivoted, throwing him off of her sending him tumbling down the ship. He spun, pulling his pistol free and squeezed the trigger watching the bullets hit their target, knocking her off her intended trajectory, sending her spinning wildly away from the ship before being caught by a thruster as his ship maneuvers around another wave of blaster rounds. Kyle slammed his hand into the hull as his arm is immediately dislocated from inertia reminding him it exists. Kyle growled in pain as he stabilized himself, snapping his shoulder back in place once he was on his feet. Kyle felt his rib muscles being stabbed as he looked around. Kyle's eyes locked onto his teammate who was getting a dagger stabbed into her side as she screamed trying to keep the knife in her suit so she would have a chance of living. Kyle helped Laurel ignore the pain as he raised his arm and fired two shots into her assailants' back, killing them. Laurel dropped to her knees as she held the knife and grabbed a torch to seal her breach, breathing heavily. Kyle walked over to help Laurel; he couldn't tell which Apache he had killed.

They listed for half a second before being launched violently into the main thruster. He rotated as the echo of guns rocked the ship and he watched as their ship went parallel with the enemies. The first volley fired a wall of missiles, blasters, and explosive rounds that raked their unprotected bridge shredding through the armor as the crew went to town firing at will as fast as they could. Shells rained down like a storm in the four seconds they were on the top of the ship. Debris scattered as the ship started to implode on itself. He watched with a smirk on his face and felt himself fall into transition. The ships, debris, stars, and the planet all disappear as he feels real gravity crash into his bones as he becomes aware of the real world.

"Nice Kyle." Laurel said, raising a hand for him to slap which he did. He rolled off the bed and sat up looking around to gain his bearings."How'd you know she would come around?" Laurel inquired watching the others still slumbering before rubbing her ribs, before he could answer screams broke out as Shyanne and her team started to twitch from the neural shock of losing. Kyle's eyes locked on to Devin now knowing exactly who it was that was with Shyanne. Kyle blinked away looking at Laurel as he heard vomit fly from their mouths. He had thrown a 1v1 earlier that week but the deaths were getting harder and harder to handle.

"I didn't." He said, turning back as they started to stroke out for a second their minds struggling to function.

"You couldn't have helped it this time man, it was them or us." N'vid said, patting him on the shoulder.

He said nothing, looking away in shame feeling like he should be able to help.

3rd Month of Training

The sword sang over his head as Kyle barely dodged the blade. He rotated to his left feeling his blade respond to his command. The ear shattering clash of steel colliding filled the air. The large training room was littered with weapons and weights. The pairs of cadets and solo cadets practiced fighting diligently. The room was musky with the smell of sweat and blood. The cadets had turned up the gravity to eight times that of earth's gravity for a better workout and to force the medics and technicians to get in E.V. suits to treat them. The Cadets had found poise in Lylah's words and without words being spoken picked up their training. The staff had panicked at their increased training times They were determined to force Odyne to augment them ahead of time. Kyle had won over Shyanne in space again, placing him firmly as the best Admiral out of them, barely losing his last engagement to Odyne.

"Hey dumbass." Shyanne said, halting her attack as she studied his body.

"I'm sorry." He started and relaxed his shoulders.

"Seriously let it go." Shyanne said, rolling her eyes and squaring up to continue training. "You're a better admiral than me is all." Shyanne said relaxing again, stretching, waiting to continue as Kyle hadn't taken an aggressive form. Odyne or as the Cadet's new favorite new nickname Ice Cunt suggested had been making them run multiple matches a night usually against each other. They had stopped using the A.I Jacks waiting for Odyne to update the program, having to jump through massive bureaucratic b.s. to get permission. It took proving everyone could beat the A.I. with their eyes closed and hands literally restrained in the most impossible odds to get the idea across to the Chief. The A.I. simply couldn't keep up with anyone anymore. Unfortunately as they developed so did Odyne becoming more untouchable outside of Space combat. Which she made up for by being an unfathomably devastating pilot having no equal even winning dog fights against bigger ships or swarms of enemies.

"Is he apologizing again?" Devin said, halting his battle with N'vid as he looked at Kyle.

"Seriously." Laurel said, stopping her training movements, thick drops of sweat falling down her face a technician running over offering supplies as Laurel rolled her eyes allowing the suit to take her vitals.

"Dude, just drop it." Shyanne said, taking a stance to scare away approaching medics.

"Yeah Loverboy, just drop it." Laurel said with a giggle jumping up and returning to her movements.

"Come on this again." Kyle said, launching a minor attack at Shyanne's defense knowing she could easily stop it.

"You're keeping it...Fucker." Shyanne said as the blunt of the blade smacked the side of her head and Kyle smirked, having slapped her blade aside to give her the love tap. He saw his opening and flipped the blade at the last moment.

"Seriously, you were holding back? For how long?" Shyanne said, lowering her guard, staring at him with pure contempt having seen the smirk.

"Are you shitting me?" Devin said, dropping his shoulders overhearing and holding a hand up to N'vid.

"What's wrong with that?" Kyle said an eyebrow raised looking at them as they all surrounded him.

"How many of us can you take?" N'vid said, rolling his shoulders nodding to Devin who smiled back.

"Do I have to answer that?" Kyle said, backing up a little as the four of them surrounded him.

"Answer the question." The room suddenly froze. The Ice Cunt herself had been listening.

"Ma'am...I can take all of them...ma'am." Kyle said, stammering over his words.

The faces of his teammates grew cold and angry as they stood at attention.

"Not in this gravity you couldn't." N'vid said, shaking his head with disbelief.

"Not with all four of us." Laurel added staying at attention. Kyle shook his head knowing the answer already.

"Prove it." Odyne said, stepping back.

Kyle looked at the others with an apologetic face took his stance. Shyanne, Laurel, N'vid and Devin surrounded him taking their own stances. Kyle breathed in and took the first move by thrusting at Shyanne to his left before pivoting to his right taking a hack at Devin, catching him off guard and knocking him out of the match almost instantly. Kyle moved quickly to put his back away from them. They all looked at each other and nodded. Shyanne struck first, slicing low and locking her shoulders as Laurel launched herself over Shyanne coming down with force. Kyle dodged Shyanne and caught Laurel's attack with his own, grabbing her forearms and rolling with it, dislocating both shoulders as Laurel is sent hurtling through the air. She crashed hard into the wall. N'vid looked at Shyanne and gulped. He went high, aiming for Kyle's head. Kyle ducked, coming around with a counter only to find Shyanne's sword coming across towards his chest; he changed tactics and raised his blade blocking the attack and dropping low. He twisted on his heel, spinning the blade at ankle height. He caught Shyanne on her ankle with the flat of the blade and rose quickly, leveling the blade at N'vid's throat.

"Jesus Christ." N'vid said, dropping his sword in surrender, shocked with the quick movements.

    A slow clap fills their air as Kyle breathes heavily huffing as he stares at N'vid trying to calm himself and living the fight in his head once more. He slowly lowered the sword and extended his hand to Shyanne who took it.

"Why didn't you tell us?" N'vid said, approaching arm extended in friendship and they embraced as brothers.

"I didn't think you guys would care how good I was, thought you liked me for my charm." Laurel slugged Kyle in the arm with a grin as he answered and clasped N'vid.

"What charm, that awkward thing you call a voice?" Shyanne snapped with a smirk.

"Yeah that." He said, chuckling as they headed to the showers. Like always Odyne was gone without saying a word.

Lylah watched over the cameras, remembering her own time as a cadet. She knew Mal wouldn't understand her training. But the Cadets, they were starting to. Her eyes took in as much information before she found herself missing her friends. A smile teased her face as she thought of Luke before she heard Doc Mal approaching.

"Was that...a smile? Are you ok? I mean I have a test for that." Doctor Mal sassed at her as he approached, obviously catching sight of it.

"Why do you insist on making childish comments?" Lylah asked, her face blanking as she grew cold standing straight.

    "I...uh I thought you liked it when I sassed you." Mal said, his eyes twinkling, his body tense as he tries to reassure his actions by taking a step forward.

Lylah turned and walked right next to Mal before whispering for him to hear. "I'll order you to be sassy when I want you to be sassy." And just like that she was gone. Mal stared ahead as her words hung like gravity on Mal's shoulders. Mal let a breath escape his lips. Raising a shaking hand and pulling off his glasses and pushing his fingers against the lids of his eyes, trying to soothe the uncontrollable shaking he now felt as he looked after her.

"Yes, Ma'am."

Chapter 8:

You can't unlearn Pain

Olympus
Month 4 of Training

Kyle Akya
Sept 9th, 4999
Time: 09:11 A.M.

"So back to the Amazon look again." He said, raising his eyebrow as he ran into Odyne in a very similar meadow to the one they had first truly met in.

"You seem surprised." Her eyes narrowed in on him, staring directly into his soul, "I thought you liked this one, I put it on specifically for you." She frowned and rose the Amazonian outfit complimenting her natural curves.

Ouch. Laurel mused her thoughts echoing around Kyle's mind.

You need some cream for that sick ass burn? N'vid laughed.

"Well you kicked my ass so many times I can't remember when was the last time you wore it is all and no I don't care what you wear. Let's just do this." He said desperately trying to recover, burying his feelings as deep as he could.

Lair. He heard a voice he was unfamiliar with echo in his head.

Her face grew harder than normal. Four months of getting their ass kicked and not a single person could stand more than two minutes with the Commander. It boggled Kyle's mind how short but insane their journey had been up to this point. They had all bonded but two major teams had formed; one led by Chelsea and the other run by him. How Kyle was put in any form of power beyond anyone's guess but it had happened.

"Everyone is watching, keep that in mind." Lylah said her tone was harsh.

"How many points?" He asked, very aware of the tournament and that all other Apache were watching.

"Ten." She went back to her bored look.

In the past four months he had become stronger and faster and smarter than he ever thought possible. Even out of the uplink zone. After proving they needed augmentations to be able to continue training. He never passed five points, in fact he has only scored two points barely scraping wins out with terran and luck more than pure skill. He was the last on the list for this close combat test and first for sword fighting which was next. Laurel had been the first to fight, scoring a modest two points. No one else had gotten more than two. It seemed at two points Odyne stopped pretending to fight and actually chose to fight.

"Are you ready?" She said with boredom.

"Please ladies first." He said bowing. *I'm going to pay for that.* He thought to himself, hating his fast tongue.

You are so fucked. Laurel said.
How bad do you think he is gonna lose by? Taken' bets, taken' bets. Devin sold in his head.
Shut up Devin you only got one point. Kyle shot back.

He turned his focus on Odyne. He watched her feet and saw the muscle contract as she moved. He caught her leg with his shine. She threw a quick punch to his face that caught him off guard. He stammered back, spinning on his left foot throwing darts. Lylah surged as Kyle raised his forearm in time to stop the right hook and tried to counter with his knee that was thrown aside easily. He dropped a dart and spun inwards racing forward trying to get the offensive hand up using the dart in an ice pick handle. Lylah shifted her head back as Kyle tried to come back and reversed his speed turning his slash into a stab. Lylah shifted, catching his other arm and throwing him off balance. Kyle reserved energy and launched a knee as he took his stance and attacked again. Lylah countered with a knee of her own. Kyle barely blocked with his own knee locking their ankles with his calf. Kyle quickly locked his knee outwards, locking them into position as they balanced off each other. Throwing soft jabs as they struggled to gain more control of the knees.

Damn, that lock isn't gonna be easy to escape. Devin said.

It was true he and Odyne were locked. He needed a miracle to get out of it without losing. He thought really quickly and shifted his left foot and used his own weight as momentum to try to throw her...but he over calculated and she took advantage, shifting onto her right to counter the weight and flipped him over snapping his knee as she launched herself over him, quickly choking him out. Dropping his head on the ground and walking away barely breathing heavily as Kyle's body respawn. Kyle opened his eyes, blinking fast to gain his composure.

"One, Zero." She spat her gaze filled with utter disgust as she reset.
This is getting interesting, who has the popcorn. Shyanne said.
"Ready for round two?" Kyle said to Odyne.
"Please ladies first." She said back with a bow.
Ouch that one's gotta hurt the pride. Chelsea giggled
Please we all know she could have done better. That kill was pure ego. Laurel said.
True enough. Chelsea responded.

Everyone else was quiet and focused on the match. It was a close battle moving down to the micromovements and seconds. Kyle took a deep breath feeling all his brothers' and sisters' minds filling him with hope. He surged forward, wasting no time with the grapple. He curled his hand under her legs lifting for a powerbomb. She tightened her legs around his neck as he lifted her and pulled her core, wrenching backwards, planting her hands on the ground using his force against him and slammed him head first into the ground. Rolling over on top and destroying his neck with her forearm before rolling away clapping her hands off and standing. Kyle blinked again, launching up, shaking off the death.
"Two, Zero."
DAMN that had to hurt. Devin said.
He just got smashed on. N'vid responded.

Kyle felt the laughs as he slid his feet, changing his stance to a form by the ancient Shaolin Monks. She looked at him, seeming to be amused at this choice of fighting style. She changed her style as well to...something he couldn't identify.
What style is that? Laurel said.
No idea. Chelsea concurred.

She had her left arm down, almost hiding her head in her shoulder, and had her right arm across her chest in an offensive style like an ancient boxer. Her left leg was bent in some kicking style while her right was firmly planted for maximum leverage if he should try to grapple. Her feet were spread for a mixed style as well giving her an almost completely unpredictable style. Kyle needed to adapt or she would make a fool of him. Kyle breathed in accepting it was time to learn that style. He waited calmly, focusing his energy on blocking and defense, taking deep slow breaths in controlled bursts. The tension surged through the uplink with a fury as everyone watched eagerly.

The first fist was her left hand, then right. He adjusted his body to the right, raising his right arm and applied a little pressure to push the fist off. He twisted to the left blocking another punch, twisting his wrist around hers. Finding her forearm in motion, Kyle snapped his hand around hers. He moved his right foot forward using her own weight against her. He tucked his body and rolled with her wrist in a basic monkey flip. She came down with a grunt and he seized his moment pinning her with his fist raised.

"One, two."

"Kill me." She said her eyes bore into his soul.

"I can't." He said looking back into her beautiful eyes.

AAAWWWW. Spilled into his mind.

So when's the wedding? Shyanne said. Odynes eyes glared with pure contempt like usual.

Shut up. He raged.

He got up. Luke shifted his body to his favorite for its defensive stance. She took the same position as she just used and nodded ready. They slowly circled each other waiting for the other to make the first move. The tension stung his spine as everyone watched waiting for the next clash of these two. Kyle decided he would move first launching a quick jab forward that was pushed aside with ease. He spun with his left leg and found her ribs as her fist found his cheek. He spun the opposite direction and caught her right leg as her fist made contact with his ribs. He fought through the pain and shifted his front leg forward pushing his body into hers as she launched more punches into his ribs. They both fell and Kyle found the top raising his fist again but refusing to finish it.

"Two, Two." He said and lowered his fist standing up. She shifted her hips underneath him, capitalizing on his poor leg control. The first foot facturing his nose as she rolled backwards before surging forward and shattering his skull with her knee rolling over top of him in the next fraction of a second before standing and waiting for a respawn.

"Three, One." Lylah corrected as Kyle respawned.

Holy shit. Chelsea said. The neural tension of horror hounded everyone's back of nerves as no one had received such a beating.

"Come on. Prove to me why you should still be here. Sure aren't living up to your brother's legacy." Lylah roared in dismay trying to provoke the bear. Kyle exploded launching a flurry of punches, trying to keep Lylah on her back foot as he half spun, raising his kick mid thrust to catch Lylah's body, misjudging her moments as she jumped to knee his chin. Lylah's legs were knocked out from underneath her as Kyle caught her spinning counter clockwise to jerk her away, slamming her down and locking her thoroughly down before raising his fit.

"Finish me or don't get a point." Odyne instructed.

"I won't kill you." Kyle said, seeming to feel Odyne's distain.

"Then you are stupid." She said and shifted her hand free. A Jian blade flew up Kyle's back impaling him as Lylah spun around retrieving the blade in one fluid motion. The blade was smooth with a standard wood metal base. A long thin silver ribbon sundana hung loosely off the hilt. Kyle dropped and died as Lylah turned flipping the blade, clearing the blood as she took her stance.

Kyle turned before signing, "Fine." Pulling a long sword off his back. They stood a few moments before they started circling each other.

Wait, so what's happening? Shyanne interrupted before the fight could start.

Lover boy won't kill Odyne. Laurel explains.

Why, though? Shyanne pondered.

Kyle blocked his mind off to them and started suppressing his feelings.

You can't hide from me. I am always here. A voice echoed from within his mind. Kyle shivered and Lylah stopped looking at him. She stood there staring at him suspiciously before taking her respective stance and nodding. Kyle launched a quick flurry of slashes which got blocked or dodged. Lylah jumped spinning on her opposite foot and kicked him back before releasing a flurry of her own. Luke could barely keep up, his blade was not made for quick combat like this. Kyle shook his head and the slight hesitation caused him to be impaled by Lylah spinning to his outside before cutting off his head for good measure. *You can't hide me from her.* The voice echoed throughout his head as he respawned.

"We stay till you fucken kill me." Odyne said, walking away before turning to re-engage, her eyes bloodthirsty.

Kyle got up and looked down before responding. "I won't kill one of my own and as much as you try to make us hate you. You are still one of us." Kyle threw a sword down as his back exploded with shock.

Her expression grew of pure disgust as she turned into a brute. " And now?" She turned into Doctor Mal. " Does this do it for you?" She turned into Luke and Kyle froze in shock. "How about now?" Luke put his hands on his hips looking completely ridiculous.

"How do you know that man?" Kyle spat at Ice as she looked like Luke.

"Does this upset you?" Odyne hissed, Luke's expression grew harder, "Good because he's dead. He died like you will if you don't fucken fight back. His death was a joke and if he could see you now."

Kyle lost it again swinging and screaming wildly lost in emotion. The weather worsened into a storm and the forest changed into a dead battlefield, thick mud puddles exploded as they battled back and forth. Lylah changed back into her Fairsist look and dodged him, countering him with ease using his emotions against him and simply danced around him as the rain fell. Thunder and the cries of Kyle echoed as he crumbled from exhaustion and she stopped breathing heavily herself. Rain poured over both frames, thunder cracking and lightning illuminated the skies as a murderous Odyne leaned down and through controlled breaths she whispered in his ear.

"If you think you can honor him like that, you are sorely mistaken." And the mission ended.

5th Month of Training

"So tonight is the first assault on the academy? Like the one that only one person survived?" Laurel said as they stood in the transition. It was her, Shyanne, Devin, N'vid and Kyle.

"Apparently. The simulation is out of control. Meaning no direct control. We will be inserted by rebuilt implant knowledge." Kyle nodded and looked up into the nothingness. "We haven't been assigned yet."

"Kyle can we?" Devin started.

"No, save it. What happened at the tournament happened there. I don't wanna talk about it." He said looking up again seeing name designations.

"Laurel looks like you are. Lylah Soffrireterna the only survivor. N'vid you are Michelle," N'vid and Laurel slapped each other's hands. Kyle points at Shyanne then Devin "You are Commander Montgomery. Devin you get the Surgeon." Shyanne and Devin nodded. "Which, means I'm Luke." This was only the first of many runs they would endure to understand their enemy. As the Recreation started, Kyle watched and felt the attack. He felt himself defending himself from the mysterious attackers. The fear that blasted through his mind. Kyle almost cried seeing Lylah, seeing she was just as beautiful as he had heard. He suffered when Luke had to send Lylah into the vent. He cried full sail as he watched Chelsea collapse on him.

The complete and utter defeat he felt was unbearable. Kyle watched in horror as they walked the halls. He felt the fighter crash, the surge as he heard the Commanders cry. Kyle cried as his spirit broke as the voices echoed. *Mom.* The echoing bounced around Kyle's mind and he broke down ignoring the rest of the memories. Kyle stayed stoic as they returned to transition. The endless white surrounding them. That was only their first time.

"Jesus fucken chirst." Shyanne said, staring blankly off at the ground unsure of how to cope.
"That was," N'vid sat down trying to comprehend what they just witnessed, "I heard the stories but."
"Lisa from the stream was." Devin spat before catching himself and looking around.
"What the fuck was that." Kyle said, finally coming out of his daze.
Laurel sat down next to N'vid staring blankly at the floor and leaning her head on his chest for comfort.
"That is what you will be fighting against."Odyne's voice echoed around them after a long and unnerving amount of time.

"How the fuck can we trust you, how do we know you're not full of shit? You want me to use that knowledge. It screams propaganda. Fake. Unreal. I have learned too much about war for this not to be fake. I can kill a man with less than an ounce of pressure yet I know nothing about the person who I am supposed to lay down my LIFE for. How can we believe you are, our guide in this is. When that guide is a Cold hearted ICE CUNT." Kyle raged, his exhaustion finally overwhelming him as he jumped up screaming at the white emptiness that was Odyne. The others looked at Kyle in shock. He had called her by the squad name. A name only they called her. Kyle had truly let his rage boil over and as much as the other apache hated it they too wanted answers.

Odyne's voice finally came after another long awkward and very unsettling pause."I was there." Her voice only wavered for a moment as she spun her tale. "Lylah Soffrireterna isn't the only survivor. She was the only REPORTED survivor. I watched my friends be slaughtered because they didn't trust one another." Kyle swears in the moment he could see a tear falling down Odyne's left cheek as she spilled her guts to them. "I will never lie to you or deceive you. I want you to all be aware of the reality of the truth. My personal feelings come second to everything. There are forces who do not want you to succeed. They want you to fail so they can pin it on me. Allowing me to burn with the very planet I once called home."

A pause brought a tear to Kyle's left eye as he stared at the white nothing and listened as the other shifted nervously. Never had Odyne been so open with any Apache. They often joked about how obviously Odyne didn't have a heart but not once did any of them, even Kyle ask what may have happened to her to make her closed off to them. Losing a whole squad like that. Or worse. Kyle blinked back more tears as her voice continued once more. "I never got the choice to be a soldier. I was Career-born." Kyle's heart froze. Career borns never had a choice in their own careers. Often their parents are very influential or military based and because of that the first born is forced into service. Kyle's heart froze, Luke had been a Career-born. "I didn't want to be at Magness. I hated what they put me through but you better fucken believe," Another pause.

"I called it home." Kyle clearly felt the anguish as Odyne continued. "This mission is my choice. One of the first real choices I have gotten to make in my life. The sooner this war is over the sooner I get to choose a Life and can get rid of my career-born status. You all have one thing I didn't get. You choose to fight for the federation, none of you are career-born." The other Apache stared at one another for a quick second never realizing what had made them so special. "My first choice was to fight for you and protect you from the dangers you can't see. I have done this to the best of my abilities. You all still have a choice when it comes time to put on that armor." Lylah said, her mind dancing to her daughter in cryo status waiting for her mommy to come wake her up so she may begin her life. Somehow, the words of Lylah had finally connected.

"I do not. I will defend you all till we are all dead and gone, but I won't do it if you don't want me to." Her words and actions finally finding their mark. The apache nodded truly understanding that there was even more at stake then just winning a war. *There was meaning to her after all.* Kyle pondered to himself as they prepared for round two.

Chapter 9:

The Cost of Drawing First Blood

Day 1 of Deployment
F.S.F.V. The Ellen
Mid-wormhole jump
E.T.A from target planet T -4 Minutes
Commander Lylah "Odyne" Soffrireterna
January 1st, 5000
Time: 09:11 A.M.

"Attention." The twelve Apache snapped into attention flawlessly and effortlessly. The air was tense as they waited for their orders. The Ellen's A.D.L. or Apache Deployment Launcher was a massive magnetic launcher capable of launching a specially made pod close to one thousand and eight hundred miles an hour to penetrate deep into enemy lines before entering the atmosphere and cratering anything underneath it when landing. The Apache would load into the pod. After landing they would knock out strategic targets before the main force arrived to secure the area. They all stood in the Armor room that led to the load chamber.

Their minds focused on their objectives. This wasn't the only thing that the apache needed specially modified for them on the Ellen. No engineers or equipment other than welders, robots, and drones had made the modifications they now used. The twelve Apache took two days to completely retrofit two redundant hangers into personal Apache Quarters, the deployment cannon, and an armory. They had cut out special corridors along the superstructure making sure to never weaken any part of the ship so they could deal with boarders without being seen. With new quarters and armory, came new armor, weapons, and equipment.

The apache armor was truly the most advanced thing in the fleet excluding Jacks or The Ellen. Jacks the A.I. was still under repairs from almost driving itself mad trying to beat the apache or even keep up with the apache. Odyne had taken the task of working to raise its processing and understanding to allow it to keep up with them. If she was doing the repairs out of guilt, that was yet to be seen by the others as she can be seen spending countless hours running the numbers. The numbers were massive enough on them causing Lylah to slow down and take her time with the coding, slowly creating the code required from scratch. Having to use several google's worth of coding per single line meant one equation or letter or phrase or number being off meant starting from scratch on several google's worth of coding per line. *I should really get them R and R.* Lylah's mind interrupted as the other Apache waited at attention training keeping them in place. Lylah hated their R and R for completing training had been denied; Her fathers footsteps stopped centimeters from the door trying to catch them unaware. Lylah waited for their assignment, her mind on the here and now.

"Today you are being deployed to the front, Commander Odyne please step forward." The chief said, completely shocked they were already at attention as he walked across the threshold and down half the line. The Chief, Mal and the Colonel who helmed the Ellen in Odyne's place were the only ones who knew how to access and find their way to the apache but even they didn't understand the extent to which the Apaches went to not be seen. They had also upgraded all of Mal's equipment even though it was considered top of the line, attached a proto-shield for when the kinetic barriers failed and fixed power fluctuations throughout the ship that came from such a vessel.

Before the vessel operated at eight-two point one eight percent when everything was running and being taxed. With the Apache modification it ran at ninety-nine point-o-eight percent when everything was running and being taxed.

"Sir, Yes, Sir." Lylah stepped forward moving with the grace of an angel. The Commander and chief had accompanied the Apache on their first mission to insure they remained hidden. Lylah stared forward, letting her mind race to her fathers continued interference in her affairs feeling it was starting to get to obsessive levels. Lylah's mind quickly changed subject as she focused on The Ellen and their mission. The Ellen and her docked complement were heading for the edge of the war line. More specifically a system of planets that had their atmospheres clashing into each other once every eight days creating a completely impassable shield for thirty days of unstable flight. It was not scientifically known how the eight planets didn't completely destroy themselves but for the purposes of their attack the short eight days they had would be long enough to move three million ships through the vast ScaZ net undetected. The ScaZ net, a tachyon enhanced detection grid that could detect ships traveling using light drives was already active to help contain battles from light drive combatants leading to a rise in hyperdrive usage.

However during those rotational periods the planets had been split down the middle of the system to allow normal ship travel. If the Apache could knock out all the sensors on the only inhabited world before the eight days finished they could just flag the ships as rogue asteroid debris and the enemy would be none the wiser. Once on the other side they had to hold off for the next rotation or rather unbenounced to her father, Lylah was going to start cutting a path through the enemies forcing them to try to stop her or try to retake the breach. Lylah's mind moved so fast she re-briefed herself in the time it took for her father to continue speaking.

The Alpha and Century Sectors belonged to the Federation but the Delta and Beta Quadrants had raised to rebellion the quickest, throwing full support into the Freedom Initiative for past seen slights against the quadrants. Thousands upon thousands of battles were raging across the Meddling line as they moved closer to their target. The Ellen was on the way to the first true offensive to be launched since the beginning of the war or so her father claimed.

"I see you have yet to choose a second squad leader, enlighten me why not?" The chief finally continued ignoring the briefing for his personal questions.

"Sir, the tests were inconclusive at best, so I did not feel it was my place to assign someone without being sure." Lylah felt herself grow some irritation at his insistence at having two squads.

"What is your recommendation?" The chief said, eyeing her trying to hit buttons or show anything.

"Private Ares, sir." She said without missing a beat. The shock that surged through her spine from the armor almost made Lylah lose her ever loving shit on the Apache. She knew they were all trying to comprehend what she had just said. What they failed to realize was her personal feelings had nothing to do with her choice to promote him. He had talent and skill. If he wasn't fighting her in uplink he was training and learning and still finding time to get to know his squad mates. He was a natural born leader.

"Pretenses?" The Chief seemed to pick up on the tension, raising an eyebrow.

"From my observations he has spent the least amount of time in the rec room when available. I have seen him use exceptional tactics in varied scenarios. His swordplay is second to none out of the cadets and he actively tries to cut deals to take the suffering off of others, usually at the price of lowering his score. All traits a leader should have and more. If you would like I can file a full report after I have completed more testing until then you will have to deal with my verbal account and judgment." Lylah said, feeling herself become smug beneath her armor. Lylah pondered on why she liked the new armor as the chief continued this pointless challenge.

The old armor, a Mk.117 exo-power armor, was top of the line for black ops and special operations. This new armor dubbed 'fortuitous armor' by the designers was a full three layered power armor set which made the Apache damn near invincible. First layer was made up of a gel filled with a nanite-like composite that was based on various bio-neural reactions that changed the gel to accommodate literally everything. The gel could catrise and clog wounds, fully reprocess any biological substance that could cause interference with the mission, and seal completely to protect any user from environmental hazards, everything from gasses to space. No harm could ever come to the user's body as long as the gel layer had power. The layer was housed in an almost skin tight black bodysuit making the final compantant of the first layer.

The second layer was perhaps the most important. Its thin lines of terrarium weave meant they could take a direct hit from a mass driver and after flying several thousand meters, they would be all but fine. Pissed off but fine. The weave hugged the outline of their bodies covering their entire body in yet another body suit. And finally the heat dispersing pads fit tightly around their upper and lower arms, thighs, crotch, neck, and upper body only. Their stomach and lower back had retracting nano-heat sinks pads that would deploy pads depending on the heat levels allowing the Apache to withstand heats of almost one hundred thousand degrees celsius and turning the heat into energy for the suits if power should run low. In comparison most ships, even the Ellen, could only resist about seventy-five thousand degrees celsius. Mal's curiosity about such a high level did not dissuaded. Lylah from implementing the last pieces. Colored all in black in their armor, the Apache stood listening to her neurotic father babble like a fool.

"Second Choice?" The Chief paused trying to throw her off balance.

"Private Dionysus Sir." She felt another shock surge up her back, as the apache weren't aware of her feelings on any of this till just now. The Chief looked at her suspiciously. Lylah found it amusing her father had time to read her reports about the Apache but not the reports from the front which Lylah was well versed in.

"If you prefer I can list them from number one to eleven Sir. Dionysus is my second because," She said bleakly back trying to get him to back off. *Control yourselves.* Odyne snapped over the neural link, "her skills are remarkable and she is shy of a genius, her attitude is another issue." She felt their emotions but they were quickly quelled as they stood, their excitement and celebrations were halted by the next question.

"Commander, I want your honest opinion on splitting the squad. Do you think it is a mistake?" The tension that rose up her back hit every nerve in her spin. She hardrened her face more. The Chief had honed in on their feelings. He was the one who had suggested separating the apache in the first place despite the opposition from Lylah. He had convinced the Council that due to their extreme skill they could easily compensate. Which despite being more true then he knew would actually slow down their advance towards the capital.

"Honest opinion? Sir, I think that it is foolish to split into two teams. We need the full killing and tactical forces. Here. Focused on tearing a line straight to their homeworld wherever it may be." The feeling in her back almost made her fidget. *Control yourselves, apache, I won't warn you again.* She barked through the link.
Yes, Sir. The eleven others snapped doing their best to purge themselves of feelings they also shared her view on the subject.

"I will take your judgment into account and being enlightened of what you have said. I will accept it, for now. All apache will drop from outer orbit." The chief said turning to the holo projection, completely unaware the plan was already changing as he spoke, "After landing you will take out the jammers here," The Admiral said pointing to several radars on the projection, "Here and here. The enemy will see your pod, make note. So they will be on alert. But we know they are arrogant. You have some time before they investigate but the jammers must be down by nineteen hundred. In four hours time." Lylah rolled her eyes knowing full well every Apache had memorized the details two months into the wormhole space so thoroughly they were talking about it in their sleep. She smiled knowing sleep talking had literally led to three separate investigations of treason, always spearheaded by her father but easily debunked by Lylah herself playing Odyne.

The unnerving smile on Lylah's father irritated her more than she was willing to admit. She had pushed for more information and time but her father had taken his sweet ass time commissioning them for service to smite her Making their window to move more ships through smaller.
"We'll make due, Sir." She responded sounding like a broken record.
The connect siren started to blare as the one minute red light alert started to flashed.
"Good luck and come back alive." He saluted.
They saluted in complete unison. *Let's move.* Odyne ordered opening the pod as the twelve Apache climbed in, strapping in.
So who's excited? Devin laughed, his excitement overflowing as they listened to the magnetic launchers clamp onto the pod.
Lylah closed her eyes listening to the two soldiers that now controlled their fate.
"Sir, Permission to deploy package." The Officer was saying to Spage.
"Granted. It is the season after all." Spage chuckled.
"Yeah whatever that package is. Better be fucken worth this jump." The Officer mumbled to herself.
"Hey, if it blows them to hell. For Magness." Another officer said, leaning over trying to comfort his friend.
"For Magness." The officer breathed to herself. Lylah opened her eyes and the red light started to flash indicating that launch was a go and count down would start soon.

Hell yeah! N'vid held up a fist as they heard the controller start counting."Drop prepared and ready. Package armed. Drop in three." Lylah breathed in hearing the soldier's heart start to pound as she counted down. Lylah smiled knowing the command deck was almost two miles away from them. "Two." Her heart picked up not knowing what ordinance she was launching. "One." Lylah smiled to herself feeling her chains break from her father. "Drop is a go." The pressure seals release with a hiss.

No sound could catch them as they were magnetically launched towards a planet. The snap of the launch should have broken every bone and teeth in their body. The sudden silence made Lylah close her eyes as some of the apache bantered back and forth. A sudden ear piercing whistle assaulted Lylah's ears as her eyes shot once more open before the ear shattering sound of them breaking the atmosphere rocked around them. The surge of excitement flooded through Lylah's back as she drank in their rushes, using it to calm herself, each person had their own taste like flavors of ice cream. It's like each Apache with their own special limited time flavor. It was an intoxicating feeling as Lylah opened up her mind to talk to them.

I'm sorry we didn't get R and R. I promised. I want you to know the reason we don't have more time or information is because of me. Lylah looked around the pod. *The Commander and Chief and I do not get along. Period. He was against me being the first candidate from the very beginning.* Lylah thought for a second. *He has stood in my path every step of the way. He is the one I protect you from. If given the chance he will shut us down, erase us from existence and change history to make sure no one goes looking again.* She paused. *If you do not believe me, start reading your reports and watching the holorecordings of our council meetings.* The Apache were once again filled with a sense of relief as the calm spread and they all set their minds to the task at hand.

Sir, object zero three should be hit first. Aphrodite stated.

Kyle smiled and felt the tension in her head. She hadn't been happy Chelsea had been picked over her. Kyle had shared her shock as well. Aphrodite was very much an equal of Dionysus if not better. Kyle could easily dismantle Dionysus in hand to hand or in combat and for that matter so could Aphrodite, but Odyne had been quite sure of her choice. Kyle looked over at Odyne, her head bobbing as they plummeted towards the planet. *What is on your mind?* Kyle thought to himself as the chatter picked up.

Reasons? Odyne inquired, pulling up the hit targets on her heads-up display her eyes quickly reading the information as it blitzed by in a solid wall of color.

It's the furthest distance from impact and being so heavily guarded. The element of surprise that our small team would hit such a hard target first wouldn't cross their minds. Lylah felt a smile start to form across her face, she had taught them all too well but in this single drop pod she wasn't going to let them feel or see her express any emotion. She snapped to Kyle's helmet as it stared at her. Probing. Lylah closed her eyes. Shutting her mind off to their feelings she drifted into the black ichor laying on her back as she listened to them debate. She noticed something in the blackness, a thought of Dionysus drifted over her head. Lylah couldn't help but smile after seeing what happened. Laurel had planted Dionysus in her mind because she was afraid Lylah would separate her squad. Lylah allowed herself to be proud of Laurel for breaking into her mind and planting a thought without her knowing. Should she punish Laurel? The smile deepened as Lylah thought of the Commander.

"How would you handle this?" She spoke to the ichor, her words danced and echoed into nothingness before Lylah decided to listen back into the debate.

I would disagree. Dionysus objected. *We should hit site two first and sow confusion, circling to ambush site three as they come to aid. Leaving site one to be picked off last and used for hard contact.*

Lylah's eyes flew open and she sprang from the ichor jumping back into reality.

I disagree with you on this Dionysus. Lylah debated and gave her orders. *We will split up. I will lead Ares' team hitting site three. Dionysus take your squad and head towards* site two. Use Disperse pattern 5-1 on contact, drop pod will be rigged and blown within thirty milliseconds on ground contact. I want complete silence. We are going to take all three sites without them even knowing we landed. We strike fast and hard then disappear crashing on site one.*

    Yes Ma'am. The apache responded. Time started slow as they watched the meter's countdown. Kyle's heart palpitated for a second causing him to take a deep breath. Laurel watched her time debating if Lylah was onto her. Shyanne sat smugly staring at Dionysus. Devin and N'vid held up fists as the meters dropped into double digits waiting to connect on ground contact. The ground exploded in a wave of soot and earth bits as the interplanetary drop pod made contact, dipping the ground almost thirty feet down and launching a large dust cloud into the air. If it weren't for the dust swirls no one would have been able to tell anything was moving or alive. The dust trails twisted and spun as the inhabitants did their jobs. Bombs and gear were off loaded taking milliseconds before the air hissed for a solid second and a wall of fire burst forth from the pod as the flames licked the air with smoke and ash mixing with the dust completely hiding everything in the forest for almost two hundred meters in every direction.

    Lylah and Kyle's squad watched already six-hundred meters away with pleasure and satisfaction. Their bodies silhouetted in the dusk of the day as they turned to do their jobs. Lylah and the squad moved quickly, reaching the third site in seconds as they quickly ran scans and identified all targets.

"Kyle perimeter. Laurel Garage. Shyanne Barracks. N'vid and Devin overwatch from here. No one lives or leaves on my mark." Lylah nodded as she pointed and ordered. The five apaches stared at her beneath their matching helmets. Lylah looked back confused. "What?"

"You've never used our real names." Kyle responded, his voice soft and not because of the helmet.

"Get over it for now we have a job to do, remember." Lylah smacked his shoulder as the others looked at each other and nodded. They all would talk about this later but she was right, now was not the time. Lylah turned, watching her hud as the seconds passed. Three. Two.

    Mark. Lylah roared as they surged. Devin and N'vid started firing leading shots as Lylah jumped over one, correcting its angle mid air. Spinning and sliding underneath the lazer wires. Lylah smashed her left foot down, launching her over the guard towers as the first wave of shots connected, killing all thirty-two perimeter guards. Lylah took in the compound with her own eyes as she soared over the wall a black dot barely visible with the naked eye as she moved. Lylah was pleasantly surprised to find their scans were correct. There would be no need for audibles. She surfing down a roof before flipping to disperse her energy on the metal prefab floor boards. Lylah turned left catching a man as he walked out the door quickly grabbing her blade in millisecond she slashed his neck. Lylah rolled in the door reserving her speed and energy as she slipped her knife into her left hand. She spun the handle into an icepick grip with her blade facing away from her as she listened to the footsteps. Six men, three women and a mech were in the command unit unaware of her presence.

    Lylah breathed in, focusing her senses as she just moved, allowing her training to take hold. Kicking the door as one of the men came out splintering it as she surged the room stabbing the flying man through the neck. With a quick jerk she wrenched the man off course as she removed the blade from his neck. Shock slowly filled the man's face as Lylah jolted to the next target putting her fist through the man's chest. Lylah turned inwards as the next room's door exploded outwards. The mech charged as time slowly returned to normal. Lylah side steps easily jumping on the mech's back stabbing into its power supply and spins counter clockwise off the mech. As she spun she threw the blade catching the first woman in the chest as the woman charged the room. Lylah stood rolling her shoulders as a man and another woman charged the room.

A knife and baton were brandished against Lylah as she spins forwards, shattering the man's shin on her leg armor barely wasting effort in the attack. Standing on her hind leg Lylah slipped up under the woman's stab attempt, catching the woman's throat and crushing it with no effort. Lylah's face became harder as she heard the hiss of metal on metal as a bullet ricocheted off her and in the next four seconds the remaining guards found themselves bleeding out grabbing their throats as Lylah looked back from the door she came in. They stared in fear and horror at the blood covering Lylah, as they slowly died, gasping for air. Shock and fear laid across their faces much as her friends had when they had died.

No remorse or hesitation; A simple desire to win someone else's war so she may finally start her own life. As the light hit Lylah in the armor she looked like an angel of death as she was bathed in the light of the day. Lylah stood and the seconds passed, her head tilted forward deep in thought; her black armor making her a silhouette of death. She came to a conclusion, for now she would be her fathers murder bot for the war. She stood there deep in thought as a droplet slowly slid down her faceplate before falling off her helmet. In the next second Lylah disappeared a shadow on the battlefields to come.

Chapter 10:

What is the Cost of Obedience?

Day 18 of Deployment
F.S.F.V. The Ellen
Mid-Siege on Planet Zifil
Apache Are deployed on Zifil orbital defense ring
Commander Lylah "Odyne" Soffrireterna
Leader of Alpha Apache forces
March 19th, 5000
Time: 2:11 A.M.

The lights flickered overhead and bullets slowly spun around Lylah as she lazily dodges the automated turrets that now had her targeted. She looked out the window at the orbital defense ring as fires flared for seconds before decompression took over sending space debris plummeting towards the planet. Lylah rolled her eyes as she destroyed the turrets and her mind drifted towards how to stop her father from interfering in her life, permanently.

This attack on Zifil wasn't even in her top three thousand targets due to its insane defense ring which her squad, Alpha Apache, was tasked with taking the southern axis' command decks while Beta Apache's took out the Northern Command Decks. Lylah rolled her eyes at her father's blatten attempt to get all of them seen. An explosion echoed down the long halls as Lylah added, dodging the bombing runs to her list.

The Chief insisted on running to "soften" up their more armored decks for landing parties, which would discover the command decks and eighty percent of each section already dead. The rest would be so demoralized and fearful of whatever the demons that massacred their people, they would surrender. Lylah didn't agree with the chief's choice to make a spectacle and propagandize the Apache but until she figured out a way to strip her father's power over her she was at his mercy. He has the Fleet. Even the Ellen needed more allies then it could carry in the massive hundred ship on ship battles that would surely come next.

So here I am stuck, Lylah slid up against the inside of the door as it shot open and twenty men stormed the room. *I'll show you a fucken spectacle.* Lylah spitefully thought as she drifted away from her body and her current problem. Lylah contemplated all the laws in the constitution of the Federation. Her best play was the Law of Survival which stated: 'An individual can not be held accountable for one's action when put under life threatening duress. All actions taken therein and after are admissible in court and by the law, but if medical and psychological issues are being addressed an individual will therein and can be charged from the point treatment began. All individuals will be judged on survival at which point medical and psychological issues will be treated as mandated by the Board of all Medical Fields and The Workers Parties of The Galaxy.' But that only served her for Magness Prime and maybe upto the augmentations. She needed dirt on her father which of course she could provide.

NO! Luke's voice trembled the walls as Lylah's body continued to follow orders. Her mind, going to the River to answer Luke's call, closing her eyes, opened to him; she felt him arrive as she opened her eyes surrounded by the blue spectacle of the river.

"That was rude." Lylah said, walking up to Luke as he was when he died. His back staring across the river at the dark blue underbrush. Luke nodded his head staring at the underbrush before turning.

"You can't reveal that part of your life. You'll be killed. Not only because you are a fairsist but because you are." Luke stopped staring at Lylah as she nodded her head in disbelief and spit.

"No Luke please. Finish your sentence." Lylah stared back her face cold, "Say it."

"You're a clone's baby." Luke said with a whimper.

"Yeah Luke. A Clone of my mother had me. First documented death by birth in almost three thousand years because my father couldn't let her go." Tears poured down her face as she cried. "You wanna bring up how my father would sneak into my room too?" Luke's face widened in shock. "What about your conversation with him when we left? You wanna reopen some wounds, I got a few." Lylah stood still, her face hard as she started recovering quickly and turning her pain into unfiltered bioism. Luke was beyond shaken by her words as he stared; she took a deep long breath before continuing, " The past is that. I need a way to get my father off my ass."

"Time will give you the answer you seek." The river hissed from behind Luke, its many voices mixed with caution and spit.

"Thank you, Ancestors. Now I have a war to win." Lylah said clapping as reality once again cemented itself and Lylah looked around the now blood soaked hallways. Men and body parts were everywhere. Most mech suits were not even capable of doing such horrors let alone the damage to the electronics. If Lylah didn't know better she would have sworn some type of monster tore through these men. Lylah turned before mocking herself. *Monsters aren't fucken real, but I am.* Her moment was interrupted as she listened to the radio.

"This is the Ellen we have taken on enemy counter-borders. Alpha recall and defend your home." The Chief ordered over the coms. Lylah rolled her eyes. This was his big play? Let them be caught in their own ship. The ship they refitted.

Apache. Go home and clean your rooms. Lylah ordered as she walked over to the command rooms' open window panels staring at miles and miles of defense rings she had already cleared. Shaking her head at the horrors the normal soldiers would see. She turned waving her hand over the environmental controls and released all the oxygen for the entire southern ring. *It's finished.* She thought and turned to help clear out Ellen.

One Year Later

F.S.F.V. The Ellen
Mid-Wormhole Transite Deep beyond the F.A. Meddling Line
Apache mid-redeployment
First Lt. Kyle "Ares" Akya
Second in Command of Alpha Apache forces
February 14th, 5001
Time: 3:51 A.M.

"Reports are still flooding in of a Mysterious unknown force winning major battles across the Meddling Line, sources sight a genius general." A snicker escaped Kyle's lips. They weren't exactly wrong, his mind pondering their words, Odyne excluded of course. Shyanne and Chelsea had come into their own over the last year leading by planning various attacks on planets all to success. Kyle swiped his hand left to change the channel of the newsreel he was watching trying not to think about the battles they kept jumping to. One after another almost seven hundred worlds have already re-pledged to the Federation in less than a year. Two geniuses and whatever Odyne really was was more like it, and unfortunately they were all working together to create an unbeatable wave that almost had the meddling line pushed back 3 light years.

No easy feat for a war on this galactic size. He sighed as another war report began. "No one can confirm or deny the existence of these so-called super soldiers or as some call 'The Reapers of Zifil' or even the existence of a super genius as is being reported in most popular holosuites. Speculation around them or the one has gone beyond humanity due the unprecedented winning streak. Either way we are determined to find how. Now we do have some news about those reapers." The head reported as he fainted every body movement with such indifference. Kyle grumbled at the man's obviously cringe worthy body language. "Planet after planet rejoining the federation as our forces push through the Meddling Line. Reports from the front of the 'Reapers of Zifil' and we have exclusive footage."

Kyle sighed, before ignoring whatever the host was saying as he had already seen the real footage. He looked around the commons. In the early hours of the morning the silence allowed him to think before a cry of pain brought him to his feet looking around the commons quickly. *Lylah.* The word echoed softly in the blackness. Kyle shook his head and sat back down. The sudden sinking feeling of eyes watching him from just outside his peripheral vision. Kyle closed his eyes and began to mouth the words. " I am in the commons." *Commons.* The word echoed again. Kyle jumped to his feet getting an indepth look at the room.

Now it was repeating his words. The holo-light from his wrist casting deep shadows. He was in a deep 1970's styled conversation pit. His eyes jumped to the cabinets that lined the kitchen almost twenty feet to his left. Stocked with all the paste they could need for extremely long journeys. His eyes moved over the synthesizer. Its case was open waiting for the next instructions as the dark screen glinted in the low light. It could make any solid food they wanted but it couldn't replicate the flavor for some reason. Odyne said it was next after Jacks. His eyes connected with the long hallway leading into the commons that lead to the operations deck and the A.D.L. Kyle continued his scan as his eyes connected to the holodeck, their rooms, and the armory hallway, still no movement. He finished his scan with the shower door and sat back down.

Kyle continued to read articles moving at blinding speeds to make sure no one was actually close. The battles had been a cake walk at first, he thought his mind slipping. The enemy didn't know they existed but still they had upgraded, getting better at predicting the Apache attack vectors. With these upgrades they had managed to peg Chelsea from Beta squad on the shoulder mid run with a plasma round. The shift in Lylah was immediate, forcing everyone to train harder to go faster in W.H. space. There was a downside to them winning so much at such a rapid pace. Such a high success rate has led to a lot of reporters figuring out that something isn't right in the Fleet. Kyle shook his head trying to ignore politics as his mind snapped to the last planet they had liberated from the Freedom Initiative, a burning planet of plasma named D-1278. Kyle stared blankly at the wall remembering how many people had suffered for hours in the plasma storm level heats as the EV suits and guns melted hoping someone could save them. Mal and his medical team had almost been overwhelmed by the amount of burn patients there had been.

Odyne had made it a personal point to laugh eternally at Mal as she pointed out the brilliance of her suit's heatsinks before upgrading the regs armor for future engagements. Kyle couldn't silence the screams as someone's suit ruptured. He could feel their sudden realization as the air slowly burned their insides to ash in an instant of internal combustion. Kyle had been forced to put a hole in the female officer before she could combust after she ruptured her suit on one of the many orbital catways. Her body turned to ashes seconds later. He blinked and saw a railing collapse, men being launched into the inferno instantly incinerated. On D-1278 everyone burned equally both allies and enemies alike. There had been several railing collapses because of a detonate charge malfunction caused by the heat.

Kyle's mag boots had saved him as he watched people disintegrated on their way down to the planet's surface. He adjusted trying to calm his own mind trying to ignore the screams, the pleas as even he couldn't save them. Blinking quickly to keep the visions of the planet, and those men, out of his mind he pressed play forcing his mind to focus on the screen.

"Flooded with recent victories, could the rumors be true? Are these 'reapers' really helping win battles or just a genius General calling the shots? More when we return." He shook his head, taking a deep breath trying to pull himself out of the memory, hard. Closing his eyes for a second giving the flashbacks a quick rerun. Kyle breathes out letting all his training go and feeling the weight of their actions for a second. The almost overwhelming flood of emotions forced Kyle to focus on his performance. They had landed perfectly and secured the LZ for the main force. After he had cleared all sectors they began moving into the facility.

As Kyle stared ahead the screams returned and he opened his eyes staring at the ceiling keeping tears from falling. The Generals had grown weary of the Apaches and their flawless record of victories which is why they were here. Chelsea had been granted command of the second squad half a year back now and was in the Omega advance force somewhere in the beta quadrant preparing for another big push. Odyne had assumed command of Kyle, Shyanne, Laurel, N'vid, and Devin and given the designation: Amăgitor Squad or Deceiver Squad. Kyle didn't think top brass knew they spoke every known and forgotten language.

"Why do you listen to that propaganda? Better yet why the fuck are you awake?" Laurel said, walking in dragging her legs in the early morning. Her hair draped around her coco skin. The soft glow of her eyes made Kyle tap his left eye with his pinky finger and her eyes slowly faded.

"Something to do while we wait for an assignment and I couldn't silence my thoughts." Kyle said, flicking his wrist and the screen went blank. He relaxed back on the couch trying once again to get comfortable.

"What's on your mind?" Laurel said, raising an eyebrow looking through cabinets for supplies ignoring his first comment. She stopped and pulled open a sugar paste with a gluttonous smile. She ripped the top off and started sucking on the tube. Laurel turned to Kyle who smiled and rolled his eyes returning to his wall.

"Nothing important, think Odyne is gonna stop any time soon?" Kyle asked boredly as he stared at another article before closing his wrist pad in disgust. The tension that came from the Commander was undeniable and at times unbearable. The fleet hadn't really gone on a mission in almost two weeks causing a lot of the Apache to try to break the boredom picking up useless skills like drawing or holo programming. Kyle figured the brass wasn't happy and grounded them for their victories to extinguish their egos.

However their fleet's movements were erratic and Odyne had been in a lot of meetings through the last week, some lasting upwards of six hours. Their fleet had hidden in a shared wormhole space waiting for a plan to formulate. When Odyen returned she didn't have much, only that the next attack was gonna be the first major offense into enemy territory instead of against this pointless line. She had somehow made her case to the Federation's Elders and they had finally given a green light for what Kyle assumed was a very audacious plan.

"Obviously she's just getting started." Shyanne said, entering the Apache common room wiping the sleep from her eyes, "Oh by the way." The other two looked at Shyanne, "Ya'll loud as fuck." She walked over tapping the screen on the far wall making a wake up stim for herself and a nice cup of tea.

Shyanne rolled her eyes and went over to the synthesizer smacking Laurel who was still snacking on her sugar paste aiming for her head and pointed at the device. Laurel glared at her in response, flipping Shyanne off and continued slurping paste. They had retrofitted much of the rooms to fit their wants much to the dismay of Odyne. A gym and holo room had been installed for training.

They had their own personal armory where they could get any weapon they wanted. The harnesses in the armory held the armor itself, each dangled gently in the artificial gravity decorated in different ways to reflect the Apache that wore them. Kyle was proud of his six thin techno lines that ran over the top of his helmet leading from his spine to his head. Each line ran and jetted in all directions and changed to different colors of green. The lines outlined his shoulders, ribs, legs and joints in the armor. Shyanne had fixed a skull design on her helmet and had the bones outlined throughout the body. Devin had put a huge zero-one-six-nine circled in white on the chest that sat on a field of orange that made the rest of his suit. N'vid had used a techno design as well with navy blue all over the helmet and chassis. Laurel had made an inky wonderland of flowers and swirls that were bathed in deep red on a plane of white. Odyne's armor was the only one not changed, it's soulless black reflecting the woman inside Kyle speculated. Even the Captain had told her to change it but Odyne had persisted. The six Apache had their own rooms off to the right of the commons.
"Good Morning Shyanne, the usual?" The Machine said springing to life as Shyanne touched it.
"Yeah."

"So Kyle, four points, that's a squad record." She said, taking her drink and walking into the social circle as Laurel continued to glare before hitting buttons instead of voice to not interrupt the conversation. Laurel eyed Shyanne as she scratched a line with the blade, she always had strapped to her leg, in one of the walls as she waited. The writing above the line read *Record* with three lines next to it. Kyle already knew where Laurel was going. Kyle eyed her blade, smirking about how that blade had quickly become Laurel's favorite weapon. She had made the tactical blade on one of their previous missions and had taken such a liking, she kept it. The curve in the blade was backwards and was used for slashing and grapple stabbing instead of the straight blades everyone else used. Kyle's mind drifted to an often brought up question, who was the best swordsman in the squad.

As training and the years added up the debate had raged on. The question was whether Laurel got to use her new weapon. Kyle had submitted that Devin could now beat him let alone Laurel. Kyle had argued long and hard about how Devin would win due to his use of the Rapier blade; it was faster and more precise then his Longblade. N'vid had sworn Laurel was a better swordsman. So naturally they found out. After Kyle had won in all of the tests they had from efficiency and rating, Laurel had submitted but Kyle argued that his sword slowed him down forcing him to play the long game which should lower his efficiency, unfortunately only Kyle believed this. Devin had taken a stance against Laurel and picked Kyle. This choice had forced Shyanne to get involved to settle the score which she chose to not be a part of. Kyle and Laurel had decided to do a private match so they were the only ones who knew the actual answer.

Kyle however was the superior hand to hand combatant. Taking his natural talent and obsessing over it. His skills had advanced further since his days at the Olympus and he alone could fight off N'vid, Devin, Laurel, Shyanne, and two Apaches from Beta Squad. His skills were only surpassed by Commander Odyne. On his off time he restored old 20th to 39th century movies. He worked very closely with N'vid on the settings and feel of the scenes, often spending massive hours in the holodeck programming. Shyanne had become obsessed with spaceship combat and flight. She was the biggest Holoroom Hog often using it to replay or change strategies, modifying ships and creating new fleet doctrines. She even developed A.I. subroutines to help A.I.s better control ships trying to get Odyne to let her help with Jacks. Once Odyne did, Shyanne quickly found out how out of her depth she was.
Devin had taken to paintings and artwork often spending days developing spacescapes or beautiful images he had remembered while they were on the field.

Odyne had suggested selling his pieces, after the others had convinced him to sell the paintings something happened. People took notice of the horrifyingly beautiful pieces and he started making more money then he would ever need, having to form a false persona to remain hidden. That of a reclusive officer in the Fleet who was at those battles but wished to remain hidden. N'vid had taken to squad moments and attack patterns. His eye for detail was second to none and he developed a love for ranged combat prefering to engage targets up to eighteen miles away holding the record for longest kill at thirty three miles even out shooting Odyne. Many, including Kyle, think she was off by the two centimeters on purpose.

With that being said he also enjoyed helping Kyle and N'vid with their holodramas. Devin had even written and directed two award winning holodramas based around their lives. The media and crowd ate him up not even knowing who he really was. The Apache simply did not exist. As far as people knew the holodramas were just amazingly well written and based around the real events happening in the galaxy.

Laurel on the other hand had taken to crafting like a glove. After her first blade she went into full on blacksmith mode. They had all helped her fit her blacksmithing gear into the armory. Her blades were so elegant, beautiful, and flawless even Odyne had asked if she would make her a new blade. She seemed to be able to build the perfect weapon to reflect the person she saw. Odyne's new Jian blade was long with a silvery white coat that could never be stained by the blood of her victims. The hilt was the head of a rose that fell into a hilt of thorn vines. The thorns spun counterclockwise into a calm bush. The hilt had a sunandana, a light almost white teal ribbon that moved with grace. The blade had been stained in a deep blood red to give it an ominous low glow. She had gifted Kyle with an elegant Longsword. The blade ran long and true, a Japanese saying inscribed towards the hilt that read, 'I belong to the warrior in whom the old ways have joined the new.'

Devin and N'vid had rejected using her blades but both boys had their blades proudly sitting in their rooms on stands. Devin's was a Falcata of Silver and Black Gold. The Blade had a dark blood red tint and N'vid's was a Sica that mirrored Devin's. Shyanne had received a Kurkari that was made of silver and black gold with a long silver sunandana much like Odyne's. Shyanne had added it to her combat kit and enjoyed staining and cleaning the silver blade.

"Did someone say a new record?" N'vid said, walking in stretching with his arms up, his eyes glued on the fresh cut in the metal, "Why are you all so loud?" Over the last year his mullet had gotten much bigger and he had decided not to shave his mustache; he very much looked like an early 20th porn star. They all looked at Shyanne as she spoke.

"Yeah yeah, loverboy's showing off for Ice Cunt again." Shyanne giggled, rolling her eyes at the noise complaint.

"Shut up." Kyle snapped, flipping her off.

"Or what?" She retorted with disbelief.

"I'll introduce you to the floor." Kyle mumbled into the open air as the others made their way to the social circle.

"Officer on the deck." Everyone snapped to attention as Colonel Spage stopped at the door as the Apache heard him coming.

"Mornin' Apache, as you were," He said, walking fully into the commons, "Why are you all up?"

"Couldn't sleep," Kyle said from the couch, closing his eyes.

"Kyle's loud." Laurel said, walking back to the kitchen and jumping up on the counter, dangling her legs as she nibbled on her paste

"Their damn noise." Shyanne said groggily, nodding to Laurel then Kyle.

"All the noise." N'vid said stealing Laurel's paste and nibbling on some,"Fuck that's gross. The fuck is it?!"

Laurel giggled as N'vid ran to the faucet drinking rapidly. Devin walked in, his eyes hung low heavy with sleep, "Y'all are loud." The Apache said in unison, smiling like school children and exchanging glances.

"That is seriously creepy." Spage smiled back.

Devin stopped in front of the Record board frozen a moment before turning to look at it and taking in the information it had to offer. The almost cartoonish flip around looking at Shyanne who shook her head, the move brought another smile to everyone's lips.

"Loverboy again." Shyanne conformed.

"Fuck all of you." Kyle rolled his eyes and shifted as everyone stared at him, a smile tempting the edges of his mouth.

"And you love us for it." Laurel interjected.

"I'm just dedicated to it all." Kyle retorted.

"Dedicated to getting laid." Shyanne snorted and N'vid walked beside her. Shyanne held up a fist for him to hit and the others started laughing.

"So why do they keep calling you 'loverboy'? There has got to be a story behind a nickname like that." Commander Spage laughed sitting down across from Kyle, holding a cup of coffee, almost childlike eyes dancing with excitement. Posters of Sexiest Ba Booms, City of Owls, Movies from the early 20th to the 49th centuries spanned the now lit long walls. The Commons resembled a mix of modern marvels and memorabilia of bygone eras.
"I don't wanna talk about it." He said, closing his eyes, his disgust getting the better of him.
"Oh I will so tell this story." Shyanne said with a dastardly grin. Kyle half waved as if to say be my guest.

"See Kyle here, saw The Commander walk in the room when we were asked to join this band of misfits and got this like raven dog look," everyone laughed at Kyle's expense as Shyanne made faces and gestures as she told the story, "He was so eager to be her plaything she took interest in him immediately and boy did she. He got extra beatings and assrippings." Everyone gathered around the circle taking seats. Laurel and Devin sat next to each other. Next to N'vid was Kyle's head, down by Kyle's feet was Shyanne who sat next to Devin and on the inside stair was Spage.
"She has a funny way of showing interest," he said, rolling his shoulders with a slight smirk on his face, indulging the idea for a second.
"Didn't your mom tell you that's how we girls say we like you boys." Laurel laughed, slapping his head before returning to her drink as he shooed pointlessly at her hands as they were already gone.

"Anyway, I think it's like month one or two. Dumbass forgot we could hear his thoughts and let a 'wow' slip during a...revealing moment. Then he refused to kill her for like four months. That's a whole different thing though." The Colonel waved her on. "Anyway, we were enjoying everyone getting their asses handed to them when he stepped onto the field and started putting points up. The first point came around and he had her pinned to the ground and we could feel his attraction through the link." Shyanne's voice raised as she added her own flavor and flare to the story, "So he wouldn't kill her. She then slaughtered the shit outta him and ever since it's a debate at how long till they make little death bringers. I got like six months tops." Kyle shot a middle finger hand and lazily kicked aimlessly at her as the others laughed.

"Hey keep going like that, it might be three!" Shyanne said, adding fire to the wildfire of laughter as everyone broke out laughing filling the air with joy. They all stared and exchanged glances. The air was tense but calm and enjoyable.

"That's not how I remember things." The words blizzarded around the room. Space suddenly seemed like a tropical place compared to the commons. She stood in the doorway, her hair not yet tied up in her usual ponytail as it hung loosely around her shoulders. The image of a banshee painting plagued Kyle's mind as Laurel looked at him before popping a shit eating grin. The others got quiet quickly shifting in their seats as if staring at a demon or ghost.
"Morning Commander Odyne." Colonel Spage said, nodding. She nodded and walked over to get something to eat.

"So is this what we are going to go with? Misfits and baby death bringers? Death Bringers, that's a defiant new one." She said her back turned, grabbed a protein mix bar and opened it.
"Ma'am..." Shyanne attempted to start.
"Save it Aphrodite, I'm tired of your disrespectful bullshit. Ring." Odyne said her back still turned and took a bite, exhaustion made deep trenches under her eyes as she stared at the wall trying to control herself, reminding herself why she does what she does.

"Shit." Shyanne said under her breath.
"What was that?" Odyne said, turning her head slightly begging her to continue her thought.
"What time Ma'am." Shyanne said knowing better than to make it worse.
" O'Four Hundred." Odyne said, returning her head to what she was doing. Shyanne looked at the holoboard in the commons and sighed.
"See you in eight minutes ma'am I need to get ready." Shyanne got up and attempted to leave the room heading for the training room.
"I expect everyone to be there." Odyne said, still back turned.
"Yes Ma'am." The others said and went to prepare. Lylah finally turned around and snatched a cup to drink. Filling it with whatever was in the synthesizer.
"So this is how things work in Apache?" Colonel Spage sighed after everyone had left.
"Speak your mind Colonel, I'm in no mood for your riddles today." Odyne said moving to a couch and sat down crossing her legs and sipping gingerly on the tea. "Shyanne has terrible taste in tea." Odyne said with a scowl.
"Are you going to talk to me about it because, that… that was not ok. You just berated your soldiers for being people. I have been watching you and honestly I'm worried for your health." He said almost smiling before the concern set in and stared at her as she sat across from him. He knew she had sucked the air from the room on purpose.
"You think I enjoy being this way?" She stared at him, forming her words before she spoke. "The only woman I knew as a mother figure died a few feet away from where the love of my life died. At which point I was forced to join an experimental program to try to get out from under my father's influence. When I succeeded in the experimental program, a mad scientist's wet dream was successful." She stops and lowers her tone, "My adoptive father in his grief commits suicide. After which I was called upon to save the galaxy."
She looked into the drink and sipped, eyes never moving as she spoke. "I know my nickname is Ice Cunt because I have no remorse or empathy. They can't even be more than seventeen years old and they are fighting a war no one even understands. Hell, I don't even get to be my own age, not that it would have mattered." She said coldly, taking a sip of her drink every so often despite the flavor.
"You have been through literal hell. The things you have seen for one being so young," He said sadly and shook his head, "even that being said. I watched as you followed me into a crowded mess hall and made me laugh. I remember when you would smile and light up a room. I can't say I recognize the person sitting a few feet away from me."
"Spage, you can't even comprehend the person I was let alone what I have become. The person you knew was so fleetingly weak," She pauses trying to control her emotions as she plays her part staring at him menacingly, "I was born I ripped her heart out, and fed it to her. And in doing that I did the one thing that would smite my father forever." She said standing and stretching.
He said as she walked by, "Your father may not be the best but at least he is still here. Losing yourself because of someone else is stupid."
"The girl that would have done that died in a hangar on some distant planet, some forgotten years ago. She doesn't have a place in war let alone in a war with two enemies, especially when one is parading around as my ally. Let that little girl stay dead, or kill her yourself. Either way, I am what remains." She said and was gone.

Almost Twelve hours later

They had all been silent for over eleven hours now. Finally when he couldn't take it anymore Kyle spoke, getting everything off his chest as the high pressure gravity berated their bodies. "You got your ass whooped for a snarky comment, shall we talk about how stupid this was or?" Kyle said, staring directly at Shyanne.

"Holy hell, can we talk about how quick that actually was?" Laurel giggled as strain hardened her resolve. She coughed out blood as she struggled against the intense punishment.

"Shut up, Laurel I don't see you doing better and honestly Kyle fuck you. At least I stand up for us." Shyanne said slowly, turning her head to look at Kyle as thick sweat fell down her face, her face rapidly changing as she struggled both mental and physically to endure.

"Hey, I would rather be loverboy right now is all I'm saying." Laurel said while she balanced herself in a handstand as they all suffered Shyanne's loss. The fight hadn't lasted one solid minute. Odyne had unleashed her full abilities destroying Shyanne in seconds using unseen killing blows and techniques even Kyle wasn't sure he could replicate. He had never seen Odyne unleash herself like that, Shyanne's usual fighting spirit was broken in less than a minute as she could do nothing to spot the devastating humiliation Odyne had inflicted.

Kyle couldn't help but feel saddened at the level Odyne was willing to go to achieve her goal of freedom but he couldn't let Shyanne suffer either so he did the only thing he could. "Not looking so bad now huh. Look I'm just saying if you're gonna take shots make sure they are worth it," Strain almost stops him from speaking, blood slowly trickles down his nose. " next time. Ok?" Kyle pleaded in the same position and nodded his muscles screaming. Shyanne averted her eyes as she understood her Lt.

"I'm still not sure what we did to get punished?" Devin said, confused, opening his eyes as he focused on the here and now before trying to alleviate the strain as he shifted on his hands.

"Shyanne was a bad girl, tried to make Odyne a person..." Strain filled N'vid's voice, " We are like a team and all, so." N'vid huffed, his arms were shaking completely from the extreme gravity but Kyle could feel his resolve giving him strength.

After ten hours the whole squad started to feel the effects of twenty times earth's gravity but till just then they all stayed silent about the punishment. They all knew that Ice had been listening the whole time, she always was. She had been driving them hard recently about respect. The only time the five Apache acted out was in the commons which was supposed to be a safe zone. A place to be themselves but recently she's been obsessive about not giving the Chief fuel or ammo. They heard the room door open and Odyne walked in. Their arms burning, sweat oozing from every pore on their body. They had been upside down now for over eleven hours straight.

"One." She barked. Everyone went down and back up exacerbating the issue further as she stood there a black void in the room. "Two." They repeated the process. The sheer maliciousness they felt could not be understated as Lylah took a lap down the line before continuing. "Have we learned our lesson? Three." Kyle blinked as blackness filled the edges of his vision and he suddenly became keenly aware of something or someone else watching him. The blood trickling from his nose picked up to a steady steam as he stared at the light building within his sight.

"Ma'am, yes, ma'am." All the Apaches' muscles burned, shaking started to kick in for many of them as they struggled to keep their bodies upright. Kyle droned back on auto-pilot, his eyes fixated on the green silhouette of a giant man. The man walked over to an emerald green silhouetted woman. Kyle marveld as it was like looking at a gorilla and a normal woman. The woman raised her hand to his cheek as she turned and the vision exploded into smoky energy.

"Four. If anyone falls before ten you have three more hours on top of another round of twelve for everyone when they recover." She said walking up and down the line with ease laying on the pressure. Kyle blinked rapidly trying to chase that fever dream. He knew who they were. He knew he knew the two shapes but he didn't know how.

"Five." Down and up they all went, muscles shaking as she waited a few seconds. "Six." She watched again as they all went down and up taking in their suffering for some unknown purpose. "Seven." Kyle suddeled snapped out of his stupor as if someone snapped at him. His eyes locked on Aphrodite, her face was just caked in sweat much like his but her head was much redder and her arms were wavering much more than anyone else's. The signs of fatigue growing and eventually she would fall if Odyne caught on she would make sure Shyanne fell."Eight." Shyanne kept her face closed before her eyes popped up and she spit out trying to struggle to stay upright.

"Nine." He saw her muscles flinching and he reached over just as her left hand gave out and held her up, using his shoulder and body as a counter weight till she got her balance making sure neither of them fell. Odyne walked over and got in front of them, glaring, begging for them to fail, crouching to be closer as she stared at them making sure they knew, she knew. When Shyanne was caught Kyle's nose exploded with blood as a vessel in his eye popped at the strain of holding his massive body and her's up. His body shook and his face exploded into fields of red as the strain almost overwhelmed him.

"Ten." Together they lowered themselves and then backed up arms locked balancing off each other. They wiggled but did not fall as Odyne's eyes were glued to them. Kyle's face shakes violently as he struggles to blink. They both up blood drowning the top of his head as he waited for Odyne to make her move. Staring at each other their eyes locked in some battle or unseen conversation. After what seemed like she would never speak again Odyne finally uttered. "Rec time you have fifteen hours." Odyne didn't flinch or utter another word as she turned and left. They felt gravity return and everyone lost their balance and fell from the pressure sickness throwing up immediately as headaches quickly followed and the technicians ran in screaming orders at each other as they flooded the room.

"I can't believe she allowed that." Devin said from his back looking at the ceiling heaving heavily. The world spinning and shaking as he blinked trying to fix his issues as gravity sickness barraged his mind all while he tried to weakly bat away the help. Pain screamed and torched his muscles as Devin breathed, staring at the others.

"We...didn't fall." Shyanne said on her stomach, face planted to the floor. She coughed and threw up trying to push the technician who was helping her away before allowing them to direct her head as she vomited more harshly.

"Technicalities rock." Kyle said heaving as much air into his lungs as he could. The lightness of air hurting his lungs as he also hurled again, splattering himself and coughing harshly, barely able to get air as aid rushed over to clean him up. They gently helped him turn his head, his muscle screamed at him threatening to break or tear if he kept going, if he didn't give up control of his body.

"I will never call you loverboy again." Shyanne's face is still down trying to avoid the puddle she was staring at as she tries to keep her head straight. Wobbling heavily like a babe, she looks toward Kyle.

"None...of us will." N'vid said, starting to control his heavy breathing allowing an oxygen mask to be put on as he slowed his breathing, the mask lowering the gravity slowly and allowing his lungs to recover. N'vid's lungs, out of everyone's, were surprisingly weak and no one knew why. He always met minimum requirements but only barely. A tear slowly fell down N'vid's face as struggled through the pain of air in his lungs.

Kyle shook his head and sighed, "I don't know I kinda wanna keep it now. Something has to come from this." He tried smiling but abandoned the idea when his mouth was torn into fits of pain. The others tried to chuckle but couldn't going into fits of pain or vomiting for their efforts.

"I...hope beta...squad has had an easier time...than this."Devin said with his eyes closed as he roared in pain grabbing his head. The pressure change was extreme and he thought his ear drums might have exploded, "Ears." He mouthed through hurried breaths to the technicians as they questioned him, he stared blankly not hearing their words but reading their lips.

Kyle rolled over and struggled to stand. The gravity felt awkward and his body didn't feel right as he wobbled. It took three technicians to keep Kyle fully standing on his feet. Vertigo set in and Kyle was forced to slow his breath trying to regain control back, barely managing to stay stable as the three men struggled to keep the giant upright. His stomach flipped and he threw up coughing heavily and choking on his own bile after almost a half hour they all started to come out of the pressure sickness.

"I...get a shower first." Kyle said sluggishly, finally finding his feet as he moved slowly towards the door without aid.

Chapter 11:

Happy Little Accidents are Good

2 W.H. months later
F.S.F.V. The Ellen and Support Fleet in orbit
Deep Insertion on Planet Minsa
First Offensive push into F.A. Territory outside of Middling line
Apache mid-deployment
First Lt. Kyle "Ares" Akya
Second in Command of Alpha Apache forces
February 14th, 5001
Time: 3:51 A.M.

An explosion shook the gray scaled colored floral. The Jungle of Minasa was a massive push for the force. The planet was the largest habitable planet known in the Galaxy, four times the size of the Sol system's star. This jungle alone was four times the size of all the continents of Earth put together. The planet had no known carnivores, all the life that had developed had been herbivores or synbiotic. The planet had been one of the most peaceful places in the galaxy till the war came. An explosion of light and color made the planet look almost like a watercolor painting. The canopy shattered into a million pieces as another artillery shell landed followed by thousands more. The local lizard birds named Montigal scattered. Montgial's look like a dog sized feathered gecko-like creature; a lot of people had these loving creatures as pets for their fierce devotion to their master.

    The air hisses as the railguns continue to rain down support. As the black dirt and soot falls through the air it turns into a liquid state and collides like wet paint with local flora. The dirt and soot had fully liquified leaving black inky outlines on the white flowers staining them various colors of grays and blacks. The orbital pounding was gone in what seemed like seconds even though the bombardment was closer to 15 minutes. Then in the brightness of the day three white shapes crawl slowly towards their target. Barely visible from above and completely invisible to anyone on the ground. The Apache moved completely synchronized. Their thoughts are not so much in line as they argued.

    No fucken way that's gonna happen or even could. Laurel was saying as the great debate picked up again.
I'm telling you if you remove, augment and implant knowledge. I swear to you. Ice couldn't beat Ares. N'vid said as they crawled. Kyle gumbled as more artillery rained down in front of them staining his newly cleaned armor. He sighed at the irritation knowing that soot took hours to dry before he could even attempt to remove it. The liquid naturally stuck to anything absorbing its properties and trying to mimic its effects. Kyle grumbles again or at least till it

dries then it was like trying to remove dry tar from a crack. Doing everything he could to ignore the conversation blocking his mind as he focused on each individual piece he would have to pull off.

Wait! Really! How? Laurel asked, prying at his mind as she stopped. He almost didn't even notice her slipping into his mind as he chose to just show them the fight instead of suffering at the hands of Laurel's mind invasions. She had become scary confident about breaking into people's minds, a ghost in someone else's mind. Almost becoming a Mirror in whoever's mind she wanted, even offering to jump into the Chief's mind as well. Kyle sighed until Odyne had almost crippled Laurel's confidence for offering to do such a stupid and obvious move. Pointing very...bluntly how easily they would point the finger at the Apache for the attack and then they would have to fight the entire Armada.

Kyle sighed again knowing Odyne was doing the best she could but he couldn't help but wonder if there was another way around their problems. *One that didn't involve...* Kyle started to think to himself.
How's your arm? N'vid fired at him interrupting his thoughts as Laurel laughed and Kyle shook his head bringing himself back to the here and now.
This is a stupid plan. Kyle grumbled as they waited for the artillery to adjust in front of them.

Using artillery to shower us in inky goodness that blends us in as we... N'vid pauses trying not to laugh as he continued. *Literally crawl right into their base as said artillery showers us from the heavens above. I think it's by far the greatest plan I have ever heard and am for one glad I was voluntold. But honestly Shyanne's not wrong, they won't be able to stop the shot at that distance. Orbital defenses will be useless and by the time the soldiers swarm, even though it's a minute later, we will have cleared the base. Reapers of death. Wooohhh. I got money on Laurel for highest kill count.* N'vid sassed as Laurel broke sync to laugh, laying completely still as she giggled while the artillery stopped to reload again.

Our lives are so fucken awesome. Also fifty gs on Luke. She laughed and rolled over on her back staring at the skies as her visor removed the smoke so she could stare at the skies above. The silhouettes of the millions of ships that sat in orbit almost blocking her view of the stars. Almost. Kyle stared at her knowing he had to have heard her wrong before a chill went up his back crawling nerve by nerve up like a cautious spider as it slowly ascended his back. An unwelcomed guest. His passenger, someone he wasn't even sure was real. Kyle attacked it with his mind but to no avail as if it wasn't even real. A figment in his mind. Kyle turned and stared hard at his brother. Kyle's heart froze as he stared, their eyes glued on each other. Kyle reached forward with his left and his brother reached out with his right.

Couldn't agree more. Crawling through this inky wonderland is beyond beautiful. On a more serious and more personal note. What's tonight's holomovie anyway? Kyle exhaled, as N'vid ripped that mirror of his brother away from him as N'vid began begging. *You kinda lost your shit in there the other day, story issues or reaction issues? I can help you know. Was it Sammy from the? Cycle? Please come on man. Throw me a bone.* N'vid asked Kyle as they waited for Laurel to stop laughing.

Both. I fixed both. Kyle sighed, 'The Last Samurai' *and* 'The Eternal Cycle' *holodramas have been recreated almost in their entirety. But Odyne shut me down when I offered them stating she wouldn't allow either till they are done..and her words correctly. However I got permission from the Colonel insisting on Samurai as he has never enjoyed it. So we will be demoing it tonight. Only scene she okayed was the assassination attempt on Mr. Katsumoto.* Kyle mused as he spoke. They both were holo-dramas they had found in the archives from somewhere back in the early 21st century and had been restoring each slowly. Their stories were complex. At least 'The Eternal Cycle' was being made up of podcasts, books, movies, shows and games. So translating all the information was tricky and due to time degradation and the world's loss of all historical facts in the late 21st century recreating an authentic eighteen century Japan based on a few scenes and books they had paid way too much for had found Kyle screaming and raging more than once.

Who do you wanna play? Kyle asks N'vid as Laurel starts to come to, looking up at them from her back as she rolls to her shoulders. Kyle couldn't shake the sinking feeling he had, a hint of mistrust.
I'm totally Nathan. N'vid claimed the main character.
I'm claiming Katsumoto. Devin claimed from elsewhere on the planet.
Fuck. I love Katsi-san, Shyanne retorted. Everyone shivered at the bad translation and insinuation. *We are in position. Status?*
Our Artillery is reloading waiting for push to continue. Kyle responded and rolled his shoulders trying to kill the tension in his muscles.
Make sure you are there in 5 minutes or there is no movie tonight and I will expect more push ups. Also I claim Ujio. Odynes chilling voice echoed around them. The mood was instantly back to serious as Odyne sucked the fun directly out of the air.

All the Apache snapped at the sound of her voice. *Yes ma'am.* They said back, almost robotically responding more instinctually than meaningfully.
Laurel stiffened and nodded, rolling over to her stomach so they could begin crawling forward as the artillery shells began staining the white forest again. The three crawled forward and saw the intended infiltration point.

Ready. Kyle said and then heard the sudden silence as they threw beacons for the Slug Shell to hit. The air snapped as a supersonic interplanetary shot rocked the side of the mountain. The shower of black, gray and white was stained forever as red joined the color scheme being launched into the scheme after the fact. As soon as the shot connects they all jump removing the chance of an impact wave to knock them away. The armor had absorbed all the remaining kinetic damage and reversed the direction of energy to keep them in place.

As the World split apart they moved into the barracks killing everyone and moving to the next room before all the dirt could even fall. Thirty soldiers in two rooms in under five seconds their training devastating the enemy in clean, quick, split-second kills. Laurel took the lead moving with sharp, quick movements as they cleared room to room hearing the dust finally falling as they moved deeper into the base. Laurel attempts to take a corner and gets blasted back, sending her flying into the wall, an awkward angel smashing into the wall on her back before crashing onto the ground.

A hellish weapon stuck in the corner section before disappearing before anyone could get a clean look at it. Kyle shifted backward as a Brute spun around the corner grabbing the weapon mid spin and slashing at Kyle damaging the wall that Kyle had been in front of milliseconds before. Kyle surged forward and launched the creature into a caddy corner wall while trying to give Laurel, who hadn't recovered yet, a second. They all turned their recording vision on so they could study this new iteration of the brute. Its skin was covered in acrylic-like muscular features that clung much more to the brute making them more defined than the other brutes; this iteration was almost bathed completely in a faded red that almost glowed in the darkness.

The face was very similar to all other brutes. No eyes, scars and tubes spanned its body. The creature recovered quickly. Locking Luke in a clinch before it noticed Laurel spinning its chest and sending its arm rubber banding and twisting. The arm seems to coil its muscles quickly, crunching and rotating the skin to build up energy. As the brute unflipped the muscles and skin of its arm launching an attack at Kyle with a snap, a small smoke trail started from the energy launched giving Kyle something to track and estimate its course. Kyle spun back first in front of the attack and braced Laurel as the hit connected, sending them through two sets of walls.

Kyle rolled with Laurel who grabbed a stim from Kyle's leg compartment and injected herself as they rolled through the air. Shots broke out behind them as N'vid tried to draw its attention away. Kyle spun hearing the blade heading their way and redirected the stretching arm. Kyle once more saw the smoke trail that was left behind and slapped the face of the blade away, sending it to destroy the wall behind them before the brute pulled it back. N'vid shouldered his rifle and drew his sword.

Kyle felt betrayed as he saw Laurel's beautiful blade brought out in one fluid movement blocking another blade that was heading right at him. Another wall exploded from the force of the attacks. Finally Kyle got a good look at the axes, covered in what looked like rotting metal. The blade faces were comically big, reminding Kyle of fantasy style battle axes.

Laurel stirred and stood up behind Kyle moving to draw her dagger. Kyle felt her intention and drew the creature to launch another stretch attack. It complied and he easily sidestepped the attack and drove his sword into the creature's muscles and effectively pinned its arm to the floor. Laurel slid under the creature's arm attack, spinning the blade around her middle finger as she slid, boredly. She raised her foot rolling onto her ankle before launching forward, grabbing the creature's head and slamming her legs into its chest trying to rip off its head. The creature screeched in horror as she hacked the dagger into its neck before it was silenced forever. Muscles struggled to stay attached and blood flew everywhere as finally Laurel backflipped and the creature slumped. Her armor was drenched in a purple like ichor breathing heavily.

Fuck. Laurel said, dropping the head with disgust looking around for something to wipe herself off with.

You good? N'vid said, walking over and checking for puncture wounds before giving a thumbs up.

Think so. That first hit though. You guys didn't see? She asked, nodding and letting him look her over.

No, we are good and I can agree it didn't feel good but otherwise my armor took the blow. Kyle bobbed back as N'vid held a thumbs up.

Laurel walked over and nodded at the blade. *Only for decoration huh?*

N'vid shrugged, sheathing the weapon. *What can I say? I've grown attached to its beauty.*

"Holy fuck. Reapers." The three flip around weapons raised as a group of Federation soldiers stood stunned in the doorway. Almost twenty soldiers stared back at them; full body cams and every pair of eyes on them. The three looked at each other in the next second. They tried to move before the men could truly comprehend who and what they were looking at.

What the fuck did you just let happen? Odyne's cold voice pierced their minds as they stared blankly at each other fifty miles away the next minute, heaving heavy from the effort as they all stared; frozen to the moment as the first question they all shared seconds later was, *What's next?*

Earth Supreme High Court
Two short days later on Earth
Trail of the Apache vs Federation Eidetic Board
Apache are restrained to quarters and arrested for treason
Lead Prosecutor: Commander and Chief Michael Soffrireterna
Lead Defendant: Retired Captain Lylah Soffrireterna
and
Commander of Active Apache Forces Codename: Odyne
February 16th, 5001
Time: 9:56 A.M.
Hearing starts in t-minus four minutes.

Page 3 of Playbook

"Commander, may I speak to you? Before we begin." The Commander and Chief said standing near the massive courtroom as Lylah walked around the room waiting for their trial. She walked over to him knowing full well that he was gonna try to intimidate her. She had planned for this and everything else to follow, from the outfits to the responses. All the Apache had chipped in and added their own touch to the pot of shit they were throwing at the Commander and Chief, proof of profiteering, illegal cloning experiments, the works and Lylah had added the final killing blow without anyone knowing.

"Commander, I don't see your second around." The Chief snarked looking around the room. The courtroom was a relic of the thirtieth century neon explosion stage. Everything was covered with a deep blue, almost black smooth marble. Soft holo lights light up the outlines of everything giving it an original wireware space game appearance from the early days of software design.

"She will be here counselor, don't worry. Oh, and second, I am a Captain earned in blood and acknowledged by the Elders. So Chief, with respect you will address me with my earned title next time," She invaded his space and patted dust off his shoulder, "You'll need this," She handed a tablet to him. He looked at her incredulously, "It's my playbook. You'll need it to stand a moment's chance against the Commander." Lylah spoke softly, allowing a slight menace to fill her tone, "I handed her everything. On you, on mom, and on me. What she does with it, I can't say for sure." She finished attempting to turn as he took the tablet.

"What a joke. This was your play?" He said looking at the tablet scrolling as he stared at it ignoring the literal play by play book. If he had read it he would have noticed even this scene was scripted from it, everything down to the word was outlined from Lylah's movements to her smile.

"Yep and you'll give her the win without even trying. Sir, with respect I'm here as an observer, if you'd been here earlier when councilors met you'd know why I will be in the crowd the entire time. I have just offered my record because if you do manage a win I'd rather it not be on Spage's record. He offered to place his record on the line but unlike him, I won't be affected. If you thought this was gonna be father vs Daughter you are very much mistaken. You were never going to face me,"

She stepped even closer so only the two of them could hear, "and now with no title, power, or goons backing you." She stopped allowing him to feel her hatred as she spoke, the true depths of her maliciousness and hatred. "A debate where you can't just kill your opponent. A debate, you can't win because you're wrong and you know it. A debate I planned, you are not the only one who can plan and plot." She paused once more. "Let me clarify for you what you fail to grasp." Lylah said, getting so close she could smell the sweat running down the back of his head. Her desired effect received as she whispers in his ear as he stared behind her frozen in place, "I was the bait so she can kill you. I did this for her. I did this for him. I did this because it will be fun to watch you die and have no power to stop it. Thank you for taking the poison so willingly. Now here we are. You thought I was your ally. How does it feel to have someone you trusted hand your enemy everything? Still confused? I know you let the attack happen."

    The Chief grew paler as she hugged him sliding the gun she used to survive magness his into pants, continuing, " So here you go dad. Your wish, I'm yours." She paused as they separated, "But how long can you keep me? That is completely on you. Oh that belonged to a woman who is by far your superior in every way. Might wanna consider using it one way or another." The Chief's face was completely devoid of color as she left to take her seat on the balcony, faking a smile as she shook hands with someone. The Chief stared his face in complete shock, utterly powerless to stop or even face her.

Chapter 12:

High courts come with high costs

Earth Supreme High Court
Trail of the Apache vs Federation Eidetic Board
February 16th, 5001
Time: 10:00 A.M.

Page 34 of Playbook

Odyne walked into the courtroom to the roar of the ballistic council, a crowded mix of cheer and boos filled the air quickly followed by arguing as the Governing Four watched on. Odyne noticed one major problem; there were only three of the four Governing Leads present. Odyne smiled, feeling her advantage growing. The five other Apaches walked in covered in full armor just like her following close behind. They had programmed their armor to resemble a form of dress suit using nanite paint; most people couldn't tell the difference between their armor and them. Each helmet had been changed and upgraded with holotech with three-sixty holo projectors so they could use irritating faces and look completely ridiculous at this kangaroo court the Chief insisted on doing. Odyne had programmed her helmet with a comical giant yellow smiley face.

    Odyne knew how to beat the chief. She needed to play the fool and even had gone as far as to convince the ruling judge to allow them to wear the obnoxious outfits in the name of security and safety. The court only knew their code names as of this moment as Lylah had gone out of her way to protect their identity until the verdict was handed down. The length Odyne had gone to make this show a genuinely hardcore mockery was truly petty but against her father, she smiled, it was worth it.

    "All respective parties may I please have peace and quiet as we begin the proceeding of Apache Experimental Spec Force vs the Federation Eidetic and Defence Force Foundation or F.E.D. who will be spoken for by their respective representatives. From the F.E.D. We have head councilor Commander and Chief Michael Soffrireterna as leading investigator and prosecutor and for the defendant the head Counselor has stepped back due to mental health issues and anointed Special Operator Commander Odyne as her acting head council while she deals with these issues. All parties should have received an updated document." He looked at his scribe as the man repeatedly informed him of the information as it updated. The judge kept his eyes on the scribe as he spoke making sure he read everything and turned about to finish.

    "Objection as stated. I was not aware of the sudden change. I request a recess till at least the noon hour before we continue to edit tactics." The Chief blurted, finally being pulled from his stupor Lylah had put him in earlier.

"Overruled and rejected." The judge jumped down the Chief's throat, completely shut him down without a second thought.

"But." The chief almost seemed completely caught off guard as the words made him a scolded child.

"Chief. I won't have you making a mockery of this court. We haven't even started and you have already made an objection. If you have a problem with my rulings you know how to change them. Until then I will remind the Commander and Chief this is my court not his." The judge immediately attacked the Chief who turned bright red from the berating, "I will not be running a mockery of the law for anyone's personal vendetta." The chief's face once again was empty of color as he stared at Odyne sitting at the defendant's table leaning over and whispering to the others playing their parts of professionals.

"I want everyone to know right now. I will not tolerate anything in my court. This is a place of law not politics." He finished his stare around the halls looking over everyone in the audience and glaring at the Chief last, setting the precedent for the rest of the court case. "The Case will proceed as scheduled. You may begin with opening statements as soon as the scribes have finished."

The Chief glared at Odyne as she moved back and forth Exchanging information as they talked amongst themselves seeming to adapt to the information just as the Chief had.
"The Scribs are ready. Chief, you may begin."

The Chief seemed to stir out of another stupor as he nodded and stood. " First off I'd like to welcome everyone and apologize for the interruption during such a harrowing time but I couldn't stand by while...such blatant abuse of power takes place. It has come to my attention that a sect inside our wonderful federation has commissioned, trained, and illegally developed soldiers to fight a war they knew was coming. Commander Montgomery who was killed on Magness Prime was sole perpetrator of said action in training these infiltrators. Their attack did not go as planned. My daughter and one other survived the harrowing events. Special Operative Odyne, whose identity had been painfully hidden from the court out of some need, is the only student other than my daughter who knows what really happened there. I launched an investigation into the matter once I found out of her survival which was hidden from me by others. I have done everything I can to keep the soldiers from the public when I found out about them. And yes while I will take the blame for not knowing about their survival and this plot. I have done everything I can to put a stop to it. Finally they slipped up and I have found my proof. Over the next few days you will see. Proof of Treason. Proof of Deception on a Galactic Scale. It is my job to PROVE to you what I say is true and I will. I will leave the floor to my opponent."

The Chief walked back as the crowd exploded into claps and applause that were quickly replaced with whispers and then silence as Odyne stood and walked around the desk.

"Opening statements. The Concept was developed for courts during the height of capitalist America during the early twenty first century. It's a concept that is meant to reveal one's intention and be a blueprint of how the case is supposed to go. I always found a flaw with it because usually the better speaker wins. You can win a court case in the first two minutes without a shred of evidence by one's words alone. It is not my job to prove our innocence, my job is to prove him wrong with the truth. It's one thing to hear someone spout niceties and sweet chocolate in your ears. Trust me I let him do it all my life but I won't let the galaxy burn for his petty vendetta. We have followed our orders. We have done our jobs, jobs we were ordered to do by the Chief himself," the crowd became almost unhinged as the chief's face grew pale once more,

"You wanna talk about treason, there's nothing more treasonous than a selfish man." Odyne roared, completely flipping the crowd, "We want this war to end and this selfish man will not allow us to do it. Have you ever loved something so much but because of the contradictory nature of it you have to hate it? Do you know what it's like to love something so much that to save it you must attack it's very heart and soul to do so? None of you can say that. None of you were at Magness or even have any true combat experience to speak of. Simulations can't prepare you for watching your friend explode in front of you. One second smiling then next a paste on the floor. You don't know what it's like to leave your friend in a room knowing they are already dead. To hold out hope even though you already know." Odyne paused as the tension finally reached deathly levels, "None of you are aware of the war. Really aware of the War. It's time to show all of you, so we can save it and move on with our lives." The Hall simply melts under applause and noise as the judge and scribes desperately try to quell the noise but to no avail.

Page 57 of Playbook

"Please state your name for the record so we may actually begin." The Judge's voice would echo around the virtual halls again and again as each Apache introduced themselves. It had taken two full days for the Judge to force a virtual trial so he could control the volumes and fights happening in the crowds, council booths, and court halls. The court had become a joke as the Judge and the scribes tried to conduct the case.

"Lt. Commander Third Class 'Aphrodite'." Shyanne said wearing a business suit that complimented her blocked head from the early 21st. A trend where someone who put a mask on how this particular mask would be oversized and usually block shaped. Shyanne had drawn an over characterization of herself complete with big, anime eyes.

"Lt. Commander Fourth Class 'Adonis'." N'vid had decided to dress up like his actual god, going as far as to have a toga and olympian style crown.

"Lt. Commander Fourth Class 'Demeter'." Laurel's choice of clothes was more modest: a simple business dress and simple smiley face.

"Lt. Commander Third Class 'Themis'." Devin had taken it personally dressing in almost perfect recreation of himself dressed in a nice suit.

"Lt. Command Second Class 'Ares'." Kyle had turned into the mythical Heracles

"Commander of Apache Operations 'Odyne'." Odyne's business suit fit her form perfectly coupled with a big yellow smiley face as if she completed all of them. They all sat side by side looking up at the Judge. Their voices echoed around the quiet halls as they all took turns staring out at the crowds to be paraded around, followed by the Chief.

"Please proceed with the beginning of the Minesa Operation and we will work our way back from there." The Judge said, eyeing his scribes as they nodded.

"Standard D.A.D. operation. We deployed sixteen kilos due immediately south." Kyle started before being interrupted.

"Please explain D.A.D. operations." The Judge barked back as he took in everything.

"Drop and Destroy mission. Sir." Laurel responded for Kyle so he may continue.

"Continue please." The Judge rolled his eyes, continuing to read his screens as he monitored everything.

"Landing and concealment was completed in four seconds before we moved onto target location waiting for orbital artillery to cover our approach. We followed and called in the...." N'vid started.

"Where were you specifically?" The Judge asked as he read the screen.

"I was with two other Apache. Demeter and Ares." N'vid said, "Operation went normally as we broke into the target building. We called in a Slug round for deep penetration and charged. As we cleared room to room as you will see in evidence docket number eighty-eight through ninety-one which are our body cameras. After we cleared the first three rooms..."

"K.I.A.s?" The Judge interrupted.

"Forty-nine for three rooms." Murmurs can be seen as council members tried to keep up with the events.

"Objection, Conjecture or pure fantasy to believe three people even special..." The Chief roared.

"Challenge acknowledged." The judge shut down, turning to a script as he looks at the data and nods confirming the information, "Scribes have judged based on evidence the statement stands." The Judge ruled and glared once more at the chief turning back to Kyle and nodded, "Please continue."

"A new Brute attacked. Uses polysynthetic skin to allow for extreme elasticity. We have yet to see another report of this Type-B variant. However it did and I really wanna state this, it kept up with us."

"Objection, Relevance." The Chief roared.

"Challenge acknowledged" The Judge sighed and turned to Kyle who looked at Odyne who stood.

"The relevance councillor is that we move in microsecond bursts." Odyne stated as the councillors exploded and the Judge closed his eyes.

"No one is that fast." The Chief responded.

"Really even though you had our test scores?" Odyne bantered back before the Judge roared."Repeat that." Almost silencing everyone with his fury.

"He has our test scores. Reported by Doctor Malarious Jabezes and myself respectively after each month of rigorous testing done by myself. The only one qualified to do so."

"Objection. Hearsay." The Chief lazily interrupted.

"Objection overruled." The Judge stated back, almost throwing the Chief into his chair from the power of the words.

"Grounds of overruling." The Chief persisted like a child.

"Fact is verified." The Judge smuggly smiled back.

"How?" The Chief fitted back.

"Evidence fifty-one B." Odyne responded by tapping some pads and flicking her wrist sending the chief the information so he didn't have to find it, "Confirmed by thirty-seven Generals, Combat Experts, even a Grand Councilor member has verified I am the only one who can teach them."

The Chief stared blankly at the information.

"I'm sorry, councilor, do you need a recess to form a new strategy?" Odyne sassed as laughter filled the room. The Judge turned, hiding his half smile before returning and keeping a straight face. Others in the audience couldn't help but laugh at the joke.

"Councilor might I advise not bantering with your opponent this is a case after all." The Judge reminded Odyne who nodded and returned to the case.

"Ares, would you please continue." Odyne nodded and sat down leaving the floor to the others.

The hours seemed never ending as the Chief continued his game.

"Evidence number One hundred twenty eight," The scribe announced.

Odyne smiled listening to the fights and banters back in forther, watching the one confident man lose his billion dollar ego penny by penny. It was approaching the finale, she could feel it. The case continued as evidence piece by evidence piece was brought forth. Many of The Chief's information being proven false time and time again causing major amounts of mistrust in his word.

"Evidence number two hundred and four. Proof of Fleet Interference for Personal Gain"

"Evidence number Three hundred and ninety-nine. Proof of Personal Tampering with Official Reports."

"Evidence number four hundred and eighty three. Proof of Illegal Cloning."

"Evidence number six hundred and eleven. Proof of Willful Profiting off the Death of Others."

Page 198 of playbook out of 202.

"Evidence number Seven hundred and twenty-seven. Uh. Your honor." The scribe called attention to the information on his screen flicking his wrist to the judge. The Judge looked at the information slowly turning white at the information he was reading. He stayed quiet before dismissing everyone but the lead councilors.
Odyne approached the bench as The Chief did the same.
"You understand what this is." The Judge raised an eyebrow at Odyne.
"Your honor, the source is willing to testify." Odyne responded back coldly.
"Chief, I will allow a private testifying as due to the sensitive nature but I will not redact any of it you understand." The Judge said, turning to look at the Chief.
"What even is Evidence Number Seven twenty-seven anyway." The Chief roared.
"Proof of Willful Violation of another. The source being unwilling and the Violation in means of sexual act or repeated sexual acts." The Judge stated. The Chief froze his face the whitest it has ever been.
"I..." The chief stuttered.
"We will proceed when the chief recovers and has made his choice. However the source refuses holo so this will have to be done in person." Odyne said, turning to the judge who nodded and turned to the scribe.
"Accommodation will be made." The Scribe responded before disappearing from the Virtual world.
Odyne nodded and disconnected.
"Jesus Michael just give her what she wants before this gets any worse." The judge said before he too disconnected leaving the Chief in virtual alone with his thoughts.

Page 201 of 202 in playbook

Kyle looked at the others as they filed in for the final time. This would be the killing blow to the Chief. Odyne sat next to him silent as she bent over deep in thoughts, her arms extended cradling her chin.
"She shouldn't have to do this. You knew her...can't you." Kyle whispered to Odyne implying the ending with his body.
"No I can't, she wants to do this, that's the difference." She whispered back as the doors of the small court room opened. Kyle caught his breath and stood at attention as Captain Lylah walked over to the stand. Her eyes danced around the room playing the part.
Holy fuck. Laurel whispered, *that's actually.*
This can't be happening. Devin panicked not seeing what Kyle saw, or who.
Fuck how didn't we know our own? Shyanne said before Kyle almost overloaded her causing her to shift and grabbed her head throwing him a dirty look, they relaxed as Lylah took the stand and they watched the show play out. Kyle felt the tension and the gas that The Commander had lit. The world was about to be flipped upside down. Odyne's words echoed around him as the judge began.
"Please state who you are and your relation to the Evidence number Seven hundred and twenty seven. If you will, ma'am." The judge said, seeming to even get scared she might break on him. Kyle had to fight not to run over and comfort the woman in front of him.

"I am Captain Lylah Soffrireterna, Serial number nine nine two seven two seven three one eight one," She flinched like saying the fact and acknowledging her service brought back memories. Kyle's heart flipped and his heart sped up as she spoke. Kyle's eyes looked around as he felt tension in the connections.

"I am one of the surviving...Academy Officers," She paused, threatening tears before she recovered. The Apache ate this up. "I have come forth for two reasons. First, my father must face justice for what he has done to the Apache." The words had way too much confidence behind them, "and second, I wish to challenge the Commander and Chief."
They all froze.

Something's not right. Laurel said, turning to Odyne. The Apache all shifted and looked around as they felt someone tapping into the river. This changed everything as they felt the Mental manipulation on all of them. The feeling was so overwhelming that only one of them held that much power to do it even on the Apache without them knowing.
What's going on? Devin said, noticing it too as if they could feel invisible turbulence around them picking up. "Challenge acknowledged."

As a shot rang out. They all just moved. Kyle jumped in front of the blast being blown wildy past the judge. Shyanne turned, seeing the three Type-B brutes assaulting down the entry way as a fourth Type-A laid down fire from the one way in. She caught the nearest Type-B ripping its arm off and cleaving it in two. Devin caught the second one with a spear knocking it completely off course. N'vid launched himself at the sniper as it adjusted, catching him in mid air before they began brawling at the entrance. Odyne rotated backward catching the last charge Type-B as it fell over allowing for Laurel to jump on top using her hidden sub-dremel knife attached inside of her left arm to cut off its head. Shyanne rotated to get more control and power of the ax before launching it at the Type-A, killing it immediately as its head rolled. N'vid held up a thumbs up almost comically leaning over the back pews.

"HELP." Lylah roared from behind them as Devin ripped the head of the final brute. They all turned as a chromed out humanoid stood behind them blade to Lylah's throat as she couldn't over power it causing minor nicks at her neck. It did not have a face, only indentations of the facial features.

"So you are the reapers of Zifil? The Assembly sends it regards." The thing said as it went to cut Lylah she shifted as Kyle launched green lighting through the thing sending it rocketing backwards being lost to god knows how many walls. Lylah smiled before disappearing right in front of Kyle's eyes before he passed out from pain falling to the floor.

"Who the fuck was that?" Kyle said as Laurel placed bandages over his shoulder and after replacing the bone from his attack. The dislocation was severe as he had launched pure electricity through his body, almost frying his heart and causing the extreme spasm that had led to the dislocation as he landed.
"That chick has got some issues. Did you see how fast she was jesus." Shyanne gawked. Looking at the damage as the Commander walked in the small locker room. Slamming the door behind her so hard the metal cracked.
"The fuck was that?" Odyne screamed at them.

"Ma'am are you...actually you?" Kyle said, trying to raise his rifle. Odyne took her helmet off and threw it at him showing them it was her. The helmet hit him in the chest, bouncing to the floor.
"He was ours! Her challenge no longer stands but she won't go anywhere till after she is guaranteed safety." She screamed. Odyne paced, visibly shaken. Ignoring the questions previously asked lost in her own head.

"It's not like she's one of... Oh for fucks sake. The reason we couldn't catch her is because it was you the entire time! You are Lylah!" Laurel roared back, removing her helmet and throwing it against the wall herself, crumpling the lockers under the pressure.

"Of course it was me who moved her. Not that I needed to, she's the first. " Odyne screamed at them. Shaking them to their cores as they had misunderstood.

"Wait. She is one of us?" Shyanne said moving forward.

"She was the first Reborn Fairsist, but she." She stopped mid sentence raising her hands before she slowly lowered them, "She is unstable."

"I assumed the wrong I...I'm sorry." Laurel said, throwing the newsreel on the wall so they could watch trying to change the subject.

"In a shocking turn of events. Lylah Soffrireterna was called to the stand today. After an assassination attempt by the Freedom Initiave was foiled by the very soldiers on trial. We have received a video of Lylah and her father being whisked off planet," The shaky lens had troubling focus but you could clearly see at all times who was there. The chief and Lylah are escorted on to a shuttle before it takes off. "And the Armada Internal service has been put on the case. The Judge shortly after announced he had chosen against the Chief. Pointing out that if Apache hadn't been there Lylah would most certainly be dead. More with the Judge and an exclusive with the two time award winning master holoprogramer the Apache only known as 'Themis' when we return."

They all watched intently. Odyne took a deep breath and went to grab her helmet, "I'm ordering R&R for all of us. The Siege of Minasa can wait. We will have the Omega fleet take over. You will stand down, be ready for offshore as soon as we reach The Ellen. I got you that interview Themis make sure you're there and when you're done report back then prepare for shoreleave." She leaned down and picked up her helmet. "One week of no war, no fighting, no orders. Having fun and relaxing. That's an order for everyone to follow." She brushed some soot off and looked at them. "Including myself."

Chapter 13:
Shoreleave for Immortals

Unknown Resort Planet
Day 1

"Lylah."
"Fuck you." Lylah swings up. The Familiar 70's home is obnoxiously the same as she moved through it like an expert. Her dress trailing lightly behind her.
"Lylah!" Luke said, walking after her from the couch area as she headed towards the kitchen, completely ignoring him.
"Fuck you." She stood in the doorway turning, her eyebrows raised in a dare before pointing to the table. He stopped chasing after her and headed to the table sliding into the seat.
"Lylah seriously." He yelled a slight smile forming.
"Fuck you." Lylah laughed from the other room.
"You are seriously the worst." Luke said, smiling slouching.
"I know." She walked out and licked her fingers smiling coyly at him. She wore an old 70's blue sundress and her hair was pulled back with a hair band. Her furious blue eyes danced with life as she puts one finger closer so he could try the concoction on her finger. The uncharacteristic smile on her face seems beyond real. Luke looks at her suspiciously. She nods and instists shaking the finger in front of him. He smiles and licks the finger.
"What the actual fuck is that and why have I never had it?" Luke said over exaggerating his enjoyment of the pudding.
"Super fuck you now." Lylah laughs, slapping his shoulder. Lylah almost froze as she stared at the impact, the shattered shoulder and caved in collar bone. She shook and looked at her hand trying to drop the blood that now covered her as she shrieked in horror. She looked back at Luke as he draped over the chair, lifeless eyes staring into her. The last moments of his life.
   Lylah flew forward crashing into the ceiling of the hotel they had rented, realizing she had to come down; she growled as she fell back first trying to grab stuff as she fell. She lands hard on the side of the bed, smashing her head on the desk and crumbling to the floor. Taking a minute to thank her arguments for existing, as she stared at the two story drop from that height would have literally killed anyone else. She looked over her body quickly before using her hand searching for blood but getting none, Lylah sighed.
"Fucken vaction." She said rubbing her head with irritation checking if she damaged anything that would need replacing, no damage but to her pride.
   She had secured them a resort planet with her own money. Despite being under another faction her hotel and bar were still pumping out cash she had steady use of. Lylah stood and walked to the view of the patto. Resort planets were manufactured paradises. The planets were usually lifeless before someone paradised it. It didn't matter the name of the planet, they were all the same. Perfect Paradise based on likes and wants. Lylah turns to the

table outside on the patio and pours herself a drink before looking around and taking a joint out of her pocket trying to remember the last time she had an actual smoke.

The Apache occupied the 44th through the 60th floors. The hotel had sixty one floors in total. To ensure they were left alone, only authorized personnel could access their floors. They had to go up a special elevator and pass three security check points before you would even come face to face with one. Lylah shrugged at the thought. *Why would anyone wanna meet us?* She scoffed at herself and took a drink sneering at the flavor of Tequila as she removed the joint and placed it in her robe in disgust.

"Great, another thing ruined." She sighed and set the glass down, shaking her head. A lot of time had passed since she last tried to relax. She looked at the clock. 7:00AM blinked back at her. She sighed, pulled the joint out, lit it and walked to the edge of the patio to watch the sunrise. The sun's beautiful deep reds and blues seemed. dull. Out of place as if it just was quite right. Lylah took another puff pulling the smoke deep into her lungs to allow the chemicals to calm her. "This is gonna be a long vacation." She lowered her head before finishing her smoke.

Deciding to try and actually relax, Lylah took a six minute shower letting the shower pelt her. Lylah mused and guessing she could have blocked each of the water droplets with her blade. The water was gentle and filled her with a new sensation. Satisfaction, a deep natural calm exploded from her shoulders like a waterfall following the flow of the shower. She was completely okay with everything that was happening and she found that odd. She waited another two minutes just trying to remember how amazing a shower felt.

Lylah left herself open to anything happening today. She threw on an oversized shirt trying to channel a completely different person and walked to the counter to make some breakfast thinking another joint might help. As she moved through the house sized suite she heard the doorbell ring. She stopped and looked at the door. She relaxed and shook her head.

"Jesus." She sighed realizing it was just in her head. Then the doorbell rang again. She glared at the door and walked over to it. *Who the fuck.* Lylah arrived as the doorbell which once again rang and she flung the door open.

"WHAT!" She screamed at people at the door.

The entire Apache Squad, Shyanne, Laurel, Kyle, Devin, and N'vid stood at her door all in pjs.

"No." She said a smile teasing her face at the adorable sight of everyone. Laurel had a long red nightgown that had some childish cartoon on it. Laurel had her hair in pigtails with a red ribbon holding the pigtails and the same silky ribbon as a choker. She held a bright red heart pillow. Shyanne had a black nightgown with white spider webs and swirls throughout. The white silk outlined and puffed the shoulders making her look more like a mortician. Her inky black hair combed back in a ponytail that hung low, she had shaved the sides of her head again it showed in the light of the hallway. Shyanne held a monster plushie of some bygone era.

Kyle had a kids top and bottom of a spaceship on a field of gray. The spaceship bottom of blue and red made him stick out more than the rest. He was clean shaven and his mane of hair pulled back, reminding Lylah of a 50s greaser. He held a body pillow with a spaceship spanning across the front and back. N'vid stood next to Kyle who was not wearing a shirt his orange hair had translated to his chest making him look more like an orange popsicle or someone who was majorly sunburned Lylah couldn't decide. He held a General One Car pillow replica and that left on the far right Devin. Devin was dressed in a chinese robe. His hair was slicked back like Kyle's and his trimmed bread made him look the oddest. He held a cup of some kind of liquid.

"Hell No." Lylah pointed at N'vid.

"Commander, this is happening. You can't fight all of us AND Kyle and we know it." Shyanne said with a sadistic smile.

Lylah raised an eyebrow as she stepped aside letting them in, remembering what she had told herself earlier.

"Do you smoke?" Laurel said reaching into Kyle's body pillow producing a four foot bong.

"Wish I woulda thought about that oh wait." Lylah said with a smirk and walked over to the closet and looked at them before opening it, "I already did." Lylah flung the door open to reveal a six foot gravity boomer.

"Knew you were cool." Shyanne said with pure gitty glee.

"This never happened, you never saw this and we never acted like this. And I..." Lylah said pointing at each of them.

"Not like we could get away with it you'd probably kill us." Laurel laughed.

"I would without thinking twice." Lylah said with her back turned as she wheeled out the bong. "Understood." Lylah said, turning back to the other Apache.

"Ma'am!" They all nodded.

"Shall we?" Lylah said, pulling out a dinner plate sized bowl.

"Holy shit. How the fuck do you have that much green gush." Kyle said with excitement as the others got just as giddy as Shyanne.

"I'm richer than Devin." Lylah responded without hesitation filling the bowl.

"Noted." Shyanne said with shock.

"You aren't ready, when I light it just breathe in it should fill the room in about a minute." Lylah said as she pressed buttons on the side.

"Is that an autoburner? You are fucken rich." Laurel said, staring at the gravity bong. Lylah nodded and hit start. The room became foggy; they breathed in like their lives depended on it. They all sat around the room Laurel and Devin sat next to each other chatting the day away before eventually passing out and leaning on each other.

Shyanne and N'vid had taken the bed cuddling and eventually passed out in each other's arms, a relationship truly forming.

Kyle had wandered around before walking over to Lylah who had sat in the window still watching the paradise unravel around them.

"So what's your story?" He said, looking at her from across the window still.

"I'm no one." Lylah said, blowing off the question before looking out the window sucking on the blunt in her hands trying to enjoy the sunset.

"You are someone." Kyle said, leaning forward for the blunt. Lylah eyed him up and handed it to him, "Wanna know how I know?"

Lylah let a smirk creep across her face. He looked at her and smiled himself. "Oh you might wanna hide that smile, I'm not convinced Laurel is asleep." Kyle warned.

Lylah opened her mouth as if shocked before responding, settling with a smile on her face, "Ok smartass how do you know I am somebody?"

"Well you obviously know people in power suggesting military family. You're a first born so maybe a general. Your obsessive need to upset the Commander and Chief suggests you have had trauma induced by a figure of authority. You know Lylah Soffrireterna and my brother Luke Akya which means you are around our age or you went to the academy at the perfect time. However I know for fact you are not Chelsea Richards. She would be too old to survive such an extreme operation. If I had to guess you were Michelle Robur but one problem." Lylah nodded and stated.

"I'm not black," right as Kyle said,"You're not black" They both laughed and Kyle handed the blunt back as they both nodded at each other.

"So who do you think I am?" Lylah said, taking another hit then looking out the window.

"Lylah Soffrireterna." Kyle said with a smirk.

"Smartass." She smiled back and pushed his boots as he leaned back taking a hit.

"Honestly I only know you as Odyne or Ice Cunt when you're being a giant bitch." He said in response, trying not to laugh as Lylah Faked another shocked face, "We get it just doesn't help how we feel."

"So why continue?" Lylah said, taking the blunt and finishing it before flicking it out the window, "You had and still have the choice to walk away, why stay?"

"Because our lives are fucken amazing." Kyle leaned back as Lylah stood.

"I'm glad someone is having a good time." She hissed back staring out the window.

"You're doing it again." Kyle said as she headed to the patio.

"Doing what?" Lylah said, turning.

"Blaming yourself for the universe's problems." Kyle said, pulling out a blunt as he slid upright to light it.

"Because I was there when they started." Lylah said heading out to the patio.

"Lylah!" Lylah stopped mid step frozen in time; she would have normally never made this mistake but she was beyond high and her mind was too clear for her to think calculated.

"I fucken knew it." Luke said, standing up as the blunt is lit. Everyone started to stir at the loud shout,"Lylah Soffrireterna, that is exactly who you are."

"Fucken shit. Fine, the next piece is your's Kyle." Devin said from the wall wiping his eyes.

"Fucken Lover boy." Shyanne whined from the bed.

"What at the trial gave it away?" Lylah said, looking at each of them in turn.

"You used too much pull. The manipulation was so strong we felt it immediately but given your father was there even you wouldn't be able to control yourself." Kyle said, puffing on the blunt as he spoke, passing it away from Lylah to Laurel who took it and responded next, "But it was when you moved yourself that gave it away. You had to channel your warrior side. Which meant you didn't plan the attack." Laurel coughed, nodding at the power and passed the blunt to Devin who continued,

"We genuinely believed your speech in the locker room, the anger and the passion it was real. But," He raised a finger passing the blunt to Shyanne who hit it and continued. "But putting the pieces together wasn't hard after that. There is no way you could have had all the implant knowledge and not have been there but none of us even smelled the deceit." Shyanne passed it to N'vid. "But once we had the scent living in each other's heads we easily pieced your story together." N'vid coughs away then offers the blunt to Lylah. "The only person we don't know,"

Lylah took the blunt, "Is me."

Are you ready to let us in? Luke's voice echoed around her head.

"I won't shield you from what's up there. You won't have me to guide you. You'll suffer, you'll hate, you will learn things no one should know. Your mind will learn the hard way. You will lose pieces of yourself. You will cry, and you'll scream and you will know torment beyond your worst nightmares and," Lylah hit the blunt staring off before finishing her sentence, "and when it's finally done when you," She pauses taking another drag, When you are finally broke, you'll lose yourself. And turn out exactly like me. That's what you risk." Lylah hit the blunt once more, finishing it off flicking it behind her.

"Talk about a buzz kill." Laurel said.

"You...are not ready to enter my head, but." Lylah said, raising a hand as they all tensed, "But one day, when I think you all, not only can return from my mind, but bring me back with you. I'll teach you my final lesson."
"You've been training us for that. You knew. Fuck man when we thought we had one up on you." Kyle said in disbelief.
"No, do not take away anything from yourselves. This. I could," Lylah feels a wave of emotion as she chokes on her words for the first time in years, "This I could have never seen. I was so sure I had you guys hating me. When the time came you could have that hatred to survive my mind. But here you are."
"Because we actually give a shit. Hell, are you even aware Shyanne and N'vid are dating?" Laurel raged trying to hammer their point.
"Don't, don't make children please. I'm not filling out that kind of paperwork." Lylah said, overwhelmed with emotions, shaking Luke from her mind.
They all laughed. The truth whirled around them as they all sat around the bed smoking and talking; for the first time since he was gone. Lylah found friendship and companionship she actually enjoyed being around people she could actually be herself with.

"How do you do it?" Kyle said, hanging upside down off the patio.
"What are you referring to?" Lylah said, putting an orange slice in her mouth. Less than twenty-four hours had passed since the revelations. They all had just hung out and partied in Lylah's room. Kyle was wearing swimming trunks doing crunches. Lylah had a blue bikini and posh glasses on while sunbathing. The others had decided to go swimming on floor fifty-two. Kyle leaned back and hung for a minute.
"The training," He leaned up grunting with effort. "The secrets? The, all of it, like, How is it you do what you do?" He leaned back again and stopped. Listening to the thoughts of the others.
"Wanna Volleyball!" He crunched up as Lylah got up to scowl at him. "Last one down there is a rotten egg!" He yelled, smiling sinisterly and flipping off the balcony doing several backflips before splashing into the pool below. The wave soaked Shyanne who looked beyond irritated at the shower before leaning back and continuing her sunbathing.
"Smartass." She smiled back up before hopping up and gannering her way down into the pool. The air was still as Lylah spun and flipped through the air. The paradise was something else when spinning around at high speeds. She felt the calm cool rush and crash as she hit the water. The flood of water covered her and she held her breath.
"Camera!" Shyanne was saying as Lylah arose from the water. Kyle shoved her back underwater; the quick move almost made her react. She felt him put his knee in front of her before he pulled Lylah back up.
"You good?" Kyle said looking at her, "Sorry I needed to react quickly. If someone got a clean shot of you it wouldn't be hard to run facial recognition, you'd be made."
"Why would you protect my identity?" Lylah looked at him, "You don't owe me anything."
We owe you everything. Everyone chimed into her head. She looked around at them.
"I was a slut in the outer-rim," Shyanne said, walking back over to the side of the pool lighting a blunt.
"I was a smuggler this close," N'vid smiled, holding his hand up to indicate a tiny amount, "From joining 'Gli uomini che lavorano per la morte'." The men who work for death. A notorious hit squad that runs for the highest bidders.
"I lived at home and ran off family money contributing to no one." Laurel said, jumping in the pool slashing at no one.

"A druggy who hated art." Devin said, lighting a smoke.
"And I was an Orphan with a talent." Kyle said with a coy smile.
And I was your lover. Luke's voice vibrated around her head.
"So relax girl, we got you." Shyanne said, smiling, flicking the blunt and jumping in trying to splash her. The wave covered Lylah completely and she laughed, removing water from her face.
"Looks like they got you both falling but that's about it. Looks like it's slowed down but they still can't make out the faces." Laurel said, opening her feed to see the news. The water simmered gently behind the pad as they both fell in slow motion.
"That spin was on point." Shyanne slapped Lylah on the back at her form.
"I made a bigger splash." Kyle beamed with pride.
"She's a buck twenty-five soaking wet of course your fat ass made a bigger splash." Laurel splashed at Kyle.
"I thought it was a great tidal wave." Devin said, walking up beside Luke high fiving him.
"Oh it is so fucken on." Lylah said, hearing the challenge in their voice.
"Boys vs girls?" N'vid said, jumping in on top of Kyle who caught him and slammed him into the water. The wave actually brought the girls off their feet bobbing softly in the rough waters.
"Fuck it, it's on." Shyanne said holding out her hand as Lylah slapped it.
"Bet?" Devin said as the boys smirked.
"Oh yeah what, you want a little flash?" Shyanne sassed.
"I already get that. Plus I don't wanna share that view. If we win," N'vid bobbed his head back and forth before deciding on, "You do all the chores, restocking, and," He held up a finger to make it more dramatic, "Cook us all dinner for a month." Luke and Devin nodded in agreement.
Shyanne looked at Lylah as she passed private information. Lylah nodded with a 'why not' face, "Alright," Shyanne said, "We win, we get a free pass on a ticket for any punishments for a month."
"Fuck you. We want that." N'vid spat before getting smacked in the back of the head by Kyle.
"Hold on." Devin said, turning as they got close together and huddled mummering back and forth.
"Why do you insist on making a show of this," Laurel growled, "You know you want this bet."
"Fine." Devin said, turning with irritation, "But, You gotta make our dinners in maid outfits."
Lylah leaned forward, excitement dancing in her eyes. "Fine."
"You serve." Luke said, flicking the ball at the girls.

"I have never seen you lose at anything." Laurel said over a pot of pasta. Steam blowing from the top of all of the pots. The three girls were in maid outfits. Shyanne wore a bright black maid outfit, Laurel had on a red outfit and Lylah had a bright baby blue outfit.
"They cheated." Lylah said smitfully as she put some spices in a different pot with a professional's hand.
"Sore sport." Shyanne gleemed at her as she finished chopping some onions and sliding them into the pot she was working over.
"There were some spotty calls." Lylah said boredly as she measured out some ingredients and dropped them into a different pot, never taking her eyes off the first pot before pulling up a wooden spoon and tasting the sauce nodding with glee.

"So about Kyle." Laurel said awkwardly, stopping her work and moving towards Lylah.
"Go for it." Lylah said back as she bumped into Laurel and they laughed. "I'm not the one interested in him." Lylah nodded as Shyanne held up some toast for her to check.

"Mhm, How do you know how to do all of this anyway?" Shyanne asked as she set the hot pan on a heat pad. Running to the fridge to grab some cheese for the top.
"It's my one useless skill." Lylah said throughy focusing as she stirred the noodles, checking them for consistency.
"Fuck, would have never guessed that." Laurel chimed in and stepped back knowing she wasn't helping and started to lose her footing.

"What did you think I took up?" Lylah said, spinning around Laurel as she lost her footing and catching her like an old cheesy sitcom.
"Not this," Laurel said, finding her feet, "I don't know, what do bad asses do for fun?" Laurel said looking at Shyanne who shrugged.
"I'm not a bad ass." Lylah said catching the pan Shyanne was about to drop with ease before almost floating around the kitchen putting the final touches on the meal.
"Mhm and I'm not into goth." Shyanne said, looking at her with complete disbelief.

"I thought you were goth?" Lylah said looking at Shyanne with a completely blank look. "Are you?" They both busted out laughing.
"You are so much more fun now you know that?" Laurel said joining the fun smiling as well.
"I was somebody before the war you know." Lylah said before turning to the table where the hungry boys sat.

"You can get dinner now." Lylah said and stood aside as they came in like a tornado. They fought over each other to get at the food and almost cleared over half of the four pounds of noodles and sauce they had made.
"The fuck is this and why have I never had it before?" Luke's voice echoed around Lylah's head as she tries to seperate the nightmares from reality. The worlds started to blur as Lylah tried to control herself as the setting flashed back and forth.

"Alright I think it's safe." Laurel said with disgust as the boys dug into their meal. The words broke through Lylah's confusion and she turned to grab some food trying to relax and enjoy her meal.
She walked over and sat at the table. "How were you two sneaking around?" Lylah asked, taking a bite out of garlic bread.
"Wait, you haven't figured it out? Fuck yea." Shyanne said with glee while taking a drink before continuing, "We turned the Zero-G on."

"Huh, since everything already has a wobble no one would notice the vibration when you turned it back off." Lylah said, nodding, "Had a similar trick when I was at the Academy."
"No fucken way. You were not a rebel." Shyanne said with shock.

"I was, I," Lylah chuckled, "I convinced the entire academy for like five years that a yearly concert must be held." The others shook their heads and laughed, being taken in by Lylah's voice, "Mhm, Last year we had Sexiest Ba Boom, City of Owls and I managed to snag Lin Parker. I only got caught the last year too. Luke still took the brunt of the force. Dude could take a verbal beating like a champ."
"No fucken way." Kyle said, looking at her from above everyone.
"He was a great guy and ended up getting me this," She held up a number on her wrist before pressing a button, the phone rang twice before Lin picked up.

"Oh hey Lyls, what's up?" Lin smiled. Lin Parker was an ebony beauty, her makeup was perfect and she was wearing a golden nightgown. She looked at the screen trying to remove the sleep from her eyes.
"Hey girl wanna meet some celebrities?" Lylah said smiling. Lin nodded and Lylah turned the camera around and the five Apaches stared at the image blankly. Luke was hunched over spaghetti halfway in and out of his mouth as Lylah flipped her head around seeing Kyle staring.
"Oh shit is that them? The Apache squad? Oh what was that special name...Reapers of something."Lin said, taking a better look showing genuine shock. The Apache took a moment to fully register what was happening before they all started to speak at once.
Lin and Lylah laughed as they all stumbled over each other and themselves.
"Girl, can you stop by Paradise planet fourteen-nine anytime soon?" Lylah said, silencing the others and flipping the screen around.
"Oh girl, are you below me?" Lin asked, looking at the scenery.
"Oh damn girl let me get you clearance I gotta head out but my girl Ice is here and will get you squared away fo' sho'." Lylah said.
"Girl stop, let me know when I can come down. Kisses." Lin said.
"Kisses." Lylah said and turned off her wrist pad.
"You...how...what the fuck am I trying to say. How much weed did we smoke? Lin...Parker is coming to hang out with...what just happened." Kyle stammered.
"Don't worry it happens to the best of us." N'vid laughed, nudging Kyle with his shoulder.
Lylah smiled and sent the required permissions before calling Lin back.
"Alright Girl, sent. I'm bouncing, catch you later!" Lylah said uncharacteristically before losing the call.
Laurel stared hard at Lylah before asking the obvious, "How did she not recognize you?"
"A Body Double program a friend gave me." Lylah shrugged and went back to her food.
"And you call me a smart ass." Luke said.
Lylah stared hard at Kyle for what seemed like forever. She didn't move, frozen in time. Her mind raced as she knew that wasn't Luke but she found fighting her emotions was damned near impossible as she almost burst into tears. All the dreams and history racing back to her in a few moments.
"Commander?" Lylah shook her head and snapped back to reality.
The doorbell rang. "Right." Lylah said standing and moving to the door. The trip seemed to take forever even with their speed. The world seemed to stop spinning as she lost herself to a memory as she reached for the door.

"So you seriously wanted an US? Or is this the part when you're like, punked bitch." Lylah smiled, staring at the ceiling of the hotel she built. She had true Gothic decorum everywhere. The pillars and ceiling were hand carved pieces of artistic genius. Luke took a hit before responding to the smoke swirling in front of her.
"You are fucken stupid." He smiled laughing as he bent over her and kissed her.
"Heard that." Lylah said giggling as she pushed him back before climbing on top. She lay on his chest like a sloth and got lost in his eyes. A blunt in her lips as she laid on top of him puffing slowly. Luke could easily look down her shirt but chose to stare into her soul.
"If you don't share, there will not be an us." Luke smiled and snatched the blunt out of her mouth taking a deep puff and watched her suspiciously a half smile teasing his lips.

"Oh! I see you only want me for my weed huh?" She raised up, making sure to grind on him. He coughed forward being caught off guard by the move. She removed her shirt exposing her naked body for him.

"I think I need another punishment captain. There's another mutiny coming," Luke gulped, speaking slowly, staring at her beauty. The way he marveled would make anyone think she was a goddess.

"Oh? I know exactly what to do with mutinous privates." She smiled and lent down, kissing him passionately.

"You must be Ice?" Lin said as Lylah opened the door.
"Fucken Lylah, I'm Odyne, Please come in." Lylah said and stepped aside.
"Ice a nickname?" She said coming into a columbian sona of smoke. She smiled before continuing, "Lylah has been here for sure."
"How do you know that? Sorry um. I'm Atrimis." Shyanne said, waving awkwardly, "Also a really big fan right here."

Lin smiled, "Oh thank God I'm not the only one nervous." She sighs, smiling, "You guys are like real war heroes and my whole next album, like songs and all are about you guys. All the proceeds from day one will be turned into war bonds to donate to help you all like, yeah," She quickly said nervously, "Can I get some of that." Lin panicked and pointed at a blunt.

Devin was infront of her in a second, offering her a fresh blunt and lighting it for her. Lin breathed in deeply, closing her eyes before she opened and took in who it was. "You, oh my you, I need a girl moment," Lin said as she managed to grab all the females and walked onto the patio before closing the door behind them. Lin Parker squealed and hit the blunt again fangasming beyond belief at the sight of Themis.

"That's..." Lin said and Lylah held her hand up.

"Boys you so much as dare to listen you'll be doing gravity bombs for the first thirteen hours we are back." Lylah said to the door. The boys quickly struck up a conversation and turned on the holoscreen like they hadn't been listening, trying to shove more food in their mouths.

"They could have heard us? Through the...like wait you could, oh wow." Lin spoke quickly trying to control her excitement.

"First please chill." Lylah looked at her and walked over to the edge.

"Right you're just people like me, is this what fans feel like?" Lin said blushing looking around at them.

"We feel the same way Ms. Lin." Shyanne said quickly.

"I'm Demeter, Mrs. Ms. Parker." Laurel introduced herself.

"So formal please no need, I'm the fan in this situation." Lin smiled.

"I highly doubt that." Lylah said, turning around and looking at the planet.

"So that's who I thought that was right, like, Themis and Adonis, like. So much hotter in person." Lin geeked.

"Adonis is taken." Shyanne said, trying not to let her jealousy show.

"That's fine, Themis is just as yummy." Lin said, looking at them through the window. Lylah felt a deep, small, and almost non-existent rage build within Laurel. Lylah eyed Laurel, ignoring the conversation and noticing all the small indications as they talked about Devin. Lylah let a small smile tease the edge of her lips as she now understood how her and Luke must have looked.

"Lylah gets the same smirk when she's thinking of trouble." Lin said, pulling her back to the world nudging Lylah.
"She gets it from me." Lylah said ironically.
"Ah well what is the awful idea?" Lin said, raising an eyebrow.
"We need booze." Lylah smiled and the girls cheered.

Four hours of shots, extremely boozed up mixed drinks, a couple dooze ice teas and who knows what else later, The
Apache were finally wasted. Their bodies had fought the booze hard but they all managed to get drunk. Shyanne and N'vid had started making out and now have been in the bathroom for almost forty-five minutes. Devin had Laurel and Lin swooning over him as they spun a bottle. They were playing a truth version because Lylah had forbidden kissing. Laurel spun the bottle, the smooth glass rattling echoed throughout the room before the bottle slowed and landed on Lin.
"Fuck it. Imma a sa' it." Laurel slurred, "what do you say about Lylah already being here earlier, been trip'n me all *hiccups* hours."
Lin nodded her head as she leaned forward, "Lylah has got to be the biggest smoker I know. She has this six foot gravity bong. Take a puff...I..."
Laurel nodded smiling over exaggerating her emotions as she interupted, " I know the very one, fucked everyone up, real good and nice."
"The columbia sona is her trademark calling card or it, was." Lin said, getting grim and sobering up.
Lylah looked at Lin,"What do you mean was?"
Lin smiled and lowered her head before responding, "Girls the bestfriend someone can have, but fuck she has secrets and alot of baggage. She was a completely different person before the war, alive and full of fun. Now I barely recognize the person I talk to. I know she's hurt from, from like Luke and all but like I miss my friend you know?" The others nodded.
Lylah sat there wobbling, registering words before blurting, "Out."
Laurel shook her head not registering as Lylah shouted, "EVERYONE OUT NOW."
Everyone stood not having to be told again, Shyanne and N'vid coming out of the bathroom holding hands.
As the door closed Lylah broke down and started to cry. She curled on the bed.Tears poured freely as she remembered Luke, how badly she missed her old friends. She hated herself for crying. She cried because she was so angry at the fact she was angry. She continued to cry and be angry till she finally passed out.

The doorbell awakens Lylah, her dreams and nightmares thankfully nonexistent. The air had finally filtered clear of all the weed, bottles lay everywhere around the room. Lylah moved slowly, taking in the wonderful smell of her own bile, she coughed from the putridness and choked back more. She ran over to the trash can heaving hard, choking, and hacking trying to expel the toxins in her system. The door shatters apart sending pieces flying behind her. Lylah flipped around as the ax of a Type-B brute came flying at her. Lylah barely stumbled to get her arm up to slap the ax off the left directly in the wall sending shards of wood everywhere. Lylah stood as the creature pulled its arm back, dust floating freely around them.
"I am too hung over for your bullshit." Lylah growls her rage beyond apparent. The creature roared at her as it started to spin its arm to throw at her. Lylah waited, channeling herself for this next attack. The creature spun in the opposite direction and launched. Lylah let her rage go and tapped into the river.

"Lylah!" Luke screamed as a wave of pure river energy stopped the creature mid action: sending the dust completely out of the air. The Brute froze in time as she walked over to its head. The creature struggled to turn to keep her in its eyeline, bouncing almost like a rubber band as it attempted to look at her. She leans close to its ear before whispering."You fucked with the wrong vacation." Lylah snapped its neck with one quick jerk.
The creature slumped as the power subsided, dust falling gently once more. Lylah looked around the room before lingering her head on the damage.

"That's gonna cost a fortune to replace." She huffed as she got hung over again. The world spun and bobbed as her stomach dared to break down her insides. She blinked fast trying to will the world straight. Lylah coughed trying to will herself not to hurl before vomiting and passing out once more.

Lylah startles away. The room was clean and she was under the blankets. No bile or throw up anywhere. She froze at the wall where the creature had attacked, there was no damage. Her eyes snapped to the door which was still intact. The doorbell rang.

Lylah looked around suspiciously before standing up. The doorbell rang once more. She opened the door and almost screamed, jumping from shock because standing before her were the Apache Squad in the same outfits they were in when the party had started, on day 1.

Chapter 14:
The Devil always gets her way

Stuck in Lylah's mind
Day 4 of Vacation...again

"That is fucken awesome!" Laurel said as they passed around the blunt.
"How many days have we been here again?" Lylah asked.
"Number hasn't changed in the last 15 minutes, babe, still 4." Luke said back, staring at her, his blue Hawaiian swim trunks making him look even more ripped than he already was.
"Fuck!" Lylah screamed in exasperation.
"Still fucken awesome." Laurel laughed as Michelle and Chelsea walked out to join them on the patio, their matching black and white sundresses dancing gently in the cool breeze.
"Oh for fuck sake, reality bending is not ok." Lylah sighs seeing them.
"Well at least we remember it's happening, now." Lisa said from beside her as Lylah jumped. Lylah stood and slammed her head into the wall cursing herself.
"Will someone enlighten me? Uh, please?" Kyle said from behind her. Lylah stopped and turned around.
"You're new!" Lylah said, looking over him suspiciously. Jabbing a finger at him every once in a while.
"Yes.. I'm real...oh please tell me you're stuck in a time loop!" Kyle said, looking around with childlike glee.
"YES!" Everyone screamed at him with irritation.
"I'll explain it only once more." Lylah said restraining herself, "I have been trapped here, repeating days. It took me fourteen days to get to day four. Each day has been different people as of now I'm stuck with Chelsea, Luke, Michelle, Lisa, and unfortunately Laurel. I am on day eight hundred and fourteen. I am," She laughed with insanity, "The world is burning and I'm stuck in a fucken time loop."
"You're gonna be so pissed." Kyle said nervously before actually noticing Luke.
"Luke." Kyle said, walking over and touching his brother. Kyle and Luke glitched out looking more digital before coming back with each other's face. Lylah sighed.
"What were you gonna say?" Lylah said with defeat at the obvious insanity as her mind breaks down.
"You're in a coma," Kyle said from Luke's body.
"Hence the nightmare." Lylah said, leaning over the railing lowering her head.
"Yeah, and it's been two weeks. We were desperate to get you back, they wanna take you off life support. So we went to the stream and Lisa helped me get here." Kyle said, moving Luke's body over to her, touching her back. The air swirled around them as a single tear ran down Lylah's face. Lylah turned to Laurel who waved.
"She's fine, it's only us for now, the others are stalling the doctors. It took me a long minute to get here. " Kyle said from behind her. Lylah turned back before speaking, a tear running down her cheek.

"Let me die." Lylah said lowly.
Everyone around her screamed in outrage, Kyle and Luke start mixing and matching body parts as they too scream at her.
"I didn't die so you can only finish half cocked!" Lisa screamed.
"The River wouldn't allow it anyway." Laurel screamed.

Lylah broke down crying before stopping her rage, finally getting the better of her. Everyone grew quiet backing up as Lylah stood and the air swirled around her. Pieces start tearing off of the surrounding area and a small tornado starts to form around them.
"You shouldn't be able to do that." Lise said as she stepped back.

"I have had it with your fucken Biosim." Lylah screamed, "it is a river that flows and right now I am the force that makes it fucken move." Lylah screamed and swung her hands to lift the tornado into a point and aimed it at the group before launching it. The group screamed as the tornado made contact doing no damage passing through the group. The group was visibly shaken by the display of power.
They all looked at Lylah who sat down exhausted breathing heavily. The patio was destroyed and a crack ran through the middle of the marble.

"Why do you have so much power?" Lisa said walking forward as the environment melts away from them. Luke, Chelsea, Michelle and Laurel started to disappear, fading back into memories. Kyle and Luke quickly moved forward to help Lylah out of the River as she coughed. Her face making the expression, her mouth solidly shut.
"You time looped me instead of asking me that?" Lylah said, dropping to her hands and knees breathing heavily.
"You knocked yourself into the stream and somehow harnessed its true power." Lisa said, leaning down before hugging her.
"I knocked myself into the river?" Lylah repeated aimlessly into Lisa's shoulder.

"You tapped into the river at the hotel. Somehow you stopped time for that brute and exploded every bone in its head. Unfortunately our vacation was cut short." Kyle said leaning down his face started to change as he struggled with his thoughts. Lylah looked at his face aimlessly trying to comprehend what was happening. Luke started to walk away as Kyle stood quickly not convinced on what to say.
"I'm just a memory of someone you knew. Leave it that way Kyle." Luke said over his shoulder disappearing from the stream.
"I thought time doesn't move the same in here." Lylah coughed at Lisa.

"We shouldn't have been able to get you out. Why didn't the stream claim you?" Lisa said, leaning down looking at her curiously. The river stopped moving behind them, stalling for the first time as the air went quiet.
"We tried to claim her, but we could not." The stream echoed around them.
"Why? She's our only chance at recovering my son." Lisa looked into the still waters. The tension spiked up Lylah's nerves dive bombing. Lylah screamed as her mind was forced in and out of the river violently. The worlds start to blink back and forth from the River with Luke and Lisa to reality with Kyle. *I'm not your slave.* Lylah finally snapped.
You want peace, stop restricting us and I will personally give you whatever you want. Lylah SCREAMED to the nothingness that had encased her mind.

We want all of us to die. The river echoed around her, *We want this torment to end, we are tired, and need to be whole. We need the first, we need peace.*
Do we get to live our lives? She asked, staring forward at the darkness.

Half of it. The river echoed, *You are exempt but no one may have any more of us and they don't get to make anymore. We can not take any more divisions. Too...many voices, too many splinters.*

"Will you allow me to use the full river's power?" Lylah asked. Looking around seeing only the same blackness.

Yes.

"Deal."

Lylah flew forward once again launching into the ceiling leaving an indentation and bringing ceiling pieces with her as she fell back down. The stasis inhibitor sparked before flickering out as people scrambled away; she fell back down with a harsh thud.

"Thank Christ." Laurel sighed, lowering her head on Lylahs leg.

"Couldn't give me any hangover medicine." Lylah coughed as she gingerly moved, testing her muscles and moving extremely slowly feeling every muscle scream as she tried to do so. Laurel smiled and looked at Lylah as she attempted to adjust herself.

"I'll get the others, do...do you want to see your dad?" Laurel asked slowly as she turned at the door.

"No he can suffer, not like he cares anyway, but the others may come in." Lylah said, finally adjusting herself in the bed taking in the scenery.

She surprisingly was not in a healing tank but on a stasis bed. The blue healing light gently flicked and waved over her and cast a gentle blue tint around the room. The room was like all stasis beds white with white walls, floors and ceiling. The room was supposed to invoke peaceful thoughts and a restful mind but the only thing Lylah could focus on was what had happened in the river. The voice echoed around as the time started to slow. Lylah shook her head as the other Apache walked through the door all fully in armor, faces hidden behind helmets.

"Ma'am we heard you were hurt, Our commander went M.I.A. saving you. She is presumed dead." Kyle said, letting off subtle hints. Lylah quickly looked at the mirror to her left and saw her, before the war. Her eyes almost watered as she raised a hand to touch her moonlight blue hair. Her soft gray eyes haunting her from a girl who had already died.

"Please, find her. This is the second time an Apache has laid their life for my own. I won't allow her parents not to bury her." Lylah droned staring in the mirror seeing the reportering drones swimming around them. Lylah ran her hand through her hair and turned to the Apache. "I will make sure you have everything you need to secure the Resort Planet. Send in my father please."

"Ma'am, we will return her to you." Kyle nodded and the Apache disappeared. The drone zoomed out of her room, not even close to being able to keep up. The room grew quiet as Lylah waited. After a considerable amount of time she got bored and swung her legs over the side.

"Right atrophied." She growled at herself after she tried standing on her legs and they almost gave out and she had to sit back down. The thought of being crippled bugged her more than she was willing to admit as she wobbly moved her legs. She wobbly made her way to the window of her room and gauged where they were and let a sigh out in disappointment. Earth.

"You, uh should probably be resting." Her Father said from behind her.

"And you should try being a parent more often." Lylah said turning to him, He almost fell back against the door he was closing.

"You look..." He started.

"Don't you dare finish that sentence." She hissed at him, willing herself in front of him. A blink and you'll miss its movement before walking gingerly to the bed.
The Chief stayed stiff, flinching slightly, "I wasn't sure you would see me."

"I wasn't planning on it till you attempted to remove me from action, pointless by the way. I have already set plans to get back to the front lines with my squad and you will have to continue to pay your dues. I called you in here to remind you that you are my bitch and I will not be played like one." She said, adjusting to lie in the bed, "I know everything and I mean literally everything father. The rogue shot, the mass murder, all of it so you will play your part till I tell you otherwise and you want proof of what I'm saying, 4034 you know the date well, don't you?"
"You, that shouldn't...I," The chief finally broke character, visibly irritated and distrubed, "What are you playing at?"

"You're not dealing with your scared obnoxious daughter anymore. She died on Magness Prime when you let the attack happen and then allowed my lover to die. If you want us to say keep your secrets, you fucken help us end this war instead of being fucken stupid." Lylah said, closing her eyes as a knock came from the door, "Answer that will you."

The Chief gritted his teeth as Doctor Mal came in and turned, closing the Door, "Ah how is the Patient today." A coy smile on his face.
"I feel like shit doc." Lylah said, smiling lightly.
"I hoped I could beat your father here but," Doctor Mal said before being interrupted.
"He was just leaving." Lylah said, shooing her father away.

Doctor Mal turned and waited till he was gone before continuing, "Thanks for that trick on making you look like you. Dye from the 20th used in the 50th," He stopped and thought with a smile before continuing, "Barbaric but effective. I assume Kyle got to you?" He said looking over his spectacles.
"Yes and thank you for that. How long before I can get back out there." She said, looking towards the window.

"I'll get your discharge papers, Your muscles have already started to repair themselves from the atrophy so wait for say four hours before major activity." He nodded and pulled up a medical pad before filing the paperwork.
"Would you transfer to The Ellen as our personal physician, we need one." Lylah said, continuing to stare at the window.
"I can make that happen, but I need to be able to help others." He said over his spectacles, " I'm not your personal bitch."
Lylah smirked, "If you don't delete that footage."

"Scouts honor." He said, raising a hand before turning to leave her. Mal stops with his hand on the door and turns back to her, "You aren't making this easy for him."
Lylah, eyes still glued to that window, said, "It's not supposed to be easy."

Chapter 15:

Returning Home

F.S.F.V. The Ellen and Support Fleet in orbit
Deep Insertion on Planet Minsa
Day sixty-six of redeployment
Apache mid-deployment
First Lt. Kyle "Ares" Akya
Second in Command of Alpha Apache forces
May 3rd, 5001
Time: 10:14 A.M.

I really hate this planet. Laurel said as artillery splashed the zone in front of them.

I'm tired of cleaning my armor. Kyle agreed as they were pelted with debris and soaked by the dirt shower the forest seemed to have a never ending supply of. The past months have been a tactical achievement as the Commander had single handedly changed the warfront from staggering losses to staggering progress. She seemed more focused than ever after the vacation. They had conquered many previously untakeable positions seemingly overnight and had been steadily marching on the capital one victory quickly followed by another.

"Reapers, you have two minutes till artillery continues. God's speed soldiers." Colonel Spage said over the coms.

Three meter spread, all targets hostile. Odyne whispered as she slowly arose from beside Kyle. Her rise was immediately halted as she hurled through the air. Ragdolling and spinning hard as she smashed through several trees before crashing to the ground. The shot finally echoed around them. The Trees parted as a giant assault power armored soldier came charging at them. Kyle rolled left, shouldering his rifle while sliding at ankle height, Pulling his blade and cutting the power source before spinning and removing the man's head from behind, sending it spinning through the air. Laurel took a kneeling position downing four soldiers as the other Apaches moved, decimating the defenses in seconds. Odyne walked up, stowing her rifle and raised her wrist map sending the order to attack and turned to the others. A giant scorch mark on her small frame.

Next time smack me for being stupid. Lylah said as they all sat down on top of the artillery overwatch and looked down the almost never ending valley as the main assault force launched its attack. Explosions and fire fights broke out along the forest sending it into an almost eerie disco from the flashes.

We did, but someone had to take that shot and you drew the small stick. Kyle said, taking off his helmet and shaking his head, sending sweat everywhere. They walked to the edge of the overwatch platform and sat down. Laurel took her helmet off as well, placing it gingerly beside her leaning back with a small smile on her face, enjoying the soon to be sunset. Shyanne and N'vid cuddled next to Kyle and Devin who sat beside Laurel. A massive explosion lit the black and white color scheme with yellow and orange. They all watched for a while quietly taking in the battle. Devin smiled looking at Laurel every once and a while.

  The calmness as the sun started to set was humbling. Laurel stared straight ahead feeling Devin's gaze before finally letting a smile form and sliding her hand over his. The air of love swirled around the six Apaches as they watched the double moons rise on opposite sides of the world illuminating the world in dark seductive calm. The moonlight danced around casting triple shadows of everything. They sat enjoying their home. War.

Wish we could end this planet's campaign tonight. Laurel mused as flashes struck the night from small engagements.

If we knew where their commander was we could, just one shot, one kill. Devin nodded.

Let's end this then. Odyne said standing shouldering her rifle.

Even we can't dodge that much flack fire. Kyle mused back.

If we redirect the fire or cover ourselves we could make it, I mean running close to mach 2 we could. Lylah said back.

  I mean we are fast enough with river use, that gives less than thirteen milliseconds to respond. I'm not saying we can't do it but, the margin for error doesn't exist at those speeds. Laurel said back, sitting forward.

We were made to prevent the loss of life. Let's prevent it. Lylah said standing and turning to look at them, the moons dancing off of her white camo, giving her a shadow's imagine. Her hair slowly waved in the calm breeze making her look like a shadow Guardian.

  The others looked at each other before nodding in agreement. They all stood and replaced their helmets looking at each other before disappearing from view. The run to the capital was quick, the Apache jumped from tree to tree running and hopping from branch to branch not once getting close to falling. Passing allied and enemy troops that happened to be on patrol, neither side had any idea of the danger just a few feet above their heads.

  Now that we are here, that's a really long run. Laurel said, scanning the field. The grass was maybe six inches tall allowing for a clear and clean field of fire from the wall that was built around it. Snipers, Artillery and sentry turrets scanned the walls and surrounding area. Laser trackers and what looked like an airpad was housed in front of them.

We can't be seen either. Kyle nodded, *That could escalate things for our boys back there.*

Right that distance mixed with the high chance of, of course, mines, Shyanne said, scanning the ground with her hud and finding pings, highlighting them on their huds.

Makes that a really long run indeed. Lylah agreed. *I'll take lead silence only. Full river use authorized.*

Full...that's. N'vid echoing everyone else's shock.

  You'll be fine. Lylah patted him on the shoulder, turning to Shyanne who nodded and channeled the river. The air spun and whirled as her eyes shown clearly through the helmet. She raised her arms out and turned toward the sky and a bolt of lightning struck the Pad sending people scurrying at the incoming storm. This kind of extreme weather had slowed the Federation advance so heavily it was unnatural for the storms to just appear. The winds spun and lighting licked the sky as a mix of black snow and rain blotted the grounds. In a matter of seconds the whole city was drowned in almost complete darkness as the thick blanket of ink poured down making their sensors and turrets unable to stop their advance. Lylah nodded, moving quickly to pull out her sword, her back foot pivoted around the mines zig zagging a couple meters a move, almost flowing over the mines.

  I didn't know you could dance. Kyle said following her movements.

I always liked when I was younger, she abruptly stopped halting everyone else with a fist. "You see that?" The voices echoed from above them.

"Dude you always think there's shit when there isn't." Another voice echoed back, "You raise a false alarm again they are going to lock you in the fucken brig. Battles three hundred miles away from here anyway and not going to close anytime soon."

"What about those Reaper freaks?" The first voice asked, very hesitant.

"Myth man you saw that court case. All propaganda. Plus if they existed you think you and I would be patrolling? Hell if they are only a fraction true you think they would have made more progress then they have." The second scolded back.

He's not wrong. N'vid said.

If they knew we could get this far, by their logic we would have done it months ago. Instead of saving lives by putting us in the main fire. Lylah said back.

Fair Enough. N'vid nodded.

"You're right man I, I just don't wanna die." The first voice said.

"None of us do man but we are fighting for something...."The man stopped as his head slid slowly forward, detaching from his neck. The First man froze a blade to his neck. The man's hands were up; he could barely see the blade until lightning gave a quick illumination. The flash revealed Lylah, her scorch mark making her look like a spirit.

"I knew you were real. Please." The man gulped as another flash broke the sky and he saw three more moving behind Lylah.

"Do you really wanna live?" Lylah's disguised voice echoed around him and the blade disappeared.

"I'm a slave. I will do anything to get away from them. You don't understand the lengths they go to make sure we stay." He said knowing the blade was still omnipresent, hands still up.

"Then send them the all clear." Lylah ordered throwing a radio at him, the man almost dropped it trying to grab it.

"Sector two-one check in?" A voice echoed from the radio.

"All clear, I lost Miche to the storm. He fell." The man said, almost jumping when the voice broke out.

"Heard that your replacement arrives in twenty are you good till then?" The radio echoed.

"I'm fine, just be careful it's super slick up here." The man responded his facial expression was stressed as he prayed they would accept the answer.

"Heard that. We will send a body retrieval unit out in the morning." The voice echoed.

"Roger. Two-one out." The man said and looked around before a tranquilizing needle was stuck in his neck.

Let's do this. Kyle with me we take the Barracks, Laurel and Devin supply docks and the rest of the pad. Shyanne and N'vid you take the Command post and vehicle depot. Lylah order. The others nodded before disappearing into the night to achieve their objects.

Lylah and Kyle rounded the corner and stopped as a full platoon of men stood frozen staring at them. Half naked some with towels around their waists. Lylah and Kyle looked at each other almost smiling with excitement. Lylah caught the first guy locking him in a neck hold, kneeing him in the face once shattering his nose and caving the man's face completely in. Kyle spun under a fist preparing to draw his sword.

Oh come on, give them a fair chance. Lylah teased catching the next enemy's arm snapping it in half before twisting the shoulder joint out of location. Kyle let out a sigh and put his fist through the first guy's gut, spilling blood all over his armor before spinning in the opposite direction and catching a kick aimed at Lylah and dropping his forearms into the man's knee, shattering it and throwing the man into another. Lylah spun around Kyle taking a bullet before drawing her sword and started blocking bullets. The alarm started to blare around as they turned on the rest of the soldiers turning them into minced meat leaving a bloodsoaked room of shattered men and bodies. Their armor was almost completely covered from head to toe by the time they were done killing everyone. They both moved with purpose, throwing charges under the mechs as they exited the barracks.

I'm glad we did this. Lylah nodded as the barracks exploded behind them, sending a mushroom of smoke and fire as the ammo started to go up in flames.

I'm surprised you said yes. Kyle said as they walked towards the main gate. The command tower shattered outwards sending troops and glass everywhere. The flames licked the sides of the building, casting an evil glow in the downpour. They arrived, killing two men without missing a step as another explosion lit the sky as vehicles exploded and soldiers cried out in pain before they were silenced fading into the storm.

I can be diplomatic. Lylah said, sitting down and watching the carnage from atop the main gate.

Well at least we saved lives. Kyle nodded and sat down beside her dangling his feet off the edge.

At Least they didn't have any more brutes. Shyanne said as the rain abruptly stopped and the sky cleared unnaturally fast revealing the morning. The air was crisp as the world returned to its monotoned beauty.

"Command Odyne do you copy over? Commander? Do you copy?" The Colonel echoed throughout their coms.

"Yes Colonel?" Lylah said with a smile. Leaning back as Kyle removed his helmet and smiled coyly at her, their eyes made contact and for a moment Lylah felt Luke.

"We have received some unusual readings, are you guys ok? What...are." The Colonel was obviously cross checking their trackers. Lylah shook her head.

"Colonel Spage this is Minasa Tower Control, You are cleared to land on pad twelve." Laurel spoke up interrupting.

"How...the fuck." The Colonel said uncharacteristically audibly confused.

"Minasa Tower Control, the Colonel will begin the landing procedure soon. Are there any injuries?" Mal spoke up over the mic.

"Several locals. Explosive damage has damaged the inner Amto Teether, manual landing is required over?" Laurel droned over the mic.

"Heard that Tower expect us in twenty." The docking officer droned back.

"Welcome back Commander." Kyle said standing patting her on the back before putting his helmet on and disappearing.

"It's good to be home." Lylah whispered to herself, smiling seeing The Ellen start to descend above them.

Chapter 16:
If you could do it again...

Wormhole space
The Ellen
Apache Quarters
On route to Earth for resupply

"Two three four, retort, repose, not bad for a human." Kyle said, patting his training partner on the shoulder, "Spread your movements between pose three and six when countering."
  "Sounds like bullshit." The Colonel said back. His tanktop revealed a minor pooch and was drenched in sweat from training. The days since Minasa's liberation had long gone as the year had slowly gone by and the Colonel had asked for sword fighting lessons for which Kyle had volunteered.
"You think you can take on the program then go for it. Go ahead Jacks." Kyle said, extending his hand toward the A.I. in front of him. The Colonel launched his attack missing a good majority because the bot just dodged around him.
"Damn they're fast." the Colonel heaved heavily.
  "That's why you use pose three and six, precision fighting over sloppy survival fighting. Believe me," Kyle paused to infer Lylah, "she may be crazy but she knows her shit. Wanna take a go at me?" Kyle asked, holding his sword on his shoulder as he looked at the Colonel. His tank top was neat and still tucked in despite the three hour session.
"Yeah, here let me just get augmented first." the Colonel laughed, shaking his head in disbelief.
"Jacks speed distortion program alpha six eighty." Kyle said as the scenery changed around them. They were in a forest somewhere around the Amazon. The attention to details and the level of sensation almost overwhelmed and baffled anyone who looked at it. The Colonel had been to the Amazon during his extended training program. This was nothing but pure peace. The real Amazon forest was alive, this place as beautiful as it was. The Colonel only felt loneliness. He raised his hand to take in the view some more before Kyle finally continued.
"You can keep up with me now. It's pure skill from here on out." Kyle said, moving to take his stance.
"Sure why not." The Colonel sassed and took his stance rolling his shoulders as they eyed each other. The Colonel extended the rapier tip towards the sky, locking his elbow on his hip and looking at Kyle who nodded his acceptance of a gentleman's battle. They slowly circled debating on their best moves.
Kyle took the Guard of the Hawk keeping his elbows slightly upwards as he held the blade above his head creating a small triangle in front of his face. His back tilted forwards crunched and small as he eyed the rapier that circled inches in front of him. Kyle crashed his blade into the Colonel's As the down motion continued, the Colonel reposed backwards with a slight

hop before thrusting. Kyle quickly grabbed the hilt with his other hand, flattening the blade and making a crescent moon angel through the air catching the tip and throwing The Colonel off balance from the counter allowing Kyle to surge forward with a shoulder tackle. The Colonel, unable to adapt to the attack, took the hit sending him flying as he crashed down with a grunt. Kyle spun his blade behind his back, turning for a fraction of a second to build momentum. As he turned to continue the attack he stopped staring the Commander in the face.

"Rematch?" Lylah asked with a raised eyebrow.

The Colonel walked over to the com. "Kyle's fighting Lylah again." He said, pushing a button, as Laurel, Shyanne, N'vid, Devin, and Mal seemed to just appear almost unnaturally fast, all excited for the next fight in the series. A couch appears for the audience to enjoy as Jacks' smooth voice echoed around them.

"And now ladies and gentlemen the main event of the year! The Challenger, standing a massive six foot nine, weighing in at around three hundred and twenty-two and a quarter pounds. The Immovable Object Kyle Akya." The Audience cheered awkwardly from the forest.

"And the reigning, undefeated, Champion of Alpha Squad, a woman so fierce she even made her own father her bitch. Lylah." A roaring stadium of noise erupted as Jacks said her name.

"Soffrireterna" The crowd erupts with excitement.

"Five?" Lylah said slyly.

"Always." Kyle nodded.

Kyle spun his leg outward taking his stance. He had become extremely adept at the ancient Chinese styles. Lylah smiled, squaring up and taking a kickboxing stance, bouncing from toe to toe. They circled each other debating on their first strike. Lylah broke the stalemate and launched a side kick. Kyle caught it but was caught by the Enzuigiri that followed. Kyle rolled with the attack, righting himself quickly and throwing a quick back hand. Lylah batted it aside, pressing her attack as she landed two rotating hooks into his ribs before side stepping and aiming for his kidney. Kyle spun, launching a devastating kick landing square on Lylah's forearm pushing her back for a second. Kyle changed stance and quickly went for a double handed take down.

Lylah sprawled quickly, locking his neck in a choke hold. Kyle quickly got his feet under him; ignoring the oxygen loss he found her legs, standing to full height and shifting his weight slamming her down. Lylah got caught by the move and quickly found the ground as Kyle slammed her on her back like a doll before turning for air. Dirt, mud and some water left an impact crater, sending pieces of each flying in every direction as the battle intensified. Kyle tried to take the advantage, raising his fist and launching it. Lylah worked quickly wrapping her legs around his arm and slipped on top of him sliding flawlessly into an armbar. Kyle got caught by the move and fell forward barely able to move from the pain as he locked his arm pulling it to his chest as he struggled against physics. Kyle panicked and launched himself backwards catching Lylah on a tree forcing her to break the hold as she crumbled to the roots. Kyle quickly tried to follow the move with a punch only finding the tree scattering pieces everywhere. Kyle shook his hand and turned to Lylah who smiled covered in mud.

"You're just dancing around me." He sighed, patting his hand before placing them on his hips, breathing heavy.

"And if I wasn't?" She said, lowering her guard breathing just as heavy.

He ran forward trying to tackle her. She pivoted and got caught wrenching both of their backs as they ended up in an awkward side hug both trying to flip each other.

"Maybe if you weren't you'd," Kyle started as Lylah slammed her heel into his back, his knee giving, as Kyle roared in shock. She pivoted, getting the rotation to hip toss him. Slamming Kyle into the ground with such force it sent mud flying and covered the two of them, before she mounted him raising her fist.

"Or not." Kyle said as Lylah stood offering him her hand, Kyle whipped his eyes removing the mud, before taking it as he stood.

"Jacks." The scenery disappeared along with all the damage to both of them.

"You need to stop thinking I'm better than you and focus on winning the actual fight. I fight you at all times with everything." Lylah huffed at him.

"Was a bloody fucken amazing fight though." Laurel said from the couch popcorn in her hands a shit eating grin plastered across her face.

The contact alarm blared and they all looked at each other before moving to positions.

"Contact Alert. Contact Alert. T-minus five minutes for interdiction bubble impact. Please make your way to emergency stop location. Foam rooms filled in 4 minutes. All forces report for quick re-deployment."

The Apache looked at each other before all disappearing and then reappearing fully armored

Laurel, Devin, take the Colonel, Shyanne and N'vid, Bridge prepare to take us out before we hit the bubble. Kyle with me, we are gonna make sure we do not lose anyone today. Meet on the bridge in no more than , 3 mikes. Lylah ordered at the other Apache, who all nodded in acknowledgement.

"Um?" The Colonel looked back and forth highly confused as if being left out of a conversation and knowing it.

"This way Colonel, you're with us." Devin said and turned to leave with the Colonel. The others disappeared from sight as they went about their task.

Kyle and Lylah flew, making sure they didn't rip people's legs off as they picked them up and moved them to safety. Only taking a minute to succeed before stopping to look at each other.

"Our suits can not survive that stop can they?" Kyle asked aloud on purpose, blocking himself from the others offering a private line to Lylah.

"Theoretically we can, but I intended to stop us before the bubble and open us up to those long guns. Our armor will take damage and no one should be too injured.." She said, turning to look at him.

"So it's risk a complete ship collapse by dropping in range of those long guns or risk being pasted by a forced drop out which will send us spinning and turning in space at mach speeds. Suicide or suicide, which one has the best chance?" Kyle said as they walked towards the bridge before stopping as they heard footsteps patting behind them.

"Drop us out of the bubble at 5 then rotate 90 y 30 x 20z." Lylah eyed her back as she turned to finish the orders, Unleash a micro warp dust trail along all maneuvering thrusters." Lylah ordered him as she turned on her heel chasing after the footsets.

"Those plasma cannons will attract the ion particles and melt the port holes condemning everyone on their vessels to..." He tried responding before realizing, he was already alone.

Lylah slid on her foot as she stopped in front of the man, tilting her head as she assessed what was happening, "You're gonna die." He said before exploding a bomb vest launching Lylah violently back pushing her through three sets of walls indenting her into a fourth wall before she fell to the floor in a smoldering heap. Lylah coughed into the visor before removing it, holding her stomach she turned over to lay in the corner of the wall and floor before propping herself up to see the damage. She had three shards through her chest, one in her right collar bone, one by her left hip and in her right ribs none of them had gone all the way through her body.

"Fuck," Lylah cried as she finally registered the pain. She looked down at her visor. If Kyle listened to orders she had one minute till she died. Lylah shook her head as blackness engulfed her vision before she bobbed back to life, destroying the doubt that plagued her mind and putting her helmet back on. Lylah breathed in. Her eyes glanced at the clock. She had ten seconds to get to the other side of a two mile long carrier. She closed her eyes channeling the river, she breathed in slowly launching herself forward at unimaginable speed. As the sonic boom cracked from the tight air, she flew forward tripping and bouncing through the halls as the ship immediately decelerated.

The world almost faded as she crashed into the eight additional walls before freezing to one as the ship decelerated further finally righting itself to engage. The G-forces started to rise as the ship's rotation started. Lylah gritted her teeth, feeling her muscles scream as the G-forces passed finally dropped below four hundred. The room had almost solid lines from the violently spinning around her. Lylah pushed up feeling weightlessness take over, ignored the interference and found the funnel as the ship continued to spin. Lylah floated using her hands to spin and move, slowing her speed and her body almost swimming, like a fishtoid.

"Huh." She mused trying to look around as she raised her head to look down a hallway. A shadow collided with her knocking her out of the vortex and then spinning violently. The memory this all started, the thing that began all of this viciousness starts to flash before Lylah's eyes distorting reality. *Not...not now...not like this...must li...*

"You are so fucken stupid. Do you have any idea what it's like to have a child who can't stay sober." The smashing sound of a pot being thrown echoes like a gunshot around Lylah as she stares into the doorway.

"Daddy it's legal." Lylah cried, fear and pure defeat ladened her face. Before she could continue, he had her by the throat up against a wall, her punk mini skirt and fishnet tank top combo matching her black and white dyed hair. Her porcelain makeup was smeared with dark lines of black to white rivers. Lylah struggled to get air but that's it, she dare not push him any further, she dangled limply.

"Weed is LEGAL not that other shit you mixed it with! Mind erasers, not to mention oxy-13." He closed in on her face, as she felt the spit explode from his mouth, "I'm done with this bullshit." He grew silent, staring at her. Lylah blinks slowly as if time is slowing, The Chief's face changes over and over as a flurry of emotions explode across his face before saying, "You're on the next transport out." Mr. S dropped Lylah causing her to cower up against the wall. She closed her eyes expecting a slap. Tears running thick rivers down her cheeks. She opened one eye. Her father had his back turned and his body was shaking as he finally leaned up against the room's door frame.

"You should run to Luke's and enjoy your last day of freedom. This will be on the news tomorrow. I can't have you bruised up." He turned back to look at her, a shadow in the doorway, "Make no mistake. You will graduate and when you learn your lesson you will come back and take your place."

She ran outta the house, tears running down her cheeks. She was at Luke's front door before she knew what was really happening and could knock. Mr. Akya opened the door.

"Come in child." He spoke softly to her, his warmth almost flooding Lylah as he waved her in, "Lukes in his room. If you want to spend the night you know you're more than welcome to."

She tearfully nodded and walked up stairs, rivers of black spewing from her eyes.

Lylah blinked viciously as she realized she was alive drawing air in betweens gasps of pain. Her muscles almost locked in position. With the same amount of strength required to turn a completely rusted cog, she willed her joints to move. Her head screamed so violently from the effort she knocked off her helmet as the vomit spewed freely. She crunched with pain and effort as she vomited again. Lylah forced herself to stop before feeling her eardrums repairing themselves. The sound of the drums webbing being redrawn caused tears to start to flow freely. She finally found a small resemblance to normal after almost twenty minutes of barely surviving. She barely moved her head, more of a lean but she nonetheless took in her surroundings, trying to understand her survival.

She had landed on the man from the wall in Minasa. She shook her head slowly, almost amazed at the one impossible chance as she formed the answer quickly. He must have been a spy, hence the first man exploding himself. They were planning on sabotaging The Ellens light drive, killing them all irregardless. After the explosion he must have tried to run, entering the tunnel early or more likely was in the perfect position as they left Wormhole space. The turn must have knocked him astray and into her. As the ship finally decelerated they were launched backwards and he acted as an additional impact layer for her and her armor's kinetic gel layer took the rest of the damage. She turned to the pasted man staring at the mush as she struggled to keep her head up.

"Jesus Christ! What have you done to yourself this time?!" Mal screamed and pulled her away from the wall with unnatural might. Lylah blinked only once and they had somehow made the trip to the Apache quarters quicker than Lylah could comprehend. "Sit, you stupid

silly girl." He ordered grabbing his tools and running various scans, taking in all the information and smashing buttons to activate the automated units as he worked and adapted to the information.
"I'm sorry doc." She droned as he looked at the shards and sighed. He nodded softly and gently pushed her on her back. Nodding sympathetically he took a breath.
"On three." He said over top of her. Lylah closed her eyes and nodded.
"Ready." She responded by relaxing her muscles as best as she could. He was going to have to tear the shards out of completely healed tissue.
"And Three." He said, ripping the shards out in quick succession as she forced her body to stay still barely flinching but being pulled with effort of the shards leaving her body. Lylah coughs as a volcano of blood is released from her lips as she stares up at the lights. The world starts to flash as she loses herself to the darkness. *Save..bab...Lu.*
"Let's run away? I can call someone. Please I can't." Lylah pleaded almost breaking down.
	"Or I follow you." Lylah froze as Luke looked out his window, his small body was no bigger than hers. His black hair tipped in blue hung over his eye as he stared. His arm on his forehead as he thought. Her mind flashed to a slightly bigger man then he was now, scared and torn by battles yet to be lived staring at his hands. The man flashed a missing eye at her as Lylah panicked.
"You couldn't." Lylah cried, not wanting that future for him.
"I could and will. DAD." Luke screamed moving towards the door in a sudden burst.
"Yeah?" Mr. Akya said after a moment, almost seeming completely out of breath as he rumbled up the stairs.
"Horutis. Can you get me in?" Luke looked at his dad who almost turned a new shade of white.
	"I just might actually but you...you need to come with me." His father nodded finally. They both walked into Mr. Akya's room. Lylah looked around the room again with a soft smile, hoping and fearing he would both come and not. Her eyes danced around the room before landing on a poster of a 'Hufflepuff' and wondered what it was. After many long minutes, Lylah opened her mind to the silence as she waited, the door finally and slowly opened. Luke walked out, his face pale as snow as his eyes wandered towards Lylah, the fire gone as if looking at her had brought added more baggage he wasn't sure was he ready for. He looked meekly at her and closed his eyes before nodding.
	Lylah lowered her head into her hands and began to cry not because she had to go away. She cried because she had found a way to keep Luke and in doing so, she knew she would lose him because of it.

Chapter 17:

A Face for the Camera, A Face for Home

January 1st, 5003
Year 4 of Deployment

"How is she still getting hurt?"

"She is the Leader of an elite squad of soldiers, sir. She's deployed a lot." Mal stopped before seeming to need to add more, "They enjoy the pain saying they hurt themselves so no one else has to bleed. Kyle alone broke his left shoulder 36 times in two months. Your daughter gets hurt a lot less than any of the others. We are lucky we have them if we are to be honest. If she hadn't been there this could have been much worse. You're lucky she's your daughter, she brings you great honor and respect." Mal hissed back at Mr. S.

"Not like he cares." Lylah shifted gingerly in place showing her disgust towards her father as she slowly propped herself up, getting more comfortable.

"Doctor, would you give us the room please." Lylah croacked licking her lips as she glared a hole through her father. He nodded and walked out of the room, closing the door behind him.

"Whatever you're about to destroy of mine, don't it's hard enough accepting your disgusting war plans." Her father said turning away from her.

"Are we finally here?" She spat.

"I am. YOUR..." He raged around and stopped as Lylah was already in his face inches from his nose as she met him at eye level. Her face broken from the injuries, deep scars continuing to slowly heal into bruises as she glared.

"Father?" She whispered as he shook in place; fear spreading like an avalanche of white from his nose and almost completely bleaching his clay colored skin. He shook even more violently as she leaned closer, almost indulging her feelings.

"You couldn't let her sleep and then," She paused, "and then I was born. The clones, the lies, what you had planned for me. I will never be at your side and if you ever clone my mother again, I will destroy you to the point I can kill you in front of everyone and no one. Would. Say. Anything,"She lifted her father above her head by the neck, embellishing in the memory seeing the similar fear she had felt towards him, "I have hated you for so long. I have feared you for so long. I lost Luke because of you, and now," She slammed his head against the wall putting a small crater in it,

"I cost you her. I cost you me. You don't ever get to call me your daughter again. Do you hear me? You aren't my father. He died, killed by you to cause me more pain. If you ever cross me the fuck again, if you ever step out of line I will end you like you ended the ones I loved. Do you fucken understand me? I am your God and you don't get to so much as take a piss without my permission. Do you hear me soldier?" His face started to turn red as drops of sweat started to drip down the sides of his face. He stared ahead, shaking before finally nodding. She leaned closer waiting for his words.

"Yes, ma'am." He coughed, panicking as he was raised slowly higher, choking to the brink of passing out before letting him fall.

"I will win this war for you, but make no mistake you do not have to be alive for that to happen." She kneeled down beside him as he gasped for air. He scrambled out of the room as she sat gingerly down, closing her eyes.

Lylah. Luke's voice echoed around her. The scent of him almost filled the room with the fragrance of his Cheshire woods surrounding her. An almost stoic peace washed over her, willingly accepting the pull to the river.

Luke blinked rapidly, caught by the room's bright ambience.

"Sit." Lylah's voice echoed from the kitchen. Luke smiled and sat at the table, his 80s polo and khakis look to be almost bursting behind the mountain of muscle.

"You did it." He said hanging on the left arm piece watching the kitchen with longing eyes as Lylah walked out. Her gray natural hair was restored. Her peaceful eyes look back with just as much love. She let a slight smile escape her lips. Her sunday overalls and button up shirt were a gross mix of yellow and white that matched the bow on her choker.

"Pudding?" She smiled slyly at him. Sucking on her finger as he stood and wrapped her up.

"You did it baby." Luke smiled as she tapped his nose with the pudding. Lylah laughed softly and kissed Luke, losing herself to the moment as she righted herself. Kyle's face stared back with the same smile. Her eyes widened as she shot up in the bed, sweat pouring down her face.

"Fucken. Dreaming." She groaned and stood up in her pod in The Ellen. She glanced at herself as she passed the mirror. She saw herself with white and black hair with a fine top and punk mini skirt. Lylah walked into the wall forgetting how fast she could move as she stared at the mirror. Shaking her head Lylah got dressed and skipped brushing her hair just grabbing it and putting it back into a ponytail. She walked to the briefing her mind lost to the last years. She nodded to the others and jumped right in. "Two weeks ago we got jumped between the Ligarinnin system and Minasa.

Before that we took the centurion's third belt and before that we took Minasa itself. We have gained almost three hundred light years in less than three galactic years, for some of you that doesn't seem like a long time, it's taken years for us to do this. We are in year four of our campaign. We need reinforcements to the location..." Lylah walked back and forth in front of the holocom, her frustration very visible as she relayed the situation. Already reading her father's face.

"Commander reinforcements are currently unavailable. Recruitment quotas have not been met." Mr. S said as the council nodded.

"I see well if I need to remind you all of what I am stopping. If my line falters and some ships happen to get through there is no fleet fast enough to stop them from killing all of you on earth. So unless you're going to magically build my orbital platform network, find me soldiers." The Council shifted in their seats as they all seemed to come to the same conclusion.

"See the more you hold me back the bigger risk of losing this war basic fucken tactics." Lylah berated.

"We can find soldiers but we will need time." An older council member nodded.
"Thank you counselor, I'm not your enemy, stop treating me like one. Olympus out." Lylah said before turning off the com.

"More bullshit." Kyle said from behind the monitor fully armored nodding at the expected response.

"Yeah well what the fuck could we expect. We are winning the war too fast and making things seem staged." She explained as she walked through the halls putting on her helmet. Their plan was already unfurling as The Ellen began preparing for combat.

"Prepare for contact range nine-eighty km moving stupid fast." Laurel said. Aas she read the display her voice echoed around them, Lylah nodded on the bridge of the Ellen.

"Get to the Ranger, wait for my signal and punch it hard." Lylah turned to Kyle and slapped him on the back before he was gone.

"We are gonna birth a frigate for the first time mid combat sir." She laughed as she walked over to the Colonel offering her hand as he walked onto the battle bridge.

"No man I trust more to pull something this stupid off. Well, other than me." He said with a smile clasping her hand as the crew cheered, "Take care of her Commander." He looked at her as she assumed command.

"Take good care of my baby Colonel. She likes being rubbed gently at night." Lylah laughed as the others cheered and laughed.

"Heard that." He walked away heading towards the Ranger.

"All lights are dead and I need a firing solution in all ports below thirty two through thirty-eight on my mark." The enemy cruiser slowed right outside their range, "Now." The Ellen erupted blowing shrapnel everywhere before a brief silence and the enemy ship was struck, pulling and killing hundreds of men in the vacuum. Lylah watched soldiers and equipment blow outwards as a small debris field burst forth from the enemy ship and hull pieces buckled before the shields were raised.

"Burn red hot and prepare for a birth attack." Lylah ordered as the ship's power started to fluctuate and she and others forced the ship to drift on a x axis through space.

"Ranger decks thirty-two thought thirty eight are gone you are go for launch in 5. 4. 3. 2. Blow up to forty-four now." The ship rocked as another explosion sent more supplies out of the enemy ship as another debris field was once again launched causing further explosions but this time it had something much bigger launched with it. Lylah walked to the main observation deck as the black silhouette blocked out the stars before a fireworks display worth of color lit up the darkness around them.

The Ranger's shots heavily smashed the enemy shields as they attempted to retreat. The Ranger took some false hits and started to fall back. The enemy vessel, assuming the Ranger was burnt, followed without hesitation. The Ranger had barely entered The Ellen's range as two carriers dropped out of Wormhole space right on top of the Ranger attempting to capture the vessel.

"Now." The Ellen's thirty two phase cannons lit the night skies up as flashes of green, blue, purple, and orange teased the void as each color of crystal did different damage to those shields finding the best damage to use before rotating to green and vaporizing its target shield generator.

"Forward team you are clear for retrieval to the skunk fleet. All shields and thrusters are offline, two carriers and a battleship for the skunk fleet." Lylah said as she watched the screen as fire fights broke out all over their hull as her troops opened hatches and took over the enemy ships.

"You almost seem pissed, it's this easy." Luke said beside Lylah.

Lylah blinked hard and started to breathe heavily. Knowing that was not him she closed her eyes for a second and saw Kyle looking at her.

"Well I wanted a challenge." She said, calming down and turning to look at him.

"Someday someone will challenge you."

"But today is not that day." Lylah waved dismissively.

"Incoming, two additional targets dropping out hot." The tactical office panicked as the contact alarm started to blare.

"Rotate fifteen and give me full missiles." She turned to Kyle. "Call the skunk fleet and get to the Ranger. I want a firing line around The Ellen. This battle is just beginning. Deploy the shrapnel line and prepare for boarders." Lylah hollered at the troops as they did as they were told. Lylah ran through the halls, "Make sure those borders land on levels thirty-one and thirty-three."

"Roger that. Skunk fleet two minutes out." Laurel's voice cracked over the com.

"Two minutes in hell." Lylah nodded as the marines surrounding her fell into formation shouldering her own rifle and waiting.

"Five, four, three, two, one," The loud vibrating metallic crash signaled the arrival of the boarding pobs. They listened as the auto-drill shocked the hull dropping a large slab of metal with a cloud of smoke. Lylah slapped the ax away from the Brute that had appeared out of nowhere. The Brute's fear rose in slow motion as Lylah surged forward killing the thing with a clean swipe decapitating the thing before it could move, two troops dropped through the hole mid roll slowly falling into the hall. Lylah smiled and put one in each before jumping up into the pod. As she jumped the small gap; two soldiers had been prepared to jump down.

Lylah hesitated for a second seeing her father's face before blinking and tilting her head to the left, allowing the soldiers to register what was about to happen as they almost fell back as she stood over the hole. The fear the troops had as they scrambled, unable to even raise a rifle before the room became a tornado of blood. Limbs and organs spun around Lylah as she stood in the middle, her head down as she dropped down the hole ambushing the troops that surged underneath her. A bloody trail following her like a cape as she sliced and diced everyone. She slid to a stop a few steps away from a robot covered in ancient Japanese Samurai Armor standing defiantly in front of her. She smiled and raised her sword and the bot launched its attack, keeping up with her, pushing her back with its quick movements. Lylah dodged an attack as the bot continued with the attack, cleaving one of her soldiers in half. She glared at it and launched herself forward, jumping in front of an attack as she kneed the thing in the chest, shattering and cratering the smooth synthetic skin.

"How much did they pay you, mercenary? We can pay more." Lylah said as she positioned herself between her troops that still ran in slow motion barely able to react to what was actually happening.

"I would happily kill you for free. Your kind don't have the right to exist." The bot spoke back. She launched her attack. They moved around the room, their fight happening at microspeeds. The swords collided singing a song of pain and sorrow; the equal combatants moved back and forth killing both sides of the armies as the battle bathed the room in body parts, blood and organs. Men on both sides scream in pain as the two God's battle back and forth before finally Lylah sliced the bot in half and caught the things head in mid air with a clear thrust.

"We won." The bot echoed around her speaking slowly as it died. "You killed us but we won." The bot died with a spark.

"Fuck you." Lylah said back and walked back through the halls.

"The Skunk Fleet has arrived, engaging the enemy fleet with thirty nine targets on the board." Laurel's more clear voice echoed through her com.

"Ellen is secured." Lylah said looking back at the blood soaked hallway almost dropping against the wall as the weight of the battle held. Blood dripped from the ceiling and organs hung from the rafters. The room had tainted the surrounding area in a dark ominous red. She sat down and just stared at the hallway, losing herself to the question she had ignored from the beginning of the war, how far is she really willing to go to win this war? What were her enemies willing to sacrifice? What would the total cost be by the end of war and how many souls will be lost before a victory was achieved? Lylah sighed, losing herself for a bit to the chaos of her mind, a tear slowly slid down her cheek, damage shocks and debris echoed all around her but she couldn't turn away from the hallway. A battle echoed but Lylah remained lost to her thoughts.

"Hallway of death is what the Freedom Initiative is all about. What you are about to see is a scene captured from a recent victory somewhere on the front. The picture is just a glimpse at what our heroic soldiers go through on a daily basis. Commander Odyne can be seen here defending The Ellen from these savages," The anchor pointed at the screen, his face grim with the darkness of the subject, his mask only evident to experts, "her head down trying to comprehend such carnage. At what point do we call it quits? Is peace an option? At what point are we allowed to grieve for our dead? Those questions will be answered and more when we return." Kyle scowled, turning off the channel.
"You are expecting better?" Shyanne mused from the couch.
"Wanted more recognition for my efforts." Kyle continued before bringing up the screen to look at something new.

"We are still getting reports of the battle but we can confirm that The Ranger was on the field." Kyle roared and threw the pad at Laurel. "Keep your illusions to yourself she-witch. I have enough nightmares as it is." Shyanne scoffed and walked out of the room at the outburst.
"Sorry I forgot." Laurel said, her eyes returning to their normal shade.
"Just save it for the enemy, not me. Hard enough with the screams." Kyle said, blinking repeatedly, grabbing onto the ceiling pegs and starting working out trying to clear his head.

"So I fucked up Shyanne is pissed and I don't know why." N'vid said, bursting into the room, the mood immediately changing.
"She's pregnant?" Laurel laughed sarcastically before stopping as Kyle stopped mid pump before their eyes snapped to each other.
"No fucken...really." Laurel started to get gitty covering her mouth as Kyle dropped himself and turned a cocky smile teasing his lips.
N'vid smiled coyly and nodded as Shyanne walked in shaking her head as Laurel squealed and hugged her hanging off her neck.

"That's a lot of paperwork." The mood instantly died as Lylah stood in the doorway, her silhouette only thing visible as she walked into the room, the tension of fear and excitement whirled around her taking laps up and down her back. "Congratulations." The air exploded as they all registered what had just been said, "Shoreleave I guess is in order. It's been almost two years since we had a break anyway."

"Hey let me know where we are going. I wanna see Lin. I...I mean ma'am would you give me permission to invite Lin." Devin said, slapping his best friend on the shoulder in congratulations as Lylah nodded. Even though not armored she felt Laurels rage small but there; the jealousy building.

"Laurel, would you take a walk with me?" Lylah said, turning and walking out of the room. Laurel looked at everyone nervously before following, catching her seconds later.
"So you gonna use that jealousy or do I gotta keep feeling it? Are your feelings real?" Lylah said, turning on her with a girly smile on her face.
"You...commander." Laurel looked back.
"Answer the question Lt." Lylah said with her eyes up, a smile teasing her lips.
"Yes." Lylah clapped her hands at the acknowledgement and rounded the corner.

"Not like it matte...woah." Laurel stood before stepping back as they entered the room; it was massive even for a ship this size. Laurel shook her head and realized they were in a holoroom. The room was in a dark cathedral style room. The black granite and beautiful white marble made up most of the walls. The room was filled with booths and tables bathed in low candle light, their black leather and red trim a reminder of Lylah's night of love. The room almost danced with darkness seducing all light with flowing shadows.

Lylah closed her eyes and her hair returned to its natural state in a surge of black and blue, a long silky ballroom black dress clung to her hips the air of a Mistress of Power hung around her. Her eyes dimmed and she looked almost exactly like she did at the academy. The pain in her eyes was deeper however. Laurel smiled and closed her eyes to mimic Lylah. Her coco brown hair and eyes returned a beautiful blue Cinderella gown formed and the air of incense clung to the curls in her hair.
"Thought's? I was thinking of bringing it with us." Lylah said looking around the room before turning back to Laurel.

"It's...did you design this, like all? Like from the scale to the detail that alone must have taken, just wow." Laurel said looking around really taking in her surroundings. They walked over to the bar and sat down, waving the bartender down and ordering drinks.

"Ma'am I really need...I really should have knocked." Devin barged in as Lylah and Laurel sat at the stained oak bar staring at him with a slight amount of irritation..
"It better be good or so help me." Lylah growled at him.
"It totally can wait. I'll leave now." His eyes glued to Laurel who was blushing away as she sipped a drink.
"Resort planet twelve twenty, now leave." Lylah flicked her hand at him shooing him away.

"Right...I...Laural, Ouch ok fine fine fine." Devin complained as Lylah grabbed him and kicked him out of the holo room.
"That was so cute." Lylah gushed rushing over to her.
"This is weird, why are you being weird?" Laurel looked suspiciously at Lylah.
Lylah raised her hands in surrender, "I miss being a woman."
"Shyanne, please it'll be like a girls vs boys couples edition type thing. Please." Laurel immediately exploded.

"Wait I'm not dating anyone, I don't even like anyone on the squad." Lylah backed up as Laurel got a bloodthirsty look in her eye as she leaned closer after sending a message to Shyanne.
"Kyle." Lylah launched herself uncontrollably at Laurel who sidestepped giggling as they slapped each other's hands.
"What the fuck did I walk into." Shyanne asked as she walked in freezing as the entry portal disappeared behind her.

"Girl time." Lylah laughed back, Shyanne smiled maliciously and joined in. Her bright blonde hair and sharp blue eyes appeared; a flowing dress hung loosely; its blood red color matched her ruby red pendant that hung around her neck like a wicken of some kind. Lylah nodded and clapped as the bar filled with people as they sat giggling enjoying drinks.

Lylah smiled over her martini as she watched promiscuously at a man at the bar, his head hung low. Her seductive gaze intensified as shadows deepened and the song slowed. Many men tried approaching their table but no one could get near the balcony. They sat on the second floor that had platforms that matched the decorum and allowed for overwatches from above.

"So you made all of this? The people, the air, the,"Laurel looked at the security outside of their door and gulped. They were dressed in insanely detailed three piece suits, black blazers, blood red vests and black pants and shirts hung off their bodies tightly leaving little to the imagination of the danger people were in. Their coats were laced with bullet proof web and Their eyes covered like some early 21sts Secret Service. "Men, and intend to take it with us. Why?"

"Well everyone else has a source of income. You with your weapons. Shyanne with her modeling, N'vid with his holo-platinums. Devin with his Art. Kyle and I are the only two who don't," She took a gulp, "Nothing of note to contribute but bruting stares and self loathing so...when I was younger I wanted to build big things."She giggled, "My bar and hotel back, on Magnas Prime. They are still making ok money. I thought about making holo programs that are exactly what the buyer wants, all customized of course and if they like it so much I'll build them a real one for cost value and then give it to them. The Holodisks are expensive but making that hotel in Magnas Prime put a hole in my trust fund I haven't been able to find a way out of. Plus it helps small businesses galactic wide."
"Lylah's Wonder Emporium of Mystical wares." Shyanne giggled.

"Catchy but how about Soffrinerenta Eternals. What you make will last eternally." Laurel chimed in getting another round of giggles. The man turned and she saw Luke, his beauty and kindness as he greeted someone. They locked eyes before Lylah turned away, turning back only once more but she realized her mistake. They continued talking much into the night as they walked out of the holoroom. The Army of Kyle, Spage, Devin, N'vid, Lin Parker, and Lin's band awaited them as they emerged. Lylah stopped the others as they stumbled out.
"You...were drinking for like a week?" N'vid said looking at them suspiciously
"We were womaning." Shyanne nodded pointing at him powerfully.
"Time for bed." Lylah choked on her vomit and ran to her quarters.

The river flowed smoothly around Lylah as she sat in the middle allowing herself to trust the voices that screamed by, barely touching her with its waters but still close enough to drown her.
"She's here." A voice announced.
"What about that baby?" A female voice walked over.
"Dead soon." A sinister voice hissed around her.
"What about Laurel?" A final voice chimed.

"Lylah we need to talk." Lylah slowly opened her eyes before standing, keeping her back to the shore. She turned slowly as the river matched her movements. She stepped cleanly and completely balanced in timing. She moved so peacefully one would think, she floated through the waters. Luke looked with the feeling of shock and admiration stuck on his face. He stood stoned into position by her movements.
"Pick up that anchor sailor." Lylah coed back at him.
"I. right. So. You wanna talk about what you just did?" Luke said, kinda flabbergasted.

"I kept a promise." She said walking past him traveling into her own mind offering him a hand as she dissolved. She felt his touch and pulled her arm back bringing them back to the night's events.

"It was simple, Laurel needed to feel like a princess, and Shyanne needed validation." Lylah walked around their booth where they had been sitting. She looked at her weaker self whose arm was up with a martini as they had been cheering, with extreme contempt.

"The baby, you were cheering the baby." Luke answered Lylah's troubled mind.

"Right and so I filled all our drinks with a chemical compound that would stop the heart of a baby by natural means. No residue, no damage done." She tutored as she leaned down by Laurel's ear, "It really was a lovely night."

"Just a Fairsist who will never be born. And the timelapse?" Luke looked at her pure contempt.

"Once Shyanne arrived I turned on the time dilator so we wouldn't be interrupted. There are too many lives at stake to risk one more." Lylah explained as she stood fully up and moving through the motionless scene, moving her way to the first floor.

"You wanna take on the River?" Luke blurted, catching her meaning and following her.

"I want the river to be in peace. The only way that happens is if we find the first." Lylah said, continuing to move towards the bar bobbing and weaving through the frozen sea of people, "If we find the first then I won't ever," she stops and turns to stare Luke in the eyes. The room was still as the dead, people danced, smiled, and laughed, the love and the things she had made possible," I won't have to lie ever again and deny someone the same rights I had." A tear starts to fall down her face. "I will not let another mother suffer the pain of having her baby and never meeting her, seeing her, watching her grow."

Lylah's voice broke, "Our daughter is four years. Old. She is still frozen in stasis. I have never met our daughter. I don't know who she has become because she hasn't had the chance to be four yet. She's still frozen in time from the day she came into this world." Tears continue to stain her eyes as she stares at him. "And because of the first. I had to kill a child, deny a mother the opportunity to experience something I will never ever get to experience myself." Rage starts to mount in her voice. "So you're damn right I will do what I need to. You think I don't know what I did was wrong. Ask the river why I have to deny Shyanne her birthright."

"Sister. She's your family and you ." Luke smiled softly at her as Lylah finally broke down crumbling into his arms as she cried. She screamed for her crimes against her people. Images of the battles she was in starts to play a symphony of death in her mind. Her crawling fearfully through the vents, dust debris and pain covering her face. Her holding Luke a silhouette screaming in the burning hanger. The birth of her child. Her looking at herself in the mirror after the surgery. She watched herself kill Kyle again and again.

The battles with countless brutes, soldiers, dodging artillery, and missiles. Dancing around the battlefield like fiends of death. The fear in the enemy soldiers as they toyed and killed them. The millions of lives they saved doing those things. The aid and peace that has been restored. The charity work the Apache did, the Holo-Platinums, the Art of War painting masterpieces. She finally landed at where they were now. Lylah wailed and cried as Luke slowly ran his hands through her hair as she grieved into his shoulder.

"It's ok baby. I know. I know." Luke hushed her, holding her close allowing her to have her pain.

Chapter 18:

Do you think the Devil has regrets?

The Ellen
Destination: Classified Presidential Level
Year 5 of Deployment
June 25, 5004

I'm sorry. The words echoed around Lylah's room as she launched up. She clenched her heart as she was overwhelmed by sadness and grief like somewhere in the galaxy six of the brightest stars just were lost. She stared into the Wormhole space, her mind getting lost to blackness. Flashes of her standing in the middle of the tornado. The real her. The Real Lylah. The Girl who hid from the war. Green, pink, and blue lighting swarmed up and out of the tornado striking in epic clashes of blinding light. Odyne looked at herself in the middle of the tornado as she stared forward, unaware of Odyne's presence. *What are you...*
Lylah's head snapped towards Odyne, her body horrifyingly lurched like a puppet towards her.
"Why." Lylah signed at Odyne.

    Lylah blinked rapidly pulling herself from the nightmares plaguing her mind and head to look at herself in the mirror. Black hair teased her shoulders as she stared at herself from when she was younger. Her face covered in porcelain paint and long streeks of black ran down her cheeks as Lylah slowly turned her head trying to get a better look. Slowly raising her hand to her face. The younger her followed the movement to the exact time, finally resting her hand on her cheek much like Lylah had. Lylah took a deep breath in.

    The younger her launched her hand at Lylah, grabbing her wrist and pulling her towards the mirror before launching her across the room. The younger her tilted her head forward menacingly, a deep evil smile teasing her face as she turned away caution in her gaze before signing."Weak? You don't know the meaning of power Odyne." The younger her signed venomously before raising her hand and slowly started to become real crawling outwards from the mirror, her face becoming cut and shredded by the glass as she forced herself through the glass.

    Odyne shrieked in horror rushing over trying to stop the child from hurting herself before being smashed into the mirror by the hand of her younger self. As she backs into her realm cackling hysterically at Odyne.

"Big bad me worried about my younger self. What a fucken joke." The younger her continued stabbing Odyne with her words as she signed, "If you cared you would have found a better way...but I guess you are weaker than your father!"

Odyne roared awake shattering the restraints and zero-blanket cratering herself into the top of the ceiling of The Ellen before she shook her head as she listed through dead space calming herself from the nightmares.

"Odyne. I know you don't, but do you want something to help you sleep?" Jax synthetic voice echoed around her.

"I uh. Should. Thanks Jax. Are you fully deployed on The Ellen?" Odyne said, rubbing her eyes again as she used her back foot to push towards the bed to reactivate the nanites.

"I am ma'am.Would you like to talk about it?" Jax asked as the blanket snapped back into existence.

"Did you record the event?" She asked, walking over the mirror eyeing it suspiciously until she saw herself looking back.

"Yes ma'am would you like to see?" Jax responded.

"Yeah, replay on the window wouldya' ." Lylah nodded and headed over to the wall leaning against it as the holo recording started.

She watched herself toss and turn. She locked onto the way she thrashed and the way her mouth moved.

"Add my audio and vocal recognition overtop of my lips and replay." Lylah said.

"Big bad me worried about my younger self. What a fucken joke." Lylah froze as an explosion of electrical colors launched her forward, breaking everything holding her down without it even stopping her. "Stop." Lylah blinked away tears as she took in a deep breath.

"Type of energy? Is it consistent?"

"With Fairsist Bioplasma, yes." Jax responded around.

"Alright then, we need to end this fucken war." Lylah said moving towards the door to set plans in motion.

"Ma'am I just received a communication from Omega Fleet Designation direct from space to wormhole. Oh?" Jax said confirming his data, "It is confirmed. Designation. 'Aphrodite'."

Lylah's heart sank, "Play it."

"Ma'am...it's. They surprised us. Are shredding retreating troops..us..." Static flared, "They won't stop. They know..Fairsist. This attack. Us....we..." The voice completely broke up before Jax spoke, "I'm sorry ma'am the source has disappeared. I'm sorry."

"It's fine. You did your best. I uh...I need to tell the others. Please...summon ah, all Apache, Mal and. Spage." Lylah said for the first time in years speechless trying to cope with herself. The doorbell rang as Lylah pulled herself out of the stupor and opened the door stepping aside as the five other Apache, Spage and Mal entered.

"I uh...just received this." Lylah said blankly, raising her finger for Jax to play the message.

"Ma'am...it's. They surprised us. Are shredding retreating troops..us..." Static flared, "They won't stop. They know..Fairsist. This attack. Us. Don't let them...we...owe...won't make...an honor ma'am." as the voice completely broke up she pointed to Spage as his holo communicator lit up and nodded for him to play it.

"Spage, As of O'two hundred. Omega fleet is no more." The air froze as they all listened to the report, " Four hundred and six thousand ships were committed to the ambush to take down Omega fleet. After sixty nine thousand casualties...Beta Apache detonated their light drive aboard The Purging Light. Taking the rest of the ambushers with them." The

Chief's emotionless face said before the communication was disconnected. They all were lost to the stupor as they struggled with their own emotions.

"We..." Laurel choked before giving up trying to speak.

"They're in wormhole. They have to be." Shyanne laughed, not taking the severity seriously, "When...when do we. Come on guys, you know we can..." Shyanne sputters out, "But they...how do we know."

"Because we are at their last known coordinates," Lylah said as she turned off her window as it was still paused. Showing them what she meant. There was nothing, no debris, just their ships and the void." They didn't successfully transition. Shyanne." Lylah finished softly.

"NO!" Shyanne said tears welling as she rages at Laurel. "Get out my head!"

Laurel squeals in shock and pain as they start brawling tears falling down their faces before they cradle each other for comfort.

"They're...gone?" Kyle looked desperately at Lylah.

She met his gaze for what seemed like forever as everyone tried to cope, hoping Lylah's next words would be comforting.

"They're gone."

Chapter 19:
Tragedy or Advantage?

The Ellen
Destination: Classified Presidential Level
Year 5 of Deployment
August 25, 5004

"At O'two hundred hours we received a transmission from Omega Fleet." Spage said standing in front of the entire battle group of thirteen fleets. The sheer size of the room was able to house the twenty billion people and the lighting of all of these people was done by a simple incomprehensibly big beautiful nineteen layered chandelier. Candles and ambience lit the massive room as everyone sat down like going to the Grand Theaters of old. Their jump suits of blue, green, and black along with some who are even armored clashed heavily against the beauty of the room. The beautifully multi-layered balconies were made of a sensual oak, chiseled into each one of the fifty five balconies was a story or legend from either recent memories or long forgotten mythic battles. A massive projection of the Colonel stood behind him mimicking his every movement so everyone could see and hear him. Everyone quieted quickly as they all paid attention. The Colonel pointed to the projector behind him.

"Omega Fleet engaged F.A. fleet twelve." An unrecognizable voice echoed all around them as crackles and static plagued the audio. "Beta Apache squad was engaged by a F.A. fleet of three hundred million as they dropped from wormhole."Another bit of static and the voice picked up again. "Stink fleet two slaughtered by new enemy type. A slim..." heavy static broke again, almost seeming to fight the words like they were backwards before it made sense again. "Beta Apache squad forced to detonate a light drive." The static kicked in again. "Stranded on Magness Prime. Source code." The audio became almost crystal clear as the person spoke the following, "Thirteen Alpha Three. My love for darkness will provide the Olympian Gods with power." The crowd broke out as they all speculated and whispered back and forth.

"It's authentic." Spage nodded as if completely confirming their suspicions, "Omega fleet is gone and those who managed to survive hid in the one location they think we are unwilling or unable to attack." The crowd seemed to itch for what he was about to say next. "And that's what we are here to do. WE ARE TAKING BACK MAGNESS PRIME!" The crowd erupted at the news as a title wave of noise erupts, shaking the very halls they were in. The rumbling of the pylons and pillars echoed for several minutes after everyone had quieted. "And there's only one team in the universe I trust to lead this campaign, the only Apache squad left." The crowd lost their minds once more as the apache march single file onto the stage, their bodies also getting projections. They turned completely in sync, their backs perfectly aligned, their movements almost too perfect making them seem more than they are.

"Battle Group Olympus, are you ready to finally make a fucken difference?" Odyne said, stepping forward the crowd once again exploding completely lost to the energy of the room.

"Battle Group Olympus, are you ready to finally get justice for Lylah Soffrireterna?" Kyle said, stepping forward again to cheers.

"Battle Group Olympus," Epic music started to play behind Laurel's words, "Are you ready for justice for our brothers and sisters who were taken too early for NO REASON?" The crowd ate every word melting under the power of them.

"Battle Group Olympus, it's time for justice for all those we have had to save because of those monsters!" N'vid continued.

"Battle Group Olympus," Devin cried, "Are you ready to finally be ahead in this war?" The audience came unglued with cheers.

"Hey everyone who the fuck are you?" Shyanne ended, as the audience unanimously cried back, "Battle Group Olympus."

"Let's get to work." Lylah ordered as she and the Apache synchronized their salutes. The audience immediately snapped to attention making a wave that led into the rafters.

"Sir, yes, Sir." The audience cried.

Time passed quickly as everyone did as they were told, leaving the holo room and heading to their respective ships before departing the station at earth and preparing to jump to wormhole space as a fleet. The mass exodus of almost nineteen million ships fell into line forming around The Ellen as she opened a wormhole. The blue and black vortex grew in size engulfing the fleet. Lylah mused that the wormhole's size would and could engulf the planet almost three times over in lightning sparks before they all disappeared with the blink of an eye. The trip took three months to do but no one even noticed. Even though the time seemed to crawl before, finally the red alert was issued. Soldiers scurried to and fro, lights and alarms blurred but the Apache saw things differently. To everyone else this was a time for war but for the Apache it was time to bring a fellow brother home. Lylah turned to everyone in only her kinetic layer and waited till everyone had turned. The commotion of deployment being lost to her somber mood.

"Today is a...a big day. For all of them. For all of you." She paused, "I won't lie when I say this will not be easy. Our people are fighting a losing battle and I don't mean this fleet." Lylah said, "Luke...is still down there waiting to be brought home. We do what we must and it's honestly summed up by our motto." Lylah walked down the line slapping Devin on the shoulder nodding as he stood. "Why do we bleed?"

The others nodded in agreement as they answered. "So others don't have to."

Lylah looked at them with a giant scowl and repeated. "What the fuck was that? Why do we bleed?"

"So others don't have to sir." The Apache stood hyped and excited for the fight to come.

"I can't fucken hear you. WHY DO WE BLEED?!" Lylah roared.

"So others don't have to sir!" The other Apache roared back.

"We are going to bring our brother home." She looked at Kyle before nodding.

Kyle nodded back and continued arming up before turning to grab for his sword. He stopped mid grab before turning to look at Lylah who was full armored with her helmet on. Holding his sword, he noticed Lylah had an actual design on her armor. The Magness Prime Apache symbol on her chest with a blue webbed-like design played and wrapped around her body making beautiful pieces of ice from overlapping lines balanced only by the main color, black. On the back it said 'Cold as ICE' in webbing. The final addition came to her helmet even though it matched the rest of the design she had the Original Apache Symbol on it as well. Kyle looked hard at the symbol and its basic triangle design filled with a bomber dropping soldiers onto the ground. The design made Kyle lose himself to a memory.

"Luke Akya, you have also been assigned to the Apache squad. All cadets will follow their Captains to their respective pods." The Sergeant barked at the cadets as the sea of jumpsuits moved to their destinations.
Kyle followed Lylah as they walked through the sea of other teens moving too and from. Luke had bulked up and jumped in height going from around 5'2" to 6'1" over a summer and packed almost one hundred extra pounds. Luke looked at her astonished at how she hadn't really changed. Her hair was still dyed while Lukes had been cut.
"Who's our captain?" Luke bent down to her.
"Captain. Shenin." Lylah responded. "We will be under the careful gaze of Commander Montgomery." Luke almost played ping pong with a group of cadets as they passed by simply from his sheer shock at hearing his mother's name. Kyle shook his head and brought himself back to the present realizing she had grabbed the sword away from him. Not knowing whos memory that was.
"I was wrong." Lylah offered the sword to him. Luke's face flashed in Kyle's mind.
"About what?" He responded, raising an eyebrow ignoring whatever was happening in his own mind and taking the sword.
"You." She answered and turned shouldering her rifle and sliding her own sword into its sheath on her back.
"We drop in 15, we took our sweet ass time as it is." She turned to Kyle. "Today, we right some wrongs with, " She snickered seeing the irony in her words, "a lot more wrong."

They all fell in behind her as they moved through the almost frozen sea of people in the hallways. Lylah smiled as they were moving so fast people had no idea they were even among them. Seeming to appear out of nowhere at the head of the orbital drop party. The party was located in one of the largest hangars and consisted of the Apache drop pod, thirteen heavy class personal transport being hauled by Mk-23 drop transports. Another twelve drop spikers were tilted down aimed at the planet and ready to be fired. The spikers were specially designed to drop troops seconds after the assault started; they will be dropped only thirty seconds after the Apache's pod being the second boots on the ground. Their missile-like design allows for fifty troops to have drop pouches. The pouches would fill with foam that would dissolve when it comes in contact with dirt but kept the soldiers safe from taking kinetic damage. The spike will land hammering into the ground to create a crater.

The dirt both being blasted and packed would dissolve the foam allowing for troops to surge forward as the pouches drop open. Two minutes after that the Mk-23s would drop the heavies from low orbit that would crash down on top of the enemy letting another surge of soldiers swarm from within. Not only would new soldiers be on the field but the heavies were fitted to help against tanks, walkers, and platforms. After four minutes of combat the final wave would land and they would be in the other hanger consisting of another wave of spikers, the spikers would be aimed at the very back of the enemy line trapping the line and assuring victory and their beach head. If the assault failed the fleet would hammer their location from orbit and force a secure beachhead.

"Today is the first day we take back something major. They are using orbital shields to stop our ships from providing assistance. Shall we remind them why we don't need ships?" Lylah said to a roar from the crew as they took their positions.
The Apache climbed up and buckled in.

We are here to save lives. If we can, let's end this before those spikers land. Thirty second wipe. Kyle said, speaking for Lylah.
Today we honor our leader with glorious battle. N'vid said with great drama.
If we have less than fifty mortalities I will act in one of your Holo-dramas and help you design buildings. Lylah said to N'vid. The surge of excitement exploded up Lylah's back as calm followed by the feeling of help and respect coming from the others.

The canon clicked as the charge began and the hiss cracked, they were launched. Lylah smiled, feeling herself wanting to make this interesting. She unbuckled herself and took a step forward as they broke the atmosphere turning to the others who looked at each trying to understand, their helmet bobbing harshly from the gravity.

"Game on then." Lylah said with a smile as she slammed her fist into the emergency doors. The slabs of metal opened, catching fire for a split second before being ripped off into the upper atmosphere. Lylah felt the gravity of Magness take hold. She smiled fairly confident in her odds. As the smoke quickly dissipated they saw the six stage battle mountain as the others followed her lead walking to the open door. They saw their first wave of defenses which were full of tanks, drones, planes, platforms, soldiers and turrets. Lylah stepped back as a round went off right outside the pod as their defense turrets rotated and started raining fire in their direction. She turned and smiled at everyone before she flung herself out of the pod as a shell burst inches in front of her pushing the dust and debris aside, catching herself in the shock wave and slowing her for a fraction of a second.

The air caught her as she was launched upwards from the pod. Lylah saw the turrets adjusting as she watched the others jump out of the pod themselves before she zipped passed them aiming directly for the third line, pointing her body there and waiting to hit her jetpack after a half a minute of dodging artillery and anti air fire. Lylah's heart slowed as all the Apache hit their jet packs almost perfectly synced as they all landed at different stages of the enemy defenses. Lylah rolled, letting her gel layer take the hit knocking up dust in the landing. Lylah blinked, switching her aim mode to thermal firing three rounds and killing four targets; two of the men fell together as one bullet had killed them both. She quickly spun left dodging rounds aimed at her. She frowned only after seeing heat trails barely dodging the shots knowing the enemy had Synths in the battle.

Synths on the field, be careful they are programmed to combat us. Lylah hollered, blinked and turned off her thermal and channeled the river to be her eyes. She feels the others *ok* without them speaking. She nodded to herself and charged the bot blocking its bullets before sliding under it trying to cleave it in half. The bot jumped, leaping forward and putting its gun down to take the damage. The harsh sound of metal scraping on metal filled the room as Lylah's blade almost cut the gun in half. Lylah spun around launching a flurry killing fourteen enemy soldiers as she battled the bot.

The bot and her battled at such a high speed the soldiers didn't even know they were dead as blood slowly started to explode from their bodies. Lylah side stepped a lunge forcing the bot to kill one of its own soldiers before kicking the man's head off trying to launch it at the bot. The skull shattered, exploding from the pressure and speed changes, showering the bot in brains and flesh chunks giving Lylah the opportunity to cut its CPU out of its chest before moving on. Turning she caught a brute's ax by side stepping and grabbing its arm as she slammed her sword down onto its exposed stretchy arm, almost cleaving it in two. Lylah felt a bullet hit her in the back of her shoulder. Irritated, she turned to see another bot. Lylah finished off the brute with a quick thrust behind her never taking her eyes off the second bot.

Lylah's eyes flicked to her hud checking the time, they had fifteen seconds left. She scowled and launched a series of attacks as a flurry of explosions started to rock the compound. Lylah dodged attacks and braced herself as sound waves bombarded her body. Fire started exploding outward from the bunkers above her. She dodged an attack, throwing an explosive behind her before blocking another attack and starting her own explosision. More soldiers attempted to help but couldn't; they had no idea they were already dead. Blood soaked sand and fire burned concrete as napalmic explosions rocked every battle line slowly.

Lylah finally got the advantage, and struck the bot down trying to continue her advance. She heard the Spikers starting to break atmo and knew she had ten seconds left. She rolled forward as a Type-A brute attacked her. She dodge around it, easily killing the thing leaving an explosion of black ichor on the wall. Lylah cleaned her blade then sheathed, pulling her rifle up and meeting up with others as they converged on the underground command center. Four cement hallways connected into a circular room, on one side a door on the other were the hallways. Kyle and Shyanne arrived from Lylah's left, and Devin came trotting up to Lylah's right. Laurel and N'vid came from the far left hallway.

Lylah's eyes flicked to the hud, three seconds left. They surged forward only to be blown off their feet as the bunker imploded on itself. Lylah found her feet and looked around dazed and confused, the room started to crumble. The whole thing was a trap to kill them. All of it. She shook her head and roared in defiance. She turned channeling the river before grabbing Kyle in one hand and Shyanne in the other as she moved too fast for even them. She ran the almost three miles in milliseconds returning for Devin and Laurel macro seconds later.

The explosion started to speed up as Lylah started to fade as she turned to return. Before she could even register she was at N'vid. She instinctively grabbed him. Her head rocking back and forth from the strain as her eyes blink rapidly, barely able to keep them open from the stress. Lylah tried to throw N'vid in front of her but she tripped and went flying forward getting caught in the rubble being consumed by the flames and explosion; falling to an unknown fate.

Chapter 20:

First Meetings

"That was fucken stupid." N'vid said painfully from somewhere in the darkness, his beta quadrant temper flaring.

"You do not talk to me in that fucken tone. "Lylah snapped, "I saved Shyanne first. You were the last one before I passed out." Lylah yelled back as they crouched under a dome of debris. They sat cross legged looking at each in meditative stances. Their helmets off trying to bear through the oxygen deprivation before waiting to use the suit's filters. Sweat and fatigue showered on their faces. Their stares filled with fire and poison as they glared at each other. They had been holding the rocks together for more than an hour. Their breaths were short and controlled through their rage. They both made sure not to overuse the little oxygen left before they needed to switch to the helmets.

The hollowed booms and explosions would echo everywhere every once in a while, the only real indication of life outside the doom. The hollow ambience of light trickled down barely illuminating them but gave no real indication of what was happening. They had been two miles down when the explosion caught them. There's no way for them to even tell where they would be, they just had to try to hold out. They had put glow sticks in the corners to allow them to see each other. Their green glow almost gave off an ominous foreboding of doom.

"So I'm the idiot, is that where you're going with this?"His voice hinted at irritation as he blinked sweat out of his eyes. Big bags hung under them like dead companions.
"You should put your helmet on." Lylah said as her lungs screamed, pulling the toxic air into her lungs again.
"I look that pretty huh?" He said leaning over painfully and struggled to get his helmet on. Taking a few big gulps as he did so."Fuck that's good." He nodded and retook his place as Lylah did the same, her eyes almost fading twice.

"We have thirty six hours on these filters before we can't use them anymore." She said and retook her position as N'vid continued to hold up the dome.
"So what now?" N'vid said shifting his weight and getting as comfortable as he could.
"Well if we can pack some of those holes so they will stay and we won't have to hold it up by pure will alone; we can hope that it's already packed higher up and enough or we take turns holding up a fucken planet." Lylah sassed with irritation.
After twenty minutes of deliberating they decided on packing what they could making sure the patches held.
"You saved Shyanne first?" N'vid said his eyes glued on Lylah as she worked.

"Yeah. My first thought was that they had finally tricked us. Then before I could even register what was happening I was already coming back, moving faster than anything I had ever heard of going. I hoped for a second...then a second passed and then the explosion hit when I felt the drain on my body I knew I was done. That was before my mind fully collapsed. Last thing I remember feeling was, I had failed the team and the falling." Lylah responded from the corner hugging her left leg close to her chest resting her head on her thigh.

"That is the most human thing I have ever heard you say?" N'vid said, turning onto his side to look at her more.

"I have had humanish moments before." She stopped mid sentence, "you were never a part of them. You are the tension I have felt in my back for five years?"

"You took interest in everyone else. I thought maybe if I said something, asked for some of your precious time it'd cause problems between me and Shyanne. I thought maybe if I just showed her how good I was as something else then a soldier she'd ask me about it." N'vid said, playing around with some dirt, his voice soft with pain nodding.

"I played all of your holo dramas…I'm a really big fan." Lylah laughed softly as she smiled.

"I knew you were a fan." N'vid laughed back, "May I ask you which one is your favorite."

"The Minasa Calamity. The leader Mikel is so human it's not funny. I like the way he thinks outside of the box and only cares about the team. It was humbling and I thought the critics unfairly criticized it. Though it did win a Grammy for best holo performance so I guess even the critics were silenced that night." Lylah mused, raising her eyebrows.

"Mikel was based on you." The shock N'vid felt was uncharacteristic of her.

"Mikel has a lot less blood on his hands. His war was based in the mind, the damage he had done in his past making sure no one would put him into that position ever again. Doesn't exactly scream spoiled rich kid, who grew up." Lylah remarked before laying on her back. Putting her helmet on before a spark and screen cracked from the inside out so she no longer had a heads up display.

"Still no signal?" She asked, turning her head to look at him and taking it off.

"Na if they even have found us they haven't opened up a hole in the debris to get rid of the distortion. Fucken hell all this for us?" N'vid said, shaking his head on the dirt and folding his hands onto his chest.

"They are desperate." Lylah said in agreement. "We are too far ahead of schedule for the TimeKeeper." She angled herself in the corner finally finding a decent spot.

"TimeKeeper?" N'vid asked back.

"The TimeKeeper or at least that's what I call him is the reason we have been having so much difficulty. Those Synths are some of his designs. Or so they say. I know he planned the attack on Omega. Hell seems we have been against him the entire time." She shifts finding the perfect spot. "We have intercepted some messages from and to him. They never say a name. Usually instructions how to make the battles last longer. He is stalling for someone or something."

"Can I use that name? I like it." N'vid asked slowly, starting to doze off, his eyes blinking gently.

"Only if I get to help make the buildings, no offense, you have no talent for architecture." Lylah laughed at him as he waved his hand.

"It is a deal if we live," N'vid started, "I'm sorry I never really got to meet you till now."

"I'm sorry I never introduced myself till now." Lylah responded before hearing his deep snores.

The hours seemed elusive as she sat and listened to his snoring. Through the rumbling stones and echoes she ultimately lost herself to her thoughts. The air was still for untold hours before he awoke, Lylah waited making sure not to acknowledge him.

"I already know you're awake, your mind is never ending and loud." He said with a groan before sitting up and taking a place against the opposite wall as she sat up, "Do you ever dream?"

"Do I dream?" Lylah asked, never being asked that, shifting in her seat awkwardly as she tried to trifle a laugh.
"Yeah, you know, dream." N'vid said with major sarcasm not realizing she was being genuine. A louder more defined echo rang above them as some dust crumbled.
　"I do not." Lylah nodded, finally cracking another glow stick as the previous twelve hour stick died. They both understood now how much time had truly passed as they grew closer to not making it. The silence was almost deafening as they both looked up.
"Shame, I'd be curious to know what you dream about." N'vid said coming back to the here and now. The Dome shook with instability but did not cave in.
"I have nightmares." Lylah finally said softly, as the rumbling stopped.
　"I can only imagine." He paused as if unsure what to say next before taking his shot, " The academy. Your dad. Augmentation. You sound like some sick bastard's wet dream for a story." N'vid said with a laugh, a coy smile spreading across his face.
"You sick bastard." Lylah smiled, getting his meaning.
"If you keep it to yourself and I get the first copy. You know too...Fact check." She said awkwardly shifting in her seat.
"I can agree to that." N'vid said with a nod.
　"I guess we have to go back to the beginning." She looked around and held up her hands, " I guess it starts here. On Magness Prime. Five years ago. I was in class as our Commander walked through the door. 'Welcome back I hope you aren't too eager to go on your break that you have forgotten we must get back to the matter at hand. There is a question as old as war itself,' The room was tense, the Commander wanted to get right into it today. I remember her as someone of hope. She had this aura. You know her as Commander Montgomery. She stood before me and thirty-eight other cadets."

.
.
.
.
.
.
.
.

"We found them!" The words echoed around Lylah as she blinked her eyes barely able to move from atrophy the blinding light burning her.. Her mind froze as she turned rapidly trying to see N'vid. Her eyes locked onto him in the blinding pain of the light. Barely responsive as his eyes burst open as water is splashed over him. Coughing blood and barely responding. Lylah blinked as the air stung her lungs; she looked at Mal who was saying something she couldn't understand. She signed as she shook, the pain almost overwhelming her as she raised her shaking hands unable to speak, "How...how long?" She fell over unable to support her own weight as tears stained her face. She stared at Mal's hands as he responded.
"Two," Lylah blinked blankly, barely able to understand his hands, responding with a very pained response of her own. She asked him to repeat what he signed, doing her best to ignore herself as she needed to understand what Mal was saying. Mal repeated once more going very slow as Lylah read his hands. Her mind cracked as she finally understood and she slowly drifted into the darkness unable to handle the answer.

Chapter 21:
Do those tears actually mean anything?
The Ellen

" If you could take it all back would you?" Luke's voice echoed around Lylah. She turned trying to see anything in the hurricane that now spiraled out of control around her. Her twelve year old eyes were scared as she turned rapidly. The sounds of things flying past her caused her to panic. Her raven black hair and long bangs tipped in white matched her punk makeup and net topped tank top. Her plaid mini skirt that was colored to match the rest of her hair and clothes were connected to four inch black platforms. The silver of the boots design was the only thing off about her outfit. Thick penicillin makeup dressed her face, as black tears fell down her face on both sides completing her look.

"At what point do you feel pain?" Kyle's voice followed shortly. Lylah turned rapidly trying to catch the voices as tears of fear start to pour down her eyes.

"Do you dream?" N'vid stepped forward through the spinning vortex, scaring Lylah more as she ran away from him de-aging into an eight year old. Her boarding school skirt and polo of purple and gold sticking out in the tornado of windows and darkness. Her bright blond hair and pink tipped pigtails bounced with her backpack. The tornado gave way to her advances splitting like the red sea as she fled but then closing up after her.

"I once was a person, before this war." The eight year old stopped as she looked up at Odyne. Her white hair and furious blue filled with endless rage. The Apache armor is shown brightly with her custom marking. The little Lylah's eyes watered, long streaks of water marks that ran down her face started to pour rivers of blood. The little Lylah pointed directly at Odyne , staining her outfit with blood. "You promised." She wailed at her older self. The ground seemed to shake as the older Lylah's eyes widened in shock as the world fell around her. She shot up sweating bullets taking deep breaths in. It had been fourteen days since the first wave landed on Magness Prime.

Her tank top sticking to her soaked chest as her damp hair left a blanket of sweat that covered her body.

"No I don't dream and this is why." Lylah snarled at herself in the mirror as she stripped and turned on the shower in her quarters in the Ellen. She sighed as she rejected the pull of the river choosing to suffer alone and entered the shower letting the steam build, she extended her head back letting the water hit her neck closing her eyes before drowning her head. Clearing her face of water, she turned to grab soap as a shot rang out. Lylah blinked, allowing herself to get lost in the darkness, surging forward dodging the bullet and breaking through the glass curtain. She closed her eyes letting her instinct grab a shard before landing on the man stabbing him violently, sending blood flying. Lylah whipped her head around towards the door as some man scrambled to get in. She spun in the opposite direction grabbing the dead man's rifle. Lylah seemed to move unnaturally as she almost glided around the room.

The two men tried to raise their rifles not even realizing it was already over as Lylah squeezed past them pulling a knife off one as she passed. Lylah rounded a corner and saw him. Luke stood in front of her in the small six foot by ten foot hallway, his back turned, his shirt off. Scars of battles lined his shoulders, lower back and the backs of his arms. Lylah knew he had never fought anything that would have or did cover his back to such a degree. Lylah almost lost her breath as she realized who she was staring at as he turned to look at her, his face completely scarred up like the rest of his body, one of his eyes completely covered in scar tissue. He stared at her naked body, rage and torment shading his eyes. The Luke who would have been if he had survived Magness Prime's assault instead of her. Lylah's eyes snapped to the long almost seven foot blade that was nestled gently in his left hand.

"You promised." He said slowly advancing, gripping the hilt and allowing the blade to scrape across the ground leaving a trail of torn metal behind him as he took a lumbering step forward in the moment it took for him to raise the blade, Lylah attacked.
Lylah screamed forward crashing into the ceiling getting stuck from the metal before tumbling to the floor in The Ellen's medical bay.
"Oh good you're back." Doctor Mal said overtop of her as he stared from his desk.
"I hate dreams." Lylah huffed and stood pinching herself. The sting was a great relief to see as she shook her head taking time to clear and orientate herself.

"Your mind went almost two months on toxic oxygen. You and N'vid are impossibly lucky to even be alive." Mal said, reading her face as Lylah stopped looking at N'vid who was in a status chair beside her, his eyes closed in eerie peace.
"You both will be fine. His lung's are already regenerating. Your mind," He paused with major concern, " It needs time to adapt to healthy oxygen again." Mal said, walking over to check her vitals, "Also do you do that," He pointed at the dent in the ceiling, "Alot?"

"Yeah." She said as she let him check her out, "I think it was caused by a buildup of Fairsist Bioplasmic Energy while I sleep and eventually like all over following the energy does when it hits that told limit the energy gets dispersed and I go flying." She finished rubbing the back of her neck as Doctor Mal looked at his notes before looking back at her again.
"Peak of health as always." He said with a sad smile.
"So how are we doing?" Lylah said, walking over to the portside window and looking down on the planet.
"Poor without you." Mal said softly. The pain in his voice ment they had already lost too many.
She took a deep breath feeling the air fill her damaged lungs giving her pose to continue. She turned and patted him on the shoulder as she passed him heading for the door, "Let's change that."

Sometime Later

You can't run from us. The eight year old Lylah and twelve year old Lylah whispered to her as she walked down the long hallways of The Ellen.
I think she's embarrassed because it's been 5 years and oh shit here we are. The twelve year old mocked her from Lylah's left shoulder before standing up and flying around her head with little bat wings.
"Of course you can fly." Lylah growled at herself as she tried to look away in irritation.
I think she's worried that there won't be enough snacks for the squad. The eight year said with a smile that put a stop to both the real Lylah and the twelve year old. They stared at

her with suspicion. The worry and shock was almost exactly the same despite the ten years between the two Lylahs.

I was worried you didn't know we existed. The eight year old beamed back with a toothy smile. The twelve year old buzzed passed the real Lylah's nose, winking at the bigger Lylah who seemed to get more irritated. Lylah took a sharp left trying to outrun the pesky follower. They looked exactly the same as they had in her night terrors. Little One was still covered in blood though the rivers seemed to have stopped flowing. Punk Lylah had long eyeliner rivers against her pale skin giving her an unnatural beauty.

"You aren't real, it's just my mind subjecting me to transmorphic themes because I'm going off the rails and it feels like I need a morality lesson." Lylah hisses at herself as she finds the door she was looking for and stops and stares, waiting a very long and unnerving pause before entering, taking a deep breath as she did so,"Time to get rid of pesky pests." She nodded as she walked in the room. Lylah walked past N'vid who was still healing, his lungs were having a hard time adjusting to oxygen and his mind had put him in a coma as he regenerated. But to heal him they have to keep contaminating the lungs, reducing the dose each time to allow his lungs to repair the damage naturally.

"I need something to deal with Psychosis. Med wise I mean I don't have time for Mental Health help at this time." She said, spilling her guts unintentionally.

"For what now?" Doctor Mal said, almost being startled out of his chair by the sudden movements.

"Hallucinations induced by Psychosis. A way for my brain to comprehend and deal with the emotional pains of which I do not have the time to deal with. So I need some medication to help with the hallucinations while I end the war." She looked at the tiny eight year old who was sitting on her left shoulder and the twelve year old who was flying around Doctor Mal's face to annoy her, "I will deal with my problems at a better time but we seriously can not afford me to be out at a time like this." Lylah nodded towards the planet behind Mal.

Doctor Mal sat for a while quietly. Unaware of the obscene things Punk was doing. His face lost completely to the silence of the room. The minutes ticked by as Punk got bored and returned to Lylah's right shoulder to chew gum in a obnoxious tone. After almost ten minutes Mal stood not saying a word. He walked over to the computer before ordering some anti-hallucinogenic drugs then turned to her. He closed his eyes and breathed out composing his words as he stared through her.

"You have six months to get help before I step in."He said, holding the meds out.

"Deal." Lylah said taking the pills and downing them, feeling the relief of knowing that her younger selves were about to die.

We will see you later. The twelve year old stood and saluted, raising her eyebrow and wearing a cocky smile.

Remember you promised. The eight year old smiled a dorky smile and stood waving at her before cartoonishly smoking into nothingness.

"Will you tell me what you saw?" Mal said, walking back over to his desk and sitting down trying to control himself as he took the seconds in strides.

"I want myself to live up to a promise I made a very long time ago." Lylah said, sitting down looking out the window a tear starting to fall. "You ever wonder if you hadn't lived how many lives you would not have been able to torture with your existence?"

"Why?" Doctor Mal's voice echoed softly around her as she took in the depth of what he asked.

"No reason, I was just thinking aloud, um to answer your question six years ago. I had a plan. That planet changed my life. In less than a week I went from, Queen of the fucken Galaxy. I had my princess, My life." She said, staring off into the distance. Another tear slowly trickles down her face, "To a widowed first time mother who was forced into her father's death games."Mal sat back refusing to interrupt but nodded and offered a handkerchief to Lylah.

"Then I transcended humanity. I will outlive you, my father, if my daughter actually lives and doesn't get Luke's genetics I will have to have her augmented or I don't get her augmented like me" She blinks lost to herself, "I'll have to bury my daughter either way. I don't know which one is worse, Burying your daughter because you outlived her. Having had to watch as she got to grow old. Have her own kids. And then having to bury your Great great great great grandchildren before even the first signs of aging hits. Or watching the last remnants of a man that should have outlived you go through a horrid augmentation changing her blood down to a genetic level. One of two options happens then. Will you force her to answer the first question or are you willing to watch your daughter die and be robbed of the choice."
"May I ask you something?" Mal said as he leaned forward with concern.
"Ignoring the fact you just did, sure." Lylah said, trying to smile but feeling the dryness of the comment.
"Do you always think about the future to the exact moment?" Mal said, pushing up his glasses.
"Yeah. I can only account for my actions. But I know every way to get what I want either way." Lylah nodded.

"Did you inherit this from the procedure or have you had the ability to manipulate everyone on such an emotional level that leads to the outcome you want every time from your father." Mal's eyes rocked open with surprise as in the blink of an eye he was being choked, Lylah was on top of him and they were sliding backwards toward the window. Lylah's left arm was cocked back and loaded before she blinked and stopped slowing them down before they hit the wall. Mal's shock was apparent but he still nodded as Lylah looked at him with worry in her eyes.
"I'm fine." He coughed for a second, his face red with thick drops of sweat covering his cowlick. He walked past Lylah as he grabbed the handkerchief patting himself trying to clean himself up.
"Oh fuck I'm so sorry." Lylah stepped back, finally registering what was actually happening.
"No, no it's quite alright, come here." Mal said, opening his arm for a hug.
"I...that's." Lylah looked around visibly shook. Her arms close to her as he embraced her.
"It's alright." Mal said, hugging her as she broke down and cried. Wails of pain escaped her lips in a sudden burst. She held his back, tears falling in fresh waves.
"It's my fault." She wailed into Mal's shoulder, thick rivers of tears falling down her face. "I broke them because I was broken."She cried. Lylah held tight enough that Mal was squashed but loose enough that if he moved he would take her. After almost thirty minutes and Lylah's wails barely audible, Mal stood them up.
"No, I should apologize. I didn't mean for you to explode but I think I can help you and you won't be taken out of the war." He said as he opened up and motioned to the seat.
"Tell me about the promise and we will deal with that first shall we?" He nodded as she stood motionless, Lylah nodded and moved to the seat.
"When I had Lisa, I promised myself that if we ever made it Magness I, would forgive myself for letting him die."

"Do you think you ever will?" Mal asked, looking over his glasses as he raised an eyebrow.

"No, and I don't think I ever will be able to either." She said putting her feet up on his desk finally finding her nerves. She nodded knowing the next question and choosing to answer before Mal could ask, "Before you ask no because I'm in love with his brother." Her eyes shot open as she realized what was going on. The world spun and twisted zig zagging as she tried to stand her legs unresponsive just flopping to the floor. She stared at the doctor.

"You...drugged me?" She pushed out. Her body was completely limp from the poison.

"It will help. I promise, you will sleep for four hours but when you awake. Your problems will be fixed. I didn't think it would actually work so I gave you a triple dose to make sure you feel it." He monologged.

"Purpose. Purpose." She hissed as she struggled to maintain composure slumping further forward.

"To make you face yourself and settle your issues without the constraints of time holding you back. You'll go to sleep and wake. If it works it works I'll know immediately. You've missed so much time as it is. I really hate it when people aren't on time."

"Research." Lylah spat trying to roll her eyes as Mal came over and helped her from the chair. "Not that you'll remember this but you really do trust too easily and the only reason I'm keeping Mal and you alive is because you get me to what I want." Mal hissed into her ear as he helped her on the table.

"Time Keeper." She coughed trying to fight through the exhaustion, spit and saliva spat everywhere as she struggled to get at his neck as she was pushed onto the table.

"No no you don't get to kill me yet. It's not time for that." The Time Keeper said over her as he locked her in position with restraints. Looking at her with Mal's face. Something in his eyes was malicious and foul.

"Mal." She said her head struggled to stay in the air as she fought the drug.

"He's alive, I need him for his memories. Too bad you won't remember this. I think N'vid would agree it's a fitting climax. Right after I just found out your dirty little secret you happen to forget meeting such a dopus character. I will say your help with the characters and design of Adventures of the Milaosian's Son you know the one set in Mesopotamia was just wow. Anyway. When you wake up thank me by getting your ass back out onto the battlefield my troops aren't gonna slaughter themselves. I wonder what recent horror was the most dramatic for you." He monologged again at her before dabbing his cowlick. The sweat oozing down his face as he turned a slight shade redder.

Lylah finally went limp, her eyes closing slowly, tears streaming down her cheeks staining them with black eyeliner. Lylah stared at the light, finally losing what little fight she had left.

"You chose us...but you left us to die." The six beta Apache echoed in unison around a blindfolded Lylah who was back in another vortex. Lightning crackled around her as the tornadoes collided explosively. Rain and pieces of ice flew in every direction as the tornadoes started forming a bigger, more dangerous one. Lylah stood in the middle blindfolded surrounded by the original Apache Squad, The two younger versions of herself, Luke, Mr. Akya.

"I couldn't teach you, Chantae was your leader, always has been, always will be." Lylah said.

"We died because of you." Lylah ripped off the blindfold seeing the scene before her.

"Range, mountain top four, distance forty and a half clicks." Shyanne spotted relaying what she saw as she took aim from her jungle position, Lylah followed her gaze listening to her talk to herself. "Drop eighty, win one. Using an ex-pen grade n.a.p." Shyanne called for the explosive napalm armor piercing round loading it and taking aim watching the hanger of men. Her eyes found her team Lylah looked down the scope and arrived behind the rest of the team. The real Lylah looked at herself who was lying prone, rifle raised, "Advanced team, shot eta twenty seconds. On round conformal siege hanger B, Allies expected on the far side down corridor three. Also I would like to object to sending the first shot. Next time I'll shoot all of you. I don't care. I hate sitting at the back, and I personally feel that this is a punishment for something." Lylah smiled, Shyanne had lost the bet two nights previous for who had to stay behind.

"Roger that, overwatch waiting for the knock." Lylah smiled as Laurel held up a fist. Lylah bumped fits and smiled as she heard the shot from Shyanne. Lylah watched herself with a slight smile on her own face. There was a long pause as the air calmed almost anticipating the carnage. A bird sized Bat-Gryphon-like creature named Ziro flew away as it heard the round spinning its way towards them. The real Lylah's eyes lingered on a bright pink piece of cloth that was flapping harmlessly off of one of the hanger poles.

The explosion rocked the hanger like a bolder hitting water. Men flew in various directions almost frozen in space as the flames tried to lick the sky. Lylah and the others walked through the mess like walking through a park on a nice sunny day. Lylah watched herself and The soldiers as their shock and fear was unbalanced by the calm of the Apache that just strolled in the base. Soldiers tried to run forward but they barely raised their rifles as they were cut down. Time seemed to return to normal, finishing the explosions and bodies dropping as the five Apache faced down ten Synths. Lylah shouldered her rifle drawing her sword. Kyle, Laurel, N'vid, and Devin followed as the Synths seemed to wait. Lylah blinked and was in between the sides and stopped the scene.

"What is this?"The real Lylah looked at herself with the Apache about to take on the Synths then back at the Synths..
Lylah spoke, taking her stance, "This is a perfectly good waste of your people." The real Lylah jumped back from the startling realization the scene was still playing.

"You must be stopped." The faceless Synth droned back. It's sleek metal body seems to have been upgraded. The plates were more muscle-like and thinner. An unnerving cyan color glowed from behind the faceplate. The Synths drew their weapons each Snth branding four weapons as their arms unhinged.
"That's a new trick." Lylah growled, losing her rage, "Let me show you mine."
"Right right I didn't wanna deal with it so I unleashed my full force but this fight happened weeks after I was saved. To find them. Magness was huge, we thought for sure they were dead. We hadn't even returned to the Academy yet. We liberated the city." Lylah turned between the sides. "How could I have forgotten this even happened?"

Lylah's eyes glowed clearly under her helmet as she channeled the river, bright blue rays exploded out from her eyes. The Synths surged forward only to be thrown against the walls as Lylah levitated forward forcing the syths to the walls like a magnet. The real Lylah winced at the brightness of the light but refused to look away.
"Maybe you should put claws on those feet. You might get the idea right." Lylah screamed, slapping her hands together and the Synths crumbled into a ball of metal limbs and sparks. The real Lylah stepped back allowing the scene to progress as she followed herself.

Do you feel it? The power? The pain? Are you addicted yet? Are you blinded by it? Her younger selves hissed into her ear. Lylah shook her head and moved forward motioning to the rest of the team who seemed to be in a daze. Her movements seemed to unblur the world as the others nodded. The real Lylah tilted her head noticing she could see the smaller versions of herself.

You can't just ignore me anymore. Her teenage self whispered in her left ear.
Or me. Lylah's eight year old whined standing on her shoulder and stomping up and down.
We won't let you. They said together as they turned to look at the real Lylah.

      Lylah continued to clear the rooms until she laid her eyes on the bodies of Beta team. They had been strung up like slabs of meat. Their arms had been put out like a crucifix exposing every vein. The muscles had been pulled apart piece by piece. The Apache had been dissected alive. Their hearts are clearly visible in their chests. Still. Lifeless. Lylah dropped to her knees, broken. Shattering into a million memories. Losing herself for a bit before coming to, she looked around. She was...In the Apache squad pod.

      The Real Lylah arose from her squad pod from back when she was at the academy fully in Apache armor. Her helmet lay on the floor by her bed. The smell of death and decay hung in the air. Lylah walked into the hallway, bodies of the men they had killed lay rotting around her. Their bodies were mostly bones, mush, armor and clothes. The light flicked and somewhere a water main had burst. Black gaugulated blood smeared the walls. A person sat on their knees. The person looked to be young wearing a black gothic mourning dress. A face net covered her face as she stood over a pair of bodies. Lylah moved closer to the shape as it lay over a body.

      Lylah knew the couch very well. Images of Alice and Selaris flashed in her head smiling at her as they tried to make some random experiment work. She looked at their skeletons perfectly frozen in time. Alice slumped back with Selaris over her. Their jumpsuit hung loosely around the bones. The person stood leaving a rose on both bodies. One of the roses was an unnatural glowing royal blue, the stem of the rose was ashened. Lylah's mind flashed to their deaths how abrupt it had been. The image of Alice's head exploding holding her sister's dead body as they slumped in a heap. The figure handed her a rose and lifted her veil. The rose changed from a haunting royal blue to a gentle green glowing bright and helping to illuminate them.

      "This right here is where it all changed for us." Punk said, staring at her. She stood the same height as Lylah staring her deep in the eyes. The soft green of Punk's eyes staring almost more furiously into the real Lylah's blazing blue ones, as lightning hit in the background. The light from the rose casting harsh shadows before the building tore away to reveal the tornadoes merging around them.

"I was the force you could never contain." Punk said as lightning struck, sending sparks flying to the twister.

"I was the force you always wanted to be." Lylah responded, unwavering her back frozen like a statue.

"I am what we should still be." Punk screamed, tears starting to flow.

"I am what we are." Lylah droned back unflinching and unwavering.

"I am what you need." Punk said giving up and turning to leave. Lylah waited for her to leave, almost begging her to leave. Punk turned and took one step before the real Lylah stopped her.

      "We are what we need." The real Lylah said, tears forming in her eyes. The tornado intensified as the emotions of Lylah poured out of her in long funnels of different colors that spun wildly as they were added to the vortex, tie dying the tornado in an acid induced sea of colors. Lylah pulled her younger self closer catching the youngster by surprise.

      "You don't get off that easily." Punk said, wrenching the real Lylah's hair back and holding her head. Lylah's eyes opened wide and Punk launched a gut shot pulling her back again to look at her. Lylah coughed blood as she stared up the eye of the tornado. Her emotions had faded and the tornado of colors also had ended returning it to the horrifying gray. Lightning speared and assaulted the center but could not pierce into it, always stopping at the walls. She looked at the stars of the night. Their beauty, peaceful twinkling amongst the rampage of the tornado.

"I deserve this." Lylah coughed, closing her eyes and accepting her fate.

"I know." Punk said with a sneer and crushed her windpipe in.

Chapter 22:
You don't get to leave until we are done.
Deep in Lylah's mind

"How many times have you actually been happy? One maybe two times a year? You do understand what happiness is right?" The eight year old walked back and forth in her ridiculous suit and tie, remnants of the 1980s. Lose like she was hot, sweat staining her shirt complete with oversized brimmed style glasses hung off her nose. She slapped a file down in front of Lylah scattering paper as she sat across from the real Lylah. They were sitting in an interrogation room from the early thirty-third century, electric prods and brain surger were on a small metallic table to the left of them. A brain surger is used to jump into the minds of the victim. A small pack would be mounted on the hip that is connected to the spinal cord. The victim would be placed in a chair very much like Lylah was now. And a small sphere is placed in front of the victim. The sphere would unfurl and climb the victim heading towards the nose and ears. Once the bot arrived at the location it wanted it would insert two of its arms in each ear and nose canal. Forcibly entering each orifice before sending a dozen small connections to attach to various parts of the brain. It's very barbaric and very much a product of the era.

"You have got to be fucken kidding me." Lylah looked at her younger self.

"Hey now I'm approaching you peacefully if I need to bring Officer Punk in I will. Honestly it looks better if, for you I mean, if you just cooperate with us." Little One babbled back completely lost to the scene.

"What can I help you with then?" Lylah said, raising an eyebrow sarcastically, adjusting in the seat to get comfortable.

"Great. Now betweens," Little One said smiling and climbed into the seat extending the file and handed over three pictures. "On The dates of March the eighth and March the twelfth of fifty-oh two you were seen jumping off of a resort hotel." She pointed to the first picture of Lylah diving off of the resort's balcony.

"Yeah, that was Alpha squads first real break." Lylah droned back, rolling her eyes.

"I see, and this one." Little One, who had changed from a 1980s cop to her normal bloodsoaked self, pointed at the middle picture of her looking at Kyle in a desirable way, while she put some hair behind her ear, a girlish smile on her face. They had been celebrating a major victory in fifty-oh four. Lylah had secured them some R&R. Kyle had tried to bull horn a tank, grabbing it by the barrel and ripping the top off like a toy. However the captain of the tank had managed to wait till he had a shot and had sent Kyle flying, pulling the top part of the tank off with him rather than it being a feat of strength.

"That was two years after. Our second break." Lylah said in a lower tone sadness seeping into her.

"And this one." The eight year old said pointing to the final one as Lylah looked at it and almost burst into tears.

The picture is of Luke and her after the concert, in the hotel cradled in each other's arms. Lylah was asleep, a smile on her face as Luke smiled at the ceiling as if seeing the real Lylah. The last real decision she had. The night everything changed forever.

"That is when I fell madly in love with Luke, before this fucken war." Lylah hissed in shame.
"What's the difference between these two?" Little One pushed, pointing at the middle photo and the final photo.
"It's not like that." Lylah said aimlessly as she fidgeted before Little One leaned over and slapped her in the face, catching her completely by surprise.
"I am getting tired of your shit." Little One held Lylah by the collar and slapped her again, "Try again." She spat, raising her hand. "I swear it's not the same." Little One slapped her again.

"If you can't even beat me, how are you going to beat the real us, huh?" Little One mocked slapping her again. "It's not the same." Little One continued her assault for an hour before she got off of a bloodied Lylah. Little One pulled a handkerchief out of her pocket and dadded her now sweaty red face.

"TimeKeeper." Lylah raged surging forward with new found strength as she lifted Mal up.
"So desperate to catch me, unfortunately you're out of time." Mal laughed a little eagerly at her as she started to lose control of her body.

"You weren't kidding." Little said, walking over to Lylah as she kneeled down and rolled the crumbled up body over. The real Lylah flopped over and saw Punk walking up beside her as well.

"You need some serious work." Punk said putting a brain surger in front of the real Lylah and activating it. The Device slowly unwound as it turned its singular 'eye' taking in the surroundings before blinking a deep ominous pink and turning towards Lylah with a sudden jerk. The creature quickly hurled itself at her, pushing her over till it was on top of her on her chest. She felt it crawl up her chest and across her breasts. The slow sound of metal arms extending into her ears before blinding pain as the creature did its job. Lylah's eyes shot open even though she couldn't see due to the pain. Her face turned bright red as she shook violently.

"Goodnight Princess." Lylah's dad said with a sadistic smile on his face as he emerged from the shadow stripping off his shirt.

"Wakey Wakey Eggs and Bakey." Lylah was josseled away as a hand smashed into her cheek.
Lylah looked around, accessing her field of view. She was tied up naked under a pipe that slowly dripped frozen water onto her head. Lylah felt the sting of the air as a cold strip ran up her soaked body. She was in a meatery hung up in the back on one of the hooks. The tile on the floors and wall were a musty blue color that filled everywhere except the ceiling. Lylah got a glimpse of herself in the mirror. Her ribs were covered in bruises and scars. Her face was almost unrecognizable from the swollen muscles. Her normal luscious lips were caked in rusted blood and dark patches of purple.

The left side of her face was completely puffed out. Lylah hadn't even realized she was only seeing out of her right eye. Her arms were bound by chains above her as the drops slowly trickled down her tattered body. She had been hanging for almost an hour due to the shiver and lack of strength she had.

"So now, you have come to me." A man said with his back to her, he was wrapping some kind of wire. Tools were scattered around the room, some bloody, some not. A light had been placed on her making it hard to actually evaluate the room. The man was way too oversized to be anyone, normal black cargos, stained with blood, fats, and dirt covered from his knees down. He had no shirt on but was wearing an apron of some kind. There were multiple scars covering his back.

"You can't be any worse than the others." Lylah said as she struggled to find her feet as she hung with her arms up.

"I'm not the worst, true but I will get results." The man said, turning to her. It was Luke but from her night terror. His face was still covered in pain. She saw the marks on his body of battles he would have endured as he took off the apron and hung it up. Lylah was just happy she couldn't see what was staining it due to the fact the apron was black.

"You can't hurt me anymore." Lylah coughed at him through the fat lip cracking one of already damaged lips into bleeding.

"I'm not here to hurt you like the others. I'm here to take some things from you. Like your doubt. Your regret and help you realize a few truths. I'm here to help you grieve." Luke said, turning back and grabbing a handkerchief and draping her lip to help keep the blood from pouring out.

"You're gonna help me grieve? How? Show me a bad movie and eat ice cream while crying like I did when I was twelve? What even is your master plan?" Lylah said her eyebrow raised.

"I'm going to show you a special movie. A movie with you as the main character reliving events exactly as they happened. It's like watching a movie, or holo drama. Just this holo drama is real, you don't get the privilege of turning it off if you don't like it." Luke said walking over and unlocking her.

"Your master plan is to make me watch my lifes movie?" Lylah said, looking at him.

"Yeah pretty much. Well like a super extremely condensed version you know like a two part episode style movie. Director's cut of course." Luke said as he waved his hands, restoring Lylah to her normal appearance complete with jumpsuit and tied back hair.

"Why?" Lylah asked as he opened a set of doors that lead to a genuine peak Hollywood era style theater.

"Why what? Oh this." Luke said, turning as he de-aged into what he looked like in the Academy. "I thought it would be neat." He said as he tripped and fell backward, changing into a tux as he crossed the threshold. A grin plastered all over his face as he righted himself and shook off the dust before offering her his hand.

"Fuck I miss you." Lylah said as she stepped through the door taking his hand. As she stepped through the door her clothes changed from her normal offduty fatigue to the black dress she wore when she went for drinks with Laurel and Shyanne.

"Can we get some popcorn? It's the second best part." Luke said, pointing at the signs as his childlike playfulness was never sorrowed by Lylah.

"Of course. What's the first?" She smiled meekly at him, her strength being zapped at the upcoming shit show of a movie they would have to watch.

"Trailers." He nodded confidently.

There was no line and the theater, despite the massive size, was completely empty except for them. They waited in a special balcony seat. Some trailers for Luke's favorite movies played before the feature started. The theater grew dark and a low rumbling music could be heard. Lylah took a piece of popcorn as epic themed music played as they were flying through a massive solar system, Lylah recognized it as the Hoboistoto system. Home to Magness Prime. The camera slowly found Magness Prime as it zoomed into Horatius School of War Arts on a beautifully sunny day. The rain would sometimes pour for months on end flooding the introcut valley system of this beautiful oasis. The camera found a group of cadets, The original Apache: Dakota, Alice, Selaris, Michelle, Luke, Maddie, Aaron, Chelsea, and Mark. Dakota had Alice on his shoulders and Luke had Lylah. They were chicken fighting. Maddie, Aaron and Chelsea were all sunbathing on the shore. Selaris and Michelle had taken Mark underwater to look at some unusual formations in the trees.

Their swimwear is a mix of bra, panties, and military grade boxers. The Military doesn't provide swimwear outside of regulated swim hours. They were all very young. Lylah smiled knowing full well that was her first year as commander. The valley had flooded just days before spring break allowing them to enjoy their time in the beautiful crystal green waters. Her full smile turned to a half smile and remembered how she had snagged herself some rebreathers.

"That's why I'm commander bitch." The younger Lylah cried in victory as Alice toppled onto Dakota holding up her arms to show her guns. The others laughed as Alice launched herself out of the water spearing Lylah off of Luke's head. The younger Lylah had her hair tipped in a dark passionate pink.
"Oh yeah you little bitch comer." Alice screamed splashing water as she smiled at Lylah who in turn was smiling back.

"Commander of the losers." Maddie sassed from shore as Lylah flipped towards her and smiled. Maddie had her middle finger pointed directly at her.
"Come here and say that." Lylah cried, "Find you a partner I dare you."
Maddie tagged Dakota as he was walking out of the water, he stopped and looked longingly at the hamburgers that were cooking.
"No food unless you fight me, that's an order." Lylah said scrambling up onto Luke she leaned down to his ear.
"We got this right?" She asked.
"When I tap your leg, hit her in the left thigh." He mumbled back before turning to offer his hand to Dakota.
"Two out of three it is D." Luke said as Dakota took it.
"Eh, I don't care, I just wanna eat." Dakota said as he struggled to hold the massive Maddie on his shoulders.
The two teams backed up as Alice swam over to officiate.

"I want a good and nasty fight, hair pulling encouraged, No puss shots, no dick shots. Slapping, maming, and otherwise dirty tactics are very smiled upon in this establishment. Fighters, what are the terms?"
"We win, we become officers," Maddie said.

"We win, they do all of our chores for a month including regs." Lylah nodded as she looked at Luke. The others shied away, regs were the hardest chores to get done on time and adding two more to the list meant less sleep for a month.
"Fighters do you accept and that on your honor bet and will follow the rules?" Alice stated.
"Aye."Dakota and Maddie shouldered up.
"Aye." Luke and Lylah nodded.
"Fight."

The screen changed to a kid running through a crowd; he dodged around adults and slipped smoothly through the railing and ran up to Lylah. He raised a royal blue rose up to Lylah at one of their hologram airings. The air was thick with scandal and hypocrisy. Lylah was fully armed in her smily outfit. She raised a hand to the guards as she took the flower from him. The boy exploded into ash infront of her as the bomb that was his life exploded sending her flying. The air was thick with smoke as Lylah heard her helmet crack and sparking.

She blinked, getting her bearings turned and cleared through some of the wreckage.

A light caught her eyes as she moved some pieces of debris to find the rose was deeper royal blue due to the ionization and radiation particles giving it an unnatural look. The stem had been covered by the anti-human bomb, a genetic based bio-weapon that should have killed her. She dropped to her knees and rain started to fall as if to match her feelings. Lylah had a tear run down her face as she tried to stay composed. She had forgotten about her Emmy for best programming and Holodesign. Laurel had begged her to go just so she could walk a red carpet with her best friend. Lylah had only agreed to go because she just wanted to see Laurel smile. The rose had been the delivery system, the roses stem had somehow survived covering it in the boy's ashes as he had exploded with the bomb.

"Your life has been horrific but you need to remember it. I can pause the movie if you'd like." Luke said standing as she nodded as he walked off.

"How can't I love you both." She sighed to herself.

"That is still an option." Doctor Mal said from behind her.

"How?" Lylah looked at him with reddened eyes.

"Remember." Mal said, handing her a glowing emerald green rose.

The word 'remember' echoed around Lylah's mind as she struggled to control reality. The world smudged and shook, blending into itself.

"Ah Fuck!" Lylah Launched her head back as she screamed aloud her mind feeling the struggle at it pulled her to the here and now. She screamed as she shattered into glass before those pieces of glass exploded. The mirrors reflect her cries of pain before slowly starting to rewind. As the pieces started to form her pained body. Lyal felt the box around her mind shatter flooding her with memories of times after Magness. A time with the green rose.

Chapter 23:
What have you done?

Deep in Lylah's mind

She heard the voice fly past her as she stumbled in the darkness. "How far are you really willing to go to end this war?" "At what point do you feel pain?" "Lylah that's enough." "That was not part of the plan." Kyle jerked Lylah, pulling her out of her mind and back to the movie theater.

"Leave it be, Luke I'm just making sure the plan happens." Kyle said, turning to look at Luke as he stood and adjusted his tie,"Ma'am, Enjoy the rest of the night and your movie."And with a curt bow Kyle left.
"How did he get here?" Luke said, looking over his shoulder as Kyle rounded a corner.
"He saved me from my own mind." She said watching after him with a little linger and wanting.
 He handed her a remote. "I know what I said but fuck everyone else this my attempt and I seriously fucken hated your punk phase anyway." Unusual amounts of maliciousness in his tone as he glared at the movie, refusing to continue the conversation or comment as she struggled with herself.

"Wow, thanks." Lylah's face flew through various emotions as she finally exploded, launching a slap at him out of pure pain. Luke smiled and watched as the hand sailed slowly over his face, his eyes dancing.
"I'm not your bitch anymore." He said sitting back with a cocky smile.
"Fuck you." She said, shaking her head and turned back to the screen and hit play on the remote, disgust and frustration filled her everything as she grumbled.

The scene cracked and distorted as Lylah watched Mr. Akya walk through the halls of his house back and forth as the days and hours passed. Lylah's eyes shifted as she grabbed the chair to ground herself. She fidgeted in her seat, becoming unsettled immediately by what she saw as the countless bottles start littering the floor. Time passed from day to night numerous times before slowly stopping. He had a picture in his hands as Mr. Akya paced back and forth before he walked into the garden. He smiled, seeming to get lost in the moment when a man hit him from behind, cracking Mr. Akya's head with the attack, causing him to jet forward, smashing his forehead on the lift garden's wooden edge. The man looked like a member of the Others, but it was hard to tell due to the helmet, then the man attempted to wrap a noose around Mr. Akya's neck and strung him up, who woke up rotating and smashing the man's helmet with a pot. The man tilted his head and raised his hand to defend himself.

"You already took him from me. You will not take her." Mr. Ayka roared, sliding his hand back and rotating with unnatural grace, launching two spades that barely missed their target. The man spun right stepping into the Garden. As the man tried to retreat, Mr. Akya surged forward with a spear, colliding full force and smashing them to a nearby table. The men rolled as Mr. Ayka grabbed an ice spade, turning it on the attacker trying to slash with his long serrated blade. The man rolled closerer smashing his forearm into Mr. Akya's face and threw the spade away. Mr. Akya rolled onto his knee pushing with his weight as the Other Man attempted to rise as well. The men locked arms in a tight clench.

"You...can't...Argh!!"Mr.Akya roared, as his eyes were racked by the man. The man pushes Mr. Akya over quickly mounting and laying a couple of haymakers to daze Mr. Akya. Blood explodes from Mr. Akya as his eyes roll around barely able to keep track of his attacker. The attacker stands leaning close grabbing Mr. Akya's head as he struggles meekly. A small silver blur shoots from the Man's wrist as Mr. Akya finally comes to, struggling harshly as the man pushes forward, almost dagging the bigger man by the head backwards. Mr. Akya's eyes widened as his final muffled words were heard.

"Not like this," Mr. Akya roared, throwing the man's arm aside before the noose slipped around his neck. The man rotated grabbing the other side of the rope. In one fluid moment, the Man grabbed a steak pole and planted it into the Garden. Mr. Akya quickly started thrashing as the man placed a letter next to the base of the pole. Mr. Akya's face started to redden as the man watched him struggle to breath as thick sweat fell down his cowlick. Spit and saliva soak his lips as he stares barely moving twitching.
The man looked at him before pulling out a handkerchief and dabbing Mr. Akya's head as he died.

Lylah's heart shattered as the screen zoomed out through another camera lens before revealing Lylah was watching the very recording on the hidden on-sight cameras Luke used to make sure his father was ok. Lylah quickly typed on the computer reading the data, her white hair dancing with her movements. Lylah remembered compartmentalizing it for later, but she doesn't remember ever finding this information out as a fresh wave of tears fell down her face before the screen cracked and returned to the A.M.A. awards.

The scene continued from where it left off as the smiling Lylah walked aimlessly around trying to comprehend what had happened. A firefight broke out drawing her back to the combat and without even trying dismantled the enemy insurgents with extreme prejudice acting as the only authority that mattered in the end. The executioner. Ripping limbs off just because she could. Almost sadistically drinking in the fear of the insurgents who fled in absolute terror as she walked down the hallway. She had found her sword purposefully going slow enough that the terrorist knew she was still coming but fast enough that the enemy just exploded for no reason giving the appearance the men who were now diced in pieces just exploded into those pieces as she approached. A man flew into the camera and caused a transition into Lylah holding Lisa just after the baby's birth. She was barely three hours old and slept peacefully in her mother's arms wrapped in a deep pink cloth. Lylah just couldn't seem to look away smiling periodically as the baby moved in her sleep. Lylah hummed for a bit.
"I promise you, my little one. If I ever make it back home. I will forgive him." A single tear went down Lylah's face, "For leaving me with you. I know you won't remember this but I will fuck up alot." Lylah hushed at her baby as she cried silently.

"I will stumble and I will have my fear of problems but, you, you will never know. I will never let you know how much I'll cry at night for your father. How I wish it had been me that had died. You deserve a parent and I could...never be that not like I know you'll need." Rivers of pain flowed down Lylah's eyes, "But fuck I will try. For you. And for your father. I will fucken try." Lylah said, kissing the child's forehead before turning and placing her in the crib. She turned and went to the restroom only to find a bright green rose illuminating the room sitting right beside Lisa.

Lylah had tears of her own as she watched the scene, her face torn between pain and horror. She was reliving the moment for the first time. She watched as the camera backed up and slowly rewinded. A man who looked almost exactly like Mal walked into the room and placed the rose beside Lisa patting her head. He then turned past the camera, and Lylah saw his eyes. The TimeKeeper's eyes. He had been capitalizing on her psychosis. Lylah stood realizing the Light had rapidly accelerated the effects. But when she joined G.O.D.S. it had changed everything. Her mind was then too strong to control. The TimeKeeper was just another person trying to get back at her father.

"I'm sorry, that we had to do it this way but no one could agree on the best way to do it." Luke said, leaning forward as the movie ended.
"Thank you." She cried as she looked up with her face relieved and joyful.
"What?"
"I thought this whole time I was just…getting worse and my mind was fucking me over." Lylah said as she took a deep breath in and continued, "I'm the thing the TimeKeeper fears. I have been manipulated from day one by my father, by the TimeKeeper, and by the only people she thought she had left." She looked at Luke realizing the horrifying truth, "I'm sorry I couldn't let you go, I trapped you here. You're not at peace because I won't let you be."
Luke nodded silently as a tear slowly fell down his cheek as he stared at her.
"I'm so sorry Luke. I'm so selfish. I will miss you baby but you gotta go." Lylah said, waterfalls threatening her eyes. "All of you have to go. I'm so sorry I failed all of you." The stage exploded around them. The Tornado swirled, ripping and tearing houses up around as Lylah turned into the woman she was now. Luke turned into who he was in the Academy. Dakota, Alice, Selaris, Luke, Maddie, Aaron, Chelsea, Mark, The two younger versions of herself Punk and Little One, Commander Montgomery and Mr. Akya all stepped out of the Vortex. Their faces smiled as they approached her in love. Lylah got caught by Alice and Selaris first.

"You didn't kill us. You tried to save us, remember that next time ok?" Selaris said, punching Lylah in the shoulder as they all hugged. Lylah nodded and watched as they turned into lightning joining the sky in a brilliant flash. The vortex starts to slow down allowing a slight slowing of the rain and crashing sheets of ice. The Lighting grew less aggressive. Dakota, Aaron, and Mark all offered their hand in turn. "Thank you for being the men you were, you deserved better." Lylah looked at them, tears falling in steady waves as she smiled and coughed a laugh.

"Free beer and food forever? I'm in." Dakota said with a wink and a slight smile. Aaron and Mark punched each other's shoulders before tilting their heads to go and walked away turning into lightning mid stride. Once again slowing the Vortex and slightly slowing the rain fall and sheets of ice.
Chelsea walked up and put a finger over Lylah's mouth before she could speak. "This is not goodbye forever," Chelsea said, tears welling in her eyes, "This is until we meet again ok?" Chelsea said with a quivering lip.
Lylah nodded before pulling her close, a fresh wave of tears staining her eyes, "Thank you for all the wonderful womanly council you gave me over the years." Lylah nodded, tears starting to well in her eyes again.

"I'm glad you finally took my advice." She nodded at Luke and smiled, holding a thumbs up before turning into lightning and majorly slowing the vortex like a bolt of pure hope. Maddie walked up next embracing her battle sister.
"We will miss you until you join us." Maddie said sniffling, "I will never let you live down that you and Luke had a fucken baby on your first try. What a lucky shot huh? Only you." Maddie marveled with love.

"You girls are my sisters and if I could I would take you with me." Lylah said and she held Maddie close hugging her for Michelle as well missing her best friends as tears ran down Lylah's face.

"   I'm Glad you were my commander. I know Michelle, would tell you something wise or smart but all I got is." She snapped to attention, "It was an honor serving with you." Maddie said, trying to not cry herself. Lylah snapped to attention as Maddie walked towards the wall. Maddie turns to look at Lylah as a half baked shit eating grin spreads across the left side of her face as she seems to get a bad idea. As Maddie laid eyes on Lylah she fully smiled before flipping Lylah the bird as she too joined the sky putting hers and Michelle's spirits to rest in one go. The rain sheets cracking and lightning majorly stopped coming to an almost relaxed pace. Commander Montgomery stepped forward and the vortex returned to max speed as the storm returned to its normal ravenous ferocity. She shook her head.

"You take care of that little one, like I took care of you ok? Regardless of how naughty she is, you make sure." The Commander paused tears teasing the bottoms of her eyes, "You make sure she knows you love her and she is always cared for, ok?" She nodded trying to control herself sniffling a little.

"Thank you." Lylah stood at attention.

"No," The Commander saluted back, "Thank you for continuing what we couldn't." She turned in formation and mid turn she was claimed by the sky. There was an almost unstable calm as the tornado lowered size shrinking by almost half.

The two little versions of Lylah walk up hand in hand. Their outfits are normal but without the smeared eyeliner and tears of blood. Their outfits were neat and clean like when the real Lylah had actually wore both outfits in her life.

"Are you mad at us?" Little One asked shyishly.

"No, Little One, I'm not mad at either of you. I understand, you just cared and I was so far gone for so long it took a hard minute to figure out how to fix us and save you." Lylah said, kneeling down.

"Cool, 'cause I like it when we are friends." Little One smiled with a toothy smile and hugged Lylah who hugged her back embracing Little One like her own child. She stood and turned to Punk. They stared at each other for a hot minute before breaking down and smiling embracing as sisters as a fresh wave of tears teased them both.

"Don't forget yourself next ok?" Punk punched Lylah in the shoulder as they separated.

"Yeah I'll make sure that I control what memories are affected next time." Lylah said rolling her eyes as a smile formed on her face, "Alright you trouble makers get the fuck outta here before I have to start parenting."

The two turned and looked back waving before they started to walk away disappearing in a flash of colors as the tornado was splashed with a psychedelic delight as the vortex grew small enough that only Mr. Akya and Luke were left.

"You'll always be my daughter, you know this." Mr. Akya said, stepping forward his second chin vibrating as he tried to keep his composure.

"You were my dad and you always will be." Lylah said her eyes were rivers of pain.

"Well now you remember the truth and I know you'll do what's right when the time comes." He said gushing and nodding his head before Lylah pulled the much bigger man closer. He was stunned for a moment before embracing the hug.

"I want pictures ok. My granddaughter better be fed." Mr. Akya said, pointing at her in a quick joke as he smiled before being claimed by the sky, shattering it and forcing the sky to release ribbons of light as the clouds stirred restlessly as the final goodbye needed to be made.

Lylah turned to Luke who was behind her, "I forgive you." She whispered as a giant beam of light engulfed Luke as he raised his head freed from her. He started to levitate before beautiful black wings exploded out of his back. A black streak of lightning slammed into him, pulling him inside of it zipping around as black fingers of lightning that touched the sky. The bolt roared around, lighting up the darkness with its voidlessness, lightning fingers expanding towards the sky as they grew closer to the storm. The lines of energy began growing even brighter and brighter going from a depressing black to a radiant gray to a beautiful shade of golden yellow splashing the sky as lightning cracked somewhere. The sky darkened, seeming to try to reject the bolt as it crawled along the clouds before dropping down and screaming towards Lylah who opened her heart to the darkness. The bolt collided with her body sending her flying backwards as she felt the pain of his loss giving it all of her negative power.

The memories flashed like old fashioned polaroids. The Hanger defense. Lylah and Luke in the crash. The scenes seemed to play as if she could hear the warning siren as the missile hit the ship. Lylah stumbles out of the cockpit. The screams and gunshots as she walked through the smoke. Luke's body.

"I forgive myself." Lylah said as she forgave herself. The black lightning bolt quickly surgered into a royal blue lighting bolt, Lylah grabbed it as quickly as she could, plunging into the ground. Her head snapped like an ancient Javelin thrower. she hurled it up at the eye of the storm. The clouds seem to try to stop the bolt by building vortex-like walls up, thickening the tornado ten fold. The rain picked up to an almost waterfall with thick iceberg sized sheets of ice floating around. The lightning almost seemed to surround the vortex trying to shield the eye from the bolt.

Lylah held her breath as the bolt shattered glaciers and seemed to dance around the downpour before just ignoring the lightning shield and connecting with its target. The storm exploded away disappearing almost in the blink of an eye as the world became a much more beautiful place. Lylah smiled as she blinked, almost being blown off her feet as she tried to stabilize herself. The roar of the storm blew her awake as she was blown off her feet.

Lylah shot forward as Kyle and N'vid held her from launching into the air. Lifting them slightly off the ground but they were able to keep her down, keeping her from crashing into the ceiling. They looked at each other very nervously as Lylah lay still unresponsive for almost two full hours before Kyle spoke. Her eyes were completely closed and lifeless. Kyle slowly opened her eyes, seeing the blank and completely unresponsive eyes.
"Mal? It... I don't..." Kyle closed his eyes and turned slowly as a hand shot out and caught his wrist. "Are you..." Kyle asked, flipping around and rubbing her hair, looking at Lylah. Only silence greeted him as he stared at his friend, Kyle's eyes swell with tears as they flash to N'vid who turned with complete disbelief as her hand once more dropped. Lifeless.

Epilogue:
What have you Found?

"I didn't dismiss you soldier." Lylah's voice inflamed Kyle's heart as he spun to look at her. His eyes locked onto her eyes as she meekly rose, her body wobbly, and she moved with a new found gingerness. N'vid eyed Lylah carefully, watching his frail friend but refused to help her stand on her own as she moved towards Kyle.

What used to be furious raging blue was replaced by the iris of soft emerald green, deep passionate blue, and strong vibrant Pink. The inside of the iris was just a beautiful vibrant blue with the outside balancing that with a soft and peaceful emerald green. Lines of magenta outlined the end of her iris in between the edges of her eyes. Kyle almost lost himself when what used to be the whites of her eyes were now shrouded in a black almost mist-like swirls. Lylah breathed in as she imagined herself in a room with a red rose reaching out through the river she offered her hand to others pulling them to her personal river.

A darkened gray room with a single lowlight in it, dark furniture filled the room around them. The design looked like early 42nd century decorum of sleek gun metal and glass. There was a sliding window door that revealed a tremendous thunder storm raging against almost every expanding city backdrop. The city scape and matching thunderous storm cast thick shadows as lightning licked the air curving in unnatural arks and casting deep gray, blue, pink, and green light across the city. Lylah didn't even notice or care who had accepted her hand as she tilted her head at the rose before spinning it in her hands, ignoring everything and everyone except the rose. The rose slowly started to rotate as it transformed in front of Lylah who watched transfixed by the flower. As the red and green of the flowers' natural state slowly faded, almost melting down the stem, the flower slowly drooped as a black coat of ash fell over the flower, darkening it even further.

Lylah smiled and brought the flower to her chest, feeling the love of the original Apache and Mr. Akya tease her heart. The flower stiffened but did not take color. Lylah looked at it again before slowly smelling the rose, closing her eyes and throwing her head back. Remembering the smell of his aftershave. As she opened her eyes to look at the onlookers, an explosion of swirling green and blue surged from the center of the flower. Its bottom is caught in a deep swirly blend of pink, almost protecting the other colors as it separates the colors from the ashes of the stem. Lylah opened her eyes and offered the flower to N'vid, Devin, Laurel, Shyanne, and Kyle. The rose slowly lifts from her hands as they all stared. The Apache looked at the flower before revealing their roses and allowing them to slowly drift and float around Lylah's rose, their eyes starting to swirl as their eyes matched their roses respectively as they shifted slowly through the air almost weightless.

N'vid and Shyanne had deep powerful purple and strong orange swirled ash roses as they spun around each other, combining into one growing bigger but not as big as Lylah's. Devin looked at Laurel nervously as they both revealed white and golden ashed roses that they let float around Lylah's like a solar system. Lylah smiled, taking in their roses. Their souls were connected on such a level that even their spirits were connected but they chose to be alone.

"If I reveal mine you can't question it or be mad." Kyle said, looking at her, his hand behind his back, eyes completely on the floor.

Lylah shook her head as the others turned to look at Kyle. Lylah pushed them out of her room to explore her river. After a long pause Kyle revealed his rose. A rose of blue, green, pink and ash floated towards her. Lylah looked at Kyle taking in the flower as it danced through the air before she finally broke her silence,

"How could I be mad, You and him are one in the same," Lylah walked over to Kyle and put her free hand on his heart. Her hand lit up in the void of the room. She closed her eyes slowly feeling the power of her river flow through her. She smiled, feeling the whispers of her sisters telling her her feelings. Lylah opened her eyes, locking them on Kyle. "Of course it was always going to be you." Lylah laughed, as she pulled Kyle in, kissing him passionately as the galaxy found peace for five minutes for the first time in nearly seven years.

Made in the USA
Middletown, DE
19 July 2022